The Story in the Stars

Book 1,
Gateway to Gannah

Gannah's Gate

THE STORY IN THE STARS

Gateway to Gannah 1

Third Edition

Yvonne Anderson

The heavens declare the glory of God;
and the firmament sheweth his handywork.
Day unto day uttereth speech,
and night unto night sheweth knowledge.
There is no speech nor language,
where their voice is not heard.
Psalm 19:1-3

1

Dassa trudged through the Ayin Forest across crusted snow, her weary steps fueled by the nearness of her goal.

Soon, she told herself. *Soon this will all be over.*

On much of the planet Gannah, winter was drab as an old faded photo, but here in Ayin, the foliage boasted the colors of a prism. The trees kept their leaves until the new spring growth pushed them aside, so now, the frosty forest pulsed with color.

Dassa quickened her pace despite her exhaustion and the steepness of the slope. Labored breath billowing like smoke from a puffing firedrake, she crested the ridge and cast her gaze into the valley below.

A rush of delight coursed through her weary body. There it was—home—the comforting outlines of the domed green roof barely discernable through the trees. Revived by the sight, she hastened down the hill across the sun-spangled snow.

She smiled as the round, two-storied house came into full view. Unlike her childhood home, it was no mansion. It couldn't compare to any of the seven provincial palaces from which her father, the toqeph, reigned as the ruler of all Gannah. But she could think of nowhere she'd rather live than in this yellow stone cottage at the edge of the forest with her husband, Rosh, and their two boys.

Nor could she imagine a more perfect late-winter's day. Gannah's volatile temper was mild that afternoon, with the sun smiling down from a brilliant blue sky and breezes caressing with a mother's gentleness. And today, this most beautiful of days, she,

Atarah Hadassah Hagah Natsach, would finish her quest and be named a Nasi.

As she plunged toward the house and the last lap of her race, she felt no euphoria. But, the test had been grueling, and she still must prepare the metheq and take it to her father. Surely once he approved her offering and declared her Nasi, her elation would know no bounds.

She left the woods and traversed unbroken drifts. A shroud of abandonment lay over all. Of course it was quiet, she reminded herself. Her mother kept the children at Armown, and Rosh traveled Outside.

So why did the silence seem so unnatural?

At the house, she removed her snowshoes and used a booted foot to sweep the snow from the threshold. Once inside, she closed her eyes and heaved a sigh.

Then she shivered.

Before embarking on her trek, she'd set the temptrol to just above freezing, but the empty house felt frigid, with a chill of the spirit more than the body.

Dassa tugged off her boots, took thick slippers from the shoe-warmer by the door, then slid her feet into them. Next she shuffled through the dining area to the climate panel nestled in the gently curved, fabric-covered wall, and adjusted the control to a more comfortable temperature.

The heater rumbled awake then settled into its familiar hum as Dassa toured the vacant rooms. She hugged herself as the emptiness formed a shadow of foreboding in her heart. Nothing had been touched in her absence, but somehow, nothing was the same.

She had neither time nor strength to waste on the puzzle. Back in the kitchen, she shrugged off her travel-stained pack, laid it on the table, and pulled out a heavy tin. Though mossberries weren't much bigger than the blue spots on a damebug's back, they were weighty, and this tin was full of them.

She removed her hooded coat and draped it on the back of a chair, then opened the tin and admired the glistening purple berries. Their rich fragrance made her mouth water. Hungry as she was, though, she wouldn't steal a taste.

Every Gannahan knew the legend of the would-be Nasi who completed his quest with valor, but sampled a berry while preparing the metheq. When he then came before the toqeph, his purple-stained tongue told all. Because he'd yielded to temptation, he was disqualified from the Nasihood for the rest of his life.

The knights of Gannah wore neither badge nor uniform. The color from the mossberries eaten at their induction never left their tongues, and that was the mark of their rank. Some toqephs' mouths were black because they ate each time a new Nasi pledged.

Dassa assembled the ingredients for a pie shell. Though the metheq could be any sort of treat in which mossberries played a role, her father loved pies, and she'd picked enough berries for a nice one. Thinking of the pleasure it would give him, she scooped and measured, mixed and rolled.

An hour later, Dassa left the house with a bubbling-hot mossberry pie in a basket over her arm and ice skates slung over her shoulder. The ancient rules stated the Last Requirement must be performed entirely on foot, so she trudged past the hangar without stopping for the motorsled. If she continued on through the woods then cut across the frozen lake, she'd be at Armown in less than two hours. A baby step, compared to the distance she'd already come. She'd easily make it before nightfall.

The sun still shone undimmed by clouds, but the shadow in her heart grew darker the farther she trudged. Fear knotted in her chest, though she smelled no dangerous animals near nor sensed treacherous changes in weather.

She cast her mind toward Rosh, and their meahs connected faintly. Good. He was well. Her children, though… A mother shouldn't lose touch with her children, even under stresses like these. But when she reached for them in her meah, she felt nothing.

Perhaps she'd been away too long. She reached her meah upward, toward her Yasha. That connection remained as clear as ever. *Finish your mission,* was the message she sensed. *Finish your mission.*

So that's it. The children would be restored to her once her quest was completed. Odd, though, how she felt so desolate. Almost as if… No, she wouldn't think it.

On the bank of the lake, she sat on a rock to change into her skates. After that, the colorful tree line fell behind as she sped to her destination.

But the closer she drew to the palace, gleaming in the sun across the frozen expanse, the larger the emptiness yawned within her. What was going on? Was this part of the test? She drew the crisp Gannahan air deep into her lungs, but it failed to calm her.

Fourteen days ago, when she'd clung to the frozen cliffs, buffeted by gusts and sprayed by the icy breakers, filling her tin with the tiny mossberries, she'd envisioned this moment. Nearing the palace, carrying her prize. Lightheaded from fasting, weak from exertion, but energized by the impending victory. Then presenting her offering to the toqeph. He'd sample it. She pictured his azure eyes widening in delight as a smile stole across his face. "Not bad," he'd say, or some such grudging praise. Once he'd eaten, he would pronounce her a Nasi, and the rest of the metheq would be hers.

It would be the first food to cross her lips in a fortnight, but it was reputed to be worth the wait. They said a man could fight for seven days and nights on seven mossberries. An exaggeration, no doubt, but the tiny fruits did seem to impart unusual strength and refreshment to those who had earned the right to eat them. Her mouth watered at the scent wafting up from the basket she held in both arms.

As she neared her destination, she wondered at the absence of skate marks on the ice. Usually the surface was scarred with them, especially here, near the palace.

She glided to the pavilion on the shore. After stumping on her skates across the snow, she sat on a bench to change into her boots then started up the path to the plateau, where Armown reigned in noble splendor. Her legs felt wobbly, the basket heavy on her arm, as she plodded upward.

Intent on her purpose, Dassa maintained communion with the Yasha, putting all else out of her mind.

Then she reached the stairway cut into the stone face of the mountain, leading up to the palace. Before she'd climbed three steps, waves of sorrow radiating from the ancient pinkstone walls drove her to her knees, and she barely rescued the precious metheq from sliding down the slope behind her. A vision of death—many deaths—passed across her meah, sucking the air from her lungs. Eyes closed, she forced herself to inhale, and the frigid air cut like a blade.

She rose slowly, casting with her meah into the palace. She could make no connection with her sons. Her heart nearly stopped—they were gone. *No!* Her mother? Gone. Her father? Dim. Very dim.

A great many souls had vanished from inside those walls, from the whole city of Ayar. She spread herself farther. This death ravaged as far as she could sense.

Dropping her skates, she clutched her basket and ran up the stairs.

2

In his office aboard the hospital starship *LSS Barton*, Pik studied a computer image. Was it an actual woman of strange and wonderful breeding, or a computer-generated compilation?

And was it pornography? Perhaps. But he was conducting an anatomical study. To settle an argument.

His eyes followed the gyrating image on the screen. She was a remarkable specimen. Clinically speaking, of course. The breasts were Glenmarrian, no doubt about that. His focus lingered there to confirm his first impression. Definitely Glenmarrian. And definitely delicious. His gaze moved south. Ah, the umbilicus sprang from a different gene pool. Unlike the one undulating before him, the Glenmarrian navel is—

"Dr. Pik."

Pik's heart jumped and he exited the site, feigning deep interest in the medical page that came up in its place—a treatise on toenail fungus in elderly Eutarians.

Though Broward's thinning brown hair and stubby frame made him a less-than-imposing figure, his position commanded respect. Probably the only man in the galaxy with both a medical degree and a ship captain's credentials, his resume was impressive indeed. Besides that, Pik liked the man. Considered him one of his few Earthish friends.

Nevertheless, he felt superior to the captain, in height, looks, intelligence, and especially fashion sense. Pik didn't lift his gaze. "Yes, Captain?"

Broward got right to the point. "You have a new project."

"Already? We haven't completed our assignment here yet."

"No, but a distress signal takes precedence."

Pik looked up. "Distress signal?"

"From Gannah. They're dying in a plague and require immediate assistance."

Pik blinked, not sure he heard right. "They're dying *where*?"

"Gannah."

Something clumped in Pik's gut like a not-quite-done Cephargian blood pudding. "What sort of plague?"

"The message calls it the Karkar plague."

The pudding rolled over. "I had no idea it still existed."

"Nor did I." Broward paused. "Gannah's never asked for help before. Ever. For anything."

Pik said nothing. He couldn't fathom the proud Gannahans being brought so low.

The shorter man looked at Pik with accusation in his brown eyes. "What do you know about this disease?"

Pik returned his glare with a Karkar impassivity no Terrestrial could match. "That was centuries ago. I'm not that old."

"But you are head of my Infectious Disease Unit, and it originated on your planet. How do we stop it?"

"I have no idea." Neither did he have any idea why they'd want to.

"But you can research it."

Pik's ears swiveled in a Karkar shrug. He felt confident the captain, being a Terrestrial, would be unable to interpret the subtle gesture of casual disrespect, even if he noticed it.

But Broward frowned, perhaps picking up on Pik's attitude through his hesitation. "Well? You Karkar might not have the musculature to make faces, but I know there's something going on behind that expressionless mask of yours."

The Karkar sighed. "Research the plague?" He paused again. "I suppose I could..."

"And you will. Quickly. We should be there in two standard-weeks. A great many more Gannahans will likely have died by then. Your plague just about wiped them out last time, did it not?"

"It's a shame it didn't."

Broward's brows rose. "You're a doctor. How can you say that?"

Remaining seated, Pik pulled himself up to his full, proud height, putting him eye to eye with the standing captain. "I don't see that Gannah has made any contribution to the galaxy, save to provide a template for pure evil."

If Broward was impressed with Pik's superior size, he didn't let on. "It's good you're a cool, dispassionate professional, then, because as an agency of the League of Planets, it's our job to save them." He let that sink in a moment then went on. "What do you know of Gannahan physiology?"

"Very little. Only that it's markedly different from yours or mine."

"How so? Are their livers in their armpits and their hearts in their backsides?"

Pik ignored the captain's Earthish humor. "The systems are comparably arranged, but their chemistry is different and their functions are enhanced. Muscle mass is greater, senses are sharper, organs more efficient and less subject to wear. Their immune systems are impervious to all known diseases..."

"Except this plague."

Pik turned to his computer and began a search, but answered according to his own knowledge. "That's caused by a musculophage engineered by Karkar biochemists to attack

Gannahan muscle tissue. I believe it's the only illness they're susceptible to, and it's harmless to all other life forms."

Broward crossed his arms. "So those biochemists must have been familiar with how the Gannahans are put together. And they must have kept records."

"I'm sure they did." Pik scanned the various entries. Not much came up at first glance.

"And with their data, you can stop the plague."

Pik cocked his head to the left in acquiescence. "I shall try."

"And you'll succeed. Once you and your people figure it out, get a team working around the clock to manufacture as many doses of the cure as possible. If you need more help, I'll take personnel from other duty. This is our top priority."

"I'll do my best, Captain."

"Your best is all I ask. But you've already shown me how good your best can be. If you fail me this time, I'll be demanding some answers."

If Pik could have scowled, his look would have been enough to get him demoted to records clerk. "I understand, sir."

"Very good." Broward nodded and started to go, then turned back. "But Dr. Pik…"

"Yes?"

"Those people who sent the distress signal are generations removed from the ones who ravaged Karkar. They've been living peaceably for hundreds of years, ever since your forefathers sent theirs running for home with their tails between their legs. You should have no axe to grind with them after all this time."

Pik swallowed a snort of derision. "I'm familiar with your overworked Earth adages, but our Karkar proverb says it better: 'Deep wounds heal, but the scar reminds, and the memory makes the wound bleed fresh.'"

"Your sayings are morbid. I like ours better."

"It sounds smoother in our own language."

"Your language sets my teeth on edge. Spare me."

Before Pik could decide whether to take offense, the captain had left the office.

He stared at the door as it swished closed. Ordinarily, Pik enjoyed his job. The assignments were challenging but satisfying, and when he pillowed his head at dimlights, he felt as content as a luglit with a bellyful of well-aged zikzak. But requiring him to come to the aid of the filthy Gannahans pressed his loyalty to the edge.

He should have listened to his mother. She'd told him to keep all twelve toes on Karkar where they belonged and not get mixed up in the Earthers' affairs. Just because our governments have joined in league, she said, doesn't mean we should forget who we are.

She was a fine one to talk. She, who married a Terrestrial. Fortunately, that mistake hadn't tainted her progeny. Pik's appearance was as striking as anyone's on his planet, and his mind was sharper than most. That was why he wanted to travel. There was too much to see, too much to learn to stay in one place his whole life. He'd come home when he was ready to settle down.

But he didn't expect that would be soon. In fact, he'd released his betrothed from her promise two years ago.

Deen would have made him a worthy wife; his mother had chosen her well. But it wasn't right to keep her bound to a man who might not claim her until her fertility was past.

It had been comforting, though, to picture her waiting. It pained him more than he cared to admit when she married Llllaarrr less than a year after he released her.

Now here he was, forever single, far from home, and required to rescue the people who would have annihilated his own had they not been stopped in their tracks by what some called a miracle.

As a scientist, Pik didn't believe in miracles. But he had to admit the way those ancient chemists stumbled upon the one thing that could bring down their ultrahuman opponents seemed supernatural. And their success at surreptitiously introducing it into the enemy starcrafts' ventilation systems certainly beat all odds. Every last fiend not only left the planet within days, but their bloody surge across the galaxy was halted once and for all. The Karkars' stroke of luck—or genius, Pik preferred to think—saved every civilization in the path of the ravening Gannahan onslaught. As far as Pik was concerned, his people were the saviors of the universe.

At the computer, Pik delved deeper into the records. Surely somebody, at some time, had digitalized the chemists' notes and entered them into the database. Not that anyone could have predicted a resurgence of the plague, but such a notable achievement should be properly memorialized.

While he searched, his mind rehearsed what he knew of modern Gannah. The sum of it would fit on a sticky note. The villains had burst from anonymity to become an unstoppable scourge—nearly unstoppable, anyway—then vanished from sight as quickly as they'd appeared. Thereafter they were relegated to the realm of legend, in which they always played the bad guy.

Except for that swarthy musician. Since first rocketing onto the music scene about two years ago, Ross Knapsack, as he called himself, had been improving his people's public image at the speed of sound. Adolescent girls swooned over his well-muscled physique and startling violet eyes, the boys admired his manliness, and adults appreciated his talent. Having seen videos of his performances, even Pik was grudgingly impressed with Knapsack's smooth, agile voice and natural showmanship.

Pik tried to ignore the popular Knapsack tune that came unbidden to mind as he scoured the records.

After an hour of poring over the data, jotting notes, and sketching diagrams, Pik sat back and rubbed his eyes. The ancient Karkar had discovered that the invaders' inordinate strength lay, at least in part, in the extra CD155 receptors in their muscle cells. Pik's ancestors then were able to engineer an organism that attacked those receptors. Because of the Gannahans' unique neuromuscular junction, the virus readily slipped into their central nervous system through the retrograde axonal transport. That led to paralysis, respiratory arrest and death.

It was a masterful piece of molecular engineering—a thing of beauty, really. Now, what about undoing its damage? It would take a few days in the lab, but he was pretty sure he could—

He stopped short, realizing he was humming that Knapsack song again. Catchy tune, though. And the lyrics were clever, for a love song.

He thought of Deen, and his ears sagged. A Karkar didn't marry for love, but feelings usually formed between spouses over time.

Pik wondered with a touch of bitterness what his wanderlust had cost him.

3

Broward was right, Pik thought, in saying he was a cool and dispassionate professional.

Or perhaps more accurately, he was passionate about his profession.

His position on the *Barton* had been complicated and expensive to finagle, and he would do nothing to jeopardize it. If he must climb over a mountain of inbred anti-Gannahism to reach the top of his career, then so be it. Whatever it took.

Turned out it took more than swallowing his resentment. So many false starts in the lab, so many self-recriminations about betraying his fellow Karkar, so little time to manufacture the antidote. And the nagging fear that, in the end, it would all be for naught.

When he at last learned how to combat the disease, new uncertainties set in. What would Gannah be like? What would the remaining inhabitants do to the landing team? He could barely eat. His lean, pale Karkar form began to fade into a hollow-eyed wraith. If a wraith could be seven feet tall.

By the time Pik stood on the command center observing the landing preparations, he felt like a fly zooming in on a spider web.

"What do you see, Mr. Norinaga?" Broward asked the first mate.

"The continent is coming into view, sir. I see cloud cover, but not too much for the sensors to penetrate." Norinaga fell silent as he read the incoming data.

"Well, what's it look like? Where's the largest population center?"

Pik's innards cringed at the thought of facing a large population of plague-crazed Gannahans as he watched Norinaga scan the data flowing past his eyes.

The first mate's face took on the image of puzzlement. "There…there is no population center, sir."

Broward frowned. "What do you mean?"

"I'm getting—" Norinaga shook his head. "I see no human life readings at all."

While Pik's mind struggled with that concept, the captain turned to his communications officer. "Ruiz, didn't you say they responded to our message?"

"Yes, sir." From the tone of her voice, you'd think they were on a routine exercise, not approaching the spookiest place in the galaxy.

"Then someone was there ten minutes ago," the captain said. "Where did the signal originate?"

"Just west of the continent's center, sir."

Broward swung back to Norinaga. "You see people?"

The first mate paused as he scanned. Then he looked up. "Just one, sir."

The command deck fell silent.

"One living person on that whole planet?" Broward's voice was hushed.

Norinaga stared at the information flowing across his screen. "That's all I can locate, sir. Only one."

Pik felt like the air had been punched from his lungs. The whole planet dead. "That can't be, Mr. Norinaga. Keep looking."

Several moments passed as a crew of technicians scanned again and reviewed the data repeatedly. No matter how they came at it, they could detect only one living human.

"Tell him to hang on, Ruiz," the captain said. "We're coming down."

Broward turned to Pik, his face ashen as a Karkar's. "You won't need much of a medical team after all. One other doctor should be sufficient. And call a halt to production. We won't need any more doses."

While a jumble of conflicting emotions converted his lunch into boiling acid, Pik contacted the lab and gave the order.

He wasn't sure how to deal with all this. Though he'd been prepared to save the accursed Gannahans, he felt personally responsible for their extinction. Partly because his people had created the disease. But mostly because this was what he'd secretly hoped for.

The whole team seemed to share Pik's anxiety as they watched the planet come into view. From their comments, no one knew what an infernal world would look like, but when it rose before them in a blaze of brilliant blue, it took them by surprise.

The landing craft drew closer an1d the planet's single continent spread before them, its clean, bright colors pleasing to the eye. By the time the craft hovered over their destination, the party's amazement had rendered them speechless.

A sprawling structure of rose-colored stone surrounded the approaching courtyard, which looked to be roughly four hundred meters across. As seen from above, the pavement of multi-hued stone slabs formed a mosaic in the detailed design of a spreading tree with red foliage.

Curving in a graceful oval, the palace enclosed the yard in its embrace. Only two stories high on either side of the main gate, the building grew to majestic heights on the opposite end, where a massive tower looked down upon the compound and surrounding environs. Gannah's flag, white with a green tree design, flapped from a pole on the tower's peak. Pik stared at the fluttering banner. Such a peaceful emblem for this warlike people.

The shuttle settled down left of a central fountain surrounded by resplendent shrubs in full bloom despite the just-above-freezing temperatures. Wind whipped across the wet pavement, scattering shed petals across dirty remnants of melting snow. Gray clouds raced across the cold, pale sky as the landing party exited their craft, clad in biohazard gear as was the normal precaution.

Not that anything about this situation was normal.

The *Barton* had come to the aid of many suffering civilizations, but never before had Pik encountered such a destructive disease. The vacuous courtyard, the empty windows staring blankly down, the leaf litter blowing across the pavement—it made Pik's skin crawl beneath his suit.

The name of Gannah had always summoned a dark mystery in his mind. It represented a place as vile as the mythical hell itself. But what he saw here didn't fit the image.

Even on a cloudy day, the beauty of this world was unlike anything he'd ever seen. The architecture could only be described as poetic. Colors glowed clear and distinct, and the very stone seemed living and wholesome. Islands of flora dotted the plaza like miniature parks, artistically plotted and lovingly tended.

Through his protective headgear, Pik heard a strange, organic music. The wind didn't howl, it sang, and the blowing litter danced to the tune. A formation of birds flew overhead, warbling in harmony, and a small creature scampered in rhythm across the courtyard. It seemed the whole planet had the same pulse.

Yet someone lay dying nearby.

Pik pointed to a wide portal at the foot of the tallest section of the building some two hundred meters away. "Looks like the main entrance."

He led the way, followed by Dr. Webb, the shuttle's pilot, and the navigator, all trying to survey their surroundings through the restricted view of their headgear. Rather than echoing across the vacant courtyard, the clatter of their footsteps seemed to be swallowed up by the emptiness, or maybe hushed by the wind, as if the planet were making a deliberate effort to muffle the foreign sounds.

Though massive and intricately carved, the heavy double doors of the main entrance were opened with an easy pull. The team slipped through into a broad, curving entrance hall with many passages branching off and fading into the gloom. In the center of the hall, opposite the doors, a living tree grew, its trunk meters in diameter, its massive branches reaching toward a distant skylight in the tower above.

Pik gazed around. "Which way, Duval?"

The navigator looked at his hand-held directional instrument then pointed past the tree. "That way, sir. "

As they edged forward into the darkness, a soft glow appeared within the walls to illuminate their way. It seemed as if the stone itself radiated with a cool, pink light. Once the hall was lit, the crew saw balconies rising in courses, like layers of a cake.

Palumbo, the shuttle pilot, craned his neck to look. "We're not going way up there, I hope?"

Duval shook his head. "No, he's on this level."

Pik motioned them forward. "Let's go. We've no time to waste."

The group tagged along behind Duval as he traversed the flagstone floor to the far end of the hall, following the instrument's signal.

"That's funny," he said shortly. He shook the handheld instrument and tapped it against his palm. "It just went dead." Looking around, he pointed to an open doorway. "I think it was taking us there."

Suppressing his annoyance at Duval's incompetence—the fool probably forgot to charge the batteries—Pik entered with others hard on his heels.

One window lit the room, and a light blinked from what appeared to be communications equipment on a central console. Ruiz's voice came faintly from it, broken by interference. "Landing…on the wa…Ackno…ing party…knowledge, please."

In front of the station, a woman sprawled in a chair, head thrown back, eyes closed, jaw slack. Her thick braid of black hair nearly grazed the floor.

Surprised to see a female, Pik hesitated for half a second before striding toward his patient.

The only living Gannahan didn't seem aware of their presence until Pik swiveled the chair to get a better look. Even then, her only response was a catch in her labored breathing. Her skin hung loose on a once-sturdy frame, the muscles beneath it wasted away. The body temperature was 36.46 Celsius, but Pik didn't know what was normal for a Gannahan. The heartbeat was slow but steady. One hopeful sign, at least.

Duval went to the console and tried to figure out the communications equipment while Pik spoke to the patient in the Standard Language.

"My name is Dr. Pik." She had sent and received transmissions in that tongue, so he assumed she could understand it, but she registered no response.

He tried again. "We came in answer to your distress signal. Are any others still alive?"

Duval found the right control to activate and spoke into the transmitter. "Landing party to *Barton*. We're here. Do you read?" As the speaker crackled an affirmative answer, Duval looked at the woman, awaiting her response to Pik's question.

Her eyelids shuddered but didn't open, and she breathed the word, "No."

Duval met Pik's gaze before he turned back to his task. Dr. Webb prepared the respirator while Pik continued his examination.

How strange, to enter the heart of hell and find it altogether pleasant. But not so strange as to examine a dying demon. Whose tongue—surely *that* wasn't normal—whose tongue was a uniform, deep purple.

"Ready, Doctor," said Webb.

Pik took the mask from her and placed it over the Gannahan's mouth and nose.

"This treatment has never been tested," he told the patient, "but it should arrest the progress of the disease. Inhale as deeply as you can."

The Gannahan's respirations remained shallow. Crouched beside her, Pik watched for a reaction, but got none. No color flickered through the cadaverous complexion, and the patient made no attempt to communicate.

Pik stood. "Let's get her up to the ship. The sooner we get her out of the contamination, the better."

Dr. Webb helped him lift the woman and lay her on the stretcher. She didn't weigh much.

"We're taking you to the ship's hospital," Pik told her, a little alarmed at the increase in her heart rate. "You'll be well cared for there."

The adjustments Duval had been making on the communications equipment cleared the reception somewhat, and Norinaga's voice came through well enough to understand most of the words. "Dr. Pik, are you there?"

Pik stepped toward the transmitter. "Yes, we're all here."

"There's a storm moving your way, and fast. Heavy rain, large hail, hurricane-force winds, and more lightning than a shark has teeth. If you don't get back up here soon, you'll be stuck on Gannah until it passes, and from the look of things, that could be a while. It's bizarre the way the storm came out of nowhere, but it's a monster."

Pik fought down a wave of panic. A confirmed indoorsman, he hated weather of any sort, but nothing filled him with terror like a storm. "Thanks. We're on our way." He turned to Webb, who monitored the patient. "If she's stable, let's hustle."

Webb nodded. "Should be okay to transport."

They all snatched up the stretcher and their equipment and hurried out. Once they'd passed through the great hall and reached the main entrance, Pik paused despite his haste. "A moment please." Somehow he felt compelled to close the door and make sure it latched securely. Then, at a deep rumbling that could be felt as well as heard, Duval pointed across the courtyard.

"Take a look at that sky."

Clouds black as space barreled toward them, and the music in the air played dueling kettledrums. Pik's heart leapt. "Run!"

Gusts sucked at their clothing as the landing party raced across the pavement, sharing the load of the stretcher. Halfway to the shuttle, Pik's visor fogged from the steam of his exertions, but he continued in a blind dash to the landing craft. They loaded in record time, and, buffeted by the winds, lifted up and out of the way as a heavy black curtain drew beneath them, flashing daggers of lightning.

Heart pounding, Pik tried to quell his terror and focus on the patient. If he made it back to the *Barton* alive, nothing would induce him to set foot on that planet again.

Dr. Webb removed her headgear, shook out her hair and wiped the sweat from her brow. "I'd heard Gannah can have some pretty hellacious weather. Guess that rumor's true."

Duval peered through the shuttle window at the fury falling behind. "I've never heard anything about Gannah at all."

"Me, neither," said the pilot. "Just that the bogeyman came from there. But it sure didn't look like I expected."

"Neither does the bogeyman," said Duval, staring at the emaciated woman on the stretcher.

Pik monitored the patient's signs, wishing he knew the difference between normal and cause for alarm. With readings like this, if she were any other race, she'd be dead.

4

Dassa knew what was happening—the arrival of the Outsiders, the inhalation treatment, her kidnapping by these aliens—but couldn't squander her fast-fading strength by responding.

As they secured her mobile bed into the landing craft and the doctor turned his attentions to her again, she wondered about him. Where did he get an antidote for this plague? No one had ever seen it before except its victims, and they'd all died before finding a cure. How could he counter an illness he knew nothing about? Unless...

His speech was somewhat impeded, as if he lacked the fine muscle control required to form the sounds, and the timbre of his voice was reedier than an Earther's. And though she hadn't opened her eyes, she was aware of his towering height, could feel his massive presence. Yes, he must be a Karkar.

And he was touching her with those grotesque, six-fingered hands.

But she wouldn't think about it. She'd allow these Outsiders to do as they wished. So long as they moved her toward her next objective.

Even now, her husband, Rosh, negotiated with the Eutarians for passage to League Station 27. The speeding vessel in which she was imprisoned closed the distance between them, for she'd heard one of her captors say they were on a course for that same station.

After Dassa completed her quest, she'd contacted Rosh through meah communion. He'd already learned from his twin sister, Ra'anan, of the tragedy at home, abandoned his tour with no explanation to the Earthers in the band that accompanied him, and headed for Gannah by any and every route he could find. By the time Dassa arrived at Armown, he was already on his way.

As the horrors had unfolded before Dassa's eyes, only Rosh and the Yasha kept her from losing her mind as everything else slipped away. Their families. Their friends. Everyone they'd ever known and those they'd never met. How could the entire world be emptied of souls? How could there be no one left but Dassa and Rosh?

Their loss was incalculable. Beyond devastating. Past comprehension. For some reason, their Yasha spared just the two of them, and they clung to each other with desperation.

But Dassa couldn't hasten their reunion. All she could do was heal.

She willed her body into a comatose state to escape her pain and commence her recovery.

Pik's ears frowned as he stood outside the captain's cabin, his stiff, blond brush of hair scrubbing the doorframe. This situation was becoming a nightmare. "You wanted to see me, sir?"

"Yes, come in." Broward gestured toward a chair. "I need a report on our patient's progress."

Pik sank into the seat, feeling as if he'd go all the way to the floor. Spacecraft furniture was seldom suited to people of his stature. "Nothing has changed. The Gannahan is still not responding."

"It's been ten days. The treatment should have kicked in by now."

"It has. That is, the progress of the disease has been arrested. She's breathing easier, the heartbeat's stronger, and the brain's shooting impulses all over the place. But she remains unconscious."

Broward's stubby fingers tapped the desktop. "Why?"

"Haven't a clue. From the cerebral activity, I'd say she's fully aware of what's going on around her, but she doesn't respond to stimuli."

"So what are you doing about it? I need something constructive to give High Command."

"As my report indicates"—Pik nodded to the open file on the captain's desktop screen as he shifted in the uncomfortable chair—"I'm giving electrical stimulation to the limbs to help rebuild the muscles. Also, high-protein liquid nutrition. But the body chemistry is so outlandish it's hard to know what else to do. Her blood contains elements I've never seen before, and I believe conventional pharmacology would be contraindicated, even if I knew what to treat for."

"In other words, you're doing nothing."

"I'm…monitoring her."

More closely than he let on.

Though he personally abhorred the race, the chance to study a live Gannahan was a rare gift. As far as he knew, no physician from a civilized world had ever had such an opportunity, and he'd never be accused of passing up a chance for advancement.

Broward grunted. "HC is hounding me for answers. What am I supposed to tell them?"

"That she's resting comfortably."

Pik's messenger sounded, and he answered. "What is it?"

Kamchatka, one of Pik's assistants, sounded a little breathless. "Sorry to bother you, sir, but Dr. Webb is having a problem with our patient."

Pik exchanged glances with Broward. "What sort of problem?"

"She can't get her to settle down."

"She what?" Pik sprang from his seat as if launched. "I'm on my way."

Less than two minutes after acknowledging the message, Pik and Broward arrived—a bit breathless themselves—on the patient's floor and hurried toward the Gannahan's room, where Pik heard Dr. Webb pleading, "Please, ma'am, you can't…No, no, stop that, please, you must settle down."

Pik strode in. "What's the problem?"

The Gannahan's IV and feeding tube lay scattered around the room. Her arms had been flailing when Pik entered, but, breathing heavily from exertion, she dropped them at the sound of his voice. Her eyes flew open to reveal brilliant green orbs, which searched his proximity a half second before fixing on his face.

Webb spun around, her face as distraught as an Earther's could be. "Dr. Pik! The patient is…she's…well, look at her."

He did. And suppressed a shiver. Despite his close association with the patient, it was the first time he'd ever felt the infamous Gannahan gaze. He kept his attention on Webb. "Tell me what happened."

"When I started setting up for her stimulation treatment, she opened her eyes and looked at me." Webb's voice cracked with distress. "I was so startled I dropped the gel. When I straightened up after picking it off the floor, she was trying to pull the feeding tube out of her nose."

Those green eyes drilled into him steadily, but he continued to look only at Webb. "And then?"

"She hit me in the face, and I had Kamchatka call you." Webb's glance darted between the Gannahan and Pik, and the red mark on her cheek verified that much of the tale.

The patient still stared at him, but at least she'd quieted down. It was probably best to humor her for now. Speaking to Webb, Pik stooped and grabbed the IV needle and tubes from the floor. "Might as well take these things out of here. The stimulation machine, too. It doesn't appear we'll be needing them anymore."

With tremulous hands, Webb loaded the equipment on the machine's cart and pushed it swiftly out without a backward look.

Once Webb was gone, the captain had room to step toward the patient, hand extended. "I'm Edwin Broward, captain of this vessel, the *LSS Barton*, research hospital. Allow me to offer you a belated welcome aboard. I was unable greet you properly when you first joined us."

The creature on the bed wordlessly shifted her gaze to Broward, relieving Pik of its sharp scrutiny.

When the patient made no move to shake the captain's hand, he withdrew it. "What a terrible tragedy your planet has undergone. Are you aware of…the extent of the losses?"

She expelled a long breath, then nodded.

Broward's forehead creased. "Though I'm thankful we were able to save you, I deeply regret that we came too late to help the others. Please accept my deepest condolences on your unspeakable loss."

She stared at him but made no further response.

Broward swallowed. That gaze must unnerve him, too. "But…you have me at advantage. I'm afraid I don't know your name."

Her lips parted and she made a grunting sound, as if trying out her voice. Then followed a hoarse and foreign-sounding rasp. "I am…Atarah…Hadassah…Haga…Natsach."

Broward seemed to hang on every inexplicable word. When it appeared her speech was finished, he leaned forward ever so slightly. "Did you say your name is Atarah? May I call you that, or would you prefer—"

The Gannahan breathed deeply, licked her lips, and spoke again. "Atarah is title of my father's family. My given name is Hadassah."

Broward opened his mouth to speak, but the patient wasn't finished. "You may call me..." She seemed to search for the word. "Mrs. Natsach."

The captain nodded. "Very well, Mrs. Natsack. Let me again offer my condolences." His voice grew soft and sympathetic. "You've lost everything, everyone, you've ever known. I can't begin to comprehend what that must be like."

A small tremor convulsed her body, and she shifted her gaze to the ceiling, as if seeking a response up there. Wherever she found the words, they came out less hoarsely, but her meaning was no easier to follow. "You speak truly, you cannot comprehend. But it is also untrue. I have not lost my husband."

Pik glanced at Broward, whose raised brows indicated he found that statement as confusing as Pik did. "Pardon me?"

"He is a minstrel. He travels the planets. Natsach Rosh."

The captain's face registered no recognition, but something resonated in Pik's head and then a thought took shape. "Ross Knapsack? He's your husband?"

She turned her gaze on him again, but the green spark of malevolence had faded. "You know him?"

"The whole galaxy does."

Recognition lit Broward's face. "Oh, yes, the singer. He's your husband? Really?" Then sympathy faded his countenance. "Do you know how we might reach him?"

The woman hesitated. Pik watched her face, wondering if she could possibly not know how to get in touch with her husband. Or was there something she wasn't telling?

Finally she spoke in that husky accent. "Perhaps his manager can assist you. Gareth Oza."

The captain nodded. "I'll look into it immediately. Again, please accept my condolences. I'll see if we can reach your husband. He needs to know there's one bright spot to report in this catastrophe." He looked up at Pik. "I believe I have something to report to HC after all. And Mrs. Knapsack—"

"Natsach."

"Mrs. Natsack. I hope you'll be as comfortable as possible here in our care. After you've rested a bit more, and if Dr. Pik here will allow it, perhaps we can talk again. Meanwhile, if there's anything I can do for you, please let me know. Anything at all."

She studied him as if measuring his veracity with some unknown power of discernment. "Thank you. Your kindness is great."

"Don't mention it."

Broward turned to Pik. "Once you've seen to her needs, Doctor, I'd like to speak with you."

Pik tipped his head. "Of course."

After a farewell nod to the patient, Broward turned and left, dispersing the curious crowd gathered outside.

The door slid shut behind the captain, and Pik swallowed. He was alone with a wild Gannahan.

But she was an invalid. Even if the stories of Gannahan ferocity were true, he should have nothing to fear.

Watching her out of the corner of his eye, he opened a cabinet drawer and selected a fast-acting sedative and a syringe, which he slipped into his lab coat pocket. "The captain is right, Ms. Natsach. You should rest."

She turned that weapon-like glare back on him. "You are Karkar."

His blood ran cold, and he kept his hands in his pockets to hide their trembling. How fast could he load that needle?

"I am."

Rather than leaping from the bed, fangs bared, as he half expected, she shifted her gaze to the ceiling. "You saved my life. Why?"

The question, though a good one, took him by surprise. "I was under orders. Acting as an agent of the League of Planets, not as a Karkar."

Her wasted condition gave her a cadaverous appearance as she stared upward, unmoving. "That must have been difficult for you. But your duty is done. You may leave me now."

He'd like nothing better than to do just that. But how dare she suggest it? And how dare she show sympathy for his position? "It is also my duty to assist your recovery."

That gaze turned and speared him again. "Is that what you call it? I would have continued my healing sleep, had not your peoples' tortures forced me to act."

"Tortures? You've received nothing but the finest care."

"You pierce me with needles. Violate my body with tubes. Pollute it with chemicals, which I must waste energy to excrete." Now that her vocal cords were warmed up, her voice rang clear, though the words still slurred. "You drain my blood, scrape off cell samples, plug me into barbaric devices and jolt me with electrical shocks. Is this not torture?"

Pik's ears jerked. "That is basic medical procedure."

"It is cruelty." She closed her eyes. "If you wish me to heal, let me rest."

This was one patient he'd like to keep permanently unconscious. "I'll give you a sedative."

"No!" She tried to sit up but fell back. "Your potion would poison me. The best way to help, if that is in fact your aim, is to leave me be."

"Very well." Was that really how Gannahans healed themselves? Simply through deep sleep? "But if you need—"

"I do not." The patient let out a long sigh as if breathing her last then lay still as death.

She spoke as if the Gannahans didn't believe in medicine. Surely they didn't achieve their unusual health through sleeping. It went against his grain and his training. "Before I go, may I ask one question?"

She stirred a little and grunted, which he took for assent.

"Why is your tongue purple?"

She answered without deigning to look at him. "You have never heard of the purple-tongued knights of Gannah?"

"Of course. In fairytales designed to frighten children into behaving."

She opened her eyes and turned her head. "Then you had best behave, Dr. Pik."

A chill rippled across his skin. "What are you saying?"

"I am Nasi."

His mind spun around that bizarre possibility. One of the Gannahan knights? He'd never considered there to be any truth to those stories. Did she possess supernatural powers? Was he—was the whole ship in danger? "Is the tongue purple from birth?"

She lay silent while Pik's curiosity screamed for satisfaction.

"Where does the color come from?"

When no answer came and her breathing grew measured and slow, Pik turned down the light with a shaking hand and left the room. What sort of monster had they brought on board?

5

Hours later Dassa awoke with a cry and a stabbing pain in her chest.

With the eyes of her meah she saw spurting blood and jagged metal protruding from her body, grasped by red-stained hands. The pain was hers, but the hands were Rosh's. Her own hands grasped only the front of her hospital gown. She heard his cry, felt his pain, shared his terror—and then their connection was broken.

She sagged into the mattress. His heart beat no longer—so why did hers? Why were her sheets not covered with blood? Why was she still alive, when everyone…everyone…everyone else was gone?

6

ik stared at the message on the screen. This nightmare went on forever.

He tried closing his eyes, but when he reopened them, the words hadn't changed.

"Subject: Sole Survivor of Gannahan Plague. Due to insufficient information from attending physician, High Command is sending an investigative commission to meet the *LSS Barton* at Station 27." The commission's estimated arrival date was in twenty-two days.

Pik uttered a nasal moan. In twenty-two days, his soaring career would fizzle out like a dying flare. Curse that little goblin and her whole damnable race.

He had been trying to unravel the Gannahan snarl for weeks now, but he had precious little string loosed from the ball. The commission would be no more impressed with his excuses than Captain Broward.

"What do you mean she's in a coma?" Broward had demanded when Pik tried to explain. "Day before yesterday she was awake and talking."

"She was, but she's slipped out of consciousness again."

The captain had clenched and re-clenched his fist. "And you're not even keeping her hydrated? You're sorry you saved her, is that it, and now you're trying to kill her?"

"Not at all." Pik kept his voice as expressionless as his face. "I'm acting on the advice of the galaxy's foremost expert in Gannahan physiology."

"Who would that be? And why didn't you consult him before?"

"Because she was unconscious before."

Broward's eyes narrowed. "The patient herself, you mean? She's hardly in a position to—"

"She was fully lucid yesterday. And she made it quite clear that our efforts on her behalf did nothing but hinder. She insisted her body is capable of healing itself, and I agreed to stop getting in the way of its natural processes."

"Well, I don't like it, and neither will HC." Broward scowled and paced. "I can't let you stand around doing nothing but wag your ears while the only survivor of her planet's disaster dies of inanition. Not when she's under my care. I won't have it."

Pik couldn't blame the captain. If his and Broward's positions were reversed, he'd be saying the same thing, but more loudly. Nevertheless he stood his ground. "I have no training in Gannahan medicine, so I must rely on what she says. Even if she's not a physician, she has to know more about how Gannahans heal than you or I."

Broward glared up at Pik, opened his mouth as if to speak, then snapped it shut.

It occurred to Pik that if he were ordered to take action and the Gannahan died as a result, it might not be a bad thing. The patient would be out of his hair for good, but he would be in the clear. "What would you have me do, Captain?"

"I will trust your judgment on this. Keep doing what you're doing. That is, keep not doing what you're not doing." Broward rubbed his eyes. "Just let me know the instant something changes."

But of course nothing did. And now, while Pik contemplated the message of doom on his screen, Broward slipped in and helped himself to a chair across the room.

Pik looked up from his gloom. "Hello, Captain. To what do I owe the pleasure?"

"Any change in the Gannahan?"

"None." Pik's ears sagged.

"I figured as much." Broward crossed one leg over the other. "But we did finally get word on the husband."

"I wondered. A public figure like that should be easy to locate."

"One would think so. But there's more here than meets the eye."

"How so?"

Broward shook his head. "You tell me. Five standard-months ago, he disappeared. Left word with his crew and his manager that he was canceling the tour. Going home."

Up went the ears. "How long ago?"

"Five months, plus or minus. About the same time we estimate the plague struck Gannah."

Pik leaned back in his chair. "It must be a coincidence. No message could travel through space that fast. He couldn't have known what was happening at home."

Broward shrugged. "Sure seems like he did. He hopped a freight for League Station 2. Another took him to Uranus 1, and then he somehow turned up on Eutare. About the time we entered Gannahan space, he was boarding a merchant ship for Station 27."

Pik's ears stiffened. "Why would he go there? He couldn't have known we'd take his wife there. He couldn't even have known if she was still alive."

"It gets even stranger." The captain ran his hand over his shiny pate. "A little over two standard-weeks ago, a fire broke out in the engine area, trapping seven crewmen. The Knapsack fellow came to their rescue. He saved them all, but before he was able to escape, an explosion slammed him against a wall and impaled him with a shard of Pyetronium." The captain jabbed a thumb toward his chest. "Right through the heart. Instant death."

Pik sat up straighter. "Two weeks ago, you said?"

"That's right. The same time his wife went back into hibernation."

The men exchanged uncomfortable looks. "What are we dealing with here, doctor?"

Pik visualized the small form lying immobile in the dark and an unexpected wave of sorrow overwhelmed him. "An individual utterly alone in the universe."

Dassa lay on the slab of a bed alone in the darkened room as if dead. Her heart beat but faintly. Her lungs inflated and deflated with no noticeable rise and fall of her chest. She hadn't moved a flicker in days.

At first after Rosh's death, the Yasha's presence was as a friend, giving comfort without speaking. He understood her pain as no mortal could.

But after she had mourned in silence some days, the communication became more direct.

Arise.

I have not the strength.

Then I shall give thee of mine. Arise.

How can I, with Gannah dead?

Gannah lives. Remember what I promised thy ancestor, Hoseh?

Yea, my Yasha. That as long as his descendants served Thee faithfully, Gannah would never die.

That was my promise then, and I shall not repent of it. Art thou not a daughter of Hoseh?

I am, Lord.

And my promises are sure.

Yes, Lord. Every word is true. She had no doubt of that. But how could He expect her to just get up as if nothing had happened?

Arise.

How can Gannah live? I have no husband. Gannah will die with me.

Thou would question thy King?

Nay, Lord. Never. But I do not understand.

True, child, it is past thine understanding. But understanding is not necessary for obedience. Now, hearken and heed. Arise. Thy King commandeth thee.

"Mrs. Natsach?"

Dassa's eyes opened slowly at the sound of the familiar reedy voice. Her mouth felt as if it had been dried in a desert wind. She tried to form saliva, but what little came was thick and sticky.

"Mrs. Natsach, I have news of your husband."

"Wha—t?" The word crumbled from her throat like a brittle page from an ancient book. Her eyes felt as gritty as her mouth, but she searched until her bleary gaze found the Karkar doctor. The unwholesome image swam before her like a bad dream.

"What about"—she tried to wet her cracked lips with a wooden tongue—"my husband?"

The Karkar paused before answering, his placid face as unreadable as a statue's. "You know he's dead, don't you?"

She closed her eyes and exhaled all her air. She would have taken no more in again, except for her King's command. "Yes."

"How did you learn of it?"

Her throat swallowed reflexively and nearly stuck together. "I felt him go." She relived the vision briefly. "But I know not how…he was taken."

The story he told her fit both Rosh's character and the few details she already knew. She listened in silence, longing to abandon all and sleep forever.

But her Yasha spoke again. *Arise!*

Gathering the remaining shreds of her strength, she opened her eyes and raised her arms slowly, flexing her fingers, marveling at the effort the simple motion required. "That explains many things. But...my time of mourning is past." She forced herself to sit, though her wasted muscles screamed with pain.

When Pik tried to help, she recoiled from his touch.

He withdrew his hand. "I merely wanted to help. It's extraordinary that you can move at all. You should have died long ago. Did all Gannahans have this ability? To go into a sort of suspended animation at will?"

She flexed her neck. "How else does one heal?"

"Most of us require food and water. Where does your body get the energy to rebuild?"

Dassa stretched her arms out to her sides, swiveled them, moved them forward, then lowered them, muscles burning. It was all she could do to keep from crying out with pain. "My reserves are exhausted. I, too, shall need sustenance for my healing to continue."

"I can arrange that. What does a Gannahan eat just out of hibernation?"

For a physician, he sure didn't know much. "Something soft, easy to process. But my greatest need is water."

The words seemed to stick in her mouth and she forced them out, realizing the Yasha had roused her at the last possible moment. Had she slept another hour, she would never have awakened.

Her eyes burned with absent tears. Her head felt like it was floating. Just when she thought she'd swoon back onto the bed, the doctor placed a receptacle of water in her hand and the tactile sensation brought her back to full consciousness.

She accepted the cup, careful not to allow their fingers to touch, then raised it to her lips. The flimsy disposable vessel contained only a small amount of water, but even that negligible weight made her arm tremble.

"Take it easy," the Karkar advised. "It wouldn't be wise to overdo it at first."

Did he think her an idiot? But he was right. She allowed the first life-giving drops to soothe her tongue before letting them trickle down her swollen throat. Her stomach recoiled in pain at the unaccustomed intrusion, but she took another slow swallow, feeling the water absorb into her gasping tissues.

The cup slipped from her trembling hand and clattered to the floor, spilling the life-giving fluid. She gave a cry, riven with shame at her weakness.

But the Karkar merely said, "It's not a problem," and reached for another identical cup from a counter nearby. The room was so small and his arm so long, he could grab it without even shifting his weight. He then picked up a pitcher from a small table beside her bed.

The sound of the water pouring into the cup was the loveliest thing she'd ever heard, and when he extended it toward her, she reached for it eagerly.

When his long fingers wrapped around hers to help lift the cup to her lips, his touch made her stomach spasm all the more, but the water was already absorbed and there was nothing to come up.

The pale giant beside her waited for the spasm to pass, holding the cup to keep it from dropping. "Perhaps a bottle with a straw would work better."

She pulled her hand away, leaving him to hold the water himself. "Perhaps." The Outsiders' casual attitude about touching was offensive enough, but when the one doing the touching was a Karkar, the horror was multiplied tenfold.

He set the cup on the table beside the bed. "I'll get you something a little easier to handle."

She shivered. Though she tried to hide it, he'd been watching. Instead of a water bottle, he pulled a pillow and blanket out of a cabinet. "If you will allow me to place this behind you to raise your upper body, you'll be able to drink without having to hold yourself upright." He brought the pillow to the bed. "May I?"

Gratified he asked permission, she nodded.

He arranged the pillows behind her and she settled back into them with relief. Then he covered her trembling body with the blanket before turning away and opening another cabinet. After a thorough but fruitless search, he spoke into his messenger. "I need a self-hydration bottle. And a floorbot, please. We have a spill."

Dassa watched the doctor as he went about his business. It was disturbing the way his face never changed. Even his mouth barely moved when he spoke. It was unnatural.

Unnatural for most creatures. Normal for a Karkar.

Karkar. The very name was almost a curse word. Yet here he stood, taller than any human should be, pale as a cadaver and blank-faced as a manikin in a mask. With six gaunt fingers on each oversized hand.

Her gut tightened in revulsion, remembering the many times those hands had touched her in the weeks since her capture. She tried not to hate him, but it was difficult. He didn't know any better. He didn't realize that on Gannah, a man never touched a woman who was not his wife, mother, sister, or daughter. Not even casually. Not even during courting. Only in the case of extreme emergency.

She supposed he could argue that this was an emergency. But—and here the hate bubbled up again and her body stiffened at the thought—there would be no emergency if not for the Karkar, the creators of the plague, the abominable creatures who plotted the extinction of the Gannahan race.

As fast as the hatred flared, a quiet word from her Yasha doused it. *Oh?*

She sank back into the pillows.

No, this Karkar was not at fault for her people's recent devastation. She knew who was, and it was no pale giant.

Dassa tried to blot out the memory of her father, burned in her mind, she feared, forever. The toqeph, Atarah Degel Jachin. Her powerful father, his strength devoured by the plague. Her handsome father, his sagging, disease-ravaged face barely recognizable. Her eloquent father, speaking his final anguished words with a mouth that could scarcely do his bidding. "I have erred, Hadassah. I alone deserve to die...but the people...are punished...for my sin." And his last words, uttered in despair. "I disobeyed...my King."

Her father. He was the one who was responsible for this. Not the tall doctor.

But the doctor was easier to hate.

7

Slouched in his favorite chair, Broward stared at the painting of the old-timey Interplanetary Station, seeking comfort from the past while contemplating the uncertainties of the future.

He thought about the upcoming meeting with the League Investigative Commission, wondering what they'd have to say about his breaking protocol, squandering metric tons of fuel, wasting three hundred thousand Leaguepounds' worth of laboratory supplies, and endangering the safety of the ship, all to save one life.

One Gannahan life. Which, officially, the League didn't consider worth saving.

Gannah had never joined the League of Planets. Gannah had never contributed to League efforts. Historically, Gannahans were bloodthirsty and aggressive. Recently, they were aloof and self-righteous. Why fly to their rescue?

Broward's brow puckered, thinking of the small, solitary patient in his hospital, on the mend at last. Protocol notwithstanding, if he had it to do over, he'd do the same thing.

Except next time, he'd take more risks, get there faster. Maybe save more than one.

He swallowed hard. There would be no second chances. Not for Gannah. And not for him.

He'd have to find a ship of some sort. An independent, not under League control. If that wasn't possible, maybe a job on a Station. But nothing on the ground, if he could help it. He didn't like breathing unfiltered air. Didn't think he could handle the unpredictability of weather, the changing daylight cycles, the myriad other inconstancies of life on a planet. The very thought seemed foreign. Unnatural.

He sorted through his mental list of professional contacts, looking for favors he could call in, people who might have the influence to help. A few possibilities came to mind, all of them iffy. Not many would be willing to help someone the League had blackballed.

Broward's gaze slipped from the painting to the clock on the other wall.

In twelve standard-hours they'd be docking at Station 27. Six hours later, the commission would convene.

He ran his hand along his forty-one-year-old-but-probably-done-for head, reminding himself that it was an investigative commission. They had no authority to make decisions, just discover the facts and make recommendations.

But those who pass judgment would rely on the commission's report. If he couldn't convince the commissioners of the rightness of his decision, he'd be in neck-deep sewage.

By this time tomorrow, he'd know if he should buy a snorkel.

While Broward agonized, Pik reviewed his notes. Fact after figure. Result after result of test after test.

He'd found scores of small differences between the Gannahan and the galaxy's other races. This came as no surprise, for he knew the Gannahans were different. He'd hoped to learn the root of those differences and translate that knowledge into better medicine for everyone. But the answers continued to elude him.

The smooth, regal Karkar, the furry, sawed-off Glenmarrians, and the fleshy, mid-sized Earthers looked dissimilar, but they were so essentially the same that it was possible to match blood and tissue types for transfusion, grafts, or transplants. The

Gannahan, however, while indistinguishable from an Earther in general appearance (except for her eye color), was subtly distinct. Her sharper senses, powers of recovery, and resilience against toxins and diseases surpassed anyone else's.

And, as much as it pained Pik to admit it, so did her intellect. Although he had only one specimen to observe, she told him that her near-flawless skill in memorizing, remembering, and understanding new facts and unfamiliar concepts was fairly typical of her race.

Their weakness, according to his patient, was their lack of inventive curiosity. Until they were attacked by the Fueraqis, Gannah had only the most primitive technologies. Nearly all of their advancements were learned from other societies.

But they learned extremely well. If the ancient Gannahans were as superpowered as this one, it was small wonder they'd been able to take over half the galaxy.

And all the more remarkable that the Karkar had brought them to a permanent halt. Why had they not regathered their strength and sought revenge? He couldn't believe they lacked the ability. For some reason, they must have lacked the will.

Of all the mysteries about Gannah yet to be solved, this was the most puzzling. Pik couldn't fathom them not burning to avenge the staggering blow his forefathers dealt them.

He found it extremely disquieting. The sooner he could turn the patient over to the authorities and relieve himself of her care, the better he'd like it.

He saved her life, facilitated her recovery, and secured his name in medical history. He didn't need to play babysitter as well.

While Broward and Pik brooded, Dassa rested.

She'd been doing a lot of that. Though she had regained

some use of her limbs, the new muscle tissue was still weak and unreliable, and the rebuilding process was painful. She hurt wherever she had muscle, which was everywhere. And Gannahan or not, the constant pain wore on her. She didn't even object when the Karkar announced that she'd be transported around the station in a wheelchair.

Although Dassa was aware there were 243 people aboard the *Barton*, she had seen no one but Dr. Pik and a couple of assistants. The Karkar hovered over her protectively, supervising if not performing every medical test, even uselessly attending the physical therapy sessions like a surveillance camera on an oversized pole.

It took her a while to figure out why. He hoped to somehow gain fame and fortune from her calamity, and he wanted to share it with as few others as possible.

She knew this because she'd been watching him as intently as he had her.

It wasn't a particularly pleasant study. The extra digits on his hands both fascinated and repelled her. The sound of his voice sometimes made her skin crawl. His pale complexion bespoke weakness and ill health, which made his exaggerated size seem like overcompensation. But the thing that bothered her the most was the way his expression was always the same. Between that and his lack of a decent meah, it made him difficult to read.

She'd met Karkar before and found them repugnant. What with their insufferable arrogance, distasteful scent, nerve-grating language, and ridiculous, elongated proportions, she couldn't understand why the Yasha created them.

This Pik person was different, though. He was hard to read, but not impossible. She could connect with a glimmer of a soul that no respectable Karkar should have. Despite his abhorrence of her race, he was not unkind. And she could see that his actions were not entirely self-serving. Somewhere, buried deep within and probably invisible even to himself, sputtered an un-Karkar-like flame of compassion.

If his people ever found out, they'd probably try him for treason.

Treason. The word made her ache within. Her father had been guilty of it, and this is the result. The destruction of their people and her captivity by the Outsiders.

She remembered the Yasha's words. Remembered His authority over all planets. All peoples. All situations.

And the absolute trustworthiness of His promises.

Because of those promises, the future of Gannah was in her hands, but she needn't fear. She must merely follow the Yasha faithfully, wherever He led, and He would take care of the rest.

But, oh, the places He led...

8

The double doors opened and Captain Broward wheeled Dassa into the brightly lit conference room.

The investigative commission seated around the massive table wore matching dark blue jackets decorated with wide white diagonal sashes. As Broward brought her to the table, she scanned their faces and read what she could of their thoughts. They eyed Dassa with a mixture of curiosity, sympathy, and revulsion.

Earlier, the captain had given her a run-down of what such an inquiry was like, and she'd done some reading about League procedures and laws. He had also made her aware that the commission held his career in their hands.

The outcome of the meeting would affect her future as well, but she felt no trepidation. She had nothing more to lose.

The commission exchanged glances with one another, then an imposing Terrestrial woman spoke. Her voice was small and childlike in contrast to her large build and obvious maturity.

"It's a little early, but since we are all here now, I'll call the meeting to order." She nodded to a man at the far end of the table, apparently a secretary. "Begin recording."

She looked at a notebook screen. "This meeting of this League of Planets Investigative Commission has been assembled for a two-fold purpose: first, to investigate the facts surrounding abandonment by the medical vessel *LSS Barton* of a mission to a member planet of the League; and, secondly, to discuss a medical catastrophe that reportedly resulted in an unprecedented number of deaths on a planet not associated with the League. Once we have obtained sufficient facts, we will make our recommendation to League Headquarters as to further action."

She turned to Dassa and Broward. "I am Felicia Hammond, of Earth. My fellow commissioners will introduce themselves before they begin their questioning.

"You understand this is just an investigation. No one is accused of any crime, and no one is on trial. We are, however, trying to discover the accurate facts of these situations, and you are required to answer all questions truthfully. Do you both understand the procedure?" She looked at Dassa as if she expected trouble.

Broward nodded. "I do, Madam Commissioner."

When Dassa answered the same, Commissioner Hammond gave her another sharp glance before continuing.

"The first set of interrogatories will be directed to Edwin Broward, captain of the medical research vessel, League Starship *Barton*." Hammond gave a solemn nod at Broward.

The Karkar on the commission, who had eyed Dassa with open hostility from the moment she entered the room, rose first. "Captain Broward, I am Kiik." She spoke into a mouthpiece that translated her words into the Standard Language, since, like most Karkar, she was unable to pronounce the language intelligibly. "It is my understanding that you were orbiting the planet Beeheehoohaa for the purpose of studying the results of a vaccination program instituted five standard-years ago. What sort of vaccinations were these?"

The few syllables of the Karkar tongue were varied by inflection, volume and pitch. As Kiik's voice went from throaty to shrill, from shriek to whisper, Dassa tried not to cringe at the assault on her ears.

"Honorable Kiik," the captain answered after the woman resumed her seat. "The vaccination was for a respiratory illness peculiar to that planet. The children were especially vulnerable. In fact, the Beeheehoohaaan infant mortality rate was roughly sixty percent before we developed the vaccine. Our mission was to see how thoroughly the program was being implemented and what impact it had made thus far."

The other Terrestrial, Tagore, stood up, stroking his neat mustache as he glanced from his notes to Broward and back. "Captain Broward. Where did the Beeheehoohaaans get this vaccine? Did you provide it?"

On and on they talked. It was all Dassa could do to stay awake as the laborious process dragged even the shortest question into a matter of long minutes. The interrogation about the vaccinations continued for nearly a quarter hour before Hammond brought the subject back to the matter at hand. "About the distress signal you received while orbiting Beeheehoohaa. What did it say?"

Broward shifted in his chair. "The initial message said, 'The Karkar Plague is loose on Gannah. Assistance needed.'"

A short, copper-haired Glenmarrian seated to Hammond's left hopped to his feet, his chin barely clearing the tabletop. "I am Tig Roso, of the planet Glenmarria. Why did you not worry it might be a trap?"

The captain's brows lifted. "I had no reason to suspect such a thing."

"How dare you abandon your mission to go chasing after something so vague?" Kiik said. "Do you value the lives of innocent Beeheehoohaaan children so lightly?"

Broward's jaw line grew taut. "There was nothing vague about our choices. We are a hospital ship. When we learn masses of people are dying in a pandemic, the first priority is to answer the call. Our leaving Beeheehoohaa endangered no one, but had the potential to save millions."

"Captain Broward," said Tagore. "Did you request permission from the League High Command before abandoning this mission?"

"Saving lives is our first mission. We left Beeheehoohaaan space immediately and messaged HC of our actions en route."

Listening to the meeting drone on, Dassa fought to stay still. The rapid regrowth of her muscle tissue caused continual pain, but it paled beside the grief throbbing like a wound in her chest. What was wrong with these people? Did they consider only the residents of League planets worthy of life? Or was it just Gannah they despised?

To keep from exploding from pain and frustration, Dassa let her mind venture elsewhere as the commissioners went over the same material from every conceivable angle, until she realized Hammond was directing the attention to her.

"We will now hear from the plague survivor herself. Madam, first let me extend to you our deepest condolences. I know your sorrow is great."

Dassa nodded. "Thank you."

"We cannot undo the events, but we do want to find out what happened. So if you would, please introduce yourself."

Dassa stood slowly, relieved to be able to change her position at last. "Honorable Hammond, I am Atarah Hadassah Hagah Natsach, Toqeph of Gannah." She then sat, regretful that protocol did not allow her to move around more.

"Toqeph?" Kiik squawked like an injured bird. "You claim to be ruler of Gannah? How are we to accept such an astonishing statement? For all we know, you could be a Gannahan swineherd, since there is no one to contradict you. Is that not so?"

Dassa glared at the Karkar, her fingers twitching as she wrestled a flash of anger to the ground. "Gannah does not lie."

"Madam," said Tagore as Kiik glared at Dassa with palpable contempt. "We are aware you've been through a terrible ordeal, but please understand that our purpose is to ascertain the truth. We must ask, therefore, whether you can prove you are whom you say. Could it be that you call yourself toqeph by default, because there's no one left to fill the position?"

The suggestion was so insulting Dassa hardly knew how to respond. "I am the daughter of the toqeph, Atarah Degel Jachin. I completed my training and fulfilled the Last Requirement. My late father received my offering and pronounced me Nasi. As his only child thus qualified to succeed him, I am Toqeph Atarah Hadassah Hagah Natsach, not by chance nor by choice, but by right and the will of the King."

"You, madam," said Hammond with an air of affront, "a Nasi of Gannah? You speak of legends and myths."

Dassa could take no more. She stood, and everyone in the room stared at her in shock the breach of etiquette.

"Honorable Commissioners, I must lodge a complaint, as I believe is my right as a dignitary visiting a League outpost. I have complied with your customs and violated no law. Yet from the moment I entered this room I have been treated with suspicion and contempt. I have been called a swineherd—and I suspect I know what that term means on your planet, Commissioner Kiik— a liar, and an imposter to the throne of Gannah. Any one of those offenses would be a serious charge on my own planet. You have, therefore, accused me of being three times a criminal.

"If that is your opinion, I ask to be formally charged and tried. Otherwise, I demand these accusations cease. I believe I am also entitled to fines and sanctions, but I waive that right. I understand you are ignorant of my culture and I wish to cause no ill will. I will, therefore, be satisfied with the cessation of this sort of hostile interrogation.

"Now, am I to be charged with these crimes you insinuate? Or will I be treated with the respect due a visiting head of state?" She looked around the room, fixing each stunned commissioner in turn with her intense stare. "While you deliberate, I shall return to my quarters to await your decision."

Trembling with rage, she turned and stumped stiffly toward the doors before the stunned commissioners could recover their senses. As she reached the exit, she heard the captain say, "Ladies, gentlemen, if you'll excuse me, I must see the toqeph safely to her room."

She didn't turn to look, but he must have slipped through the doors before they slupped closed behind her, because the next thing she heard was his voice.

"Ah, Mrs. Natsack. Or Madam Toqeph. Or—"

She stopped and turned. "I suppose Madam Toqeph would be appropriate."

He'd brought the wheelchair. "You shouldn't be walking, Madam Toqeph. May I assist you?"

"Thank you, but I've been inactive for too long." She resumed walking, flexing her arms and stretching every aching muscle she could. "I apologize for my outburst. I hope it will not reflect poorly on you. But I could no longer bear those…those self-obsessed, bent-beaked pufftsipporim."

Walking beside her and pushing the empty chair, he looked at her, eyebrows raised.

"Small Gannahan birds that puff themselves up when they feel threatened, to make themselves appear less vulnerable to predators."

"Does it work?"

"That depends upon the predator." She almost smiled. "But why did you leave, too? Do you not fear they will view that as insubordination?"

He shook his head. "I couldn't very well let you find your way alone, especially in your weakened condition. And they'd probably prefer to discuss the questions you raised without my being there. I think you shook them up pretty badly. They're not used to people challenging them."

"Was I not within my rights? From what you'd told me about the commission, I thought—"

"You were well within your rights. Your speech was perfect, spoken like a lawyer. That's what took them by surprise. They thought they could intimidate you, but now you've backed them against the wall."

"Will they come out fighting?"

Broward shook his head. "Hard to say for sure, but I suspect they'll backpedal big time."

Never having heard the phrase, Dassa gave him a curious look.

Broward chuckled. "They'll try to gloss over everything that happened and resume the inquiry tomorrow with a new attitude. Do everything they can to make it look like they've always been your most ardent supporters."

"And what about the matter of your career? Have I harmed or helped your cause?"

Dassa's steps had slowed, and Broward motioned to the chair. "Sure you wouldn't like to sit for a while?"

She shook her head. "The exercise is good for me."

"The chair is here whenever you need it. But regarding your question, I believe you've put me in an excellent position as well. Recommending disciplinary action against me would be the same as saying they wish you were dead." He laughed. "Which, of course, might be true, but they won't admit it. No, Madam Toqeph, they'll do all they can to befriend you. And that might very well include commending me for my efforts to save your people."

Dassa smiled. "I'm glad I did it, then. Because you deserve to be commended."

He shrugged. "The *Barton* is a medical research vessel. We could scarcely have done anything else."

They walked in silence for a few paces, then Broward said, "I noticed you fingering your ring when the question was raised about your claims to the throne. Is it a signet ring, something only the toqeph would wear? You could have offered it as proof of your claim."

She raised her hand and twisted the ring on the middle finger of her left hand. "Yes. It is the Ring of Atarah. But it would be proof of nothing if they chose to disbelieve me. A Gannahan does not lie. My word should be more reliable than any physical evidence."

"A people who don't lie?" Broward chuckled. "There's a concept the League won't be able to handle."

"Can *you* handle it, as you say?"

"Do I believe you, you mean?" He seemed to study the empty wheelchair as he walked. "I believe your people were probably generally truthful. But I've never met anyone who would never lie under any circumstances."

Dassa smiled. "And how many Gannahans have you met?"

"Just one, Madam. And I have found that one to be without guile. But tell me, if you don't mind, about that ring. I've never seen anything like it. What sort of metal is it?"

She stopped walking and extended her hand. "Yes, Dr. Pik was interested in it too. It is called livingore. It is found only on Gannah, and in very limited quantities. It might be the rarest metal in the universe. The stone is ayinstone. This same ring has been passed down from one toqeph to another for almost three hundred years. It has fit every hand that wore it, and matched the eye color of every toqeph."

The captain looked dubious. "How can that be?"

"Refined livingore grows or shrinks to take the size and shape of whatever warm object is pressed against it. When this ring was given me by my father, it was too large for my finger. But over time it adapted. As for the stone, it changes color depending upon the chemical make-up of whatever it touches. It looks gray and ordinary when it comes out of the ground, but when it touches a warm living thing, it changes. I do not know the science behind it."

He looked into her eyes and smiled. "I was afraid you were going to call it magic."

She didn't smile back. "Magic always has an explanation."

He nodded and turned his attention back to the ring. "I see it's showing its age. I can hardly make out the etchings."

"Yes. It must be re-carved every fifty years or so because of wear. The tree on the stone is the symbol of life on Gannah. The writing on the band says, 'Atarah, King.' According to legend, this is a reproduction of the ring made by the Bara Himself and given to Atarah, the first man, whom the Bara placed on Gannah to rule His Creation. The ring passed down from father to son until it became too worn to be repaired, and another was made to replace it. This is the twenty-first such ring. The House of Archives holds the first twenty, but the oldest are so deteriorated it is hard to know what they once looked like."

The captain stared at her. "You're saying the same family has ruled in unbroken succession since the beginning of history? I've never heard of such a thing."

She began walking again. "It is true."

"None were ever assassinated, deposed, or defeated in war? The line never died out from lack of heirs?"

"If a king or regent died without heir, a brother or nephew took the throne. On one occasion—or rather, two now, counting me—a daughter reigned. And the Atarah has never failed to fulfill his duty to his people." *Until now*, she thought with a pang, but continued. "Nor has Atarah's right to reign ever been challenged. Insistence on questioning authority is an Earthish flaw, not a Gannahan."

Broward shook his head in amazement. "That's remarkable. But...sometimes on Earth, a leader is deposed because he's not fit to lead. Were none of Atarah's heirs weak? Did none ever lead your people astray?"

The pain in Dassa's chest sharpened. "None were weak. The requirement that the regent be Nasi takes care of that. But they have occasionally shown poor judgment. "

Dassa was glad they'd finally reached her suite. "Thank you for seeing me safely back, Captain."

Broward smiled. "I have enjoyed our conversation, Madam Toqeph. Almost as much as I enjoyed your challenge to the commission. But whatever they decide in our absence, you will still be expected to attend this evening's reception, which the Eutarians are giving to honor your late husband's heroism on their behalf."

She nodded. "I have not forgotten."

"Very good. Shall I call at nineteen hundred to escort you?"

"I would like that, Captain."

He gestured toward the empty wheelchair he'd been pushing. "Would you like me to put it inside for you?"

"No, thank you. I'll take it. Thank you again for seeing me safely here."

He nodded. "My pleasure. I'll see you this evening."

She watched him walk down the long, curved hallway until he was out of sight. Then she turned to the door, searching for the lock. She wished she'd paid more attention to how it opened. On Gannah, a lock symbol was always found in the center of a door. But though this one was decorated with an abstract pattern of indentations, she could find no distinctive mark. She ran her gaze from side to side and top to bottom. If there was a lock there, it was invisible.

Embarrassed, she glanced down the hall in both directions, but no one was around to witness her dilemma. She knew the lock worked with a fingerprint scan, so she pressed her fingertips to various places on the door. Nothing. Pressing both hands to the cool surface, she tried to slide the door open manually. It was like trying to move a wall. Frustrated, she pounded a fist against the unyielding panel.

The words echoed in her head as her fists thudded against the door: *the Atarah has never failed to fulfill his duty to his people.*

Until now.

She sagged against the door. *I am willing to complete my mission, my Yasha. But what is my mission?*

The answer was the same as before. *Arise.*

9

Immersed in a pricy nirrtsik facial, Pik felt the tension slough off with the dead epidermal cells. Then his ears jerked in sudden annoyance, causing the cosmetologist to pull back from massaging his forehead.

"Did I pinch?"

Hearing her speak his native tongue was music to his ears, and they lifted in pleasure.

"No," he answered in the same language. "I just remembered something I forgot to do."

"Ah." She resumed her ministrations. "Nothing that can't wait, I hope."

"Well, no. That is, it can wait until we're through here, but I really must cut my shopping trip short. I promised to call my mother as soon as I arrived on Station 27."

The cosmetologist chuckled. "If you know what's good for you, you'll do that right away. We can't have you upsetting the mimsey, now, can we?"

Pik sank deeper into the chair with a moan of contentment. "No. We definitely cannot have that."

An hour later he returned to the Gannahan's suite, which he shared in his capacity as nursemaid. The fact that it was the best the station had to offer eased the sting of his servitude somewhat.

Upon entering, he paused at the mirrored wall just inside the entrance to admire the results of his abbreviated spa visit. His complexion glowed, with no trace of whisker roots visible. Elaborately lined and shadowed eyes stared out at him from beneath a trim and exquisitely bristled haircut. The treatment had set him back a bit, but it was worth it.

The wine he found in the wet bar was free, though. Or at least, paid for by whoever was footing his patient's bill. He made himself comfortable in front of the computer, from which he called his mother. Once that chore was out of the way, he could enjoy the rest of his freedom before the captain brought the Gannahan back.

When his mother's face appeared on the screen, though, all thoughts of enjoyment fled. "What's this I hear?" she said in Karkar, the shrieks and shrills of her voice both familiar and grating. "Is this what I put you through medical school for? To disgrace yourself? To smear the family name?"

Pik heaved a sigh. It was public knowledge, then. She knew he'd saved the Gannahan's life. Would she give him a chance to explain? "Please, Mother. Tell me what you've heard. In his message yesterday, my father called me a celebrity."

To kill time during the delay between the sending and receiving of the transmissions, he switched to a game of Gonk, hoping the game would go better than the conversation. Only two moves in, however, a pounding outside drew his attention. He looked at the door, trying to place the sound, then said to the computer with his mother's image waiting on the screen, "Excuse me, someone's knocking."

Curious, he opened the door to find the Gannahan standing before him, her wheelchair in the middle of the hall. He leaned out and looked around, but she was alone. "What are you doing here? And where is the captain? Surely the meeting's not over already."

"It is not, but I am finished with it. How does one work the lock to this door?"

"Fingerprint scan. Like the Station Head told us."

"But I cannot find the lock."

Pik stepped out of the room and let the door close. "It's right where it's supposed to be." He pressed his left index finger against a small box, not in the door itself but in the doorframe, and the portal opened obediently.

Dassa nodded. "Things are much different here than on Gannah."

She passed through into the suite as Pik retrieved her wheelchair from the hall. "What are locks like there?" And why did he ask that? He couldn't care less.

"We seldom have reason to secure things on Gannah. When we do, we mark them with a symbol, like this." She drew in the air with her finger, a triangle with a dot inside. "That tells others not to open. A door, a drawer, a box, a file, whatever."

Pik wondered if she was joking in some strange, unfunny Gannahan way. "That's ridiculous. It would stop no one."

She fixed him with that horrible stare. "We would not consider opening something with such a sign."

Unable to wrap his mind around the concept, Pik decided to drop it. "Why are you here?"

"These are my quarters, are they not?"

At that moment, his mother's voice found its way across space. "You know perfectly well that's not the family I meant. Your father knows nothing of honor, nor much of anything else. Despite what he thinks in his idiotic Earthish pride, you've brought dishonor upon all of us. He doesn't grasp the implications of what you've done. You have—" She paused, seeing Pik excuse himself and head for the door. "Oh, very well. Go see who it is, I'll wait."

Interested, the Gannahan moved toward the sound. "I did not mean to interrupt. Please, finish your conversation."

Pik's long stride carried him to the computer before Dassa got there. "I must go," he said to it. "I'll talk to you later." He terminated the connection and the screen went dark.

Dassa raised her eyebrows in surprise. "You need not have done that on my account."

"No, we were done." He hoped his mother hadn't caught a glimpse of Dassa.

"Was that your wife? You fear her jealousy?"

"No, it was my mother. And if she sees who you are, she might rupture something."

Dassa nodded. "From the way she spoke, it sounds as if she agrees with your sister Karkar on the commission that I should have been left to die."

Pik blinked. "You understood what my mother said?"

"Karkar is a fascinating tongue. I find it unintelligible when written, but when spoken, I can usually pick up the high points. "

That was a new one. "Most non-Karkars find it obnoxious."

"It is." She shrugged. "But it is interesting nonetheless. Will your mother not think it rude that you halted the conversation so abruptly?"

Apparently she did, because the computer hummed. "Your mother is calling, Dr. Pik," its electronic voice said. "Will you accept the call, or shall I take a message?"

"Take a message." He turned back to the Gannahan. "Don't worry about that, tell me about the meeting. Why are you back so soon?"

"I have been a burden to you and the League, and I regret that."

That wasn't an answer, and it irritated him. So why did he let her continue?

"I shall, therefore, regain my strength as quickly as possible and learn to make my own way in this strange society of yours. I am Gannah, and as such should be beholden to no one."

He had no idea what she was talking about, but it didn't matter. "The meeting. What happened at the meeting?"

She sank into the oversized sofa, tipped her head back and closed her eyes. "Absolutely nothing. Tell me, Dr. Pik. When a Karkar refers to a swineherd, he really means a prostitute, doesn't he?"

"It is a common euphemism. Why?"

"Because Commissioner Kiik called me one."

"I'm sure you're mistaken. We Karkar are notoriously hard to understand."

Dassa opened her eyes and looked up at him. "She spoke into a translator, and I understood her perfectly. Both her words and her meaning. But" —she cocked her head slightly—"why is your impediment so much less than that of your other countrymen? I have never known a Karkar to speak the Standard Tongue half as well as you. Most cannot do it at all."

Pik preferred not to discuss his mixed heritage. "And how many Karkar have you known?"

Her eyes seemed to scan his mind. "Enough to see you are unique. Your face is more pliable than most. Your mother is obviously a Karkar, but…perhaps your father is not?"

This truth usually made him feel dirty, but Dassa's question was gentle. Not thrown in his face as an accusation. To his surprise, he responded without going on the defensive. "My father was born in Sweden, in the area of Earth called Scandinavia. He is a doctor, like my mother. They met while studying neurology on Bappas. For some reason she was quite taken with him. For a time, at least."

"They are no longer married?"

"Since Karkar law makes no provision for divorce, they're stuck in their union. But they have as little to do with one another as possible."

"Are you their only child?"

He tilted his head in a Karkar nod.

"I had no idea intermarriage ever occurred between Karkar and Earth."

"To my knowledge, it has never happened before or since."

Her green gaze was thoughtful. "Then you and I are both one of a kind."

Before that shocking thought fully registered with Pik, Dassa rose. "Well, as I said, I have made a decision, but I shall need your help. First off, teach me everything you know about dinner etiquette at League functions. I have a reception to attend."

Pik joined Dassa at the computer, where he helped her find what she was looking for. He watched as she pored over the sites, voracious green eyes devouring screen after screen. "It is well you showed me this, or I would have behaved like the barbarian everyone thinks me to be." She stood. "I am weary. I shall lie down for an hour or so."

"That might be wise." Pik took her place at the computer, intending to catch up on the news. "Would you like me to call you?"

She answered as she moved stiffly across the room. "No, I shall awaken when I must. But you needn't stay here guarding the door. Why not venture forth and enjoy yourself? You so looked forward to visiting the Station."

He felt a strange tugging within as conflicting desires grappled in the lower part of his chest. "There is no urgency. I explored a bit while you were in the meeting, and I have things to do here before I go out again."

"Oh, yes. You must call your mother." She disappeared into her room.

Pik's ears frowned as the door closed behind her. He supposed he should call his mother back, but first he wanted to see what he could find about himself in the latest medical journals.

About an hour later Dassa emerged, yawning, and shuffled toward the kitchen area, where she took a bottle of water from the shelf.

"There's some in the chillbox," he said without glancing up from his reading.

Drinking deeply, she didn't answer right away. When she came up for air, she said, "I do not like it so cold. Did you return your mother's call?"

He looked up, ears jerking. "I see a Gannahan female nags as much as any other."

"I merely asked a question."

"Women are always 'just asking.' They start with a question and end with a tirade. But no, I did not call my mother. Why do you care?"

"Because I know what it is to be parted from my children." Her voice grew husky.

Trying to ignore the reappearance of that strange inner grappling, he directed his attention back to his screen.

"I apologize. I should tend to my own business and not meddle in yours. But could you help me with one more thing? Your computers are unlike ours on Gannah, and I have not been able to figure them out. Can you find me a site that teaches the proper application of cosmetics? I fear I looked out of place at the meeting today, and I should like to learn to…how do you say it? Do myself up right."

Pik exited the medical journal he'd been reading. "Wasn't my earlier instruction adequate?"

"I should like to go with a minimalist look, as Gannahans do not ordinarily use cosmetics."

"And you wonder why people think you barbaric."

"I thought it was our taste for wholesale slaughter that marred our reputation."

At least she admitted it. "No, that's what made your reputation. And it will take more than cosmetics to change it."

She drained the water bottle. "I have heard it said that people will buy anything if it is packaged attractively."

He located a suitable site and opened it. "You want to sell the galaxy the notion that the Bogeyman is benign?"

"I do not deny history. I merely want it known that Gannah is no longer a threat."

Pik's ears twitched, for he felt her presence quite threatening. But not for the reasons he did formerly. "Why do I get the impression that's not entirely true?"

She chuckled, and it occurred to him he'd never heard her laugh before. It warmed his bones as much as her glare chilled them.

Shortly before nineteen hundred hours, Pik opened the door for Captain Broward, who stepped in, small but dapper in his dress whites.

The Gannahan emerged from her chamber on cue. She'd wound her lush hair in a black coil atop her head. Her dusky complexion glowed, and hints of color framed her brilliant eyes. A floor-length gown of jade green draped with shimmering grace around a body that hinted of the robust shape it must once have boasted. She was, indeed, an attractive package.

Himself in his finest, Pik surveyed his patient with surprised appreciation, but the captain spoke first. "Madam Toqeph. You look very…well rested."

"Thank you, Captain. You look well yourself."

Broward beamed as he offered her the wheelchair. "Why, thank you, Madam. Our dinner awaits. Shall we?"

"I think I shall walk. I am, as you said, well rested." Smiling, she took his arm.

Seeing the two, Pik felt a twinge of something, he wasn't sure what. But when Broward looked up at him, with the woman on his arm, and said, "After you, Dr. Pik," he knew what it was.

He was jealous.

Impossible. How could he, the proud Karkar, be attracted to a barbarous Gannahan? It could never happen.

He left the suite, ears back in a scowl, and the green dress rustled behind. With the captain attached.

Curse it all anyway.

10

Dassa allowed the captain and Pik to escort her to a table near a raised platform at the front of the room.

Several hundred well-dressed people, all of whom seemed to sport a different artificial scent, watched the trio pass through their midst. To Dassa's surprise, many smiled and spoke kindly to her. She replied as politely as she could, but when they reached the table, she sank weakly into the chair the captain pulled out for her.

On Gannah, a celebratory meal was a long, drawn-out affair with music, dancing, and entertainment interspersed between courses. Dassa wondered where those activities would take place, as the tables were so close together. But mostly, she worried that her strength would give out long before the festivities ended.

She was about to ask the captain what sort of dances could be performed in such limited space when Zim, the Stationmaster, approached.

He took her hand. "Madam Toqeph. How good to see you out of the wheelchair tonight and walking on your own."

"Yes, thank you. I'm getting a little stronger every day."

"I trust your accommodations are to your liking?"

"They're splendid. I could ask for nothing more."

His broad grin nearly split his face. "It's an honor to serve you, Madam. You will let me know if there's anything you need?"

"I will, Mr. Zim. Thank you."

He moved on, and others stepped in to greet the guest of honor. She conversed with each politely, though all she could think about was getting back to the room, crawling into bed and losing consciousness.

But she couldn't make an early exit tonight the way she'd escaped the commissioners this afternoon. She was a guest of these people, and, as the Yasha reminded her, she must start acting more graciously.

When the announcement was made that the meal would be served, the stream of curious well-wishers slowed to a trickle, allowing Dassa some respite. In addition to Broward and Pik, five others dined at Dassa's table: Commissioner Hammond and her companion; the captain of the Eutarian freighter upon which Rosh had died; and two of the men whose lives Rosh had saved. Dassa was grateful they spoke among themselves throughout most of the meal, rather than to her.

The room soon grew stuffy. More than half of the people here were Eutarians, and their strong, natural scent permeated everything, despite the many and varied fragrances that competed with it. The food, on the other hand, contributed nothing to the olfactory mélange, for it had little odor or flavor.

Being Gannahan, she shunned the alcoholic beverages it seemed everyone else enjoyed before and during the meal. But she did her best to eat the food, knowing it was necessary to build strength. Even though it did keep threatening to come back up.

After sampling the soup course and the thin, crispy square of dry, crumbly material that came with it, Dassa turned to Pik and spoke in low tones. "Are you certain this is edible? It seems to have originated in a laboratory rather than a farm."

His ears lifted almost imperceptibly in a subtle movement she discerned as amusement. "It was manufactured right here on Station 27." He patted some oily soup residue from his lips with a napkin. "How did you guess?"

She waited for the pseudo-food to settle back down a bit before answering. "I've heard of such things." She resisted the temptation to add, "But I'd hoped never to experience them."

Truly, the Yasha had strange ways. But He paved those paths with grace, and despite being swathed in a veil of black grief, she saw His blessings. These alien people treated her kindly. Even the commissioners spoke with respect, addressing her as Madam Toqeph without a hint of sarcasm. The meal moved quickly from one course to another. Her physical pain was great, but tolerable.

More tolerable than the ache of her sorrow, which never ebbed.

When the servebots removed the last of the dishes, the Eutarian captain and his two men got up from the table. Expecting everyone else to stand as well, Dassa gathered her strength to rise until she noticed that those three were the only ones on their feet. As they made their way to the platform in the front of the room, she whispered to Captain Broward, "What is next?"

"The main event." His smile suggested it would be something she'd enjoy. "They're doing a presentation in honor of your husband."

The chemical material in her stomach churned and she stared at the table, fists clenched. She didn't know what to expect, but she was certain the program would be agonizing.

It was.

When the Eutarian captain presented her with Rosh's personal effects, it took all her strength to not shed tears before the Outsiders. She only escaped that defilement by imagining his horror if she shamed his memory in such a demeaning way.

The Eutarians' gratitude was touching, but she only wanted to flee.

When Dassa returned to her suite, she instructed the baggagebot to stack the cartons of Rosh's belongings against a wall in her room. Once the bot chugged out, she fell into bed without even bidding the captain and Pik good night. She must flee her sorrow through sleep before the pain killed her.

Except the throbbing grief kept her awake.

When she closed her eyes, she saw him. Remembered the smell of his hair, the taste of his kisses, the warmth and power of his body. But she could make no more connection with him than with a fantasy. He was out of range of her mortal meah.

The boxes of his belongings drew her. She hadn't been able to bring herself to look at them at first, but now she couldn't stop herself.

Climbing stiffly out of bed, she turned on a light and approached, wondering what was inside. Did she have the strength to open them? She imagined seeing his clothing, smelling his sweet Gannahan scent, running her fingers over the embroidery of his favorite tunic.

Perhaps finding a black hair on the collar.

No, she wasn't ready for that yet. Instead, she picked up his guitar.

He had gotten it six years before, when they traveled to the cliff city of Aruwts to celebrate the annual Festival of Voices. The whole royal family was there: the Toqeph Atarah Degel and his wife, Yachad; Dassa's brother, Arodi, and his wife, Malah; Dassa's sister and brother-in-law, Kannah and Ozni; and all their various offspring.

On the flight back to Armown in the royal aircarriage, they practiced new songs introduced at the Festival and sang some old favorites. Their voices blended in rich harmonies fluttering with layers of descants. They chased frivolous fugues and complex counterpoints, yelped in lively yodels, and crooned gentle tunes. After an hour or more the children began to grow restless, so Yachad and Malah herded them to the back of the aircarriage for a snack.

The remaining adults launched into a discussion of how the toqeph and his father before him had made numerous overtures to the Outsiders, but Gannah remained universally despised.

"When we do well, they are filled with envy," Degel said. "And when we err—" He slapped his hand on the arm of his chair, his ring cracking against the wood frame. "Just because one Gannahan is a murderer, they think we all want to kill. We must begin again to show them they have nothing to fear and much to gain by dealing with Gannah."

Rosh strummed his new guitar thoughtfully. "Their heroes are athletes and entertainers, milord. Mayhap we might win them over through music. A popular entertainer would have a forum. The people would hearken to him with respect."

Knowing what he was getting at, Dassa followed the conversation with foreboding. But why should she worry? Her father wouldn't agree to what Rosh was about to propose.

But to Dassa's dismay, this idea intrigued him. He leaned back in his seat and studied Rosh. "Thy thoughts have merit. Whoever would thus venture forth, however, must be a man who would not intimidate. One neither overly clever nor overly talented."

"That is my thought as well, milord."

Arodi scowled. "Why should a Gannahan rise to fame when so many of the Outsiders themselves try without success?"

Rosh turned to him. "Because Gannah is a mystery. Are not all people drawn to a mystery?"

Thoughtful, Ozni smoothed his black mustache with thumb and forefinger, tracing it all the way down his chin. "Yea, it might be possible."

The toqeph nodded. "Yet it is no small thing for a man to leave Gannah. He severs himself from all that is good and right. He places himself in continual danger. The Outsiders are untrustworthy, their customs obtuse, their laws unjust. There is no morality without, no truth. I send knights Outside to acquire knowledge, but I would not send one Out to sing, to be made a laughingstock. Nay, I cannot send a Nasi on such a mission."

Dassa hoped that would be the end of it, but Rosh spoke again. "True, milord. A Purpletongue would not be accepted, but a common minstrel might be received."

The Toqeph fixed his son-in-law with a striking sapphire stare. "And how would a common man survive such an ordeal?"

"He could, if the Yasha were with him."

Degel raised a thoughtful eyebrow. "Am I to understand you volunteer for this duty?"

Rosh swallowed, avoiding Dassa's gaze. "I do, milord."

"Thou wouldst leave thy wife and children? Why?"

"Because Gannah is in need of an ambassador, and I believe I am gifted to be such a one."

"Gifted?" The toqeph drummed the chair arm with his fingers then nodded. "I would never have described thee so, but I believe it be true." He turned to Dassa. "What thinkest thou, my daughter?"

She hesitated. "My husband speaketh well. But… could such a minstrel travel with his family? As thou knoweth, I have visited the Outside before with no ill effects. And think what an education it would be for Johanan and Jehu."

"Certainly not," her father said.

"Nay," Rosh said at the same moment.

Dassa's heart sank.

The toqeph's tone didn't invite discussion. "My grandchildren are too tender to be exposed to the corruption Outside."

"Hast thou forgotten what we spoke of earlier?" Rosh asked her.

She bowed her head. "That is so, milord," she answered her father. "My suggestion was ill-considered." She turned to her husband, eyes cast down. "And nay, Rosh, I have not forgotten our discussion."

When her father looked at them with a question in his meah, Rosh reached over his guitar to put his hand on her arm. "Methinks now is the time to make thy petition to the toqeph."

With a small bow to Rosh, she turned to the toqeph and took a deep breath. "Milord, as thou knowest, I have completed the Sixth Level of education. Ordinarily that is enough for a woman, but Rosh thinks it might behoove me to continue further."

The toqeph nodded. "That would be appropriate. My own mother was a Seven."

"Yes, Father. I would emulate her. And even… and if I might have thy permission, milord, I would go beyond that, and seek the Nasihood."

Kannah and Ozni gasped. Arodi glanced at their father, then turned to glare at Dassa, hurt and anger emanating from his meah. Dassa couldn't meet his gaze. It had been six years since their eldest brother Areli died while performing his Last Requirement, and her heart still ached to think of him.

Her father looked back and forth between Dassa and Rosh, silent for a long moment. "Thou art a woman," he said at last. "And married. A mother. The Nasihood carrieth great responsibility, and thy duties would take thee from thy family."

"Yea, milord. But Rosh is in agreement with this course. And when I must be absent, the children will be well cared for by my mother and his."

"Hmmm. Few women have attempted such a thing. But thou might possibly succeed, for thou art stubborn enough to see a hard thing through to the end. Art thou willing to make the necessary sacrifices? To serve the toqeph without question? To forsake all, to live and die for the good of Gannah?"

She glanced at Rosh, whose violet eyes gave encouragement.

"I am, milord."

After a pause, Degel nodded. "Then I will allow it." He tossed a brief glance at Arodi. "And I hope another of my children will see fit to undertake the same endeavor. Though I am yet young, only the Yasha liveth forever." He snorted. "I love thy children but wouldst not have a Natsach as heir."

Dassa opened her mouth, then closed it again at Rosh's look of warning.

Rosh bowed. "Thou art gracious, milord. We shall make arrangements for Hadassah to begin her training."

It was almost as if he knew what would happen. That he must prepare the way for her to follow him into the Outside, and that she must take the throne upon her father's untimely death.

Even that death, Rosh had foreseen.

For some time before the conversation in the aircarriage, Dassa had feared that her father was not wholly obedient to the Yasha as a toqeph must be. It wasn't the sort of thing one liked to think about, let alone talk about, but in her meah, she knew Rosh shared her concerns.

Finally her worries grew so great she had to speak of them. "The Yasha promised Atarah Hoseh the Wise that so long as his heirs remain faithful, Gannah shall live. Now seeing my father's mind, I fear he putteth all Gannah in jeopardy. But I dare not broach the matter."

Rosh shook his head. "Nay, one may not question the toqeph."

"But how can I keep quiet with Gannah in danger?"

"We must be patient. Remember the story of David in the Book of Earth? Though King Saul treated him wickedly, David never ceased to honor him as king, and Jehovah rewarded his obedience. We must now do the same. However the toqeph's obedience might fail, we must be certain to give him all respect due Atarah's heir."

"But I fear for all Gannah if the toqeph should step too far from the Yasha's will. Why do none of his advisors warn him?"

"My heart is one with thine, my love. I think, however, there is something thou might do."

"What is that?"

"If thy father continues on his present course, the Yasha shall surely not stand idly by."

"Thou speakest of his secret search for the vessels that bore the dead from Karkar?"

Rosh nodded, his face sober. "The Yasha will not allow him to raise them. Hoseh the Wise commanded they be sunk deep in the sea, never to be touched nor entered again as long as Gannah shall live. If thy father disobeys that command, it will be the end of him."

"I fear the same."

"But few others do. Of all who might be his heir, you are the only one who sees the danger in his actions. If they share his disobedience, would they not share his fate?"

Dassa could hardly believe what he was saying. "I cannot be toqeph. I am the youngest, and a woman, and—"

"And married to a Natsach. Yes, I know well, no Natsach hath ever been heir. But Natsach or no, thou must be ready to lead our people if and when that time cometh."

"I hoped thy words would comfort me, but they have disturbed me more."

Rosh took her into his arms. "Our comfort must be in our Yasha, who saves, guides and empowers. We pray that Atarah Degel be delivered from his error, but the Yasha forceth no man to obey against his will. We must prepare for the possibility that the toqeph may not choose rightly."

Dassa wished she'd left this discussion to the nonverbal meah communication. Speaking plainly made hard things seem harder. She had no desire to seek the Nasihood, nor, worse yet, to reign as toqeph if the need arose. She was unfit for such a burden.

"Let us pray," Rosh said. "If this is the Yasha's desire for thee, He shall make it known to us both."

Rosh prayed beautifully. He loved the Yasha with all his heart, and his prayers were like music — far sweeter than the songs he sang in the Outside.

Lying in her bed now in the darkened room on League Station 27, separated from the love of her life, light-years from Gannah and deeply alone, Dassa remembered his prayers, and his music, and his love, and her heart swelled and ached.

But she didn't weep. A Nasi neither wept for himself, nor grieved for his losses. When he was knocked down, a Nasi picked himself up and rose to fight again.

Or to die standing.

11

Three days later, Dassa entered the conference room on her own two feet, with Captain Broward a pace behind. Since the last meeting, she'd regained most of her strength. If not for the fact that she had no people to lead, she might have felt like the toqeph she was.

This time, the commissioners rose and bowed with proper respect. She nodded at each, greeting them by name. Then they all took their seats around the vast, gleaming table.

Once all were seated, Commissioner Hammond began the proceedings. "Madam Toqeph. We thank you for consenting to meet with us. I hope you will allow me to apologize for our discourtesy earlier, which stemmed from our ignorance."

"No apology necessary, Ms. Hammond. I do not expect you to be familiar with Gannah's customs."

"You are very gracious, Madam, but nevertheless, I do apologize." Hammond looked around the room. "Well, now. We already know each other, so we shall dispense with the usual introductions." She directed her attention back to Dassa. "We know the subject is painful for you, but the League must learn more about what transpired on your planet. Please, if you would, begin at the beginning. Tell us what happened." She took her seat.

"The beginning?" Dassa glanced at Kiik. "That was centuries ago."

"Yes, of course." The corners of Hammond's mouth turned down. "But you needn't go back so far. Can you tell us if the illness had lain dormant all those years? Or were there smaller outbreaks previously?"

Dassa wondered how much she should divulge. "Perhaps, if I may, some early background is necessary after all."

Hammond nodded. "Whatever you'd like."

After another moment of consideration, Dassa began. "Some eight hundred and fifty years ago, my many-times-great grandfather, Atarah Nacah Marrah, began Gannah's notorious rampage across the galaxy. He was succeeded by his son, Atarah Hoseh Charash, whom we now know as Hoseh the Wise. By the time Hoseh was forty years old, he was the proud annihilator of Nobo and conqueror of Karkar. Once he had the Karkar under subjection, Hoseh left the rule of the planet to his knights while he scouted ahead, looking for another people to conquer. Even as the Karkar were designing the plague, Hoseh was reconnoitering the planet Earth."

"Earth?" echoed Tagore, the other Terrestrial on the commission, and all at the table exchanged looks of surprise.

"Yes, Earth." She wouldn't deny her people's past, unwholesome as it may be. "My ancestors' success was due in part to thorough planning. They knew their victims' customs, languages, weaknesses, and strengths before ever making a move."

"Gannahans visited Earth that long ago," Hammond asked, "and no one knew it?"

Dassa wanted to remind the commissioner there was much about Gannah no one knew. Instead, she just answered the question. "In your eighteenth century AD, Terrestrials had no way of detecting an orbiting ship. Hoseh and his reconnaissance teams wore local dress, disguised the bright color of their eyes with tinted lenses, and followed Earth customs in order to learn all they could about their intended victims."

"You're saying that if Karkar hadn't stopped them, we would have been next?" Tagore said.

"We cannot say what might have happened. We can only say what did. The Gannahans were stopped at Karkar. And what occurred on Gannah recently is directly related to that event."

Roso, the Glenmarrian, hopped up. "But what did happen? That's what we want to know."

"And that is what I am telling you, if you will please be patient." Dassa moistened her lips. "Hoseh the Wise was on Earth at the time the plague ravaged the marauders at Karkar. They notified him of what was happening, but he had no physical contact with any of the diseased. He ordered them back to Gannah, and he and his exploration team followed. He arrived home to find the warships orbiting the planet without a living soul on board.

"Did no one check for survivors?" asked Kiik.

Dassa scowled at the ridiculous question. "The disease was contained within the vessels. Why would he expose a search party to contamination? No, the vessels were never boarded. Hoseh ordered that they be towed to the surface, weighted heavily, and sunk into the depths of the sea, never to be disturbed as long as time remained.

"A large number of Gannah's leadership—that is, the Nasi— were lost, and after three generations that knew little but war, we underwent a period of dramatic restructuring. Then, in the days of my grandfather, the Toqeph Atarah Naphtali Adin, another change began. Perhaps even before. I believe it was the result of Gannah's new ventures into the galaxy. Not to conquer this time, but to build relations with others for the mutual benefit of all. Through this outreach I think we contracted a different sort of contamination. A nonbiological one. Unlike the rapid Karkar plague, it was slow and insidious. It was the foreign notion of questioning authority."

Recalling her conversations with Rosh about their concerns, she went on with a heavy heart.

"Some years ago, the thoughts of my father, the Toqeph Atarah Degel Jachin, turned to those buried warships. He wondered what they contained. He speculated how long the disease could survive without oxygen, in such cold temperatures and under such pressure deep in the ocean.

"And he ventured where no Gannahan must ever go. He contemplated disobedience to the command of Atarah Hoseh the Wise. To even consider it was a crime. To discuss it made him worthy of death. When he tossed out the suggestion of raising the warships, his Nasi advisors were horrified to a man.

"Seeing their reaction, he backed down. But he never forsook the idea, and later began working in secret to execute his plan. Gannah has always obeyed the Atarah implicitly, and seldom has he led them wrong throughout the history of our planet. Therefore the people whose aid he enlisted, though sworn to silence, had no reason to distrust this new interest in undersea exploration." If only they had! Surely, someone could have intervened.

But no one did. Not even her.

Hating the truth but unable to hide from it, she went on. "Finally, after years of quiet preparation, he began to bring up the ships. The Nasi realized at last what was happening, but it was too late to stop him. I was unaware when the ships were raised."

Hammond looked surprised. "You were off the planet?"

"No, I was fulfilling the Last Requirement. That involves weeks of traveling alone through the wilderness, cut off from all communication with the rest of the world, in the final test for the Nasihood. When I completed my quest and returned to Armown, I found all Gannah either dead or dying. I was told that a warship had been raised, and as it reached the surface it exploded, releasing the plague in a poisonous cloud."

Cold questions came from all sides, each a razor-sharp accusation against her father. How far out at sea was this explosion? How long did it take the cloud to travel to land? Was the disease spread only by the cloud, or was it also carried person to person?

"I am not certain," she answered, bleeding within. "I do not know. I cannot say. I have no idea."

"Did it also condense and fall as rain?"

"I believe it precipitated, yes, as rain or snow, depending on the location."

"How did the organism grow and multiply under the sea?"

Dassa swallowed. She couldn't go on. "My apologies, but I have told you all I know of the matter. I have many questions myself, but no answers beyond those you have already heard."

Broward stood. "If I may, Commissioners, Madam Toqeph has told you all she knows, and there are no other witnesses we might call to shed further light on the events. I suggest this commission make their report to HC with what information we have and close the matter."

Dassa gave him a small smile of gratitude when he sat down.

"Captain Broward makes a good point," Hammond said. "Further questioning would be useless. Touching the events leading up to the explosion and immediately following, therefore, I think we can let this rest. But do any of you have any questions for Madam Toqeph on other matters?"

Roso stood, shaking his red mane from his eyes. "Yes. I would like to know what our guest intends to do next. She cannot live forever on the League's largesse."

Dassa had lately been giving that very matter a great deal of thought and prayer.

"I think that can be determined later—" Hammond began, but Dassa interrupted.

"Excuse me, Ms. Hammond, but Mr. Roso is right. It is not proper to accept your generosity without offering something in return. Since the League possesses limited knowledge of my planet and my people, I would like to offer my services as an instructor in a League university."

A ripple of surprise passed through the room.

Hammond appeared thoughtful. "HC might consider that. Are you qualified to teach? Have you a degree from a League-certified institution?"

"I have completed the seventh and highest level of education on my planet, but I have never been to a school of any sort, for Gannah does not have them. Education, much like diplomacy, is carried out in a less formal atmosphere than on League planets."

"You say seventh level," said Roso. "What does that mean?"

"Education begins at a very young age," Dassa explained, "carried out within the family setting as a natural part of everyday living. When a child is older, he learns various subjects at greater length, often under the tutelage of a local person with particular knowledge of the subject. Learning is accomplished through hands-on activities, demonstrations, games, and competitions. By the time a Gannahan child is ten years old, he is literate in two languages, proficient in simple arithmetic, and familiar with scientific principles. He knows basic Gannahan history and geography and has a smattering of knowledge about other planets. Children are also taught a wide variety of practical skills from an early age, along with athletics and the arts. They are, I believe you would say, well rounded."

The commissioners again had many questions. "Was there no governmental oversight? Did the child have to pass a test to move on to the next level?"

"There are tests for advancement," Dassa answered, "and the student's development in every area is examined, not merely academic studies. For instance, if a Second Level child cannot handle his *lahab* with dexterity, he will not pass to the Third even if he can do complex math problems and recite whole books."

"His lahab?" Tagore asked, his voice sharp with suspicion.

"The retractable circular blade which every Gannahan carries at all times. He practices with it until it becomes an extension of his arm." She felt the weight of hers in her pocket.

"Your children were routinely given weapons?" Kiik squawked.

"A small, bladeless version is given to each child in infancy. When he is older, he receives instruction in the use of a real one. By the time he is six or seven, he is fairly proficient with it. Anyone beyond the Second Level of education is required to carry a sharpened lahab with him at all times."

Hammond was aghast. "How could a child be trusted with such a thing?"

"The lahab is carried as protection against wild animals and other dangers, and even young children understand it is not a toy. Life on Gannah has always been hazardous, and we only survive by being prepared. Skill with the lahab is one way we do that."

"Do you have one on your person right now?" Kiik asked.

The woman had a gift for asking idiotic questions. "I am never without it."

The Karkar rose quickly. "I will not sit in the room with an armed Gannahan. How did this get past security?"

Hammond raised a hand. "Sit down, Ms. Kiik. If Madam Toqeph didn't cut your throat when you insulted her earlier, I doubt you're in danger now."

Dassa gazed up at the Karkar. "I have no interest in drawing your blood nor anyone else's. However, in answer to what I believe is the root of Mr. Roso's question, I shall submit to your own examiner's testing if it will help you determine my qualifications for teaching. If there is any lack in my education, I would be happy to rectify it. In fact, it would be good for me to attend your schools. I should see the workings of your educational process before I participate as an instructor."

"I expect HC will be very interested," said Hammond. "We will relay your offer to them." She looked around the table. "Are there any other questions?"

The Karkar had resumed her seat but continued to eye Dassa, who had a sudden, impish idea.

"Are you curious what a lahab looks like, Ms. Kiik?"

The Karkar's eyelids fluttered. "I have no interest in it, thank you."

From a fold of her garment, Dassa pulled a flat, blue disc, pressed a button between her thumb and middle finger, and a series of curved blades appeared around the disc's edge like glittering, evil teeth. Everyone in the room started with dismay.

"Be careful," Dassa said as she slid the lahab across the table toward the Karkar. "It is sharp enough to shave a spider."

They all watched in dumb fascination as the glittering object skimmed toward Kiik and stopped half a meter from her.

"I said I had no interest," the Karkar said.

"My apologies, Ms. Kiik, but you cannot lie to a Gannahan. Go ahead, look at it. If you wish to retract the blades, press the button from both sides at once."

Kiik gingerly picked up the instrument with both hands. "It has writing on it of some sort."

"My name. The lahab serves as both self-defense and identification."

Kiik pressed one long finger to each side of the button, and the blades disappeared. "Does it never open in your pocket?"

"It does not open so easily. There is a trick to it, to prevent accidents. Feel free to pass it around. The others are curious, too."

Holding it as if it might bite, Kiik handed it to Tagore beside her. The Terrestrial pressed the button, but nothing happened. "I see what you mean, there is a trick to it. But this writing..." He peered at it closely then looked up in surprise. "It's Hebrew!"

The others leaned toward him to get a better look. "What? How can that be?"

"The characters do look somewhat familiar."

"What's 'Hebrew'?"

"Why Hebrew?" Tagore asked, "rather than the native Gannahan language?"

Dassa smiled. "Hebrew *is* the native Gannahan language. Or, it was originally. Our tongue eventually became a mixture of Hebrew and King James English, but the original characters are still used."

"What is King James English?" asked Roso.

"How could your language be the same as the Jews'? Hammond's voice was tinged with skepticism. "It's not possible for the same language to evolve in separate societies, let alone on separate planets."

"It did not evolve," Dassa said. "It was given to us at creation."

When the commissioners looked at her blankly, she explained. "In Earth terms, you might say it is the language of God."

12

Dassa wondered why Captain Broward seemed so brusque as he hurried her back to her quarters. Good thing she'd regained her strength. A few days ago she wouldn't have been able to keep up with his determined stride.

He offered no explanation for his mood, and probing with her meah revealed only a confusing jumble of high emotions. When they were nearly to her room, she had to ask. "I do not understand, Captain. After what happened in there, you have every reason to be upset, but not with me."

He snorted. "No? I realize you're not used to the way we do things, but why did you have to bring out your weapon? Worse yet, why did you bring up religion? Weapons and religion don't mix."

"Religion? We were discussing languages."

"Yes, until you brought God into it."

Stopping to unlock the door, Dassa frowned at Broward. "Do not blame that pandemonium on me. I was asked a question and I answered truthfully. What would you rather I said?"

The captain followed her into the sitting room. "I'd rather you'd stuck to the facts and kept your opinions to yourself."

"That is what I did."

"Hardly! Calling your native tongue the language of God is an insult to others. The League encourages tolerance of—" He glanced around the room. "I don't see Pik. Where is he?"

"He is my keeper, not I his. How can you say the League encourages tolerance of all religions, when my innocent statement caused a small-scale riot?"

"You're putting words in my mouth. And where is the doctor?"

The door opened at that moment, and in strode Pik. "I heard about the brouhaha. What exactly went on in that meeting?"

"What did you hear?" the captain asked.

"The whole station's talking about it, but nobody seems to know anything."

Dassa sank into a voluminous chair. "I do not understand it myself."

Pik stared down at her from his great height. "I heard you attacked Commissioner Tagore."

Feeling as if the chair was swallowing her, she leaned forward out of its clutches. "No, I merely asked him to give me back my lahab."

"Your what?"

"My blade. The weapon we Gannahans are famous for slitting throats with. The commissioners were curious to see it, so I showed it to them. When the ruckus started, I thought it should be put away before someone got hurt, so I asked Mr. Tagore to return it."

The captain crossed his arms. "He thought you were attacking him. He was trying to defend himself."

"He had no reason to fear me. I merely asked him, in the calmest of voices, to return my lahab. Instead, he tried to open it and sliced his hand."

"You're a Gannahan," said Broward. "Moving toward him was enough to make him feel threatened." He shook his head, and his anger seemed to slip away. "I realize you didn't do it deliberately, but you've got the whole station in an uproar. Once things calm down, you'll owe a lot of people an apology."

Dassa frowned. "I shall apologize to anyone and everyone once I understand my error. But it was not I who started the shouting—I never raised my voice. I shook no fist, I drew no blood, and it was not I who stood on the table stamping my feet and screaming—"

Dassa started when a volcanic laugh erupted from Pik. "I heard about that. Was that Roso? What was he screaming, something about some ancient Earth king?"

Dassa wondered how Pik found humor in the Glenmarrian's appalling behavior. "He asked what was meant by the term *King James English.* When everyone was too busy shouting at each other to answer, he jumped onto the table and yelled, 'What is King James English? Why will nobody tell me? What is King James English?'"

"What *is* King James English?" Pik and Broward both asked.

"It refers to the language used in an ancient translation of some Earthish holy writings. It's named for the English king who ordered the translation.

Broward's expression was blank as the Karkar's.

"He hoped that by making God's words available for the common man to read and understand, it might free them from the lies of the corrupt clergy. Since then—"

"Just how would you know that?" Broward interrupted. "You've never been off Gannah in your life before, and now all of a sudden you're an expert in ancient Earth history?"

"I never said I had not been off Gannah."

The captain stared at her for a moment before spinning around to Pik. "I've got to try to straighten things out with the commission. Do not let her leave the suite. She's a walking war zone."

Pik gazed down at her with that empty, plastic expression. "No surprise there."

"HC's going to have my head on a silver platter." Broward turned back to Dassa. "Whatever openness you're accustomed to on your planet, I'd thank you to keep your opinions to yourself from now on. We don't need incendiary talk from the likes of… Well, from anyone. But particularly from someone whose ancestors used to run around wiping out entire civilizations. Please do not ever, under any circumstances, discuss religion with anyone as long as you are associated with my ship. Do you understand?"

"I do not understand, but I shall do as you ask." Dassa sank back into her chair. "I am sorry to have created such a stir. Be assured, I shall henceforth cause you no trouble."

Broward didn't look convinced. "Don't let her out of your sight, Pik. Keep a tight lid on her until I get back."

The captain left the suite, and Pik glared at Dassa in a silence dripping with disapproval.

"Relax, doctor," she said. "I shall cause you no trouble either."

"Oh? And when did you cease to be Gannahan?" He ambled to a nearby chair and collapsed his lanky frame into it, stretching out his legs before him.

"When you ceased to be bitter. But truly, I had no idea speaking the name of God would cause such a furor."

"Superstition often tends to arouse strong feelings. What exactly did you say?"

Dassa repeated her statement about the origins of the Gannahan language, and Pik nodded. "Yes, I see where that could cause problems. What I don't see is how a people evolved enough to master space travel can cling to these ancient myths."

"Myths?"

"Yes. Belief in a powerful, transcendent being. That sort of immature thinking has no place in an advanced society."

Dassa pulled her legs into the chair and sat cross-legged. "How then do you explain the fact that the early native Gannahan language is the same as ancient Earth Hebrew?"

"It cannot be true."

"It is verifiable fact."

"If that's so, then there's an explanation I haven't yet learned."

"I just gave it to you, but you refuse to believe it. Is it not a scientific principle that the simplest explanation is usually the best?"

"Yes. But your explanation requires too great an assumption and therefore cannot be valid."

Dassa studied the doctor's long, pale face, its blank expression a jarring contrast to the emotion charging his words. She sensed he recoiled from some shameful memory. "I am happy you disagree with me."

His ears stiffened. "You are?"

"Perhaps I should have said I am happy you do not pretend to agree. A less honest person might declare both our viewpoints valid. It speaks of your intellectual integrity that you believe unchanging truth exists."

Pik snorted. "I believe no such thing. Where'd you ever come up with that?"

"Because you think my beliefs to be wrong and your own correct. Such conviction requires a belief in the existence of absolute truth."

"You're misconstruing what I said. If there were such a thing as truth, I'd think someone would have found it by now."

Dassa stood. "How do you know someone hasn't?" She crossed the room, dimmed the lights then pressed a button on the back wall. The decorative ceiling rolled away to reveal the stars glittering through a skylight. "What do you know of Karkar's constellations?"

"Next to nothing." Pik pointed upward. "But I do know you won't find them up there."

"True." Dassa curled up in the massive chair. "We are too far from your planet or mine to see either of our home skies. But do you know anything of the constellations at all?"

"Only that the ancients had vivid imaginations."

"What sort of things did they imagine?"

Pik slouched low in the chair with head tilted toward the stars. "There is a woman, supposedly, called Xnikkii. That's from an ancient word meaning virgin."

"Do you recall what she looks like?"

"Like a collection of unrelated pinpricks of light."

Dassa continued to gaze upward but kept half an eye on Pik's reactions. "Not like a woman?"

"Not that I've been able to see."

"What other constellations do you recall?"

"There's Glng. That's a sort of half-man, half ng, which is a hoofed beast."

"But he looks like neither?"

"Not even a little."

"What else?"

Pik yawned. "I seem to remember a slithery monster of some sort, stretching far across the sky. No legs, just a head, tail, and enormous body. It's called Szsznaak. There is no creature on Karkar that corresponds with it."

"And again, when the stars that comprise that shape are pointed out to you, you can see no resemblance to such a creature?"

"None whatsoever." He looked over at her. "What are you getting at?"

Dassa returned his gaze. "Are you aware that every human culture we know of, on every planet, has the same constellations?"

He averted his eyes with a snort of disdain. "Not likely."

"They are not the same stars, of course. But the ancient peoples of all the planets imagined the same shapes in the heavens and gave them all the same fanciful names."

"How can that be?"

"That is what Hoseh the Wise wanted to know." She shifted to lie sideways in the chair, her head resting on one of its arms and her legs on the other.

"And who was he?"

"The Gannahan king who conquered Nobo and Karkar."

Pik's ears tilted back. "That's what made him wise?"

"No. He had an avid curiosity. A hunger to acquire knowledge that drove him to seek and explore ever farther afield. He discovered, in his roaming, that all the peoples he'd run across had the same legends concerning the stars. Every planet's ancient constellations were in the same position in the skies, had similar names, and told the same story. And none of them looked like what they were supposed to depict."

"What do you mean, they told the same story?"

"The ancients believed the heavens illustrated a universal story"—she gestured toward the ceiling—"with all the constellations its characters."

"I've never heard of such thing."

"Perhaps not. For many centuries, even for centuries before Hoseh's day, the story was largely forgotten on all the planets, Gannah included. Hoseh only uncovered it by digging into the most ancient records."

"So what was this story in the stars?"

She'd thought he'd never ask. But how could she tell him without breaking her promise to the captain? "It deals with the virgin you mentioned, giving birth to a child who was both man and not man. This child would grow up to suffer and die. His death would involve a cross. A result would be the pouring out of life like water, and he would one day return and vanquish the monstrous serpent forever."

Pik merely blinked.

"You do not believe me? Check the archives for yourself. If you dig deep enough, you should find record of that basic theme in the astrological antiquity of every peopled planet."

Pik rubbed the back of his neck. "Until I have the opportunity to do that, I'll withhold judgment. In the meantime, please continue." He got up and went to the chillbox. "Your fables are quaintly interesting."

Surprised he was willing to listen, Dassa continued. "Hoseh found such striking similarities in the legends he couldn't help but be curious. By the time he reached Karkar, his curiosity was nearly an obsession."

"Our history portrays his obsession somewhat differently."

"I'm sure it does." She took the bottle of water he handed her. "Thank you. I do not deny Hoseh and his knights were as cold and brutal as deep space itself. They dispatched all who stood in their way and refused to be burdened with prisoners. When they grew weary, they drank their victims' blood to renew their strength and continued in a drunken frenzy until every opponent was dead."

Pik settled back into his chair. "You mean when he wasn't pondering the constellations. Or did he contemplate the universe while slitting throats?"

His sarcasm was understandable. "I do not think so. When one is in a blooddrunk, one thinks of nothing else. And it takes some time to clear the head afterward."

Pik's voice was edged with suspicion. "You speak from experience?"

"You have your professional training, I have mine." She didn't wait for a response. "After learning all he could from Karkar, Hoseh continued to hunger. His curiosity about the stars gave him no rest. He felt there must be an answer. Perhaps on the next planet. As I explained to the commissioners, he left Karkar under the iron-fisted rule of his knights, and in a small but powerful craft manned by a minimal crew, he headed farther into the galaxy.

"They came across a lush, fruitful planet and stopped to take a closer look. What Hoseh found there changed all of Gannah forever."

13

While Pik slouched in his chair nursing a soft drink, Dassa continued her story.

"The people of the planet Hoseh discovered were primitive, highly emotional, and rabidly religious. Most other worlds, like Gannah and Karkar, had some old creation myths—which were strikingly similar, by the way—but their religious beliefs were either vague or nonexistent. This planet, however, was rife with conflicting religions, and Hoseh could see that this was the primary reason for their backward condition. Their pointless disputes fueled by self-righteous fervor kept them from realizing their potential.

"This would have made them easy to conquer, except for one thing. Hoseh and his chief Nasi, Chen Shakak Hagah, traveled the planet's surface disguised as natives so as to cause no alarm. And almost immediately they came across an obscure people who, unbelievably, spoke a language similar to Gannah's. These people had no country of their own, but could be found in pockets nearly everywhere."

Pik sat up straighter. "You mean they visited Earth? And these people were the Hebrews? I had no idea Gannah had its sights on Earth, let alone actually set foot there."

"No one but Gannah knew it, until now. In any event, Hoseh found himself plagued by uncertainty for the first time. Vanquishing the Terrestrials would be as easy as burning out a nest of vermin, but he held back, sensing something of extreme import surrounded the phenomenon of these nationless people.

"He and his Nasi traversed the planet gathering masses of information, but nothing satisfied him. He felt sure the answers to every question in the universe could be found in that place and was determined not to leave until he had uncovered them."

Dassa looked up at the stars. "Did you ever lie on your back on a summer night, gazing at the heavens and wondering what was out there?"

"No. Thanks to the way your relatives ravaged my planet, all Karkar cities are built within domes. No stars are visible."

She stared, surprised by his rancor. "That is not true. Karkar's surface is uninhabitable, yes, but Gannah did not make it so. Instead of restoring what remained and rebuilding your planet after we left, the peoples of Karkar continued warring with one another. You compounded the destruction we began, and within a century had wiped out two of your own races and rendered the atmosphere irredeemably poisonous."

Pik cleared his throat. "Be that as it may, the only Karkar constellations I've seen were in pictures, and they bored me. But if I'd had the opportunity to look at the stars, I doubt they'd have called to me. In my youth I had no desire to leave home." He looked vacantly across the room. "Funny, though. Now that I'm gone, I feel little desire to return."

The probing fingers of Dassa's meah found a crack in his detachment. "As I never wished to leave Gannah. But unlike you, I plan to return as soon as I am able."

"Why? There's nothing there anymore."

"But it is Gannah still. I merely need to find a few people to put on it."

"You want to play God and create a new race?"

"No one who tries to play God gets away with it." The familiar sorrow pressed so against her chest, she wondered why her sternum wasn't crushed. "What do you miss most about Karkar?"

"I don't miss it."

"Everyone misses something from home."

Pik continued to stare at nothing, and Dassa waited.

He raised a finger. "I miss…" He dropped his hand. "Oh, forget it."

"You may speak your mind. I shall not belittle you."

Without looking at her, he said slowly, "Of all the things on Karkar, I most miss…my mother."

Dassa blinked, fighting tears. "I miss mine as well. Though it is hard to say what, or who, I miss the most." Memories of faces passed before her vision, laughter and song, the warm weight of babies in her arms.

They were silent together for a moment before she added, "I miss the music."

Still leaning back in the chair, he turned this head to look at her.

"You know, the music. You heard it when you were there. You were the only one."

He raised his head. "How do you know that?"

She unfolded herself from the chair and leapt up in one fluid motion. "I must dance."

"What?"

She went to the entertainment terminal. "Show me how they dance on Karkar."

"What are you talking about?"

"Teach me a Karkar dance. What music shall I play?"

Pik got up and came toward her, a look of bemusement about his ears. "Fast or slow?"

"I don't care, whatever you like. I just need to move."

He viewed the selections. "How about this?" He made a clicking sound in the back of his throat.

"That is what it is called? What does it mean?"

"Just that." He made the sound again and selected the song. "It has no translation."

Dassa hurried to shove the furniture out of the way. "How much of a dance floor will this require?"

"That's plenty. What do you think? Do you like Karkar music?"

She listened, bobbing in rhythm. "I do. At first it seemed to be entirely percussion, but now I see it is not quite." She rocked her body to the beat. "If you were on Karkar, how would you dance to this? Show me."

He watched as she swayed. "How did you know I heard the music on Gannah?"

"It matters not. Come, dance."

"Answer my question first."

How could he stand like a stick with that music playing? "What question?"

"How did you know I heard the music? Or, if you won't tell me that, I'll ask another: you said Hoseh the Wise found something on Earth that changed all Gannah forever. What did he find?"

She allowed the music to flow through her, moving with its pulse. "I am not permitted to speak of that. I promised the captain, remember?"

"Hoseh found religion?"

"No, he found the truth. Show me how you dance to this."

"You didn't answer a question yet. How about this one: why is your tongue purple?"

"I already told you. I am Nasi."

"Is it purple from birth?"

"No one is Nasi from birth. How does a Karkar dance? Show me."

"How does it get that color, then?"

Her movement ended when the music concluded. "You have wasted so much time, the song has ended. I shall play it again, and if you will not show me the proper steps I shall make up my own."

He reached the audio player before her and pulled her hand away. "No dancing until you answer at least one of my questions. Choose one to answer, then I'll teach you how to dance the—" He made that clicking sound again.

He still held her hand. And the sensation didn't distress her as it should have. Though his face revealed no more than usual, she saw a new light in his amber eyes, and behind them a new awakening.

"I know you heard the music because…I felt it in my meah."

"I need an answer I can understand. What's a meah?"

She pulled her hand away—slowly, so as not to seem rude. "It is the Gannahan's sixth sense, so to speak. We are aware of others' thoughts and feelings through it."

His ears stiffened. "You read minds?"

That could be a little alarming to someone who wasn't used to the concept. "Not the way you're thinking. It's more like…like empathy than telepathy."

It seemed his inner medical researcher took over the questioning. "Is it a physical organ? Where is it?"

"It is an area of the brain. And it is one reason Gannahans are natural linguists. We can understand much of any spoken language because we know the person's thoughts without comprehending the words."

He nodded. "Is that how you understood my mother?"

"Yes. And how I knew you heard the music. I felt you appreciating it, and it surprised me. I thought no Outsider could hear it." She glanced at the audio player. "Does that answer your question?"

"Well enough." He turned the music on then led her back into the center of the room. "This is how it goes."

She stifled a smile as he demonstrated the jerky movements suggested by the music. After watching briefly, she imitated them.

"You might be a natural linguist, but you haven't captured the spirit of Karkar dance. You're too graceful."

"My apologies." She made her movements less smooth. "Is this better?"

"It's a start. Okay, next we do this." He lurched and turned around, moving his feet in spastic rhythm.

She repeated his maneuvers, and he corrected her foot positions.

After going over the entire routine one time, he played the music again, and they danced in unison. "You learn quickly, but your moves are still too smooth."

"I shall master it. One more try?"

"If you insist."

This time she inserted a few finger snaps, hand claps, and foot stomps of her own, tossing him a mischievous grin.

"Nothing wrong with a little improvisation," he said, panting, but made no move to embellish his own rendition.

The song ended. "I like that," said Dassa, still dancing even after the sounds faded away. "Teach me another." She headed for the entertainment terminal. "What should we put on next?"

He again reached the audio player first. "You must choose another question to answer. Which will it be?"

She looked at her hands enclosed in his six-fingered ones. And didn't shudder. "I promised Captain Broward I would not discuss religion, and I am also forbidden to speak of the other."

"Then answer a different one. Have you ever been blooddrunk?"

All warm feelings suddenly gone, Dassa pulled away and busied herself pushing the furniture back into place. "Thank you for teaching me the"—she tried to click the name of the song, but it didn't sound even close to the way Pik uttered it—"the whatever-you-call-it. I enjoyed the experience. But I shall go to my room now. Good night, Dr. Pik."

"It's not even dinnertime yet. What do you mean, 'good night'?"

Pausing with hands on the back of a chair, she looked up at him. "I mean I do not wish to discuss it."

"I told you I missed my mother. That's as intimate a confession as it gets for me. I told you that, because I know you'll never mention it to anyone. As I will never betray your confidence."

Dassa knew he meant what he said, for the moment. But she doubted he could be trusted in the long run. "You have touched me where none should touch me, examined and explored every region of my body, and shared your findings with the galaxy. Why should I think you would not make public anything else you learn of me?"

"Because it's not Dr. Pik who's asking."

"What?"

"This time it's Pik the man."

She felt him reaching for her in the tortured half Karkar/half Terrestrial version of the meah he didn't have. Reaching in hunger.

Not a lust to claim and conquer, but a deeper hunger, and a compelling one.

She turned away. "The Nasi training is not discussed with anyone. Particularly an Outsider."

But that is a human rule, not Mine, the Yasha whispered.

"Does it matter anymore?" Pik asked.

Dassa walked to another chair and sat, uncomfortable with the feelings swirling within. What did He mean, special? "You are an Outsider wherever you go, are you not? Even on Karkar?"

He didn't speak, but he didn't need to. They both knew the answer.

A trickle of relief seeped through her. Relief that she could share secrets with this strange, lonely creature who, like her, was the only one of his kind. "I will explain the blooddrunk to the man who has no people. But the doctor must never hear a word of it. Can the Solitary Pik keep a secret from the Medical Pik?"

"The Solitary Pik never speaks to anyone. That's why he's solitary."

Dassa smiled. "Everyone needs someone to talk to."

His voice sounded even more pinched than usual. "He's lately finding that out."

"I know someone he might want to acquaint himself with, then, if…if he is not repulsed by what he learns."

Pik took a chair opposite her. "He's listening."

"You may think the Gannahans a cold and unfeeling people, but—"

"'Cold and brutal as deep space itself,' is the way you worded it moments ago."

"That is the impression we give, yes. The fact is, we are subject to the same range of emotions as any other human but are taught early on to keep our feelings in check. The only thing that makes a

Gannahan lose that control is the ingestion of either alcohol or blood. It makes us mad. We acquire a strength and stamina that can only be described as demonic. It enables us to commit the horrible deeds that made us legendary."

Pik watched her but didn't interrupt.

"For that reason, alcohol in any form is banned on Gannah. Merely to possess it is a capital crime. Blood, of course, cannot be outlawed, but the drinking of it is. That, too, is punishable by death.

"Blood can only be swallowed in two situations. When it is necessary for defensive survival, and…and under very controlled conditions, for training purposes. So a Nasi might know what the effect is on his mind and body. One must practice with any weapon to be capable of using it properly, though one hopes its employment shall not be necessary."

Pik's ears pricked with interest. "How much does it take to cause this intoxication?"

"A very small amount."

His ears moved back and forth as he digested the information. "The doctor would find this interesting. But he will never know about it."

The weight on her chest began to ease. "And the Solitary Pik? Does he abhor the Gannahan now more than ever?"

"No." He cleared his throat. "He is glad to learn of this. In fact, he'd like to know more. Show me how they danced on Gannah." He rose and headed to the entertainment terminal.

Dassa remained in her chair. "We dance to anything, or even to nothing, with very little provocation. In fact, at the conclusion of our annual Festival of Voices, we participate in a magnificent dance that lasts for nearly two hours. The steps are quite intricate and take months to learn."

"I guess I won't ask you to teach me that one."

"I suppose not. I saw no Gannahan music in the available selections, but that doesn't matter. Choose a tune, and I will show you some simple steps."

Pik surveyed the choices. "This one's nice." He turned on a slow song. "What would a Gannahan do with something like this?" He approached her chair and extended his hand.

She took it and rose, a smile playing at her lips. "We could do any number of things with that."

14

After Dassa retired for the night, Pik retreated to the sunken theater area of their suite and selected a movie from the extensive playlist.

The wide, curving screen wrapped him in a comfortable world of make-believe, and though he had the volume turned low so as not to disturb the sleeping Gannahan, the audio filled the room like a lulling fragrance.

Then a buzzer sounded, and Captain Broward's voice came over the door speaker, breaking Pik's trance. "I need to see you."

Pik jumped and blinked, muttering a Karkar curse.

He paused the scene and went to the door. "I was starting a movie."

"Oh? What is it?" Broward followed Pik into the darkened alcove.

"*The Treasure of Bande Kor.*"

"That's a good one. And what a system you've got here! This nursemaid job has its perks, eh?"

Pik grunted, handing the captain a beer he'd snatched from the chillbox on his way past.

"Thanks." Broward glanced at the bottle as he took a seat. "Whoa, Klarson's Premium from Bappas. You're a first-class host. At least, when the League's footing the bill."

Sprawling on the sofa, Pik gargled a chuckle. "So you've seen this?" He unpaused the movie.

"One of my top ten." Broward leaned back and surveyed the surrounding screen with evident pleasure. "I've never watched it on a set-up like this, though. It's like seeing it for the first time."

Two minutes into the movie, Broward said, "Did you talk to her?"

Annoyed, Pik tore his attention away from the action. "Who? About what?"

"The Gannahan. About how a civilized person should behave in polite society."

Pik kept his gaze on the screen. "We discussed it."

"And?"

"I agree her comments were inconsiderate. It doesn't sound like she was the uncivilized one, though. The fault was with the commissioners who overreacted. I missed what he said just now." He turned up the volume. "Did you catch it?"

"He said Cephargian pirates attacked the ship, killed the crew and took the treasure. Didn't you say you'd seen this before?"

Pik's right head-tilt signaled a negative. "No."

"About time you did, it's a classic. Did you make her understand how wrong it is to discuss religion?"

"We talked at length." Pik still felt her hand in his, saw her small, graceful body dancing before his eyes. "But she insists she wasn't talking about religion, she was discussing languages. I don't think she grasps the issue."

"Seems like a lot of things she doesn't quite get. Ever take a good look at her? As a woman, I mean. Her body looks like the peak of health these days, but she's still comatose as far as romance is concerned."

Pik's ears smiled. "She does have a way of keeping people at arm's length."

"I expect she's still in mourning. At least I hope that's not the usual Gannahan way."

Pik imagined the captain's reaction if he knew how he and Dassa had danced that afternoon. Best not to mention it. "I'm sure that's it. But she does tell me her people had no sexual relations outside of marriage."

Broward snorted. "I'll bet."

"No, she meant it. She was horrified to learn that we were assigned the same suite here on the station. Even with separate bedrooms, she said such an arrangement would be unthinkable on Gannah."

"Might need a little cultural training, then, after a decent interval. She does seem to be a fast learner."

"That's for sure."

"So the two of you talk quite a bit, then?" Broward gave him a shrewd glance.

"I answer her questions." Pik shrugged. "What did you want to talk to me about?"

Broward looked surprised at the question, then sheepish. "I didn't really need to talk to you, I merely wanted some company. It's been a rough day."

"Did you make any headway with the commission?"

The captain took a long pull on the beer. "I think so. They admit the commotion was as much the result of their overreaction as it was to the Gannahan's statement, which they concede wasn't intended to be inflammatory."

Pik stifled a burp. "Very reasonable of them."

"I thought so. Commissioner Hammond tells me they've concluded their investigation. In their report to HC, they'll recommend accepting the toqeph's offer to teach Gannahan history and culture on one of their university campuses. The commissioner is going to stop by tomorrow at ten to talk to her about where we go from here."

"Where *do* we go from here?"

"I'm taking the *Barton* back to Beeheehoohaa to finish what we started. The commissioners will take the Gannahan to Earth on the *LSS Comet*. They want you to accompany her and continue overseeing her recovery. First, though, you'd better come aboard the *Barton* and remove your personal belongings. I'm not sure when you'll be rejoining us."

"Very well." Though his words didn't quite reflect his feelings, the thought of traveling with the Gannahan no longer seemed as odious as it did yesterday. "I've enjoyed my service on your ship and regret having to leave."

Broward smiled. "You'll be greatly missed, both professionally and personally."

Pik reviewed a mental list of the ongoing projects he had back on board. "There are a couple things I'll need to take care of first, though."

"I'll give you time to tie up any loose ends."

"Speaking of which, what did the commissioner say about our leaving Beeheehoohaa before our mission was complete?"

"I believe the word she used in that context was 'commendation.'" Broward grinned.

"Really! How'd you pull that off?"

"I'm not sure. She didn't promise anything, but the hints she dropped were very encouraging." He rose. "Another beer?"

"Sure, thanks."

Broward opened the chillbox then chuckled. "I wish you could have seen Roso up there on the table throwing that tantrum." One beer in each hand, he performed a low-volume impersonation.

"'What is King James English? Why will no one tell me? What is King James English?'"

Pik choked a throaty laugh. "Are those characters the best HC had to send?"

"I don't know." The captain handed Pik a bottle. "They're probably competent under ordinary circumstances, but that green-eyed Gannahan does something to you." He popped off the lid and drank deeply. "I envy you, you know."

"Why is that?"

"Because you've had a chance to get to know her. From what I've seen, she's got it all—looks, smarts, royalty—the whole package. Just a little stand-offish. I'd sure like to know how to loosen her up."

Action on the big screen caught Pik's attention, and his ears scowled. "And I'd sure like to watch this movie."

Broward laughed. "All right, I'll shut up. I can take a hint."

Pik reversed to the place where the captain had first interrupted. Dassa would never loosen up with Broward the way she had with him. Only Pik had heard the music.

15

Aboard the *Comet*—in separate quarters this time—Pik allowed his Medical side to take control, throwing the Solitary Pik back into confinement.

His past consortium with the Gannahan embarrassed him. Made him curl up in shame as if before his mother's scolding. He still felt drawn to her on a base, elemental level, but smacked down the attraction with a solid backhand whenever it raised its head. The less he saw of her, the more at peace he was with himself.

In the company of Commissioner Kiik's husband, Kasan, he enjoyed endless matches of hmmmjckt, discussed Karkar politics, and relished the simple joy of speaking in the vivid Karkar language. When Kasan was otherwise occupied, Pik flirted with the female crew even though they were Terrestrials. Sometimes he challenged one or another to a game of plink in the recreation room. He often let them win so he could see them jump and squeal with delight.

Dassa seemed to be trying to make friends too. She kept her distance from the men, of course, but there were females aboard. Besides Hammond and her companion, and Commissioner Kiik, three other women traveled from Station 27 on business. Not to mention Pik's new plink-mates.

But none of the women seemed interested in striking up a friendship with a Gannahan, and she didn't force the issue. When he inquired in a professional capacity, she told him she was concentrating on the healing process, jogging for kilometers around the circular corridors and working out in the ship's small weight room. He also noted that she spent hours scouring the ship's data library, researching the ways of the Terrestrials and other League worlds.

It was probably a lonely existence. But she never complained to her doctor.

Two weeks out from Station 27, his rumbling stomach sent Pik to the dining room, where he saw Dassa eating lunch alone and frowning at something on the computer.

He chose a sandwich of veggie chicken, a side of roasted Ilyria strips, and fortified water. At each selection, a scanner read Pik's subdermal chip, debiting the total from his Leaguebank account.

Next, he surveyed the dining area for a seat. If Kasan were here, he'd have sat with him. But the sight of the solitary Gannahan stabbed him with guilt, and in hope of soothing the sting, he carried his lunch to her table.

Noting the intensity of her concentration, he asked, "What are you studying?"

Her gaze lifted to meet his, sending a thrill throughout his body, and her fierce face gave way to a welcoming smile.

She closed the computer and it sank flush with the tabletop. "Still trying to figure out the League's financial markets. Such things are beyond me."

He cut his sandwich into small pieces, as the Karkar mouth was unsuited to biting and tearing. "What's beyond me is how Gannah could function without money."

"We manage quite well, as I've explained before."

Speaking the standard language was difficult under any circumstances. Pik couldn't even attempt it with his mouth full. As he chewed, he wordlessly offered her some of his Ilyria strips.

"Thank you, but I've had enough." She gathered her empty wrappers into a neat bundle and wiped her place at the table with a napkin.

After swallowing, he continued the conversation. "They tried the communal method on Karkar centuries ago. Some nations on Earth and Eutare did, too, I'm told. But in every case the system soon collapsed. It's unworkable."

"I've read about those experiments, but they were nothing at all like our way. On Gannah, all resources are Gannah, all people are Gannah, so everything is everyone's and no one lacks."

"You can't merely consume, you must also produce. Where is the incentive to work, and how are goods and services provided?"

"Perhaps one must be a Gannahan to understand."

"Perhaps." Pik took another bite, thinking it must be nice to be able to eat and converse at the same time.

By the time Dassa threw her trash in the receptacle and returned to the table, Pik's mouth was again empty.

"I haven't seen you since your last check-up a week ago. How have you been?" He gave her a visual once-over. "You look in the peak of health."

"I'm well, for the most part, but I feel as if I'm lacking something."

Pik thought of the hours she'd spent the last week working out. "It doesn't seem to affect your energy levels."

"Not seriously, but something's missing nevertheless. Not just an element in the food, but something's also lacking in this artificial atmosphere. I'd kill for some fresh air."

Pik cast a glance around the room, but no one seemed to have heard her. "Don't say things like that. People will take you seriously."

"I am serious."

He nearly choked, but she soothed her words with a smile. "Almost. But don't worry, killing would accomplish nothing. There's no fresh air to be had in space at any price."

He took a gulp of fortified water. "No wonder people avoid you."

"That has nothing to do with it. If I joked like that with anyone but you, I'd frighten the feathers off them, so I'm always careful what I say."

"Feathers?"

Dassa fiddled with the lid to Pik's water bottle as she talked. "It's an old Gannahan expression. When you scare a notsah bird, it runs away in a cloud of feathers."

"Doesn't sound like a good defense mechanism. If its feathers fall out, how can it fly from danger?"

"It can't. It weighs something like 175 kilograms, and its wings are too small to lift it off the ground. But it can do some damage with its hooked beak and ten-centimeter claws. And when it's frightened, it excretes a foul smell. The stench of the falling feathers is enough to make you vomit."

"Sounds delightf—"

The unfinished word was knocked out of Pik's mouth by a violent jolt and a deep rumble that shook the whole ship.

"What...?" Dassa gasped as the floor listed, the lights went out, and lunch trays slid off tables in a surround-sound clatter.

The ship tilted again. A dim glow returned as the auxiliary power kicked in, and an alarm whooped.

Hanging onto the table, which was bolted to the floor, Pik swallowed hard as his half-eaten lunch scrambled to get out of his stomach.

A recorded announcement shouted above the alarm's din as the ship slowly leveled. "Attention. Stage Four Alert. All hands, report to your stations. Passengers, please remain where you are. Do not move about the ship. Repeat: Stage Four Alert."

The other diners shrieked. Pik couldn't release his grip on the table. Dassa cringed as if the alarm hurt her ears.

A live voice replaced the canned announcement. "This is Captain Jorge Quintana. We are under attack by Cephargian raiders. This is not a drill. I repeat, we are under attack."

Pik locked stares with Dassa.

The captain's voice continued. "It would seem their ship was cloaked. Just moments ago, it appeared from nowhere and knocked out our shields. Prepare to be boarded."

The transmission ceased.

"Raiders?" Terror made the word catch in Pik's throat.

"That's what he said," she answered. "Does he mean—"

Their attention swung toward the door at the sound of shouting and hurried footfalls outside.

"Cephargian pirates!" Pik's choked reply answered her question and identified the bald, burly men who burst into the room, weapons drawn.

16

Terror sapped Pik's strength, numbed his senses, and drained his mind of reason.

It was like a horror movie, but worse, because he couldn't walk away. The way his legs trembled, he doubted he could walk at all.

The planet Cepharge never joined the League of Worlds. They didn't like the rules. Even the most law-abiding Cephargians were vulgar, but those who made their living raiding League starships had developed their native cruel streak to poetic proportions. They tormented Karkar travelers in particular, frequently cutting off the sixth finger from each hand just for fun.

Pik flexed his fingers and shuddered.

The swarming pirates hustled the passengers out of the dining room, shouting commands in a crude rendition of the Standard Tongue. When a crewman at another table tried to resist, a pirate knocked him senseless with a savage blow then grabbed his wrist and dragged him out with the rest of the prisoners. He might have dislocated the crewman's shoulder, but Pik wasn't inclined to investigate.

With the screaming alarm feeding his fear, he dumbly obeyed the pirates' commands, keeping barely enough wit to stay close to Dassa. Whether through desire to protect or be protected, he wasn't sure.

Her face revealed little, and she said nothing as she complied with the Cephargians' barked orders, allowing herself to be herded through the corridors with the rest of the passengers and crew. Pik wondered at such un-Gannahan docility.

His heart almost leaped from his chest when she grabbed his arm.

"There's Captain Quintana," she muttered, "up there with Commissioner Hammond. I must speak with him."

Pik looked. The captain had the swaying stance of a man recovering from a laser stun, and what looked like a burn on the side of his head supported the diagnosis. "Tell him he should sit down before he falls."

But Dassa released his arm and weaved through the press of bodies toward her target. Unwilling to be left behind, he followed.

The pirates, tattooed faces glistening with sweat, shouted and poked and yanked at their captives until they'd forced all the passengers and crew into the multi-purpose room. The place droned with frightened murmuring, punctuated by the Cephargians' shouted orders and the moans of the injured. An infusion of perspiration, fear, lost lunches, and uncontrolled bladders mingled in a stench that must have rivaled the notsah bird's excretions. Pik was tempted to look for feathers—a thought that almost sent him into hysterical laughter. He only kept it at bay by visualizing his hand with the sixth finger hacked off.

Once everyone was gathered, a silence fell and all eyes watched as a tall Cephargian strode from a side entrance and strode to the podium on the small stage. The tattooed mural on his naked head featured plenty of blood red. His garish attire was loudly expensive, and he carried himself with an air of authority.

Pik flexed his fingers, wishing his height didn't make him stand out in the crowd.

Dassa continued edging her way toward the *Comet*'s captain. She managed to squeeze close behind Quintana and murmur something to him, but Pik couldn't hear what. He only saw the look of consternation on the captain's face when he turned around and shook his head. She then whispered something to Hammond, whose response was a fierce, "No! Never!"

The pirate found a microphone, tapped it, then spoke. "Attention, attention, all you rich swine. I'd like to thank you for coming, and for having such a neat little ship. We're delighted to be able to add it to our fleet. But first things first, as they say. We don't like taking jewelry and things off corpses, so if you don't mind, I'd like you all to line up real nice and orderly so's my friends can make sure they don't miss no one when they collect your valuables."

The prisoners exchanged terrified looks while the pirate continued.

"Now queue up here so we can see who's who and what's what. Don't give us no trouble now, 'cause that makes us peevish."

The pirates shoved people into four lines with aisles between for the pirates to pass.

Quintana called up to the man on the platform. "Who's the leader here? Is it you, sir?"

"Yeah, it's me. Who's askin'?" The Cephargian grinned down at the captives.

"I am Captain Jorge Quintana, and I demand that you leave this vessel at once."

The pirates erupted in hilarity. "Your request is duly noted, Cappy," said the head Cephargian. "Now, line up with the rest of the pigs."

The back of Quintana's neck grew crimson. "You, sir, are in violation of Section 1404.25 of the Code of Interspace Passage, which states—"

"I don't care what it states," the pirate chief roared. "If you don't do as you're told, I'll have you cooked on a spit with an apple in your mouth!"

Pik hadn't been watching Dassa during this exchange, but to his horror, he now saw her making her way through the crowd toward the Cephargian.

"Excuse me, sir," she called as she moved toward him. "As I understand it, a Cephargian likes nothing better than a test of skill. Is that so?"

The pirate eyed Dassa's approach with interest. "Could be. What sort of skill?"

"A fighting competition. We have a proposition for you."

"Come back here, madam, please!" Hammond called to the Gannahan.

But Dassa didn't stop until she reached the foot of the podium, directly beneath the Cephargian's lecherous eye. "Is it true what I hear? Are you a man of honor, sir?"

Pik gaped. What on Karkar was she doing?

"Of course. A Cephargian's always true to his word. Right, men?"

"Aye, right!" the hijackers thundered from all corners of the room.

"So if we come to an agreement," Dassa said, "you will abide by its terms?"

"As sure as your life is in my hands, little lady." The pirate's grin broadened. "What sorta agreement are you proposing?"

"Are you aware there is a Gannahan knight aboard?"

A rumble of consternation passed through captors and captives alike.

"No," Pik murmured. "Don't do it…"

"No," said the pirate. "I weren't aware. Where is he?"

"Who would you put your money on? A Cephargian pirate or the Gannahan?"

Quintana and Hammond loudly objected until the closest pirate leveled his weapon at Hammond. Their leader barked, "Shut up your squawking, you two." He turned back to Dassa. "What are you saying?"

"I propose a contest. Our Gannahan knight against your best fighter. You win, you get the ship along with everyone and everything aboard. You lose, we all go free. With our valuables."

The pirate looked interested, but wary. "To the death?"

"To the death."

Pik felt faint.

"Well, now. A Gannahan, huh? Them knights is supposed to be like magic almost. Let's make it one Gannahan against two o' my best."

"Fair enough. Provided you give us your word that if the Gannahan wins, you will immediately let us all go free and return anything your men have already taken."

"Only if my gladiators are armed and yours ain't."

"Primitive weapons only. No guns, no explosives, no lasers."

Pik couldn't believe she'd consider such terms. What did she know that he didn't?

"A blade and a spear?"

"Agreed. Two Cephargians, one with a blade, one with a spear, against the unarmed Purpletongue. If the Gannahan wins, you'll gather your dead and depart."

The Cephargian rubbed his hands. "Aye! But the dead will not be ours."

Dassa turned to the captain. "Captain Quintana, would you care to formalize the agreement with Captain…" She looked at the pirate. "I didn't get your name."

He bowed. "Hool. Hegigar Hool, captain of the *Death Knell*. At your service, little lady." He called out to Quintana. "Captain! Do we have a deal?"

"Absolutely not. This is barbaric. I will not—"

"Yes, we have a deal." Dassa turned to the captain. "Please, come here and seal it." The glint in her eye was commanding.

Pik's mind whirred. The little creature was gutsy, all right, and clever. Not to mention a genuine, purple-tongued Nasi, albeit a small one. She might be capable of anything.

Surprising himself, Pik pressed forward and murmured to Quintana, "Sir, is there help on the way, do you know?"

"No." Quintana sagged. "There is no friendly ship closer than ten days out."

"Then I suggest you do as she asks. They'll kill us all anyway. I see no other way out."

"The League doesn't do business like this," Hammond growled. "Don't allow it, Captain."

After a pause, Quintana took a deep breath. "I'm sorry, Commissioner, but I believe the doctor is right. I must do what's best for my ship and my crew. If the foolhardy little Gannahan dies, it might at least buy us some time." He stepped forward. "We have an agreement, Captain Hool."

Hool gave a gleeful chuckle as he stepped away from the podium to meet Quintana. "We will settle the matter, then, right here and now. A fight to the death, carried out according to the terms set forth by your audacious little emissary. Two armed Cephargians against one Gannahan knight's bare hands. After we kill your champion, I trust there will be no more trouble from you?"

"We will abide by the terms."

The pirate turned back to Dassa, face twisted in a sneer. "I have something special in mind for you, precious."

Showing more nerve than Pik expected, Quintana said, "You will not have the opportunity. After our Gannahan kills your pirates, you and your men will quietly leave."

"Agreed!" Hool shouted, and to his men's hoots and applause, he and Quintana grasped the others' arms and kissed on the mouth, sealing the deal in the traditional, if unsanitary, Cephargian manner.

Pik couldn't suppress a gag but he swallowed and cleared his throat, eyes threatening tears. He almost wished there was a God to call upon. The stories of Cephargian cruelties were well documented.

"All right, Cappy Quintana, let's see your Gannahan. Where is he?"

"Right here," Dassa answered.

The Cephargian laughed. "Your eyes tell me you're a Gannahan, but where's the Purpletongue? Hiding behind your skirts?"

"In a manner of speaking. I am Atarah Hadassah Hagah Natsach, Toqeph of Gannah." She stuck out her tongue. "At your service, Captain Hool."

The pirates shouted raucous objections until Hool put his fingers to his mouth and let out a shrill whistle. Glaring at Dassa, he said, "You tricked us, whore."

"I said there was a Gannahan knight aboard. I never said the knight was a man. You will keep your word, will you not?"

"I will," the pirate snarled. "But it's insultin' to fight a woman. We're gonna show you—" He gestured toward the crowded room. "We'll show all of you what an insulted Cephargian does to them that insults him." He licked his lips in anticipation. "We're gonna insult your dead body in ways you don't wanna contemplate."

Dassa stared calmly back at him. "First you must kill it. Where will this contest be held?"

"Right here. Boys!" He shouted to his men. "Clear a space and bring in a fighting ring. We'll make short work of Miss Uppity here, then we can have some fun. I'm glad you got more women aboard, Cappy, 'cause me and my boys'll want some live ones after we're through with the deceased." He pointed to Hammond. "We'll start with that one, once the little upstart's torn beyond use."

Hool ordered Dassa, "Don't you move," then shouted, "Kfay! Suddsy!"

Cephargians are always big, but the mastodons who lumbered forward at the captain's summons looked like well-muscled mountains.

"Cappy, you and that self-important wench beside you, come 'ere and wait your turn. And you there, Fingers." He pointed at Pik. "Don't be slinking off. Git over here. You three get to watch ringside."

Pik felt disembodied, disconnected, as he, Hammond, and Quintana took the positions Hool appointed them.

The Cephargians who had transported back to their ship reappeared with tall panels of some thick, clear material. After shoving back the crowd of captives to make room, they quickly assembled a circular fighting ring, open at the top and about three meters high.

They also brought a battleaxe with a huge, curved blade, a two-meter spear with a multi-bladed head, and two sets of body armor, including helmets.

"Captain Hool," Quintana said, "we didn't agree to your men wearing armor."

"And we didn't agree to fight a woman, now, did we?"

Dassa watched the preparations and her massive opponents with such concentration, Pik was afraid to interrupt. She looked so calm. Did she actually think she had a chance?

His small hope swooned in a dead faint when she muttered, "I could use a good stiff drink."

The Cephargians had the ring assembled in no time. The two monsters Dassa was to fight stripped to their shorts and donned the armor.

Dassa continued sizing them up as she slipped off her shoes. She wore a dress of filmy fabric over a short-legged leotard. Still watching her opponents, she removed the dress and handed it to Pik. Then she reached behind her neck and pulled her lahab from its pocket in the back of her tight-fitting top. In a movement so swift Pik's eye nearly missed it, she flicked open the blade, sliced the inside of her forearm, then closed the lahab and handed it to him. "Hang onto that," she told Pik. "I'll be right back."

He took it, uncomprehending.

"Combatants, take your places!" Hool called, and Dassa put her bleeding arm to her mouth.

In sudden understanding, Pik stood frozen with Dassa's dress in one hand and the lahab in the other, knees wobbling.

"What happened to your arm, little lady?" Hool asked Dassa as she passed him on her way into the ring.

"Just a scratch." Licking a smear of blood from her lips, she glanced at her waiting opponents then smiled up at the pirate captain. "Are you sure you don't want to send in a third man? These two won't last very long."

Hool laughed as he closed the transparent door behind her. "We'll risk it."

17

The Cephargians stood in one half of the ring, fearsome mountains of menace. Dassa stood in the other—only shoulder high to the beasts, but with green eyes flashing.

"Are we ready?" Hool asked.

The Cephargians raised their arms and shook their weapons, shouting something in their own tongue that made Pik's ears wilt.

Dassa crouched. "Ready."

Hool raised his arm. "Let the contest begin!"

His arm came down and the two bald monsters moved forward in small, menacing moves. Dassa circled the edge, watching, ready to dodge. The axe man took a swing and at almost the same moment the spearman jabbed.

It should have been over with the first blow, but somehow the spear point clattered against the wall behind where Dassa had crouched an instant before, and the axe swished through nothing. The spectators shouted in surprise. Dassa had dropped to the floor and rolled away so quickly it seemed she'd vanished.

With her opponents momentarily confused, Dassa sprang up and ran full tilt toward the opposite wall. Just when it seemed she'd crash headlong into it, she ran straight up it for four strides, grabbed the upper edge, and pulled herself to the top in the space of less than a second. Balanced on the rim in a crouch, she turned to face her opponents.

The Cephargians raced after her, weapons raised. As the spearman pulled back his arm, Dassa grasped the edge of the wall and lunged, kicking him hard in the face, one heel in each eye, then pulled herself back to the top like a gymnast on the bars. The Cephargian staggered backward with a yell, dropping his weapon and throwing his hands to his face, but Dassa didn't pause. She'd no sooner resumed her perch than she leapt off, landing in a sitting position on the other pirate's shoulders as his axe swished through empty air. Grasping his head in both arms, she twisted it savagely as she leaped to the floor. The pirate's neck snapped with a sickening crunch, and he fell in a heap. Wasting no time gloating, Dassa took off for the other side of the ring and ran up the wall again.

Meanwhile, the spearman had found his weapon and waved it, screaming something in Cephargian. From the way he moved, that kick had blinded him.

Dassa called to him from her perch, something Pik couldn't understand. Probably in Gannahan.

The spearman barreled over, weapon raised toward the sound. Dassa sidled like a spider away from the blindly stabbing blade then pounced on him as she had his friend, snapping his neck just as efficiently.

While the entire room stared in disbelief, she checked both opponents for signs of life. Apparently the axe man wasn't dead, because she grabbed his throat and pulled out his windpipe. Right through the skin. He made one last wheezing gasp and fell still.

The whole thing was over in two minutes.

While Pik and the other spectators stood silent from shock, Dassa wiped the axe man's blood off her hand on his leathery armor, then stood upright and faced Captain Hool. Her eyes shone with a disconcerting green gleam, her face glowed fierce, and her voice rasped with an unworldly edge. "Are you a man of your word, Hool? Or shall I have the pleasure of killing you, too?"

Voice quavering, Hool ordered the door of the fighting ring be opened, and his pirates obeyed in shaky amazement.

Dassa stepped out and surveyed the room. "Any more challenges? I'm barely warmed up."

"It weren't a fair fight," Hool said, "but we're men of honor. We'll abide by the terms. Boys!" A few of his men took a tentative step forward, but most looked too stunned to move. "Take your comrades back to the ship, then tear down the ring and let's get out of here."

Bouncing on the balls of her feet, Dassa eyed the pirate. "The contest was as we agreed. How dare you say it was unfair?"

"We were deceived," Hool said. "My fighters were too civil to strike a woman. They'd have killed you in a blink if they weren't such gawdawful gentlemen."

"Liar." Dassa growled and started toward him.

Pik found himself stepping between the Gannahan and her target. "They're leaving as agreed," he said.

She lowered her arms, which she'd thrown up as if to attack Pik. Her head and neck twitched as she studied his face. He couldn't look into those terrible eyes.

"We did. We agreed." She turned to Quintana. "Captain, if you will excuse me, I must be alone." She twitched again and took slow, deep breaths.

Her cut arm streamed blood, and Pik reached for it. "Let me tend to that."

She jerked away. "Do not touch me."

She started to go then turned around again, still bouncing. "My things."

Recalling he still held her dress and lahab, Pik handed them to her.

She ignored the dress but took the blade. "Thanks," she muttered without looking up, then turned on her heel and left, walking with a strange, springy step and another twitch of the neck.

Speechless Terrestrials and Cephargians alike parted to let her pass.

Pik followed her with his gaze until she left the room, bouncing and twitching all the way.

While some of the pirates tore down the fighting ring, Hool strode to the microphone, addressing his men in the Cephargian language. In response, a few of them unburdened their pockets and threw the contents on the floor. Several items of jewelry and other valuables clattered around the room.

With cries of, "That's mine!" and "You filthy pirates!" people chased after their liberated belongings. But their shouts were buried beneath the din of Hool's roaring as he gestured toward Pik, Hammond, and the captain.

"A Cephargian always keeps his word. But he also gets revenge. We're leaving now, like we agreed, but the League of Planets ain't seen the end of Hegigar Hool and the *Death Knell*. You'll be hearing it ring for you, soon, Quintana."

Then, in a shimmering moment, he was gone, along with the fighting ring and his men, living and dead.

Pale and showing the symptoms of shock, Quintana approached Pik. "There are a few injuries, and we are without a ship's doctor on this voyage. Could you look after them? Our facilities are limited, but I think you'll find all you need in the clinic."

"Certainly, captain. I'll be at the clinic momentarily. And I recommend you come in and let me look at that burn on your head as soon as you're able."

Quintana touched the wound tentatively. "That might be wise."

But Pik didn't go to the clinic immediately. He went instead to Dassa's quarters, where he found her washing the blood off her arm and preparing to bandage it.

He should leave her alone. Obviously, she could take care of herself. But something—probably the doctor in him—drew his eye to the neat slice in her skin. And something else made him feel genuine concern. "That should be sutured. Come to the clinic and I'll seal it for you."

"Later." Her voice sounded husky and strange. She shifted her weight from one foot to the other, practically dancing as she dried the wound and wrapped it, working as fast with one hand as a skilled nurse would with two.

"We owe you our lives."

"I don't care about that. Not my life, not yours."

Pik recoiled as if she'd spat on him. "Why did you do it, then?"

She finished securing the wrappings. "I could not let them lay hands on the ring."

"What ring?"

"The Ring of Atarah. But...I erred." She pushed past him into the corridor.

The thought that King Hoseh had worn a ring like hers when he raided Karkar had always made Pik hate the one she wore. But the suggestion that she valued it above him was almost more than he could stand.

"I should not have done this." She strode down the hall in that odd, bouncing gait, and Pik hurried after.

"Done what? Challenged them? Why in Karkar not?"

"I should not have ingested the blood. I violated the highest law of Gannah. I do not deserve to live."

Though his legs were twice the length of hers, Pik had to walk fast to keep up. "But you said it's permissible in a case like this. For self-defense."

"It was not permissible." Her voice was cold and harsh. "I would have defeated them without the benefit of the blooddrunk. Now leave me. I do not wish to kill you, too."

Alarmed, he fell back a step but continued from a safer distance. "Where are you going?" Was it safe to allow a Gannahan in that state to roam the ship?

"I will try to work this off in the gym. Eventually I will be exhausted. Then I will sleep. When I awake, I will wish I were dead." She turned to face him, eyes glowing. "Let no one disturb me. I shall not be able to control myself much longer."

Pik stopped following and watched her jerk around the bend at a rapid clip. He wondered what chemical reaction created such a dramatic effect, but didn't think this was the time to ask.

He turned and headed for the clinic, fearing he'd never forget the sight of her pulling out that thug's windpipe. He shuddered to think he'd once danced with that creature.

Most of the injuries Pik treated were minor. Commissioner Kiik fractured her wrist in a fall, and the crewman who'd been dragged from the lunchroom sustained a sprained shoulder and a concussion. But the number of patients requesting sedatives kept Pik occupied for quite some time.

From their remarks, the passengers and crew sounded both grateful to Dassa and terrified of her. They'd seen her bleeding, and most assumed the axe or spear had grazed her.

"I almost didn't come in," said a crewman sporting an egg-sized bump on his head, "because I didn't want to run into that

Gannahan woman. But the captain said I should get this checked out."

"It's always wise to have a head injury looked at," Pik said. "But you won't see the Gannahan here. She wished to be alone."

The crewman seemed relieved. "That sure is one scary lady. Not the sort of girl I'd want to cuddle up with, if you know what I mean."

"Your head will be a little tender for several days. If you experience nausea, dizziness, blurred vision, or severe headache, let me know, but I doubt you'll have any problems."

Another patient said, "I hear you know the Gannahan better than anyone. Does she get like that often? Go on a rampage, I mean, running up walls and stuff?"

Pik glanced at the man's wet pants. "Extreme situations cause extreme reactions."

The man looked down and blushed. "Yeah, I guess so. But I'm glad she did it. Otherwise we'd all be dead now, or on our way to slavery on some Cephargian ship. I always say if you've got to have a mad Gannahan around, better hope she's on your side."

"That's what you always say, is it?" Pik was glad the patient didn't know a Karkar smirk when he saw one. "Your ankle doesn't appear to be broken. Keep it elevated for the rest of the day with a cold pack on it. A little swelling is nothing to worry about, but let me know if it grows severe." He handed the patient a small packet. "And take one of these every twelve hours for pain."

After seeing the last of the patients, Pik locked the clinic, wondering if he should check on Dassa.

No, she'd asked not to be disturbed. And he suspected she meant it.

18

The door buzzer awakened Pik two minutes before 0300. He sat up in momentary confusion, and the buzz sounded again.

"What is it?" he asked, blinking.

"It's me." Dassa's voice came through the speaker. "You wanted to suture this cut on my arm."

Growling, he slipped on his pants and let her in. "It's the middle of the night."

Though she no longer exhibited that strange head twitch, she seemed bright and alert. Not ready to crash yet, apparently. "There's no night or day, just daylights and dimlights."

"My bioclock says it's night. If you waited this long, you could wait until morning."

"I gave no thought to the time. Shall I leave?"

Pik ran his fingers through his bed-flattened hair then rubbed his eyes. "No, I'm awake now. I guess. Give me a minute to get dressed, and I'll meet you at the clinic."

Six minutes later, he turned on the infirmary lights and started in surprise. The Gannahan sat on the exam table, recoiling at the sudden brightness.

"I didn't think you were here yet," he said. "The light was off."

"My head is pounding, I was trying to rest it." She unwrapped the bandage from her arm. "It's a good clean cut, not deep. It doesn't really need your attention."

He scrubbed up then examined the wound. "You're right on both counts, but to be on the safe side I'll put on some liquid suture."

She didn't flinch when he rubbed the cut with a swab.

"You could have done some serious damage. A millimeter deeper and you'd have been spurting."

"I know."

Something in her voice made him look into her face. The terrible glow in her eyes was snuffed out.

"I'll get the sutures." Deeply uncomfortable, he turned around and opened the cabinet. Where was that tube of glue? "I just used it this afternoon," he muttered, yanking open one drawer after another.

There it was, right where he'd put it.

Pik turned back to his patient, who watched with an unreadable expression. Even with the fire out, those eyes made his skin prickle. He took her arm to apply the sutures, then realized he hadn't taken off the lid. His left ear twitched with embarrassment as he let go of her arm to twist off the cap.

While he applied the glue she said, almost hesitantly, "When the doctor is through, I'd like to speak with Solitary Pik. Is he available?"

He studied the cut to make sure it was thoroughly sealed, then added a little more adhesive along one edge. Not because it needed it, but to avoid looking up. "I can summon him, I suppose. Don't touch that for a minute or two, until it dries. Then you can do anything, even shower. As the wound heals, the sutures will wear off."

She nodded.

He put the tube back in the drawer, then turned to face her. "Unless you have a question for the doctor, he's going back to sleep now. Let's see if Solitary Pik is somewhere in his room."

Pik extended his hand to help her from the table, but she hopped off without assistance.

They didn't speak as they left the clinic and walked back to Pik's cramped quarters. He offered her a seat at the desk and then sat on the edge of his bed, so close their knees would have touched if she hadn't sat cross-legged.

"What did you want to talk about?"

She cleared her throat. "I don't remember every detail, but I believe I said something to the effect that I didn't care if you died."

"You said you cared about neither your life nor mine. All you wanted was to keep that ring" — he nodded toward her left hand — "out of the hands of the Cephargians."

"Well, it's largely true. My life is of little value to me, and I couldn't bear the thought of those creatures touching the Ring of Atarah. As far as your life goes, though, I would have fought to preserve it, if need be. It's just that the loss of your life was not so directly imminent as the loss of the ring."

Pik couldn't follow her meaning and wasn't certain he wanted to.

"I'm trying to say, your death would have been a great loss indeed."

"That has long been my opinion."

"I'm serious."

"So am I. The subject of my death is the most serious matter I know."

The corner of her mouth twitched. "I'm trying to tell you I didn't mean what I said."

"You're saying it was the blooddrunk talking?" He'd been known to use that excuse himself, in his youth. Except for the "blood" part.

She looked grim. "I'm saying it was a poor choice of words. The blooddrunk is another matter."

"It's the same matter. You weren't in your right mind, and you said things you shouldn't have, like anyone else under the influence. But when we let things slip like that, we're saying exactly what we mean. We just don't have the nerve to say them sober."

"You have been drunk?"

"Everybody has. It's not so terrible." He put his hands on his knees. "Except when you wake up in the morning and you feel like there's someone inside your skull hammering to get out, and you remember what a fool you made of yourself the night before. Then it seems terrible. But about the time the headache goes away, you realize everyone else has done the same thing and no one holds it against you."

"You hold it against me."

Pik didn't answer.

"Do you at least believe that I value your life?"

How to put this? "I believe that ring means more to you than I do."

"That ring is Gannah. It is me, my people, my planet, my past, my future. It is—" She stopped in mid-sentence and sudden understanding crossed her face. "Just suppose…let's say the Cephargians took over the ship, but instead of me having this ring, you had the Kankakar Jewels."

A sudden rage flung Pik's ears back and clipped his words. "That wouldn't be possible, though, would it? Because you have those."

"I what? No. Why would you say that?"

"Because your beloved father Atarah Hoseh the Bloody Wise took them from Karkar, and they've never been seen again."

"I have heard of them, but they are not on Gannah. I have studied the archives, and I have never seen a glimpse of those jewels." She leaned forward and gestured as she spoke, imploring. "But use your imagination for a moment. If you had those jewels, and some villain came in to steal them, and you had a lasergun in your hand, wouldn't you shoot the villain to save the jewels and not even think about me, or even yourself? Wouldn't your first thought be to protect the jewels?"

Pik's heart rate increased. "A villain did take them, but he wasn't a Cephargian."

"But you see my point."

"And if the Cephargians had taken that ring, you would see mine."

The green gaze bore into him. "Is there a word in your language for forgiveness?"

Pik had to think about that. "No," he finally said. "None that I know of."

They looked at each other in silence for nearly a minute. Then Dassa pulled out her lahab, and extended it to Pik. "I would like you to take this."

He didn't look at it. "It's hardly the Kankakar Jewels."

"No. Nor is it the ring of Atarah. I wouldn't give you that. But you'll recall I also said in my blooddrunk that my behavior was inexcusable. The penalty for such a crime is death, but there's no one with the authority to administer that punishment. Only the toqeph can carry out a death sentence. If I were on Gannah, I would find myself guilty, surrender the crown to my heir, and the new toqeph would execute me."

Pik's ears stiffened in horror. "Has such a thing ever been done?"

"Yes, once."

"The new toqeph killed his own father?"

"Uncle, actually. But I have no heir. So, guilty or not, I cannot be executed. Therefore, I must sentence myself to some other punishment. I can think of nothing except to surrender my lahab, a fate similar to death. And I can think of no one more appropriate to surrender it to than you."

Pik wished his mind were more awake. He had to be missing something here. "First you ask for forgiveness, then you want to punish yourself. I don't understand you."

"Nor I you. You refuse me forgiveness for a crime I had nothing to do with, but you deny me punishment for a crime of which I am guilty." She tossed the lahab onto the bed. "If you will not take it, then give it to the doctor."

"What would he do with it?"

"I do not care."

Pik eyed the blue disc. "Tell me again why you were wrong to ingest the blood. It enabled you to defeat two armed opponents and save your own life along with more than a hundred others."

"I told you, I could have done that sober."

"No one can do what you did."

"A Nasi of Gannah can."

"If you're so sure, then why did you cut yourself?"

"Because I... I was frightened. And that itself is cause for shame. A Nasi of Gannah, afraid of inferior opponents? Even as I made the cut, I knew I shouldn't, but I did it anyway."

She had such a look of despair, Pik almost felt sorry for her. He considered a moment then stood up. "We'll see about this."

"What do you mean?"

"Come with me." He went to the door. "We'll see what you can do when you're in your right mind." He led her at a brisk pace out of the room and through the deserted corridor. "We're going to the gym. If you can do now what you did yesterday, I'll believe you could have beaten those pirates without resorting to your secret weapon. If not, then you'll take back your lahab, and I'll hear no more of this nonsense."

"You're going to throw spears and battle axes at me?"

"No, shuffaballs. But I have a wicked arm."

In the gym Pik found a dilapidated pitching machine that shot shuffaballs for practice racquet work. It took several tries before he could get it to work. Once he did, he aimed it at the back wall, adjusted the height so that it shot about level with Dassa's chest, and set the velocity to low. Shuffaballs could do some damage if they came at you fast enough.

He tossed a ball up and down in one hand. "Okay. You stand against the wall. I'll turn on the machine, and when it throws a ball at you, I'll throw one too, and you'll try to dodge them both. Then run over to that wall, go straight up four steps, jump down, and run back here and do the same thing again. If you can do that, I'll believe you could have killed those pirates in your right mind."

"When I jump off the wall, shall I land upon you?"

"No, nor break my neck. I can't enjoy proving my point if I'm dead."

"Very well. I shall do my best."

She looked as eager to meet the challenge as the Cephargians had been.

"Okay, let's go. Stand over there."

Dassa crouched in front of the wall. "I'm ready."

He turned on the machine, took three long strides to the side and let loose a ball as the machine whirred into action. She dodged, but Pik's ball grazed her back.

"If that were an axe, you'd be sliced wide open," he said.

"Let me try again."

The second time she adeptly avoided both missiles, then ran across the room and up the wall. She did a back flip off and landed on her feet before running to the other wall. Pik watched in amazement.

But two steps up the second wall, she fell.

Pik helped her up. "They've killed you twice now. Care to catch your breath and try for a third?"

"I need no rest. I shall beat them this time."

On the third try, the machine-thrown ball hit her square in the temple and knocked her out.

Pik rushed to her, heart pounding.

She regained consciousness in a second, but he couldn't believe he'd allowed such a game, let alone suggested it. What was it about this woman that addled his brain?

"Don't get up yet," he cautioned. "Sit for a few minutes. Here, lean against the wall."

"I am not harmed. My head hurt so before, it scarcely makes a difference."

"I don't care, just sit here while I put the machine away."

To Pik's surprise, she complied without argument. That made him think she might really be injured. When he returned, he squatted down and checked her pupils. Such amazing eyes. "That machine's adjustments must be faulty. How are you feeling?"

"My head is undamaged. My pride is not."

Pik sat on the floor beside her. "I'm sorry, this was a stupid idea."

"And it proves nothing."

"It most certainly does. It shows you're not capable of doing what you did yesterday unless you're under the influence. You're in the clear."

She shook her head. "As a scientist, you should know for the experiment to be valid, the exact conditions must be duplicated. Yesterday, I was refreshed and had no headache. Today, I am weary, and my head is throbbing. Yesterday, everything depended upon my winning, but today there is no danger. The circumstances are not even close to the same."

Exasperated, Pik's ears jerked. "You couldn't have done it. Admit it."

She clambered to her feet, pressing her temple and wincing. "Keep the lahab. I know I should not have taken the blood, because even as I drew my blade, God spoke through my meah and forbade me to cut myself. He said He would give me the strength to prevail. I disobeyed the law of Gannah and the command of my King."

Pik rose too. "And you saved the lives of more than a hundred innocent people. Is that a sin? Don't be an idiot."

She headed for the door. "Good night, Dr. Pik. Go back to bed. I shall disturb you no more."

Dassa drifted in and out of painful consciousness. Her head pounded, her stomach churned, and an invisible force seemed to press her into the bed. Heavy guilt mingled with the aftereffects of the blooddrunk made a poisonous mixture.

One lonely dream chased another until she found herself wandering Armown palace, playing hide and seek with her eldest brother, Areli. The game had long since ceased to be fun, for in every nook she searched she found someone dead or dying of the plague. She pulled open a drawer and found two tiny, armor-clad Cephargians, necks snapped and heads at impossible angles. *Why was I afraid of those creatures? They're mere rodents.*

She felt a presence and looked up. Her father stood in the doorway, sorrow and reproach in his bright sapphire eyes. In an agony of remorse, she fell to her knees crying, "Abba, forgive me! Abba, forgive me!"

She awoke to hear herself crying it aloud. And was aware of the presence of her Savior.

Of course you are forgiven, child. He spoke in the Standard tongue. *Why didn't you call Me sooner?*

She responded in the language of Gannah. *I disobeyed willfully. I am not worthy of Thy forgiveness.*

You were unworthy from the first, but I forgave you. For everything, past and future.

In wonderment at His mercy, Dassa made no effort to staunch her tears. But why did He use the Standard Language?

I speak in every tongue.

Was I in error, then, when I declared ours the language of God?

I speak in all languages, but not all people can hear.

She wept in confusion. *I am sorry, Lord, but I cannot understand.*

You can't expect your finite mind to comprehend the infinite. But you had no cause to give up your lahab.

What else might I have done?

You must ask forgiveness of the people who cannot pronounce it.

Dassa absorbed the thought.

There is a word for forgiveness in their language, but they have yet to discover it. We must show them what it is in My language.

But…Thou speakest in all languages.

This time He spoke in Gannahan. *Yea. The language of God is love.*

alf an hour later, Dassa emerged from the bathroom after a shower and found a large envelope on her bed. It bore no name, no message. She picked it up and peered inside, then pulled out her lahab and a note in Pik's handwriting.

"The doctor wouldn't take it either."

The note was signed, "S.P."

19

Three standard-years later…

Dr. Pik, Chief of Pathology at the League Center for Disease Control in Paris, Europe, returned to his office after a leisurely lunch.

Avoiding the waiting area, he slipped through the private entrance then hung his overcoat in the closet with a growl. He hated weather and resented the fact that dining at a decent restaurant required a venture into it.

"Dr. Pik?" His assistant's voice assailed him through the intercom. "Did I hear you come in?"

"I don't know what you heard, but I have, in fact, returned." He rubbed his icy hands together.

"Good. Because there's someone here to see you."

He stepped to his oversized desk and pulled up the day's calendar. "I have nothing scheduled until fourteen hundred."

"Yes, Doctor. She asked if you could see her without an appointment."

Pik's ears tilted back in annoyance. "You know I can't meet with just anyone who walks in. Send her to Hanley or one of my other deputies. If the matter absolutely needs my personal attention, schedule it for one day next week."

Another voice said in the background, "Next week will be too late."

Pik's heart lurched, and he stared at his closed office door as if trying to see through it.

The assistant repeated, "She says next week will be too late. It looks like you might be able to squeeze her in tomorrow morning. Would 10:30 be acceptable?"

Before her last words were uttered, Pik had crossed the room and opened the door.

His eyes lit upon a small, shapely, raven-haired woman standing before the assistant's desk.

His ears smiled and a warm flush washed all the way to his toes. "I'll see her now."

Dassa turned to Pik, her eyes even greener and brighter than Pik had remembered.

"Why, thank you. I know you're a busy man these days, so I'll only take a moment."

"I am busy. But for the Toqeph of Gannah, I shall be generous." He gestured toward the office. "You may have two moments."

Her chuckle was throaty, her grin broad. "I'm humbled by your beneficence, Doctor." As she swept past him into the office, her natural, musky fragrance stirred something within him.

He swallowed hard and waved toward the luxurious sofa across the room. "Please, have a seat." He lowered himself beside her with the vague feeling he might not have the strength to get up again. Why must he melt into a quivering wreck at the sight of her? "I thought you were in North America."

"I was. I just completed my degree at League of Worlds U."

"Degree in what?"

"Doctor of Interplanetary History."

Pik's ears stiffened with surprise. "You earned a doctorate in two years?"

"Yes. But even though I'm now qualified to teach Gannahan Studies, I don't feel fully equipped. They've given me leave to return home briefly to collect some materials. I know what I want, and I know precisely where everything is. I merely need transportation and someone to accompany me."

He wondered what that had to do with him. "The League won't provide transportation?"

"When I lived on their dole, they were lavish. Now that I've paid my debt to them, they help with nothing. I believe my independence makes them uncomfortable."

Pik cocked his head in assent. "I don't doubt it. They'd like to keep us indentured all our lives. How did you manage to pay them off?"

"Rosh continues to take care of me." She smiled. "And my study of economic principles has helped. I'll never understand it thoroughly, but I implement the basics with good results."

"I should say so." This confirmed what Pik had heard, that she'd been selling off her late husband's personal effects at great profit. Knapsack was more famous in his death than he'd been in life. The story of his mad, romantic rush to his wife's side in her hour of need, ending with his death as a hero before reaching her, had taken on epic proportions. As a result, genuine Ross Knapsack memorabilia went for astronomical prices. And Dassa owned most of it. It was like sitting on a Pyetronium mine.

Pik thought of his own burden of debt with a ripple of hopelessness. "Maybe you could give me some pointers."

"I'm sure you know more on that subject than I. But I'm sorry, I've neglected to congratulate you on your position here at the CDC. It's quite a plum."

Pik's pleasure showed only in the lift of his ears, but he suspected Dassa could sense it. "I couldn't have done it without you."

"All I did was inherit the throne of a dying planet at the time you were in the vicinity. It was an act of God."

Why did she always have to bring that up? "Whatever the cause, it was a rocket boost to my career, and you were an integral part of it. Speaking of debt, what can I do for you?"

Dassa's eyes were soft but probing as she searched his face. "I'm not sure. Who am I speaking with? I hoped to find Solitary Pik."

Pik swallowed hard. "You have found him."

She smiled then hesitated. "Then I may speak my mind?"

Solitary Pik saw the Medical one waving his arms and shouting, but chose to ignore the warning. "Please do."

Dassa leaned forward. "I understand you have many responsibilities now, and what I'm about to propose is probably out of the question. But could you take leave of your duties for a time and accompany me to Gannah?"

Pik blinked. "I'm sorry, what did you say?"

"It's not definite, but I think I've found a small ship and a crew competent enough to take me there and incurious enough not to pry into my business. But I'd like your company, and I'll need your help."

"What will a trip like that cost? If the League isn't paying, who is?"

"I'm not asking for money, if that's your concern."

"It's not," Pik lied. "But it'll take more than the sale of a few Knapsack trinkets to fund that kind of expedition."

"The cost is three million. But I've found a buyer for Rosh's hat and guitar, which will give me enough to cover it."

"I heard you'd never part with those."

She nodded and gave a sad sigh. "I never thought I would. They are so…so Rosh. His trademarks, his essence. But it's time for me to let them go."

"Yes, they're the essential Knapsack icons. But three million pounds for a hat and a guitar? I can't believe it."

"They're not paying me three million, they're paying me enough to cover the trip."

"But you just said —"

"It's complicated." She dismissed the subject with a wave. "But would you be able to get away for a year or so?"

Solitary Pik's mind fingered the idea as he turned his mental back on Medical's wild gesticulations. "What sort of small ship can get you to Gannah and back in that length of time?"

"The captain assures me none can catch it."

"I don't trust him."

"You've never met him."

"The whole thing sounds fishy."

"It is fishy. Stinks like a dagah cannery. But can you go?"

To mollify his frantic Medical self, Pik asked, "If I'm to put my life in his hands, I'll want to meet the captain and inspect his ship."

Dassa's eyebrows flew up. "You'll go?"

"Only if I'm convinced this character is legitimate."

"I already told you he's not."

Pik wrestled Medical to the ground and stuffed a gag in his mouth. "Let me see for myself. If I don't like your travel arrangements, we can make others. You said nothing's definite yet, right?"

"What about your job? Will the CDC let you resume it when you return?"

"I don't know, but if they don't, a man of my qualifications should have no trouble finding a good position somewhere else."

His employers' reaction suddenly worried him less than his mother's, whose screaming tirade would probably be heard clear across the galaxy. He tried to shove that thought into a bag with Medical Pik and tie it shut.

"I'm surprised at your cavalier attitude. It's not like you."

Pik's head tilted in agreement. "The doctor would never be so rash, but Solitary Pik is a risk-taker. I've even known him to dance with a Gannahan."

"Shocking. Will I be safe in the company of a man with so little moral restraint?"

Pik's ears smiled. "I doubt it."

"Good thing I'll be armed." Dassa stood, then watched with amusement as he struggled to pull himself out of the deep cushions. "When do you want to meet the captain?"

"Not until I get off this couch." One more upward lunge freed him. "How did you manage to get up so easily?"

"There's less of me to sink in. Did that monstrosity come with the office?"

"No, my decorator picked it out." Pik straightened his pant legs. "I don't think I've ever sat on it before. When can you arrange the meeting?"

"I'll call you."

Pik took one of his cards, scribbled on the back then handed it to her. "I've given you my personal number, in case you want to call after hours."

Those green eyes scanned the card—memorizing the numbers, Pik guessed—then she slipped it into a pocket. "I'll call you tonight. Or maybe tomorrow. Whenever I've gotten hold of the captain."

The *Swordfish* was so small Pik had to bend almost double to get through some passageways. Even in the highest sections, his head brushed the ceiling. It seemed barely spaceworthy, and the shiny-headed captain, Dortious Dmitry, could have passed for a pirate but for lack of a Cephargian's cranial tattoos.

He seemed to know his business, though, and his two-person crew, one of whom was his wife, appeared equally competent. And equally unwholesome.

"I don't like it," Pik told Dassa in hushed tones after their tour.

"It does seem a bit chancy," she murmured, "but they come highly recommended."

"By whom? An advertisement in *Buccaneer's Digest*?"

"No, by—is there such a publication?"

"Not that I'm aware. But who told you about these characters?"

"Edwin Broward. He and Dmitry were brothers-in-law at one time."

"And that makes him and his tin can reliable? I'd be afraid they'd take your three million then beam our molecules onto an uninhabitable Noboian moon."

"I know what you mean, but I trust Broward. And he says that despite appearances, Dmitry's not only reliable, but a seasoned space traveler and a technical magician. Which is probably the only way he can keep this thing afloat. In any event, Broward believes we can rely on these people and the *Swordfish* to get us there and back safely."

Dmitry must have had good ears. "If Eddie says it, you can believe it," he interrupted, "which is more than I can say for his sister, may she writhe in a thousand purgatories."

Why would Dassa deal with such people? "I cannot believe Captain Broward would knowingly send us to our doom, but I've never seen a ship so…so…"

"You've got it, tall guy, the *Swordfish* is unique. I built her myself out of scrapped-out this and crapped-out that." Dmitry chuckled. "The skeleton's an old Earth Border Guard skiff crossed with an early Eutarian Shoom. The brains are straight out of one of your own Karkar Denckisickickes, with the latest StarPak eight upgrade. It's powered by a Cephargian Gunnergeye specially modified according to my own design, which renders this little minnow the fastest fish in space. The skin's covered with scales of the highest quality Pyetronium-Efram alloy I could steal—and mind you, I only swipe the best. And the accouterments"—Dmitry slapped the back of a chair upholstered in cracked fake leather— "are top-of-the-line scrap yard. Put her all together, and she's sound as the Bank of Eutare."

Dubious, Pik's ears twitched. "Have you taken her as far as Gannah before?"

"As far, maybe. But I never had no cause to go to Gannah. I wouldn't go now, except to do Little Miss Green Eyes a favor."

"And because you're in need of funds, as I recall," Dassa said.

"Well, yes. I suppose you might say we're doing each other a favor. But all I provide is the transportation. Me and my crew won't set foot on the planet. Scary as the Gannahans were alive, their ghosts have got to be worse."

"That's fine, transportation is all I need from you." Dassa turned to Pik and winked up at him. "What do you think, tall guy? Will you join us?"

He cast his glance around, ears scowling. "Even if it were safe, which I doubt, I couldn't live hunched up for months on end. It's hard on the back and shoulders, the heart, the digestive system. I couldn't subject my body to such stresses."

"If you're claustrophobic, just say so." Dassa turned to the captain. "I guess, Mr. Dmitry, you'll have only one passenger."

Pik's ears stiffened. "You said we could make other arrangements if this ship didn't suit me."

"I didn't say that, you did. There's no time to make other arrangements. We're leaving at midnight."

The ears stiffened more. "Midnight? What kind of a crazy time is that?"

Dmitry answered for her. "It's good luck. If I can't leave at midnight, I'm better off not leaving at all, because nothing good will come of it."

Pik glared down at Dassa. "You never told me we'd be departing immediately. I haven't packed yet."

"Two days ago I said next week would be too late. Day after tomorrow will be next week. I'd think a scientist like you could do simple math without counting on his fingers, however many he may have. But if I'd known you were afraid of tight places, I wouldn't have asked you."

"I'm not afraid. It's a legitimate health risk. You need to understand how important good posture is—"

Dmitry guffawed. "You can stand as tall as you want in the cargo hold. And as you might have noticed, I've got some pretty good exercise equipment in there to keep us all fit during the trip. My bar is well stocked, you can bring whatever drugs you like to keep you happy, and you should have no concerns, healthwise or otherwise."

Pik gasped. "You fly this toy ship when you're *drugged*?"

"Not drugged. Relaxed. Seems like you could use a little of that yourself." He turned to Dassa. "You sure you want him along, princess? He's more than a bit annoying, if you ask me."

"He's actually pretty good-natured, for a Karkar," Dassa said.

At the same instant, Pik corrected, "Toqeph, not princess," then immediately added, "What do you mean, 'for a Karkar'?"

Dmitry looked back and forth between them. "If you two are going to bicker like that the whole trip, I won't have either of you. I don't care what you are, hot-shot doctor or queen of the green-eyed goblins. This is my ship and you'll behave, or I'll be compacting you into a block and shoving you out a waste tube. Got it?"

Dassa smiled. "You're the boss, Captain."

"Damn right. Remember it." He nodded. "Whoever shows up at twenty-three hundred is welcome aboard. If you're not here, I leave without you." The captain turned and started away. "Lawbby!"

"Sir!" answered the male crewman from somewhere in the bowels of the ship.

"How're we coming? About finished?" Dmitry disappeared around a corner without another glance back.

"What do you mean, 'for a Karkar'?" Pik repeated.

Dassa laughed. "Come on. If you haven't started packing, we'd better get moving." She made for the exit.

Pik followed. "What do you mean, 'good natured for a Karkar'? Are you suggesting my people are naturally unpleasant?"

"Have you thought about what to bring?"

"Because if that's what you think, you have much to learn about the Karkar, despite your quickie degree in Interplanetary History."

"This isn't a regular passenger ship, so besides clothes, we'll need towels, sheets, toiletries, all that stuff. Not to mention plenty of reading material and things to occupy our time. I've been assured there'll be sufficient food for all five of us, though it probably won't be fit to eat."

"You should know we Karkar pride ourselves on our reasonableness and sociability."

Dassa neared the bottom of the ladder and jumped past the last two rungs. "I'd rather cook my own meals from fresh ingredients, but since the *Swordfish* has no facilities for that, I'll have to survive on the usual travelers' rations. Beats starving, I suppose, but not by much."

Pik's long legs made skipping the same two rungs an easy step to the ground. "There hasn't been a war on our planet for two centuries. That's as good-natured as it gets, wouldn't you say?"

The wind whipped her hair across her face as they crossed the tarmac, and she pulled it back with both hands. "As for clothing, I think comfort should dictate. We won't have any formal occasions, so I don't plan to bring anything fancy, but if you want to dress for dinner, that's up to you."

She must know she was wrong, or she wouldn't keep changing the subject. "If everyone imitated our good nature, war would have been eliminated long ago." Hands deep in his pockets, Pik hunched his shoulders against the biting cold.

"There's been only one war fought on Gannah, and it was against the Fueraqis, not amongst ourselves. Let's quit talking about history and think about this trip. Do you have what you need, or must we go shopping? I'm already packed, so I have all evening to help you."

Pik's ears were not too frozen to tilt back in annoyance. "You really don't see us as good natured?"

"I'd sooner walk with a stone in my shoe than a Karkar by my side, because I can always take the stone out. But if I take out the Karkar, I'd be arrested for murder." She grinned up at him. "Is that the answer you were looking for?"

Hunched against the wind, he kept his eyes on the ground. "It's what I'd expect."

"By the way, I noticed all the clothes in the *Swordfish* crew's closets were exceptionally warm. They probably save on fuel by keeping the heat low. You'll want to bring your winter layers."

"Ooh, I can't wait. Will I freeze to death first, or be squeezed to death? Or maybe die of suspense, wondering which?"

"Neither. You'll be shoved out a tube for whining. Do you even have winter clothes? It's cold out here, and you're not wearing gloves."

Pik pulled his hands from his pockets and wiggled his twelve fingers. "We're in Europe. Where would I buy gloves to fit these beauties?"

"Have you looked, or do you just sit around complaining? And there's always mittens. They'll cover as many fingers as you can shove into them."

He snorted. "Mittens would make my hands look like paws."

"And the cold makes your hands look like crab claws."

"That's why coats have pockets." He plunged his hands deeper. "If nagging were an infectious disease, I'd look for a cure. But I suspect it's a chromosomal defect afflicting the female."

"I'm not nagging, I'm merely trying to help you."

"You sound more like my mother every day. And I don't care what she says about it, I'm going to Gannah."

They were at the terminal. Pik strode toward the door with renewed energy, and Dassa trotted beside him. "Do you care what the League or the CDC has to say about it?"

"No," he shouted against the wind, and they swept into the building with a rush of icy air.

"Do they even know yet?"

"They'll find my resignation in the morning, citing a family crisis."

"Family?" She pulled off her gloves.

"I never said whose family. But since you offered, I might need some help packing. How does one prepare for traveling in an unheated, homemade, and probably unlicensed ship?"

Dassa spoke in hushed tones. "Don't say that so loud, someone might hear you."

Though the building wasn't crowded at this end, he stopped and lowered his voice. "You mean it *is* unlicensed?"

Dassa kept walking. "Of course. And so's the captain. I told you from the start, the whole thing's fishy. The Space Commission's coming to seize his ship in the morning."

Pik's head tilted in new understanding. "Which is why he's leaving at midnight whether we're on board or not."

"Exactly."

He groaned. "If I hadn't already sent my resignation, that bit of news would have me changing my mind."

"We both know that's not true." Dassa shoved her gloves in her pockets. "So, do you need to buy warm clothing?"

"I suppose I must. After Captain Dmitry's threats, I can't count on keeping warm by arguing." He put his arm around Dassa's shoulders.

She picked up his arm by the hem of the sleeve and ducked out from under it.

"Bring a portable heater."

20

The *Swordfish* lurched into motion, slamming Dassa against her seat. The engine's roar hammered her eardrums, her head threatened to explode, and her stomach revolted from the violence of gravity's pull.

Eyes closed, she breathed slowly, trying to relax, reminding herself the discomfort would lessen once they broke through the atmosphere. But she wasn't suited to confinement in an artificial environment. She wouldn't be right again until her feet stood on solid ground and her lungs filled with fresh air.

And the next ground she stood on, the next air she breathed, would be Gannah's. Despite her present misery, she smiled. The old proverb was true: "I have breathed the air, drunk the water, and eaten the food grown in the soil—I am Gannah." Once Gannah got into you, you were one with it. You could never be content anywhere else.

She looked down at the Ring of Atarah. Traced the etching of the tree on the brilliant green stone, studied the worn writing on the band. A new ring must be made for her heir, once she had one. This old ring would be placed in the Archives alongside the original and its nineteen reproductions.

Or should she take it with her into the Hall of the King?

Dassa was thirteen when she and her family accompanied her grandfather, the Toqeph Atarah Naphtali Charash, on his last journey.

A piquant mix of grief and anticipation infected the whole family as they prepared. Wearing her best wide-legged pants of shimmering steel blue and a long smocked tunic, she sat while her mother braided white ribbons into her waist-length hair. "Where is the Hall of the King, Emma?"

"The way is known only to the one who must travel it," her em said. "As always, we will follow the toqeph wherever he leads."

Questions still burned in Dassa's mind, but she knew they would be answered through patient obedience. A Gannahan learned early on not to pester.

Right on time, the toqeph's driver brought the ceremonial motorcarriage, cleaned and shined, to the main entrance to the residence at Armown, then bowed and made a respectful exit. Dassa and her mother, her sister, Kannah, and her brothers, Areli and Arodi, waited outside for Abba to bring Grandfather.

Gannah's mood was as somber as the family's, with overcast skies and a damp chill in the air. Dassa shivered and rubbed a tear from her eye with a knuckle, hoping no one would notice.

The lump in her throat grew harder when she saw her father and grandfather framed in the doorway. There were no Nasi, no servants, no officers or attendants. Just her father and an old, old man.

In the usual Gannahan manner, the infirmity of age overtook Grandfather suddenly. A month ago, he'd been muscular and vibrant at the age of 114. Today, he was frail and shuffling, struggling for breath and holding his son's arm for support. Dassa swallowed a sob. She wanted to remember the toqeph in his power, but feared this last image of him would overlay all others in her memory.

Once Grandfather was settled into the carriage, the rest of the family joined him.

Abba took the vehicle's controls, and Grandfather asked in a strange quavering voice, "Do you know where you're going, son?"

"No, milord. Only that we head east on the Har Highway."

Grandfather nodded. "Yes. Head for Har."

The trip began, and so did the rain. Gannah wept at the loss of her toqeph.

The road to Har was clear of traffic, for people honored the toqeph's wish to travel his last journey in private.

Abba drove in silence. Arodi sniffled. The drenched world passed by the window at 120 kilometers an hour.

Some three hours down the deserted highway, Abba asked the toqeph if he needed a rest.

"I shall have rest enough soon," he answered, and so they continued beneath the heavy skies.

The road climbed higher, and Grandfather nodded off. More than an hour later, he awoke enough to murmur, "Turn left here," without opening his eyes. Abba turned. "To the right up ahead," he said later, and Abba directed the carriage down a narrow, unpaved road winding around rocky outcroppings beneath ancient firs.

A few hundred meters down the road, Grandfather lifted his head, fully awake. "Pull off to the side up there. We must walk a short way into the mountain."

The cloudy ceiling was a deep blue-gray, but a shaft of sunlight shone through, gilding the wet rock face before them. Abba pulled off the gravel track onto a grassy area, set the brake, and turned off the engine.

"This is it, milord?"

"This is it." Grandfather sounded eager.

After Abba helped him from the carriage, the rest of the family piled out. They followed at a respectful distance as Abba and Grandfather labored along a needle-strewn path between dripping limbs toward an opening in the side of the mountain.

With Grandfather and Abba leading the way, the family entered a room illuminated by a gap in the rocks above. A black passage plunged ahead, and at its mouth stood a low, tubular vehicle. Its pale sides glowed in the dim light as it rested on a single, wide track.

The toqeph gripped a handle and with seemingly no effort, a wide, curved door slid back and a light came on inside the pod. The opening was level with the floor, and the toqeph entered without Abba's help. Once he was seated, the rest of the family followed.

Comfortable charcoal-gray padded seats lined two sides, facing each other. Grandfather sat nearest the door, then Abba with Emma beside him. The children sat across the aisle.

No one spoke. They looked at the toqeph to see what came next. He seemed a little uncertain at first, then reached up and touched the door handle beside him. The door slowly slid back into place, sealing them in.

The interior lights dimmed. Dassa felt a faint rumble, and the vehicle moved forward. It picked up speed quickly and flew along the smooth track with scarcely a sound, carrying them deep under the mountain.

About ten minutes later, the vehicle slowed then came to a stop. The door slid open. In their meahs, the family shared an anticipation and fear that soared to near-unbearable heights.

The toqeph stood. Abba hopped up to help, but Grandfather waved away his assistance. He hung onto the sides of the doorway for balance and stepped to the platform, level with the floor of the pod.

Abba disembarked next, and the others followed in order of age, leaving Dassa to exit last.

They stood in a narrow room walled with smooth gray stone, glittering with colors as if embedded with tiny jewels. Though the ceiling was hidden by impenetrable blackness, it gave the impression of being vastly high. Both ends of the chamber were similarly swallowed up in darkness. But the area where the family stood was lit by a portal directly in front of them, opposite the vehicle's open door.

Beyond the portal swirled a sea of bright fog. Dassa knew they were deep underground, but she felt as if she were gazing at the sun through a cloud. She feared if the cloud rolled away, the light would blind her. But she couldn't tear her eyes away.

Then the realization of what lay beyond that opening made her sorrow vanish like a shadow in sunlight.

She stared at the fog for several moments, mesmerized. Finally the toqeph spoke.

"Yachad," he said to Emma.

She turned to him and bowed. "Milord."

"My son chose his mate wisely. Thou hast been a perfect wife to him, an exemplary mother to his children and a beloved daughter to me, as thou were to my wife before she passed on. May our Yasha bless thee with long life on Gannah and many rewards in eternity."

"It hath been my greatest privilege to serve thee and thy family, milord." She bowed again.

The toqeph turned to Dassa's oldest brother. "Areli."

The young man, not quite twenty years old, came forward and bowed. How handsome he was, and how regal.

"First of my grandchildren," the toqeph said, "thou hast always made me proud. Continue to strive for excellence, and thou shalt be a worthy successor to our father Atarah."

Areli cleared his throat. "Thou hast spoken, milord."

Grandfather turned to Dassa's sister. "Kannah. Like thy mother, thou art small of stature but great in wisdom. Reverence the Bara in all thou doest, and thou shalt find thine heart's desire."

Kannah nodded, but didn't answer for tears.

Next Grandfather summoned Arodi.

Dassa's second brother stepped forward, weeping as he bowed.

"Thine is a grave responsibility," the toqeph said, "for thou shalt inherit Atarah's high duty. Remember who thou art, and why the Bara hath given thee life. Serve the toqeph and reverence the Yasha, and He shall give thee a strength beyond thine own."

Arodi bowed again, speechless.

The toqeph turned. "Hadassah."

Dassa's tears flowed freely. She hadn't known it was possible to feel such emotion and not die.

Grandfather's voice sounded thin, as if it were failing him. "Thou sharest thy name with an ancient Earth woman renowned for saving her people. Thou, my daughter, must do the same. One day Gannah shall call thee Mother. Do not flee from this holy privilege."

Dassa couldn't imagine what he meant, but she nodded. "Thou hast spoken, milord."

Through her tears she saw her grandfather smile.

Then he turned to Abba. "Degel, my son and heir."

Abba bowed. "Milord." Only he and Grandfather were not weeping.

"Arise, Toqeph of Gannah." Grandfather slipped off the Ring of Atarah, took his son's hand and, fumbling, threaded Abba's finger through the ring. "The weight of the world is now on thy shoulders, Degel, but thou art strong. Wear the mantle well, and

Gannah shall smile upon thee. Forget thy duty, and Gannah shall sweep thee away like the fallen leaves of Ayin in spring."

Abba's face was somber. "Thou hast spoken, milord."

"Yea. And I have spoken my last." Grandfather's sapphire eyes widened as he turned them again to the portal. "My King hath summoned me."

While the family watched, immobile, Grandfather drew himself up straight and approached the portal with slow but even steps. As soon as his foot crossed the threshold, the cloud swirled away.

The light was not blinding, as Dassa had feared, but the scene was brighter, purer, and more clearly in focus than anything in her experience.

A long table of glowing deep-red wood carved by the most skillful of artisans stood spread for a meal. Chairs like thrones lined the table, each carved of the same unworldly material with the same indescribable craftsmanship. But at the head of the table stood the most amazing throne of all, and at the sight of the One who sat upon it, Dassa fell to her knees.

It was the Yasha Himself.

The other chairs were occupied by toqephs who had reigned before. Dassa recognized some of them from their pictures. Hoseh the Wise sat nearest the Yasha, and the rest were seated after him in chronological order. Dassa would have studied them all, but her eyes couldn't leave the Yasha.

She was aware of Grandfather approaching the table, in the full vigor of his manhood. As he made his way, the others rose and turned and bowed. All but the Yasha. He rose, but He didn't bow.

He smiled.

Dassa thought she would burst. No higher honor, no greater joy, no deeper blessing could be had than to be greeted into the presence of the Yasha with a smile.

Grandfather prostrated himself before the Throne. "My God and my King!"

The cloud again obscured the scene. It was several moments before Dassa and her family slowly rose from the floor where they had fallen in awe. They looked at her father, now the toqeph, and for a fleeting second Dassa sensed he was frightened.

Then he gathered himself together. "Goodbye, Abba," he said, and bowed toward the portal.

Only, the portal was gone. All that remained was a glittering stone wall, illuminated from above by an unseen source.

Remembering that day with the clearest of vision, Dassa trembled. No, she would not take the ring with her. Her Yasha had no need of it.

He had revealed enough of her mission that she knew she was on the right course. But how the things He promised could possibly come to pass, she couldn't imagine. How would she find a man to be her husband, father her children, and lead a group of believers to resettle Gannah, when all of her kind were dead?

According to the records, every Gannahan who traveled Outside had come home before the plague struck. Every Gannahan but Rosh. Some returned because their missions were accomplished, some because family responsibilities called them, others for other reasons. Only Rosh was spared the plague—but he died nevertheless.

When by some miracle the Yasha led her to a suitable mate, how could she love and honor him as she ought, after having loved and lost her dear Rosh? She couldn't imagine giving herself to anyone else.

Nor did she understand why the Yasha wanted her to bring Pik along. This part of the mission would be more easily accomplished without him. More pleasantly, anyway.

But the Yasha had said she must invite him, and now there he sat, brooding and grim, disgust and displeasure oozing from his being in a most unflattering vapor. All he could talk about was the discomfort of the rustic accommodations, or losing his job, his apartment, and his reputation, or the legal consequences of his sudden departure from his post. If that was such a concern, why had he come? And he needn't blame her. The choice had been his alone.

But the Yasha required her to demonstrate to the Karkar the meaning of forgiveness. *My ways are not your ways*, the Yasha had said in His revelation to the Earthers. And, like everything else in that Book, it was true. If she had her way, she'd have no further contact with the disagreeable doctor. But she was a servant of the King, and His commands were not to be questioned.

Dassa thought of the Hebrew prophet Jonah. He hadn't liked the mission Jehovah had sent him on and had tried to flee. She understood his reluctance, but had no desire to imitate his disobedience. She was a Gannahan, not an Earther. She would trust her Savior and obey His commands.

Even if it meant a long trip in close quarters with a grumbling Karkar.

20

Sitting with the captain over breakfast the first morning out, Pik gingerly felt the goose egg on his head, acquired in a collision with a cabinet door in his made-for-midgets quarters.

Dmitry sipped his coffee. "I don't care if you die of the plague while you're down there," he told Pik. "But I don't want you living just long enough to bring it back to the ship with you."

Pik's ears scowled. "As I've told you before, you have nothing to worry about." Assuming he got there alive, which was doubtful. How had he allowed himself to be talked into this? "For one thing, the plague affects only Gannahans. So even if it is still viable, it can't harm you, me, or your crew. Dassa already has immunity, so she doesn't have to worry about it either."

Dmitry's brows expressed doubt. "But don't those things mutate? Maybe it's adapted to where it can kill non-Gannahans. Or re-infect someone who already had it. I'd think an infectious disease expert like you would have thought of that."

"I have." Pik's ears jerked with annoyance. "Which is why I've brought the antidote. But I don't expect to need it, given the way its creators engineered it for such specificity. Among all the dangers we face, the plague isn't a factor." He sipped his travelration shake. "I have other concerns."

Many other concerns, in fact. Who wouldn't, heading into the dragon's lair?

Dmitry narrowed his eyes. "You don't like my ship, is that it? Don't think she can go the distance?"

"No, of course not. She's a fine vessel." Made to order for those bent on deep-space suicide. "I'm referring to what we might find when we get there. I mean, with Gannah's reputation, it's impossible to know what to expect from the planet itself. But what about grave robbers and looters and such? Surely there's no shortage of treasure hunters who'll stop at nothing to take what they want. And they won't want us nosing around."

Dmitry leaned back in his seat and crossed his arms. "Have you heard of any Gannahan artifacts being sold, other than the Knapsack stuff your girlfriend's been trickling onto the market?"

Pik's ears flew backward. "She's not my girlfriend. Where did you ever —"

"My mistake. But have you ever heard of anything like that? Artwork, weapons, jewelry, vases, anything at all?"

Pik didn't follow the virtual markets, but he was interested in rare and beautiful things. If Gannahan items were available, he'd probably have heard of it. "That's a good point. I haven't looked, but —"

"Well, I have, and I ain't seen a thing. You know why?"

Studying the smoothness of Dmitry's cranium and wondering why any man would chose to be bald as a Cephargian, Pik waited for the captain to explain.

"You said it yourself, the place is creepy. And raiders, as a rule, are a superstitious lot. They're not too keen on exploring a place piled high with dead bodies, especially when the dead folks are Gannahans. You know the stories. There's probably Purpletongue ghouls running around with their lahab blades killing each other over and over, just for something to do. Just imagine what they'd do with fresh blood to spill."

Dmitry uncrossed his arms and leaned forward. "No, I think the looters are staying away for now. Between ghosts and demons and the plague — not to mention Gannah being so far away, in that quadrant with all those weird space storms and stuff going on all the time—I figure the looters are afraid to be the first ones on the scene. Once someone goes there and comes back in one piece, they might try it. But even then, I doubt it. There's plenty of business in the rest of the galaxy. They'll wait till they're dead before they visit hell."

Pik finished his breakfast and rose. "Thank you, Captain. You've been very reassuring." So much so, in fact, he went back to his quarters and took a sedative.

After that conversation, Captain Dmitry and his crew left the passengers to themselves for the most part. Though Pik approved of their professionalism, he would have preferred a little company. Unlike the Gannahan, he was a social creature. He'd even brought a hmmmjckt set along, hoping to teach the others to play.

He might have suggested Dassa learn the game, but she showed no interest. Besides, she was too quick a study. She'd probably beat him in the second or third round, and that would take all the fun out of it.

Just as she took all the fun out of everything. He'd had plans for the two of them, involving quiet music and slow dancing, and eventually sharing much more. But although she wasn't exactly aloof, she wasn't friendly in the way Pik had hoped.

He'd had second thoughts about this trip right from the start. Then third thoughts, and fourth, all confirming the second. That is, that his first thoughts, which caused him to embark on this insane adventure, were in error. He'd made mistakes before, but none so dramatic as this. He would regret it the rest of his days.

Which might not be long. He'd probably die of boredom within the week. Or, more likely, freeze to death.

He was convinced Dmitry turned the temptrol down a degree each day in an effort to acclimate the passengers to the frigid temperatures gradually. But if that was the captain's plan, it wasn't working. Pik would never get used to this. It was good Dassa had found him some six-fingered gloves in Paris, but he wished he'd bought more than one pair.

A miserable month into the interminable journey, Pik brought his hmmmjckt set into the miniscule space where they took their meals. After wiping a few sticky drips off the table, he began setting up the board.

The big crewman, Lawbby, came in, made himself a cup of something hot and smelly, and watched with interest. "I've seen those things before, on space stations. What do you call that game again?"

"Hmmmjckt."

Lawbby set his cup on the table and took a seat. "It's sorta like Earth chess, isn't it?"

"A little, but more complex." Pik set the last piece in place. "Would you like to play?"

"Do you have to know how to pronounce it? 'Cause if you have to say it to play it, forget it. Makes you sound like you've got the dry heaves."

Pik's ears lifted in amusement. "It's not necessary to pronounce the name, so long as you play by the rules."

Lawbby took a sip of his steaming beverage. "Okay, fine, I'll take 'er for a spin. How does this boat fly?"

"If you mean how is the game played, I'll explain. It can be quite involved, though. Have you got the time?"

"Sure. I'm off duty for five more hours, unless something breaks down in the meantime."

Lawbby proved a worthy competitor, and his interest in hmmmjckt broke the ice, so to speak. Although the air in the ship was still cold enough to frost a beer mug, the crew no longer kept their distance. Now the five sardines in the *Swordfish* tin enjoyed good conversation, shared movies and games, and the time passed more pleasantly.

Until the day Pik, wrapped in a blanket, and Lawbby, in a light jacket, played hmmmjckt in the cargo bay on a table and chairs made of shipping crates. It was colder there than most other areas, but Pik liked it because it was roomier. Dassa sat cross-legged on a pile of padding used for transporting delicate electronic equipment, mending Pik's gloves. The captain's wife, Sylvia, painted a landscape in oils, working from a photograph. Dmitry was busy elsewhere.

"Is Pik your whole name?" Lawbby asked as he waited for the doctor to make his next move. "Seems kinda small for such a big fella."

Absorbed in thought, Pik took his turn before answering. "That's the abbreviated version."

"What's it short for?" Lawbby didn't consider long before moving his next piece on the board.

"Pikpeeeekpiktootakpikkakazghaghanmattsson," Pik answered, shrieking the second syllable and gargling the middle.

Lawbby jumped. "Holy excretions, you scared the creets out of me. That noise is your *name*?"

"Yes. And on Karkar, it's a very honorable one." Except for the Earthish surname on the end of it. "What sort of name is Lawbby?"

"A nickname. My real name's Lawson Bertram Beeman. Years ago Dmitry shortened it to Lawbby, and that's what I go by since."

"It hardly seems long enough to shorten." Pik moved his knight across the board and knocked over Lawbby's farmer. "Sorry, but your pitchfork is no match for my lance."

"If I hadn't lost the other forning farmers to the famine a couple moves ago, they could've ganged up on that knight and beat him to death. Excretions!" Lawbby fell silent as he studied the board.

Dassa clambered off the pile of padding and brought Pik his gloves. "All done."

"Thanks." He pulled them on then wrapped the blanket around himself again with a shiver. "I don't understand why we aren't seeing our breath in here."

Sylvia, at her easel, glanced toward the temperature gauge nearby. "It's not that cold, only 11 or 12 Celsius."

"The gauge must be malfunctioning. Feels like it's below zero." Pik looked at the hmmmjckt board, and his ears smiled. "I've got you, Lawson Bertram Beeman. Give it up."

"Not so fast, there, I can still… No, I can't. Okay, but I could… Excretions! You've got me forning cornered. Creets!"

"I don't believe the toqeph appreciates your foul language," Pik said. It was a little much even for him, but he didn't want to sound too prissy.

"Really? Excretions… I mean, shoot. Sorry, Your Highness, I didn't mean to offend you."

"It does bother me, but I realize it goes with the territory. You are a starsailor, after all." Dassa settled back into her nest of padding.

"You should have said something. I can't get used to the idea of having royalty aboard."

Sylvia dabbed at her canvas. "I can't get used to the idea of royalty doing the mending."

"Gannahan royalty does whatever is required," Dassa said. "We are not above getting our hands dirty."

"Nor bloody," Pik muttered under his breath.

Lawbby pouted, hands on his knees. "All right, I'll concede this one, tall guy. But I'll get you next game. I'd have won if not for that fornicating famine. Oops, sorry, your highness." He stood up. "I need a drink. Get you guys anything?"

"I'll have whatever you're having," Sylvia said.

Pik asked for tea, and Dassa for hot chocolate.

"Oh, so you're finally cold now too?" Pik asked her as Lawbby rummaged in a crate for the drinks.

"Not really. I just have a weakness for chocolate. It's the best-tasting thing I found on Earth."

"I fail to comprehend its popularity. It tastes like poison."

"But what a way to go." Dassa thanked Lawbby for the container he handed her. Then she popped the lid, and the contents started to steam.

Sylvia asked, "So what was it like, Dassa, being a queen? Before the plague struck, I mean."

Dassa blew at the steam wafting up from her chocolate. "Toqeph, not queen. It's more like a steward than a monarch. Gannah hasn't called its ruler king since Hoseh the Wise."

Pik's ears scowled. "Oh, yes, your favorite historical figure, and his famous ring, which you value more than my life."

Sylvia and Lawbby shot questioning glances Pik's way, but he ignored them. If their planet had suffered as his did, they'd be bitter too.

"Did you ever check out the constellations?" Dassa asked him. "Was I right?"

"It appears you were, at least to a point. But I fail to see how that makes your Hoseh a hero."

"Of course not. I didn't finish the story."

Lawbby set his coffee beside the hmmmjckt board. "Mind filling us in on what you two are talking about?"

"Dassa started telling me once," Pik explained, "about her many-times-great grandfather and what a great guy he was for conquering Karkar before moving on to Earth."

"Earth?" Sylvia echoed.

Lawbby asked, "What's that got to do with constellations?"

Dassa sat up and crossed her legs again. "I should begin at the beginning."

While Pik rearranged the hmmmjckt pieces for the start of another game, Dassa explained how her ancestors had never known war until Fueraq attacked them.

"How can that be?" Lawbby said. "Everyone has wars. It's typical human behavior. Otherwise the history books would be full of blank pages."

"Yes, but a Gannahan is not your typical human. When the Fueraqi found us, we were neither backward nor docile. But our technology and fighting instincts were used for mutual survival in a harsh world, not fighting each other. "

"Not everyone is as warlike as Earthers," Sylvia said.

"And we aren't the most violent," Lawbby added. "But I never heard of anyone who'd never had a war in the whole history of their planet."

"The Fueraqis were probably the worst." Dassa pulled one of the pads across her lap. And she'd said she wasn't cold. Obviously, she wasn't as truthful as she'd like people to believe.

"When they attacked us," she went on, "they were light-years ahead of us scientifically, even though their civilization was far younger. They merely applied their intellect to different pursuits than we. Our highest purpose had always been the good of Gannah. But once the Fueraqis came, we learned their technology and adapted it to our own uses. We learned to think as they thought. To kill as they killed. And unfortunately..." Dassa paused to sip her chocolate.

Pik knew what was coming. She was about to make excuses for the savagery of her forefathers. But he kept quiet.

"Unfortunately," she resumed, "in the process of fighting off the invaders, we discovered we liked killing people. The Gannahan bloodlust is quite literally an addiction, and the entire planet was hooked. For a short space in history, it was all we lived for. The more we killed, the more we wanted to kill."

Pik remembered the wild look in her eye when she'd killed the pirates. Yes, pleasure was certainly part of it. He huddled deeper into his blanket.

"When a Gannahan gets a taste of blood, he will always want more. And if he kills while in the power of a blooddrunk, for every waking hour of his life thereafter he will want to repeat the thrill of that experience. Once he takes that path, it is something he must continually struggle with."

Under the hood of his blanket, Pik's ears stiffened. Were none of them safe on this voyage? Would she one day snap and kill them all in their beds?

She went on to tell how, after wiping out the Fueraqi, Atarah Nacah Marrah began searching space for more peoples to conquer. How he found them and wiped them out with rabid abandon. How for two generations, Gannahans were intent on massive bloodletting wherever they set foot.

Then she told about Hoseh's discovery that all the planets had the same perplexing legends about the arrangement of the stars in their skies, and how fascinated he was with the subject.

Lawbby looked at Pik. "You say you researched that and it's true?"

He hated to admit it, but he wouldn't lie. "From what I found, yes. Apparently every ancient people of every populated planet had basically the same nonsensical interpretation of the arrangement of the stars. Upon further research, I also learned that they all believed the stars portray the same story."

"What sort of story?"

"Some ridiculous myth in which evil appears to have the upper hand but good eventually triumphs. There's a virgin birth and a savior dying on a cross and a wicked serpent and a great war. Basically the Earthers' Christianity, but on a grand scale."

Sylvia stared. "You get all that out of Leo the Lion and Sagittarius the Archer?"

"I don't," Pik said, "but the ancients did. As she says, all the ancients, on every planet."

"Curious, isn't it," Dassa said, "that all the myths are the same? How could anyone see those shapes in the stars to begin with, let alone have them tell such a story? Not just one race comes up with this, but all of them do. What are the odds?"

"Boggling," Sylvia said.

"Couldn't be coincidence," Lawbby said.

"So thought Hoseh." Dassa said. "He studied the matter for years, but it wasn't until he arrived at Karkar and again found the same perplexing legends, that he came to a conclusion. That is to say, it was on Karkar that Hoseh first believed in God."

Pik choked on his tea. If he hadn't been so busy trying to catch his breath, he'd have had plenty say about that preposterous statement.

"You see," Dassa said over Pik's coughing, "all the planets shared not only a story in the stars, but also a creation legend. A divine Creator placed one man and one woman on the planet, provided all they needed for survival, and gave certain instructions. On every orb, the people multiplied and covered the face of the planet but soon came to ignore, and in time largely forget, everything their Creator had told them. Like the story in the stars, this was such a constant in every civilization that by the time Hoseh came across the same thing on Karkar, he concluded it could be no coincidence."

Pik's ears scowled. Coincidences happened all the time. No need to dream up a fanciful explanation.

Apparently unaware of how foolish she sounded, Dassa plunged on. "How exactly it happened and who this Creator was, he didn't know, but he was convinced that some Being far more wise and powerful than he could comprehend had formed everything in the universe. Hoseh concluded that the ancients didn't imagine those shapes in the constellations nor invent the story. Rather, The Creator Himself had revealed it to them from the beginning.

"This realization on Hoseh's part did nothing to comfort him. In finding the answer to one question, he merely uncovered a dozen more. By the time he'd brought Karkar under subjection, his bloodlust was at its peak and his spiritual curiosity was nearly unbearable. He was as a man possessed."

Dassa explained how Hoseh and his men then reconnoitered Earth. Sylvia and Lawbby seemed amazed to learn that their planet had been in the Gannahans' sights, but Pik yawned. All that mattered to him was that his people had nipped that foray in the bud, a facet of history of which Terrestrials should be more appreciative.

But of course, Dassa left out that part. "Hoseh and his chief Nasi, Chen Shakak, were fascinated with the spirituality of Earth and the antiquity of its civilization. Hoseh's own land, and all the others he and his father had conquered, were far younger. But

Earth was torn by bitter religious divides, which kept them primitive and simple-minded."

Lawbby frowned. "I think I'm insulted."

"Nothing against you personally," Dassa said. "I'm just stating historical fact. Hoseh and Shakak believed that this planet had a spiritual significance beyond all others. Only there did the Creator take a visible interest in the lives of the people. Whether it was because the people of Earth were interested in knowing Him when none of the others were, or for some other reason, He continued to contact them. Revealed some of His truths to them, which He caused to be preserved in a written form that exists even today in a book called the Bible."

The Earthers raised their eyebrows at that but said nothing, and Pik didn't think it worth the effort of comment.

Dassa orated from that pile of pads like an oracle on a hill. "Hoseh and Shakak also believed the planet itself, not merely its people, had special significance. It was the site of a great spiritual war between the Creator and the Creator's Enemy. Earth was a literal battleground, and the people who lived upon it were involved in that battle every day of their lives, often unwittingly.

"This amazing reality grabbed hold of the warrior Hoseh and wouldn't let go. He came to see that if there was any hope for the constant burning of curiosity within him, he would find it on Earth, where all the spiritual forces in the universe were focused. And so, though his knights urged him to begin the attack, he held off. He was reluctant to destroy what he increasingly felt was his only hope."

Pik didn't believe a word of this, but the Terrestrials seemed interested. So he heaved a tolerant sigh and let Dassa prattle on.

"Their explorations took them to the British colonies of North America and the political subdivision called Massachusetts. They heard about a man who was going to speak at a gathering. Hoseh later wrote how he felt in his meah that his very life—indeed, the survival of his people—depended upon his hearing what that man had to say."

"Hoseh and Shakak had studied the different Earth religions. They were somewhat familiar with the various branches of Christianity and recognized the similarity with the story in the stars. But they couldn't quite grasp how it all fit together. Hoseh determined that if he hadn't figured it out by the end of the Earthmonth, he would call for his ships and commence the invasion. In a last-ditch effort to find the answers they sought, he and Shakak went into that little church in Massachusetts, sat in a pew, and listened to Jonathan Edwards deliver his droning sermon.

"He warned of God's righteous judgment, of how every creature is accountable to the Creator, and how it is only the Creator's mercy and grace that had spared them thus far. Edwards demonstrated from the Bible that every man, woman, and child must stand before God and give an account, and that apart from the forgiveness that is found only by faith in Jesus Christ, there is no hope for anyone."

Pik shivered beneath his blanket. This part was new to him, but it was also horrifying. Leave it to a Gannahan to latch onto this stuff.

"Hoseh later wrote, and Earth history concurs, that despite the preacher's bland delivery the people became hysterical." Dassa threw the pad off her lap. "They pulled up their feet to keep them from dangling into the pit of hell. They clung to the pews for dear life and screamed in terror. Hoseh and Shakak, however, sat dumbstruck. It was the first time they had ever considered that the Creator might be angry with *them.*

"All the blood they'd spilled, the atrocities they'd wrought, the cruelties they'd set in motion, flashed before their eyes, and they were acutely aware of the heinous evil of it all. They deserved the horrors the preacher described, and worse. That they couldn't escape was obvious. They thought of their families at home, and realized the entire planet of Gannah was in jeopardy.

"They didn't scream, they didn't cling to the pew in terror, but they did tremble. And that, for hardened Purpletongues, was a violent reaction."

Pik gritted his teeth. Was he supposed to feel sympathy for Hoseh?

"The terrified Earthers had a hope," Dassa said. "All they needed to do was trust Him, and they would be saved from His wrath forever.

"But Hoseh had no such hope. He was of Gannah, not Earth. While the people around them begged God for forgiveness, Hoseh and Shakak sat helpless. Their physical abilities were of no use to them here. The quickness of their minds couldn't devise a way out. The technologies at their command couldn't work any miracles. They sat directly in the path of God's vengeance, and they and their people were inevitably doomed.

"They couldn't argue with God—they had earned their fate, and they accepted that. What bothered them more than just punishment was the thought that they had squandered their lives and the lives of their people. They should have been worshiping their Creator, not destroying His creation. This was a King who deserved their devotion, a Lord before whom they should bow in allegiance, a Righteous Ruler to whom they wanted to surrender their all. Instead, they had earned His righteous wrath. Now they could never honor Him as He deserved."

The others hung on every word, but Pik nearly choked. As if any god would want Hoseh's worship!

"The service ended in pandemonium, and Hoseh and Shakak left, feeling weak as water. They went to their rented room, lit their candles, and pored over the words of the Lord in His Book, searching for hope."

Dassa adjusted her position on her nest. "The next morning, after a sleepless night, they sought out the preacher. They found him at an inn and begged an audience, which he granted.

"Since the Earthers didn't understand sojourns from other planets, Hoseh and Shakak identified themselves only as having come from afar on business, and the preacher didn't press them for details. They told him they had been at the meeting, had spent the night studying the New Testament, and had some questions about the meaning of certain passages in light of Edwards's message. For instance, when God used the word *all*, did He truly mean all?

"'What do you mean?' Edwards asked.

"'When God says He is not willing that any should perish but that *all* should come to repentance, what does that mean?' Hoseh asked.

"'Just as it says,' answered Edwards. 'God withholds His judgment to give every individual the opportunity to repent, to the saving of his or her soul.'

"Shakak asked, 'And when Paul told the Philippian jailer that *all* who call upon the name of the Lord shall be saved, both themselves and their households, what does that mean?'

"'Again, simply what it says. Any man, woman, or child who calls upon Jesus Christ in faith is heard by Him and will be spared His awful wrath.'

"'What about the Canaanite woman in the Gospel According to St. Matthew?' Hoseh pressed. 'Though the Messiah came not for her people but for the children of Israel, she said even the dogs could pick up the crumbs that fell from the master's table. Jesus agreed, and commended her faith. Tell me, Mr. Edwards. May *any* dog, however unworthy, however far removed from the children of God, pick up the crumbs?'

"The preacher looked at the two desperate men with concern. 'Why do you doubt, gentlemen? God's promises are sure, and His invitation is extended to everyone, however undeserving. Indeed, none of us deserve anything but His wrath.'

"'Is this the same God,' Hoseh said, 'who created not only the Earth, but all the heavens and everything in them?'

"'Of course,' said Edwards. 'There is none other.'

"'The redemption story was told to all peoples everywhere, in all skies, above all lands,' Hoseh went on with growing excitement. 'So God meant all people to know and to believe and to… and to be redeemed! He would deign to extend to me, to us, to all our people, eternal life in Christ?'

"'That is correct,' Edwards said, but his confirmation wasn't necessary. Hoseh and Shakak were already convinced.

"'Pray for us, sir!' Hoseh cried. 'You know the King. I beg of you, intercede for us!'

"'There is but one intermediary between God and man, the Lord Jesus Christ Himself,' Edwards said. 'But I would be happy to go to Him with you. Come.'

"And so Hoseh and Shakak fell to their knees and prayed to the God of the Universe. Through faith in Christ, they were saved from His wrath and granted everlasting life, just as God promised to all who believe."

Frustrated near the rupture point, Pik glanced at the others. Sylvia had quit painting to listen. Lawbby leaned forward, mouth half open. How could they fall for this nonsense? If he were the type to believe in witchcraft and spells, he'd say Dassa was weaving one.

"Hoseh afterward decreed that although he was heir to Atarah, he would no longer be called King of Gannah, but Steward only, or Toqeph. There is only one King, he said, and that is Christ. All Hoseh's successors have been called toqeph ever since.

"He and Shakak returned to their ship and told the others what they'd learned. The knights were similarly horror-struck to realize how they'd defiled themselves and blasphemed the Creator with their despicable acts. They were overwhelmed by the mercy and grace of God, who was not only willing to forgive them, but literally died to do so. All wept in repentance, prayed for forgiveness, received redemption and new life."

Pik shifted, preparing to rise. She was going too far now. This had to stop. But when Lawbby tossed him a "don't distract me" look, he settled back. Let the others listen if they wanted to. But his ears were shut.

"They had wrought so much destruction there was little they could do to make amends. But Hoseh decided they should repair Karkar as much as practical then pull out, leaving the battered people to heal. They would take the gospel message back to Gannah. After a time they would go back to the planets they had ransacked, make reparations, beg forgiveness, and, most importantly, tell them the truth about the Story in the Stars so that they, too, might believe."

Pik's blood pressure continued to escalate, and Dassa must have felt something in that meah she was forever talking about, for she tossed a curious glance his way as she spoke.

"But before Hoseh had a chance to act upon his resolve, a message came from the Nasi occupying Karkar. Some malignant organism had been introduced into the ventilation systems of all five of their warships, and the wrath of God's judgment had begun to fall."

No. He wouldn't listen to this any longer. He slammed his hand onto the crate in front of him, and the hmmmjckt pieces bounced and scattered. "You're trying to tell me the demons got religion? That that's what kept them from conquering Earth, and not the Karkar plague? Even if God were real, which everyone knows he isn't, that filthy Hoseh and his cutthroat sidekick didn't deserve his forgiveness. What kind of a God would do such a thing?"

Dassa's brows lifted. "What kind of a God indeed?"

Pik jumped to his feet. "Your stupid Story in the Stars makes me want to vomit. It was Karkar that stopped Gannah, not God. God is a lie. It's all a lie, from beginning to end. I am finished with you, you bloodstained, blood-addicted Toqeph of Gannah. "

He spat at her feet and, leaving his hmmmjckt set strewn across the crate and floor, strode away with an indignant swish of his blanket, quivering with a passion too deep to restrain.

He should have lied to Broward, said he couldn't find a cure, let every last abominable one of them die. The galaxy would be infinitely better off without a Gannah to defile it.

22

Stinging as if slapped, Dassa watched Pik's stormy departure from her nest of blankets.

Sylvia's eyebrows rose in surprise as she cleaned her paintbrush. "What's with him?"

Lawbby moved his gaze from Pik's empty chair to Dassa. "I always did think the doc wore his drawers too tight. But you have to admit, princess, that was quite a story. I won't call you a liar like he did, but creets, it's a lot to swallow."

"I agree," Sylvia said. "All we ever hear about Gannahans is how evil they were, never that they found religion."

Lawbby gathered the roving hmmmjckt pieces and packed them into their box. "Especially not a Christian one."

"All this makes me curious, though," Sylvia said. "I'd be interested in seeing for myself what's so special about the Bible. I've never read a word of it."

Dassa shifted her position in the pile of blankets. "I've got one if you'd like to borrow it."

"Do you really?"

"It was among Rosh's personal effects on the Eutarian ship."

Lawbby closed the hmmmjckt case. "I don't know if I'd believe a Gannahan Bible."

"Would you believe an Earth one?"

He hesitated.

"Because it's exactly the same," Dassa said. "The Bibles on Gannah are merely reproductions of what Hoseh brought back. There's nothing Gannahan about them except the materials they're made of. They even look like Earth books. Other Gannahan books are bound at the top. Only Bibles have the binding on the left side."

Dmitry's voice blared through the intercom. "Lawbby! Syl! Where the blazes are you?"

"Holy excretions!" Lawbby's eyes widened in alarm as he looked at his watch. "I was supposed to relieve him on the bridge ten minutes ago. He'll forning draw and quarter me. Creets!"

Sylvia wiped paint from her hands frantically. "And I was supposed to go on duty at the same time."

In seconds they were gone, leaving Dassa alone.

With a sad glance toward Pik's abandoned hmmmjckt set, she climbed out of her pile of padding and went to her quarters.

The easy companionship the five of them had enjoyed was gone like the innocence of youth. For the next two days, the skipper prowled the ship with a testy bark, and the crew shared his mood. Dassa left her quarters only for food and exercise.

The third day, Dmitry called to her from the kitchen as she jogged past. "Hey, there, Madam Toqeph."

She pulled up just past the kitchen, took a step or two back, and stood in the doorway. "Yes?"

Dmitry sat at a table with a half-eaten travelration in front of him. "A word, please?"

She stepped into the tiny kitchen. "Of course. What is it?"

He avoided meeting her eye. "We're a month from Gannah."

"We're making excellent time, then. You weren't exaggerating when you said this was the fastest little ship in the galaxy."

"I don't exaggerate. What are your intentions when we arrive?"

Dassa brushed back a wisp of hair. "As I told you. I want to collect books, videos, maps, that sort of thing. "

"You're coming all this way for a few books?"

"And other items of interest. Also plant cuttings and soil, so I can try to grow something Gannahan on Earth."

The captain's expression was dubious.

"I've compiled a list of what I intend to bring back. It's in my cabin. Would you like a copy?" She didn't mention that the list was written in Gannahan and he wouldn't be able to read it.

"Not necessary. You agreed to irradiate everything before removing it from the shuttle bay, remember?"

"Of course." She got the impression these questions didn't address what was really on his mind. "Is something troubling you, Captain?"

He took a deep breath and looked at her sideways. "Something new has come to light. Maybe. I need your confirmation."

"About what?"

"Is it true what the doctor said?"

As she'd suspected, Pik was at the bottom of this. "What did he say?"

"That when a Gannahan drinks blood, it induces a murderous madness. And that you yourself have killed while under its influence."

She felt her face flush. "He told you that?"

"So it's true. Is it also true that once a Gannahan has tasted blood, he'll always crave it and want to kill again?"

"You think I'm going to drink your blood once we get to Gannah?"

"No, I—"

"If I slit anyone's throat, it will not be an Earther's." She turned to leave then paused and addressed Dmitry again. "Tell the good doctor I could share his secrets too. But, unlike him, I can be trusted to keep a confidence."

She spent the next four hours on the exercise equipment, trying not to wonder what Karkar blood tasted like.

Just under one standard-month later, Pik stood outside the landing craft, feeling like a condemned man preparing to walk to his execution.

Dassa seemed to sense his reluctance. "You don't need to come if you don't want to. I can do this myself."

Pik squared his shoulders. "I said I'd go, so I'm going."

The dark look she shot his way said she didn't believe his promises could be trusted.

He ignored the unspoken accusation. "Besides, I didn't fly halfway across the galaxy in this sardine can for nothing. At least on a planet I can stand upright."

Her eyebrows lifted slightly. "You're standing upright now."

Irksome, the way she wouldn't let go of the truth.

Dmitry had been listening, his face a picture of annoyance. "Load up, you two." He slapped the side of the shuttle, charred from years of use.

Dassa climbed in, and Pik followed while Dmitry reminded them, "One standard-week. I'll wait 10,080 minutes and not one second longer. You're not aboard by then, we leave orbit without you. The clock starts when the bay doors open."

"Understood, Captain." Dassa fastened her safety restraints. "We'll see you in a week."

Pik wanted to believe that, but feared he'd never see the *Swordfish* or its crew again. Nevertheless, he waved to Dmitry and tried to exude confidence as the shuttle door closed.

While he buckled himself in, Dassa studied the control panel.

"You know how to fly this thing?" he asked.

"Dmitry gave me the run-down."

His hands paused on the buckles. "You've never actually flown one?"

She started the engines. "Not quite like this. Have you?"

"I've never flown anything but a personal hovercraft."

"According to the captain, it's not much different. Just a lot bigger. And more powerful. And more explosive, if you don't break through the atmosphere quite right. Landing's a bit trickier too. But other than that, it's a piece of pie."

Pik's ears twitched inside his helmet. He hoped she exaggerated the danger, but guessed she underplayed it. "I believe you mean cake."

"Just so it's chocolate." She spoke into the headset. "Clear?"

"Clear," came the captain's voice.

Dassa pressed a button and the bay doors peeled back. She made a few adjustments to the instruments then pulled down on a lever. The craft lifted and levitated toward the opening.

"One week," the captain's voice said.

"Ten thousand minutes," she returned.

And then they passed the bay doors and soared into the deep emptiness of space.

Pik breathed slowly, trying to will his heart to stop racing. He was alone in a shuttlecraft with a mad Purpletongue, headed for Gannah. How in Karkar had he allowed this to happen?

The planet loomed into view, a brilliant blue flashing behind swirls of thick vapor. Pik closed his eyes, certain he'd never see his mother again.

Dassa frowned. If this made the gloomy Karkar so miserable, why had he come?

She knew the answer, but didn't like to admit it. He was here because the Yasha had commanded it. Her responsibility was simply to obey. Her King knew what He was doing and would never lead her astray.

Feeling suddenly safe in the Yasha's grace, Dassa bent her concentration on flying this unfamiliar vessel, drawing from her Nasi training in the operation of small craft.

The planet came into view with a rush of brilliance, then blurred before her tear-filled eyes. Her heart alternately swelled with the sweet joy of anticipation, twisted in agony over the destruction of her people, and froze at the knowledge that her stay would be short. The strain would have stopped its beating altogether, except that it also bore the Yasha's promise that one day she would return for good.

Dassa blinked away her tears and pointed the shuttle toward home.

The deafening roar faded to a rumble, the bone-jarring shake ceased, and Pik realized he was still alive. Every muscle quivered from pent-up tension. He let out his breath, relaxed his grip on the arms of his seat, and opened his eyes.

"Whew." Dassa's voice sounded strained. "That was a rough one." Then she said something in Gannahan, which Pik guessed was a superstitious prayer of thanks for their safe landing.

He looked through the window onto the same courtyard in which he'd landed on his previous visit to this dreaded planet. He rued the day he ever saw the place, yet here he was again, and by choice. He must be mad.

Dassa undid her safety harness. "I did some calculations. I figure it's probably late spring, a little more than four years from when I left."

His trembling subsiding, Pik unfastened his restraints and peered through the smoky window. "Looks cloudy."

"Hard to tell from in here."

They removed their helmets and laid them on their seats. Then she took a deep breath. "Well, the clock's ticking. Ready?"

He glanced at her face, tight with strain. In an un-Karkarish moment of empathy, he imagined returning home to find every inhabitant dead. He cleared his throat. "I'm ready. Are you?"

She nodded.

Crouching low in the tiny craft, Pik let down the folding stair.

A damp, sweet-scented air, cool but not chilling, stole in like consciousness to a slumbering mind. He stood in the doorway trying to sort out the sensation. Fresh air always took him by surprise, but this time the jolt was a pleasant one.

Hearing Dassa behind him, he shook himself from his reverie and descended the steps.

Sky the color of a Nasi's tongue glowered overhead, but the distance looked brighter. Across the courtyard, a sunbeam made a breach in the clouds, drawing a creeping vapor from the wet pavement.

Pik breathed deeply as he moved a few hesitant paces into the courtyard. The invigorating air, permeated by that strange, subliminal music, stirred something unfamiliar but enticing within him. Still, he felt exposed and vulnerable with no dome overhead.

Dassa stepped from the craft onto the pavement, a dazed expression dulling her face. The sky lightened, the sunbeam widened, and the mist rose around her as she made her slow way to a nearby bench and sat, heedless of its wetness. Elbows on her knees, she covered her face with her hands.

Pik shifted his weight. Should he give her a moment to compose herself? Or go to her, try to comfort her? But what comfort could he give? Emptiness rang across the planet like an echo.

After several uncertain moments, he joined her on the gray stone bench. It was shockingly cold and soaked his pants instantly.

"This is worse than I expected," she said from behind her hands. "And better. Both at once."

Somehow, he almost knew what she meant.

She slid her hands down her face until her fingertips rested on her chin. When she lifted her eyes to the tower rising at the far side of the courtyard, her face brightened like the day. "Look." She pointed. "Gannah still lives."

Pik looked. "The flag?" The banner he'd noticed last time still fluttered from the highest spire, white against the purple sky, a spreading green tree in its center.

She nodded, then rose and went to the circular fountain in the center of the courtyard. Pik remembered it. Fifteen meters across, its base was low enough to sit on, but when fully functioning, the water spurted to the sky from a central fixture shaped like a cluster of exotic creatures climbing on a rock pile. The nozzles were hidden amongst the animals and arranged in such a way that the spray gave the impression of a bird flying. Now the pressure was gone and the water burbled out of the rock pile as if too disheartened to soar. Apparently the drain was clogged, for the water spilled over the fountain's edges and crept across the pavement in all directions.

Heedless of the trickle wetting her legs and feet, Dassa bent, cupped her hands beneath the flow and drank deeply. Pik shuddered to think of the impurities she must be ingesting, but after a few moments she stood upright with a look of satisfaction and shook the water from her hands. "Let's go see the Tree."

Pik surveyed the great number of plants of that description rising from garden islands dotting the courtyard. Leaves in various colors and stages of decay lay in heaps, and branches littered the pavement. "Which tree?"

"You know, the Tree. The Tree of Life."

Pik didn't know, but he followed as she hurried around piles of organic rubbish toward the entrance he had passed through four years before, when the landing party searched for the last living Gannahan. Then he remembered. An ancient tree stood like a living skyscraper in the great hall behind those doors.

When they finally reached the distant entrance, Pik breathed hard from the brisk pace. But Dassa looked fresher than he'd ever seen her as she lifted the handle and threw open the doors. "Oh, by the way. Thanks."

"For what?"

"For latching the doors when you left. I appreciated it at the time, but I didn't say anything."

Pik had a dim recollection of the incident. "Oh. Yeah. Not sure why I took the time to do that. It's not like there's anyone around to keep out."

"No people, but plenty of marauding animals, not to mention the weather. Between them, they could do as much damage as an army."

Pik scratched his head. "I figured I must have had a reason."

They walked through the outer vestibule and into the Great Hall. As before, the walls glowed as they passed, lighting their way. What sort of power source didn't need technicians to tend it? Pik followed Dassa as she made for the tree in the center of the hall.

A thick layer of leaves covered the floor in a circular carpet of red, orange, and brown for meters about the base of the tree, emitting the dank odor of decayed vegetation.

Dassa pointed toward the ceiling. "It's still alive. Look."

Pik peered upward. What he first mistook for a faint green mist, he now realized was the visual effect of millions of infant leaves unfurling high above their heads.

"It's alive," she repeated in an awed voice. "The Tree's still alive."

Pik surveyed the floor at the base of the mountain-sized trunk but saw no sprinkler system. "I see a skylight above for sunlight, but where does it get its water?"

"Through its roots, mostly, which of course go deep into the ground. But also from the nightly mists. "

"The nightly what?"

"I'll show you." Shuffling through the fallen leaves, she led the way around the tree to a vertical, tube-like enclosure on the far side of the cavernous room. To Pik's surprise, a door slid open with barely a hiss, enabling them to enter what he now saw was an elevator. Dassa said something in Gannahan, the door closed, and Pik watched through the clear glass walls as they made a slow ascent, passing the balconies one by one. The tree, which looked even bigger from this vantage point, didn't begin to branch out until the fourth level.

It took nearly a minute to get to the topmost floor, where the elevator came to a gentle stop and the door slid open. They appeared to be on an observation deck with two doors leading to rooms off the hall. The walls didn't glow, but the skylight, still far above them, provided sufficient illumination. It felt as damp up here as the rain-drenched courtyard, but stale. Not for the last time, Pik wished he had a facemask and filter. Who knew what kind of pathogens he was inhaling?

Dassa went to the railing at the edge of the deck and pointed upward. "See that circle of tubing around the edge of the skylight?"

Pik squinted against the glare. "I think so."

"That's the mister. Every night between the second and fourth hour, it sprays the tree."

The leaves, now clearly visible and just unfurling from their buds, looked scalloped and lacy.

"The leaves change color as they mature," Dassa said. "They start out green, then darken to blue, pale to yellow and finally brighten to red. The cycle takes two years. In the spring of the second year they drop off, and a new cycle begins. They were still red and on the tree when you were here last."

"I didn't notice. I was too occupied searching for my patient."

She pulled her attention from the tree to his face. "I've never told you how grateful I am."

Pik's ears swiveled a shrug. "It was my job. I didn't do it out of kindness."

Her laugh rang through the hall. "That's for sure. But I'm grateful all the same." She turned her gaze back to the tree. "It still lives. And the flag still flies." Hands lifted and face turned upward, she spoke something in Gannahan again. Another prayer of thanks, no doubt. Pik's ears frowned.

"What's your problem? I thanked you, too, didn't I?"

He found it annoying that she could read Karkar expressions. Or did she read his thoughts? Either way, it made him uncomfortable. Trying to pretend it didn't, he turned to examine the elevator. "I'm surprised this still operates. What is the power source?"

"We have a number of power centers, all with multiple collection methods. The closest one is a little south of the palace." She entered the elevator, and Pik followed. The door closed in near silence, and Dassa spoke a command that started the tube moving downward.

"The power centers just collect energy, they don't generate it?"

"The Bara provides all power. We merely discover how to appropriate and use it."

Pik suppressed a groan, and Dassa continued. "Our sun is so turbulent its surges create interruptions in any force in its range, so the Dyson-style collection methods used by other planets are unreliable here. Instead, we developed a multi-phasic system, employing the usual solar-satellite method augmented by power captured from wind and ocean currents."

Pik interrupted. "So what I've heard is true, then, that electronics and wireless transmissions don't often work here?"

She seemed surprised. "Yes, it's true, but I didn't realize that was known Outside."

"I picked up that tidbit somewhere."

They exited the elevator. While Pik made a cautious foray into the echoing hall, Dassa continued her explanation. "The key to the system is the fuel cells. The energy is collected and stored underground, and the whole subsurface of the continent is webbed with conduit carrying the power to wherever it's needed. When conditions are good and the solar collectors can work unhindered, the surplus is stockpiled. When satellite signals' paths are obstructed, the stored energy is utilized. Thanks to the bacteriophage technology, the storage cells are able to generate power when they're depleted to a certain level, but they can't go on indefinitely without some outside source feeding them."

Pik's ears perked up. "Bacteriophage technology?"

"I don't understand it well enough to explain. I only know the viruses create electricity under certain conditions, and someone discovered how to utilize that capability."

"I'm unfamiliar with the theory. Nor have I seen anything like these walls." Pik pressed his hand against the stone and his digits glowed dark red, showing the carpal bones within. "How do they do this?"

"Glass tubes filled with radiant kabod activated by a rapid pulse of power run behind a thin veneer of shayish stone. There are brighter lights here and there." She pointed to several large fixtures in the hall. "But unlike the glowlights, they're not motion-activated."

Pik's gaze climbed the layered balconies to the distant skylight until his neck ached, then peered into the gloom emanating from a wide, abandoned corridor spilling into the Hall. He imagined the place alive and bustling with Gannahans, and shivered. "Pretty dismal around here. But the building's still in good shape. How old is it?"

"If I reckon correctly, we're now in the year 812 in the Time of the Stewards. That would make the palace… something like 2,837 years old."

Pik glanced around at the mosaic floor, the detail in the carved, arching doorframes, the well-crafted furniture. It all boasted a dramatic but understated beauty, despite its dusty abandonment. "It's magnificent. Did you live here your whole life?"

"Only for six years." She picked up a multi-lobed red leaf from the floor and traced its veins with a finger. "From the time my grandfather died and my father became the toqeph when I was thirteen. After I married Rosh at nineteen, we lived in a house several kilometers from here. We'll head there next, after I pick up a few things from Armown."

Pik had wandered toward the exit to get a closer look at a gleaming rose-colored plaque on the wall. But when he saw Dassa head down the far corridor at a brisk pace, the glowlights casting their weird aura around her, he hurried after, leaving the plaque unexamined.

He'd have liked to look around him as they walked, but the light was dim and she moved quickly. He had to concentrate on keeping up.

They traveled through wide, cobwebby corridors and down dusty stairways. He couldn't believe there were no moving walkways or escalators in this immense building. The deeper they went into the palace, the staler the air smelled. Some areas seemed particularly rank. Not willing to draw in any more contaminants than necessary, he kept his lips tightly closed and breathed through his nose.

Where was she taking him? It didn't matter. Wherever she went, he wouldn't let her out of his sight as long as they were on this miserable planet.

They passed room after yawning room followed by one gaping side corridor after another. Remembering the starsailors' concerns about Gannahan ghosts, Pik tried not to think about what might lurk in those shadows. "How many people used to live here?"

"In the palace? A couple hundred at any given time, between officials, servants, and travelers. There are guest rooms available for visitors of rank. In the capital city of Ayar, the population was about nine hundred thousand, and on the entire planet, about three hundred million."

"Quite a sparse population for a planet this size," Pik mused, "but a staggering number to die in just weeks." He peered into an unlit doorway as they passed. "I hate to ask, but where are all the bodies?"

"Where do you think?"

He sidestepped a shapeless something—he didn't want to know what, but it was too small to be human—lying on the floor. "I don't know. That's why I asked."

"The first to die were buried. After that we did what we could. Mass graves, incinerators, sea burials. But soon there were too few living to dispose of them. People died wherever they were, and there their bones remain. The ones the carrion eaters didn't drag off. That's why I was surprised the air smelled so fresh when we arrived. Four years ago, the stench was terrible. You were lucky to be wearing a biosuit."

The chill that news sent shuddering through Pik's veins was colder than the air on the *Swordfish*. The planet was full of skeletons?

It was going to be a very long week.

23

Pik followed Dassa on a labyrinthine trek through the desolate palace until his feet ached. After it seemed they'd walked halfway across the planet, they exited onto a broad veranda.

The terrace overlooked a lake rimmed with trees that spread to the horizon. The rain clouds had lumbered off to make way for filmy white ones, and the sweet-smelling breeze had lost its chill. But it wasn't the fresh air that made Pik gasp in delight. It was the view.

The trees surrounding the lake were clad in every color of the spectrum, and the steaming water reflected their dazzling hues like a kaleidoscope. He and Dassa crossed the pavement, still wet from the rain, to the low wall at the edge of the veranda.

Dassa waved her arm toward the scene. "The Ayin Forest," she said, as if making formal introductions, then she gestured toward the left. "My house, which you'll see when we visit it this afternoon, is over there." She rested her arms on the moss-encrusted parapet and gazed out over the lake.

"I've never imagined anything like this." Pik took in the scene. "I thought trees were always green."

"Not in the Ayin Forest. And, like the Tree of Life in the Great Hall, most of these hold their leaves all winter."

"Do they change colors too?"

"Not usually. An elah, for instance, is always some tone of red, depending upon the variety, anywhere from crimson to deep burgundy. A libneh is pale pink, the rimmon family shades of yellow and orange, and the peqa are blue to purple. The shaqed changes color, like the Tree of Life, from green to yellow to scarlet. The firs are always green, though in varying shades."

Pik inhaled the vibrant scents deep into his lungs, and his eyes devoured the valley before him. Hazy in the vapor hovering over the lake, a flock of green and purple waterfowl bobbed a short distance from the near shore. Farther off, something long, graceful, and gray took flight with a mighty flap of wings, a silvery fish flashing in its bill. In a tree just below the veranda, a small, white-spotted animal scuttled along a bobbing teal-leafed branch, scattering radiant droplets into the air.

"Hgkch," said Pik. Even that succinct Karkar word couldn't quite express his feelings as he took in the sights, sounds, and smells of this astonishing place.

Dassa must have been similarly moved, for neither of them spoke for several long moments.

Then she broke the silence, her voice strained. "Four years ago…"

Startled by the interruption, Pik turned his attention to her.

"Four years ago, I skated across this lake. It was early spring, the water was still frozen." Her expression distant, she gazed toward the far shore. "I'd completed my Nasi training and was fulfilling the Last Requirement. The final exam, so to speak."

Pik didn't know if he should respond. Standing in this place was like standing in a fairy tale, and he felt more like an observer than a participant. He decided not to interrupt.

"One must start here at Armown and walk to the cliffs of Raqiya, 620 or so kilometers to the northwest." She gestured toward somewhere beyond the palace walls.

This was starting to sound more like a tall tale. "Wait a minute. You had to *walk* 620 kilometers?"

"Yes. The entire quest must be done on foot. To fulfill the Last Requirement, the would-be Nasi would first hike to the cliffs of Raqiya and collect mossberries. They grow no place but there. Once the berries are collected, he would fast until he returned, still on foot, to Armown. He would then present some sort of pleasing confection made with the mossberries as an offering to the toqeph. This offering is called the metheq. If the metheq pleases the toqeph, he declares the initiate a full Nasi. The fast is then over, and the new Nasi may eat the remainder of the metheq himself. That's what turns the tongue purple."

Pik's ears stiffened. "What's what turns the tongue purple?"

"The mossberries."

His brain whirred. "That's impossible. Fruit stains aren't permanent."

"Not in your experience. Much like trees are never blue."

Sure. This was Gannah they were talking about. "All right. So what's in these mossberries?"

A hint of a smile flitted across her face like the shadow of the multi-winged insect that wove an erratic flight nearby. "I only know they're delicious and satisfying, highly nutritious, and they leave a permanent stain. No one is allowed to touch them but a Nasi or an initiate performing the Last Requirement."

Dassa reached over the parapet and plucked a leaf from a nearby twig then rolled it absently between her fingers, releasing a faint but spicy-sweet smell. "On that day four years ago, I went first to my house, where I baked the toqeph a mossberry pie. I took the pie, walked through the woods to the lake, and put on my skates. The rest of the way to Armown, I traveled across the ice."

She looked out on the water below. "The closer I got to the palace, the more uncomfortable I felt, certain something was wrong. I got to the pavilion—you can just see it there through the trees."

Pik saw the curved edge of a brown roof behind a curtain of multicolored foliage.

"I changed out of my skates and started up the hill to the palace. There's a path that runs up this slope." They moved along the edge of the veranda to an opening in the wall, and beneath them Pik saw where rampant vegetation climbed broad stone steps leading up to where they stood.

"I got halfway up those steps, and then I knew. The thing Rosh and I most feared had come to pass."

Pik blinked. "You and Rosh knew the plague would strike?"

"Not exactly. But we knew my father was planning to raise the ships."

"What ships?"

Dassa tossed away the leaf she'd been holding and it fell, bruised and broken. "The ancient war ships from Karkar. The dying pilots had programmed the vessels to head for home. When Hoseh and his crew arrived from Earth, they found all five destroyers orbiting the planet with not a living man on board. He ordered them brought to the surface, weighted down and sunk in the sea, and commanded that they never be raised. Ever. But my father was intent on bringing them up."

"Whatever for?"

"I… he never said. But Rosh suggested I be ready to assume the throne if my father tried raising the ships, for no one disobeyed a supreme command of the toqeph—not even one long dead—without paying with his life. That was why I sought the rank of Nasi. I didn't really want it. But only a Nasi can be the toqeph. I never would have pursued such a course if not for Rosh."

Pik envisioned the violet-eyed singer with his broad concert smile and tried to imagine him giving such sober counsel. It didn't seem to fit.

"As I said," Dassa continued, "I knew something was wrong, so I ran the rest of the way up the stairs and into the palace." She turned and headed for the door, retracing those historic steps. "I was exhausted, out of my mind with hunger, and I couldn't believe what I was sensing in my meah. I hoped it was hysteria, the result of my ordeal."

Pik had no desire to relive with her the last awful days of Gannah but felt it best to let her speak. Reluctant, he followed her back into the ghostly palace.

She started up a wide, curving stairway. "I headed for the throne room. It's up here."

The stairs rose at a gentle pace and passed numerous curved landings and dark, cavernous hallways. Pik's breath grew labored from exertion and fear of the creepy surroundings. But he tried to hide his discomfort and managed not to pant when he asked, "Did you see anyone on your way up here?"

"Not a soul. Not at first. And that made me realize my feelings were right. That, and the smell. In the last stages of the illness you lost control of your functions, and there had been a lot of sick people all over the palace."

"How many had died by the time you arrived?"

"More than half the planet was already gone."

Pik uttered a Karkar expletive. He couldn't fathom the devastation. How could an entire population be wiped out so swiftly?

"But I didn't know that yet." They reached the end of the stairs. "I only knew something awful was happening. Fighting back terror, I arrived at the throne room."

The passage they'd been following broadened and joined a commodious room by way of a portal carved to mimic a leafy bower. Stained-glass windows lined the walls near the top, letting in dim but colorful light. Rows of pale marble pillars shaped like trees supported the ceiling. On the room's near side stood a long, oval table. The windows didn't allow enough light for Pik to see the far reaches of the place, and the walls didn't glow.

Dassa continued her story. "My brother, Arodi, was there at the table, sitting alone. He turned and saw me. 'Thank the Yasha you're back,' he said. 'I was afraid you'd come too late.'

"'What do you mean?' I asked. 'Where is everyone? Where's Emma, where are my boys?'

"'Don't you know? They're gone!' His speech was slurred from loss of muscle control. 'Everyone's gone!' He named a dozen people—his wife and children, my sister and her family, and, of course, Emma and my boys.

"I couldn't understand. Or didn't want to. 'Where did they go?' I asked.

"'They're dead. Died of the plague. Abba will be soon, and so shall I. Do you have the metheq? We must get Abba to eat it. You must be Nasi, or Gannah will have no toqeph.'

"It was too much to take in. I kept reaching for my boys in my meah, and my mother. I couldn't connect, but what Arodi was saying wasn't possible. It couldn't be true.

"With what little strength he had left, Arodi kept pestering me. 'Dassa! Do you have the metheq? We must take it to Abba, or Gannah will have no toqeph.'

"'What about Joab?' I asked. My cousin, Atarah Joab Charash, would have taken the throne if none of my father's children were qualified.

"'Dead three days.' Arodi pulled himself out of his chair and staggered toward the throne. 'Hurry. I still hear him breathing, but we haven't much time.'

"'It's a pie,' I said, stupid with deprivation and shock. 'I have nothing to cut it with, and I need a plate.'

"'Then get something. You can move faster than I.'

"So I ran out, grabbed a knife and a plate from a few rooms away, then ran up to the throne. I got there about the same time Arodi did. He'd finished the distance on hands and knees."

Pik watched in horror as she approached the throne, reliving the scene. In the spooky half-light it was easy to imagine the emotions that must have filled the room.

"The toqeph had nearly slid off his seat as he sat in his own waste. Despite the smell, Arodi and I knelt beside him. 'Milord,' I said. 'Abba. It is Hadassah. Can you hear me?'

"'There's nothing wrong with his ears,' Arodi slurred. 'It's only the muscles that are affected.' He spoke to the toqeph, his words careful and his voice breaking. 'Dassa brought you the metheq. You must pronounce her Nasi, so she can reign after you. Will you do that, Abba?'

"I looked for someplace to cut the pie, but the smell was so bad around the throne I couldn't bear to set the metheq down anywhere close. So I went back to the table, cut a piece and brought it to the toqeph." Pik glanced at the table, and his skin prickled. The empty pan was still there, the juices dried black on the bottom, like a spectre rising from the grave to testify to the truth of her story.

Dassa's voice sounded hoarse and old. "Arodi opened the toqeph's mouth and I stuffed in a pinch of the pie. 'Can you chew it, Abba? Can you swallow?'

"His jaw moved, and I held his lips closed to keep the food in his mouth. It was slow going, but he managed to swallow. Then Arodi took the toqeph's hand and laid it on my shoulder. Abba had just the strength to keep it there long enough to mumble, 'I dub thee Nasi of Gannah,' before it slid off. The weight of his falling arm would have toppled him from the throne if Arodi and I had not righted him.

"He opened an eye and looked at my brother. 'Leave us,' he gasped. 'I must…speak…with your sister…alone.'

"Arodi bowed his head and crawled several meters away, breathing as if he'd run several kilometers. It was hard for my father to speak, and I drew closer, stench and all. 'What is it, Abba?'

"Tears coursed down his face, and he sobbed weakly. 'I have erred, Hadassah. I disobeyed my King. I alone deserve to die… But the people…are punished…for my sin. I will not…feast…in the Hall…of the King.'

"His chin dropped to his chest, and I squeezed his shoulder. 'Abba! Abba!'

"Without opening his eyes, he spoke again. 'Take the ring, Hadassah. I have…no strength.'

"I slipped the Ring of Atarah from his emaciated finger and put it in his hand. 'You must put it on me,' I said. 'Can you do that, Abba?'

"He managed, with my help. Then he spoke again. 'Thou art the toqeph. Atarah Hadassah. Hagah.' I thought he forgot the Natsach, but after a long pause, he eked it out. 'Nat-sach. I have nothing left…to pass on to you…but this ring.' Then he spoke no more.

"I went to Arodi, curled up on the floor and crying.

"'Is no one well in the whole palace? Is everyone dead but you and me?' I thought I spoke in hyperbole. I had no idea how close my question was to the truth.

"'They're dead. They're all dead,' he wept."

She paused in her narration, climbed the two steps to the throne and lowered herself into it. "And now here I am. Toqeph. Of nothing."

Pik stared at her, unable to summon a word.

"But they weren't all dead. Not yet." She stepped down, passed Pik as if not seeing him, and sat at the near end of the long table before the empty pie plate. "I sat down and cut myself a piece of pie. And I ate it. My first act as Toqeph of Gannah. While my father wheezed his last labored breaths on his befouled throne and my brother lay sobbing in the shadows, I ate pie.

"All I could think of was how hungry I was. How weary, how frightened. I felt if I ate something, the pain in my stomach and the ache in my heart might lessen. I wanted to run and find my children—surely they were alive, just hiding somewhere, hiding until this horrible nightmare ended. I wanted my mother. And I wanted Rosh. Rosh. I called to him in my meah. Of all those whom I yearned for, of all that I called for, he alone could hear.

"'I'm coming,' he told me.

"'But I need you now!'

"'I'll be there as soon as I can.'

"He was so far away! But at least he was coming. The others had gone without saying good-bye."

She picked up the pie plate and looked into it. "I'm embarrassed to tell you, it was delicious. I can't describe what it tasted like, how good it was. With my father dying and my brother sobbing, I ate pie. And enjoyed it."

Pik was embarrassed as well. Why was she telling these things to him, a Karkar? He felt like a spy in the enemy's bathroom.

She set the plate down. "There were others still alive. A few were fairly healthy. Not for long, but they were then. Two of my father's Nasi, Hanoch and Gunni, came in as I sat here. 'You are back,' they said, 'and eating the metheq. Your quest was successful then? Does the toqeph still live?'

"'I am the toqeph.' I spoke the words, but didn't believe them.

"It was strange to see them bow before me. They were Nasi, and my elders. I felt like a child. I wanted to cry.

"But I didn't. I licked the mossberry juice from my fingers with a tongue that I knew was now purple like theirs, and said, 'Arise, brother Nasi. I need your help. What has happened here?'

"'They told me. As much as they were able, at least, because no one really knew. Later, they buried my father and cleaned the throne. Gunni carried my brother out. But first they advised me to get a good meal and some sleep. 'The metheq is good,' said Hanoch, 'but you need balanced sustenance, and you'll think more clearly after you've rested. I shall have a meal brought to the toqeph's residence.'

She rose and turned from the table. "The toqeph's residence is where we go now."

Glad to leave the eerie throne room behind, Pik accompanied her through a side door, down a corridor, around a bend, and down another flight of stairs. A person could definitely get his exercise around here.

The door at the end of the next corridor bore the same tree insignia as Dassa's ring, and Pik guessed the foreign lettering also said the same thing. Atarah, King. She opened the door—it had no lock—and they entered the royal suite.

Though spacious and well appointed, the rooms weren't as opulent as one might expect for a king's residence. Furniture sat grouped in cozy clusters on a plush area rug. Family portraits in bas-relief were encased in frames like flat boxes embedded in the walls—which appeared to be upholstered. Curious, Pik ran his hand along one wall as he followed Dassa through the suite, and it was, in fact thickly padded and covered with soft fabric.

Dassa took him into what appeared to be a dining room. "Here I ate the first meal I'd had in over a month that I didn't cook over a campfire."

It almost felt like a museum tour, but without a barrier to keep visitors from touching the specimens. Like the pie plate in the throne room, the soiled dishes remained on the table as if left on display, along with the dry, stripped bones of whatever animal had been sacrificed for the meal. Pik wondered why no one had sent the scrubbots to clean up. Surely the disease didn't affect Gannahan robots, too.

"And then I slept." She motioned toward another part of the suite, though she didn't take him there. "But only for about four hours. That was the longest sleep I had until I was too ill to do anything else."

While she spoke, she opened a door of a glass-fronted cabinet and removed a thin pouch of fine tan leather emblazoned with the symbol of Atarah. Then she paused to look around. "I need a box. Hmm. Oh, I know."

She laid the pouch on the bureau and headed, Pik following, through the rooms to a spiral stair and down into what must have been the royal family's sleeping quarters.

Entering a spacious bedroom, she opened a closet and disappeared inside. Before he could make up his mind whether to follow, she emerged with an unmarked box of smooth, lightweight wood of pale gray. She upended it onto the bed and dumped out a dozen or more paper notebooks bound at the top. "My mother's diaries. She wrote her diaries by hand instead of on a computer. That's fine, I suppose, but they take up a lot of space."

Dassa grabbed the empty box and carried it up the steps. Though the toqeph's residence was brighter and less oppressive than the throne room, the pervasive dustiness made Pik want to sneeze. He couldn't suppress the sensation he was intruding where he didn't belong.

In the dining room, Dassa opened a bureau drawer and grabbed a handful of red cloth napkins. Then, from another cabinet, she removed a crystal goblet, which she wrapped in a napkin and set it in the box.

Pik didn't understand why they were here. "What are you doing? I thought you came to get historical materials."

"First I need to pay my debts. Sylvia asked for Gannahan glassware, and Dmitry asked for that." She nodded to the pouch on the bureau.

"What is it?" He picked up the sack. The leather was thin, soft as velvet, and supple.

"If you knew, you wouldn't be holding it."

"Why?" He could feel an object inside, round and flattish. Almost like… He untied the satiny cord with some trepidation and peeked inside. "It's a lahab."

"Not just any lahab." Dassa held out her hand and he gave her the pouch. She pointed to the insignia. "You probably recognize this as the sign of Atarah. But this"—she slipped the lahab out of its case and pointed to the engraving around the center—"is the mark of Atarah Hoseh Charash. He carried it in his travels." She popped open the blades, which sparked with an evil glimmer. "And I'm told it saw much use."

Feeling faint, Pik sank into the closest chair. This moved the villain Hoseh out of the mists of mythology and into the world Pik walked in. Fighting the urge to run screaming from the room, he tried to think rationally. "Surely that leather isn't eight hundred years old."

"Of course not. A Gannahan doesn't hide his lahab in a pouch. It would be of no use to him there. We've put it in the leather now for long-term storage, to prevent tarnish and corrosion."

Pik's ears tilted back in disbelief. "You're giving the lahab of Hoseh — your revered ancestor, Hoseh the Wise — to Dmitry? The unlicensed captain of a maverick ship?"

"He's a collector of primitive weapons. This will be the centerpiece of his collection."

It could make the scoundrel a wealthy man as well. "Is that what he demanded as payment for this trip?"

"I offered it. It was the only way I could persuade him." She slipped the weapon back into its pouch, laid it in the box, and went back to wrapping the stemware. "Unlike the lahab, these aren't antiques. They were a wedding present to my parents from my maternal grandparents. Beautiful, aren't they?"

Though still weak at the thought he'd held Hoseh's lahab, Pik's legs found the strength to carry him to the bureau for a closer look. "They're exquisite."

The base of each goblet bore a tiny bouquet of perfect flowers made of droplets of glass. From the base rose a graceful, twisted stem supporting a delicate cup etched with twining vines. Each piece was a different shade of translucent pink, from the subtlest tint to pale salmon.

To Pik's dismay, Dassa rapped two of the glasses together. Instead of shattering, they rang like chimes, in such perfect pitch they sounded as one.

"They're as remarkable to hear as they are to see," Pik said. "But how can you be so rough with them?"

"Gannahan glass is nearly unbreakable."

His ears twitched with sudden understanding. "Oh, so that's what that means."

"That's what what means?"

"An old Karkar saying. When something's tougher than it looks, they say it's sturdy as Gannahan glass. I never understood, because as far as I knew, glass was never sturdy."

"Many things are different here."

Pik couldn't agree more. "If they don't break, why are you protecting them?"

She picked up another napkin. "Partly to keep them from ringing all the way back to the *Swordfish*, and partly because I don't want to take any chances. Gannahan glass is *almost* unbreakable."

Pik glanced at the portraits watching them from the wall in the next room. "Much like Gannahan people."

"I guess so." She inserted the last goblet in the box then put on the lid. "There. That's all I need from here for now. I'm in a hurry to get to my house. I haven't been there since I made the metheq."

Carrying the box, she led him back to the courtyard by a different, and thankfully shorter, route. After a few minutes, they exited the palace through a small door not far from their landing craft.

"Let's put this in the shuttle," she said. "You can grab your bag, then we'll get a vehicle from the livery. It should be a short drive to my house."

Pik's stomach rumbled. "Fine. But do you have any objections to a bite to eat first?"

"Not in theory. But I don't intend to eat travelrations as long as I'm in the land of real food. I could go look for some."

Pik didn't think he could walk another step. "How long will that take?"

"I don't know, but here." She thrust the box into his hands. "Take this to the shuttle, then have some lunch. I'm going grocery shopping." She hurried back toward the door they'd just exited.

With Hoseh's Karkar-killing blade in that box, he'd have thrown it to the ground if not for the goblets. Furthermore, he'd resolved never to let her out of his sight. He should leave these things here and run after her.

But he was tired of chasing her around. He needed some lunch, and if she abandoned him, he was with the shuttle, and that was the safest place to be.

At the landing craft, he stowed the box in the stern, retrieved his bag, and went to the same bench he'd sat on that morning.

Though preferable to the macabre palace, the domeless sky unnerved him. But then, everything about this planet had that effect on him.

At least the temperature was comfortable. He opened a bottle of water and took a long drink.

It tasted flat. Dassa always said the water was flat, but he never knew what she meant before. Water was water, it tasted like nothing. But now, sitting under the warm Gannahan sun, breathing the sweet Gannahan air, viewing the timeless architecture, listening to the stirring music on the breeze, and exchanging curious stares with a little three-legged bird perched on a nearby yellow-leafed shrub, Pik understood what flat meant.

He pulled a pocket lunch bar out of his bag and opened it. The familiar printing on the shiny wrapper looked foreign. And the bar tasted—his ears lifted in a smile—it tasted like a chemistry experiment. Just like Dassa always said it did.

He wished he'd stayed on the *Swordfish*. This place was bewitching him.

"Next thing you know," he said to the bird, which uttered a surprised chirp and flew off, "I'll be speaking in Hebrew."

24

Dassa jogged through the desolate halls back to the toqeph's residence. She needed to eat, yes. But first things first.

The idea had come to her as she spilled her mother's diaries onto the bed. She'd fingered the thought in her mind until it took shape. Now, she was sure.

Abba had his personal journal beside him when he died. After removing the body and cleaning the throne area, Hanoch had given the notebook to Dassa. She hadn't had the heart to look in it at the time, but now its contents interested her very much.

She dashed through the royal residence to the toqeph's private office and spied the notebook on the writing desk where she'd laid it after her father's death. Would there be charge left in the battery? Not likely. But if the palace still had power to operate the glowlights, there should be enough to run a notebook.

She opened the cover, which should have activated it. It didn't. After plugging it into a portal, she tried again. Nothing happened at first, and she bit her lip in frustration, but after another moment the screen came alive.

Trying to suppress a surge of guilt for accessing a locked file, she opened the last entry and skimmed. What she sought wasn't there, so she went back a day. Then to the day before. And the day before. Why wasn't it here? Was her theory completely wrong? He should have mentioned it somewhere.

Ah! There it was, on the first of Nisan, the 808th Year of the Toqeph.

Dassa read, transfixed.

Nodding on the bench with arms outstretched like a human solar collector, Pik lifted his head at an unfamiliar sound.

Sitting straighter and blinking away drowsiness, he stared in the direction of the noise. Something was going on in the long, curving arm of the palace near the courtyard's main gate. The wall was opening with a faint rumble, like a garage door rolling upward.

He stared, poised to run to the shuttle and seal himself inside. The shape of a vehicle appeared in the opening and emerged into the courtyard.

Remembering Dassa's promise to return with transportation, Pik eased back on the bench, though he still watched with trepidation. He knew no one was here but him and Dassa, but where Gannah was concerned, you could never be too sure. He glanced at the shuttle and wondered if it might not be safer to watch from there.

Then an arm reached out the vehicle's window and waved. He couldn't see the face that went with it, but he felt sure the limb belonged to Dassa. Letting out his pent-up breath, he sagged against the back of the bench, heart thumping. This trip would be the death of him.

The buff-colored vehicle humming over the pavement was as strange as everything else around here. It appeared to be a service truck, complete with insignia on the door and an identifying number on the side. But it looked more like an elongated version of the old interstellar exploratory vessels Earthers used to call flying saucers than anything Pik had ever seen on a road. The driver sat in a tinted bubble in the middle of the ovoid machine. The front and rear sections contained a variety of compartments and spaces for carrying equipment of who-knew what sort.

It hovered several centimeters above the ground and moved at a pretty good clip. Within a few seconds Pik recognized Dassa at the controls, and soon she drew up to within meters of where he sat, extended four wheels on the underside of the vehicle, and lowered the machine to the ground with a lazy mechanical wheeze.

"Have you thawed out yet?" she called through the window.

Pik rose and walked toward the truck, or whatever it was. "Yes. First time I've been warm in months." He looked at his watch. "That must have been some lunch you had."

"Not really. The only food I could find was no longer edible, and I didn't want to take the time to find something fresh and cook it. I'll wait to eat until I get to the house."

Pik yawned. "I think I was dozing."

Dassa grinned up at him. "I think you were burning. Your face looks like a crimson elah."

The tight, stinging sensation in his skin, unnoticed until she mentioned it, confirmed her amateur diagnosis. "I never gave that a thought. I was enjoying the warmth." Now that he was fully awake and aware of his discomfort, he couldn't wait to get out of the sun. He squinted through the bubble at the vehicle's interior. "How am I supposed to fit in that thing?"

She shrugged. "It'll be tight, but you can squeeze in. Unless you'd like to ride in the bucket." She gestured toward the area behind her.

The back portion of the vehicle, obviously intended to carry cargo, resembled a tub with unidentifiable crusty material clinging in patches to the bottom and sides.

He recalled her comment about disposing of bodies in mass graves. "I'll ride inside."

"Come around, then." She manipulated a lever, and the opposite door opened, hinged at the top. "You can throw your bag in the bucket to save space in here."

As Pik dropped his bag in the filthy compartment, he made a mental note to carry it by the handle in the future, not wear it as a backpack. Then he walked around and crammed himself in beside Dassa.

He had to tuck his knees nearly to his chin and wrap his arms around them in order to fit. But at least he was out of that poisonous sun.

His burning ears tipped back with displeasure. He'd never suffered solar erythema before. His skin would develop painful, disfiguring blisters. Then it would peel and leave patches of uneven color. Could he expect fever, chills, and vomiting? He might even slip into shock. How could he have been so foolish as to go without sunscreen?

He fingered his flaming face and neck. "What do you have to treat sunburn?"

She restarted the machine but didn't lift it off the ground. Instead they rolled across the pavement on the wheels, heading back the way she had come. "Nothing."

"Nothing? How can you have no treatment?"

"A Gannahan rarely gets sunburned. But I've got something at the house that soothes minor burns from other sources. It should work for sunburn, too, I'd think."

Pik tried rearranging his limbs to a more comfortable position but decided this was as good as it gets. "I trust it won't be harmful to tender Karkar skin?"

"It's just a tea. We drink it as well as apply it topically, so I don't see how it could hurt."

Pik felt a little faint and hoped they'd get to the house before he passed out from sunstroke.

Dassa drove into a garage area containing a number of other service-type vehicles, all with similar markings and all the same color. The door closed after they passed.

"I thought we were leaving the palace, not driving around inside."

After executing a tight turn, she stopped to shift into hover mode and raise the wheels. "We're leaving by the back door. As difficult as the main gate was to close four years ago, I didn't want to have to try opening it now." They moved forward again with a mechanical hum that echoed faintly off the walls. "Of course I was much weaker then. I'd contracted the plague myself by that time."

They traveled through a wide, curving tunnel lit only by the vehicle's headlamps."Aren't the front gates controlled electronically, like the door we just came through?"

She shook her head. "Before I closed them, they hadn't been moved in decades. They were always left open."

"Why did you close them?"

"To keep out the animals."

That didn't make sense. He'd seen animals here. Birds. Insects. Grotesque things that lurked in fine, sticky webs though Dassa insisted they weren't spiders. A few small, furred creatures scampering around the courtyard, and other sorts scurrying in the shadows within the palace. Obviously the gates didn't keep them out.

Then he remembered seeing, when they stood on the terrace, a dark, shadowy something—bigger than a Cephargian on growth hormones—melting into the trees on the edge of the lake.

Creepy as the palace was, he suddenly had second thoughts about leaving the safety of its thick walls. "Animals?" His voice sounded high and squawky, even to his own ears. "What animals?"

They approached another door, which opened. Despite the tinted glass around him, Pik flinched at the brightness on the other side of the opening.

"All animals," Dassa answered. "The billions of nonhuman residents of Gannah."

"But… they're not dangerous, right?"

She tossed him a withering look. "Chances are they'll leave us alone. But any animal on Gannah can be dangerous. Even the cute ones, even in the best of times."

They were out of the palace now, with the door closing behind them, shutting off the small measure of safety to be had on this planet. "What do you mean, even in the best of times?"

"For the past four years, the animals have been feeding on human flesh, gnawing on human bones, and lining their nests with human hair. I expect they've developed a taste for it by now."

With rising panic, Pik scanned buttons and levers near his knees. Which would close his window? He guessed right with the first try, and the curved window slupped shut, leaving barely a seam in the bubble that surrounded them. He surveyed the scenery with wide eyes, half expecting a slavering pack of vicious creatures to come barreling out of the trees.

"Relax," Dassa said. "You should be safe as long as you're with me. Even the animals respect the toqeph."

"They know who you are?"

She sighed. "I hope so."

Soon after Dassa drove the truck from the building, the service road joined another, wider route. The back road to Armown wound in a leisurely zigzag between the palace and the foot of the mesa upon which Armown stood. It made a turn, offering a fine view of Lake Gadol. At the next switchback, the bustling city of Ayar could be seen in the distance. In this fashion it looped back and forth on its way down the slope, past terraced gardens and through colorful woodlands.

But it had been half a hundred months since the roadway, once meticulously maintained, had been swept of litter by a passing motorcoach. Downed trees and branches lay, broken and rotting, wherever they fell. Weeds pried through seams and cracks in the pavement. Vines and rampant undergrowth strangled the gardens, and terrace walls mildewed in forlorn abandonment.

"What happened there?" Pik's pinched voice jarred Dassa from her gloomy reverie.

"Where?"

"Those trees, six or eight of them. Look how the bark several meters up is hanging in shreds. What would have done that?"

"Looks like dowbim."

"What are dowbim, giants with axes?"

"Large animals with long, sharp claws, which they like to clean on anything wood. Much like earthish bears, but more aggressive."

Pik gulped. "Are there…a lot of them around?"

She shrugged. "Didn't used to be, but without humans to keep them at bay, a couple of clans could have moved in. They might be fighting for dominance of the territory."

Contempt for his cowardice made her grit her teeth, but she had to admit, wildlife wars were not to be taken lightly. "Feel under your seat. There's an electrodart there in case we need it."

After a few cramped contortions, he withdrew the weapon and examined it curiously. "A phaser?"

"Not really." She swerved to avoid a large branch across the road, its dead leaves dried to the face of the pavement like crusted tears. "It shoots a dart of electricity, not a laser beam. Doesn't matter where the bolt strikes, it'll stop the target's heart in an instant. A sure kill every time."

He turned it over in his grotesque six-fingered hands. "There are no power settings? Just on and off?"

"That's right. It's good for seven shots, then it has to be recharged."

As much as was possible in the tight space, he sighted down the channel toward an imaginary target outside the vehicle. "Just aim and shoot?"

She nodded. "It's got enough voltage to kill anything, even a dowb." Sensing his fear rise, she glanced at him. "Nothing to worry about. You're a Karkar. You know all about slaying the Gannahan behemoth."

His red ears twitched, but at least he shut up.

Near the base of the mountain, the road sprouted three branches. One doubled back up the hill toward Armown, eventually entering through the main gate. The second, the Ayin highway, curved to the left toward the city.

Dassa turned onto the third branch. Like every Gannahan road that led out of a city, it was called the Migrashah Road. This particular Migrashah would take her home.

Her jaw clenched. Home. Who was she kidding? She had no home.

So what was she doing here? Why not accept the fact that Gannah was dead and start life again somewhere else? Earth wasn't so terrible, and she'd heard parts of Bappas were pleasant as well.

But the Yasha had commanded this expedition. Furthermore, He had insisted she bring the Karkar along, no matter how unsuited he seemed for the trip. The whole situation made her angry.

Why had she poured out her heart to Pik, telling him about that horrible day? Worse yet, about the Nasi's Last Requirement? That subject should never be discussed with Outsiders, especially one who had broken her confidence once already.

He'd never apologized for that. Never even acknowledged that he'd betrayed her. It was a sad day indeed when you could trust a Cephargian pirate to keep his word but not a Karkar doctor.

What was wrong with him? After seeing this desolation and hearing her story, he must understand the depth of her loneliness. And the music—he heard the music, and it touched his heart. So why did he remain so stiff and distant?

And why, in all Gannah, did she care? She shouldn't give a flea's eyebrow how he felt.

She certainly cherished no warm thoughts toward him, with his spindly limbs, anemic complexion, and ridiculous surfeit of fingers. He was vain, self-possessed, and cowardly. She'd felt his panic ebb and flow since they first entered the shuttle. Had seen those amber eyes dart about in terror. He was afraid of small spaces and open air. Afraid of nonexistent ghosts and animals he'd never seen.

Afraid of her.

Hardly able to bear the sight, smell, and feel of him at this close proximity, she gripped the steering bar in fury as they left the Migrashah and entered the forest road.

She breathed in the heavenly, earthy scents that blew in her face through the open window. How had she forgotten the Ayin

Forest's beauty? The sunbeams slicing through chromatic leaves, the sweet-smelling carpet of foliage, the branches stretching toward the pristine sky, the hum of the music vibrating from the trees—it was almost enough to make her forget her annoyance.

But only almost.

Shall I call thee Jonah?

Dassa started. She hadn't been thinking about the Yasha, hadn't expected Him to speak.

Why Jonah, Lord? I do not run from Thee as Jonah did. I perform Thy every command.

She sensed the Yasha nod. *As did Jonah, eventually. But he did so grudgingly, as you do.*

Dassa had no answer. The comparison was apt.

If thou will not forgive the doctor, thy mission shall fail.

She sighed. *It is not that I will not, Lord. I cannot.*

The Yasha's silence indicated disapproval. But she'd spoken the truth. How could He disapprove of that? Was He saying…

You mean I can?

More silence.

Dassa recalled God's ancient words: *Be ye kind one to another, tenderhearted, forgiving one another, even as God for Christ's sake hath forgiven you.*

Yea, Lord, Thy word is true. But I need Thy grace to forgive him.

In her meah, she saw the Yasha's indulgent smile. *Thou hast asked at last. Now, thou shalt receive.*

Pik's reedy voice interrupted. "What did all that? Please don't tell me some sort of animal."

Dassa turned her attention to the broad swath of fallen trees to the west, their absence revealing the open sky. "Not animals this time. More like a tornado. Two or three years ago, from the way it's all overgrown." Her eyes followed the path of the storm, realizing the road would likely be blocked around the next bend.

A few moments later Pik had the same thought, and she again felt his fear as he asked, "What will we do if we can't get through?"

"We can clear a path. There's a timbersaw in one of the truck's compartments, and I've already made sure it works." But her heart sank at the thought of how much time that would take. Her stomach moaned for food.

When they reached the area of destruction, though, they saw that only one treetop lay in their way. It was a simple matter for Dassa to remove the worst of the obstruction—with Pik cowering in the truck all the while—and they were able to hover around or over the rest.

"Sometimes," she said as she surveyed the now-open road before them, "obstacles aren't as big as they seem from a distance."

If Pik heard what she said, he didn't answer. He was too busy eyeing the 140-kilo qaran deer that had stood in the tall weeds at the forest edge the whole time, watching with wide, curious eyes. "Those horns are enormous." He twisted to get a better look as the animal trotted after them, leaping fallen timber with light, easy bounds. "And do I see spikes on his neck? Does he really need horns and spikes both?"

Pik turned and faced forward again, looking so worried and so uncomfortable in the too-small seat that Dassa actually felt sorry for him.

She smiled. The Yasha's grace was truly sufficient.

25

Dassa drove up hill and down, through tracts of wild wasteland and past shapeless, empty houses barely visible through smothering foliage. The desolation of this place would have suffocated her heart if not for the Yasha's comforting presence.

Pik seemed uncharacteristically silent as he watched their progress through his closed window.

"You've never been out of the city before, have you?" she asked.

He turned to her, banging his head on the top of the bubble. "What?"

"You've always lived in a city. Have you ever been in the suburbs before?"

"What suburbs? I'd call it wilderness."

She chuckled. "Oh, we've got wilderness, but this isn't it. Look at all the houses, every half-kilometer or so. This is a residential area."

"Of course. We're on Gannah. It can only get worse."

She turned down another road, plunging deeper into the forest, and then, after several minutes, onto a once-familiar track that was now nothing but a grassy break in the trees. The weeds flattened beneath the vehicle and sent motes and seeds flying as the truck hovered down the lane to the yellow stone house in the hollow.

Something in her gut twisted painfully at the sight. It was barely recognizable as the home she'd left four years before. Waist-high lawn obscured the flowerbeds, and verdant vines half-hid the house in an aggressive green embrace. The roof remained intact, though, and the structure still appeared sound.

She set down the truck at the end of the lane in front of the house. Pik's discomfort at being crammed inside must have overcome his fear of the outdoors, because he wasted no time throwing open the door and peeling his Karkar-sized frame out of the Gannah-sized interior.

He surveyed the house as he slowly straightened the kinks. "It's awfully small."

She exited more gracefully but with a heavy heart. "It's not Armown, no."

"And it's round."

"Of course. Square buildings are funny looking. Do you know anything in nature that's square?"

"I don't know much in nature of any shape. But buildings are supposed to have square corners." He lifted his pack from the truck's cargo area. "So now that we're here, what are we doing?"

Dassa's stomach answered with a loud growl, but she felt compelled to translate for it. "Food is the first order of business. I'd like some fish. How about you?"

He cocked his head sharply, the Karkar gesture for *Huh-uh, no way.* "I've had lunch already, and I brought supper." He gave his pack a demonstrative shake. "I don't think my digestive system could handle Gannahan food."

"Mine probably can't either, anymore." It clenched in confirmation. "I expect to be sick all night. But I don't care. I've waited four years for real food."

She turned and headed for the motorhangar. Pik swished through the tall grass after her, holding his bag aloft.

She opened the hangar door and rodents skittered in every direction. Pik jumped back with a drawn-out Karkar expletive.

Once inside, Dassa's eyes quickly adjusted to the dim light. It was all so familiar and yet so strange. She pulled a tub down from its nail on the wall, shook an abandoned birds' nest from it and scraped out thick webs with a stick.

Then, carrying the tub by one rope handle, she headed outside and around the house, where she found the vestiges of the path that led to the stream. Still holding his bag above his head, Pik tagged along with careful steps, touching as little of the encroaching vegetation as possible.

They entered the fragrant woods. At the first intake of breath, Dassa felt awash in the feeling that always overtook her here, the sensation of being in her Creator's embrace and right where she belonged. As she shuffled through the colorful fallen spring leaves, a chill of mixed delight and bereavement she could never have described rippled through her.

After a short hike they emerged from the trees into a small clearing where the path continued on, evidently maintained through regular use by wildlife. Dassa followed the descent down a gentle slope to the stream. There she lowered the tub and allowed the water to swirl into it.

Pik stood back and watched. "I don't know much about fishing, but I'm pretty sure you won't catch anything that way."

"No, but I can rinse the tub out." When it was clean enough to satisfy her, she filled the tub halfway then dragged it onto the grassy bank.

"I still don't know what you're doing."

"You'll see."

It was spawning season, and fat keceph glittered everywhere, heedless of her intrusion into their shallow breeding ground. Her mouth watered in anticipation.

Pik squinted against the sunlight glinting from the water. "There's no shortage of them, is there?"

"Not at this time of year. Try finding them in the fall, though."

He snorted. "I have no plans to be here then."

She removed her shoes and without rolling up her pantlegs waded into the knee-deep water, relishing the raw chill of the rippling stream, the earthy hominess of the coarse silt beneath her feet. She stood crouched, unmoving, arms outstretched and ready.

After a moment she plunged in her hands, snatched a wriggling keceph and threw it into the tub on the bank in one deft move. A moment later she tossed in another, then a third.

Gratified she still had the touch, she waded back to shore. "Want to help me carry this up to the house?" She grabbed a handle of the tub with one hand and both her shoes in the other.

Pik grabbed the other handle, and together they plowed back up the weed-choked path.

They set the sloshing tub in the shade of the house. Pik's sunburned face had reddened further from the exertion. "Why didn't you just carry the fish, instead of this whole tub of water?"

Dassa brushed off one foot and pulled her shoe back on. Going barefoot never used to bother her, but that little walk had proven uncomfortable. "Because once they're out of the water, their flesh starts to deteriorate and creates a foul-tasting chemical reaction." She pulled on the other shoe. "They're also best cooked over an open fire." She surveyed the broken limbs scattered about. "I'll have no trouble finding fuel."

As she cleaned out the grill pit, Dassa pictured Rosh, shirtless and brown, building it eight years before. Remembered the family gatherings. Heard the boys' shrieking laughter echo from the trees. Swallowed a throatful of tears.

Pik watched with palpable fascination and dread as she built the cook fire.

"Have you never seen fire before?"

He eyed the flames warily. "In the domes of Karkar, what you're doing would bring the Environmental Police down on our heads faster than you could say *oops*. No open flame is permitted on any League vessel or space station, either. In my world, starting a fire is criminal."

"That's true." She nodded thoughtfully. Could what she'd been interpreting as cowardice be an indication of cultural differences rather than character deficiency?

Perhaps. But he was annoying nonetheless.

Once the fire was established, Dassa headed for the house, with Pik following like an unpleasant memory.

The air smelled stale and abandoned. A thick layer of dust coated everything, and the handiwork of four generations of web-spinning weaverrats draped the walls and furniture.

She had expected that. What surprised her was Pik's remark upon entering the little kitchen. "Ah, the dishes are washed."

Puzzled, she blinked up at him. He looked and sounded terribly alien in this setting. "What?"

"At that other place, the plates were left on the table."

She shrugged off his criticism and tried to concentrate on planning her meal. "We had other things to think about in those days."

"Had you no scrubbots?"

She opened a cabinet and surveyed its contents. "We don't use scrubbots. They're demeaning."

Pik stared at her from his unnatural height, his head nearly grazing the ceiling. "No, cleaning is degrading. Scrubbots free humans from having to do it."

Dassa popped the lid off a bottle of oil and sniffed then wrinkled her nose. Rancid. "Keeping one's home clean is a privilege. To serve a loved one in that way is an honor, much like giving them a gift. It would be as unthinkable to use a 'bot to clean as it would be to… to use a machine to hug your child."

"That's warped." Pik sneezed and pawed webs from his face. "What do you have to knock these down with, other than my head?"

She opened the door to a narrow closet and pulled out a long static-duster, after freeing it from its own cluster of webs and shaking off a miniscule but angry weaverrat.

Pik stepped quickly aside as the creature skittered past, leaving a tiny trail in the dust. "Got enough spiders around here?"

"They're weaverrats."

Ears tilting back with distaste, he watched it disappear into a crack under the cabinet. "Rats don't spin webs."

"It's not really a rat, not even a rodent. That's just what we call them. But it is a mammal." She took a grill pan to the sink and turned on the spigot. It belched and coughed, then regurgitated a stream of mud-colored water. "I'll let it run awhile. It should clear soon."

An hour and a half later, Dassa spread a bright cloth on the outdoor table and laid out their dinner. Pik might rather have a roof over his head, but she craved the fresh Gannahan air.

Once everything was laid out to her satisfaction, she stood and sang the evening blessing. All seven verses. Pik had manners enough to wait, but he made no effort to conceal his annoyance.

Finally, they sat down to eat. She'd rounded up a perfect meal, one item from each of the five nutritional color groups. Enjoying the freedom of using her fingers instead of clumsy utensils, Dassa ate grilled fish seasoned with fresh herbs for the blue group; aox roots roasted in the coals for white; a mix of wild greens and blossoms tossed with vinegar for green and yellow; and for red, pickled qishshu that she'd bottled herself five years ago. With all this she drank a special blend of qay from the juice bar. She'd intended to share it with Rosh when he came home, but there was no reason to save it now.

The meal was complete but eaten in haste by the usual standards. Ordinarily a full dinner would be shared with family and friends and eaten over a couple of hours. The courses would be separated by breaks of song, and often dance, and the event would provide sustenance to the soul as well as the body. But since there was no one to join her in this celebration, she ate in silence, savoring every bite. The Gannahan flavors were richer and more complex than she'd remembered.

Across the table, Pik lingered over a travelration of spaghetti with meatballs washed down with lukewarm distilled water. He pushed the pasta around with his fork, staring down at it as if willing it to taste better.

When they were finished, Dassa chewed a freshly cut mintstick in deep contentment. "Now that was food."

Pik eyed her empty plate, his ears tipping in what she interpreted as regret. "It did smell good."

"It was better than good." She sucked every trace of flavor from her fingers then cleaned her hands with the damp napkin that was part of every Gannahan place setting. "But we'd better get inside before the storm hits."

"Storm?" His ears stiffened in alarm.

"The music has changed. Can't you hear it?"

He paused to listen. "I think I can, now that you mention it."

They gathered up their things and carried them in. The dishwasher was in need of repair before she left, so she didn't have to wonder if it worked.

Apparently washing dishes by hand was a new experience for Pik, but he took instruction without complaint—which was a new experience for Dassa. Before they finished, the sky grew dark and the wind roared through the forest, sending the spring's shed leaves fleeing in panic. Watching out the window as she dried her plate, Dassa smiled. She loved a good storm.

Once the kitchen was tidy, they went into the sitting room. Still holding the dishtowel, she surveyed the mess. "I feel like I should clean the whole house. But I guess it would be pointless."

"Yes, it would be." Pik went to the largest piece of furniture in the room. "What's this, some sort of old-fashioned piano?"

"We call it a hammerstring, but yes. Hoseh and his men brought musical instruments of every description from Earth. Craftsmen spent the next couple of centuries perfecting the art, though they made few improvements on the original designs."

With the dishtowel, she wiped the dust from the panel covering the keys, then lifted it and cleaned off the ivories as well. "Until then, Gannahan music was almost entirely limited to vocals. We had a variety of percussion instruments, but the sophisticated instruments Hoseh's men brought, as well as the concept of written notation, created quite a sensation."

While she cleaned, Pik looked at a portrait, in bas-relief like those he'd seen in the toqeph's quarters, atop the piano. "Wedding picture?"

She nodded. Even after four years, she couldn't think of Rosh without aching. The pictures of the boys displayed on either side of the wedding portrait turned the ache into a sharp pang, and she turned her eyes away.

"You were a handsome couple."

Dassa couldn't answer. Feeling drawn to the instrument like a bird to song, she sat on the piano stool she'd just wiped off. "Would you mind if I played?"

Pik's gaze darted around the room. "I don't see your videoscreen. Where is it?"

She nodded toward the far wall. "In that cabinet over there. We don't use it much except for educational purposes." Aware of his surprise but not bothering to explain further, she skimmed her fingers silently over the keyboard, relishing the native Gannahan workmanship.

He set his pack on the floor and crammed himself into an upholstered chair, creating a fog of dust, then waved his hand before his face to clear the air. "Go ahead and play, then. Serenade me."

"Don't expect much. I'm just going to plink around."

He pulled a notebook from his pack. "I'll tune you out while I work on updating my journal."

The promised rain now tapped at the windows, urged by a moaning wind.

"Do you think?" Dassa asked over the clatter.

"What do you mean?" He pressed the On button, but nothing happened. Not the first try, nor the second.

Lightning flashed in savage fury, and the ground trembled at the thunder's wrath.

"Outside batteries don't work here."

"Of course they do. Our messengers worked when I was here the last time."

"I noticed that, and it surprised me. It must have been an act of God."

Pik put away his notebook in obvious disgust as a flash of lightning brightened the room. "Never mind. I'll listen to you. Plink away."

Thunder drowned his last word and made the picture frames on the piano vibrate with a humming music of their own.

Dassa's fingers curved over the keys, and she pressed one down. The single note rang thin and lonely.

This had been her Great-aunt Zilpah's piano, given to Dassa when Zilpah died.

When she died. Would that all Gannahans could die as Zilpah had, in the fullness of age, surrounded by family. Family who lived on.

Dassa closed her eyes and allowed her fingers to travel where they would. They caressed the smooth, familiar keys, playing the comforting notes they had practiced before, years before, a lifetime before, when Gannah still lived. When her meah was knit with others. When she had loved, and was loved, and was full of love.

She rested her forehead on the instrument, listening to the music that flowed from her heart to her fingers. Watering the keys with her tears. Beyond the unbreakable Gannahan glass window, Gannah howled in mourning.

The bed was too short, of course. Pik wouldn't have expected anything different.

Too short and too rustic. Hard as a brick and altogether alien. He was used to a custom mattress with temperature control, light-blocking shades, and a sound-deadening wrap-around with built-in white noise producer. How was he to sleep under these primitive conditions?

The rain still pelted the roof, and the wind whined around the windows like a rabid animal. Knees drawn up to his chest, he pulled the heavy covers over his head. They rasped against his sunburn like sandpaper. At least the thick, upholstered walls kept the cold from creeping in.

Soon his body heat warmed the bed, the sound of the rain soothed like a lullaby, and he uncovered his face. The cool air refreshed and calmed him. He might not actually sleep, but he wasn't excruciatingly uncomfortable. Maybe he'd be able to get a little rest after all.

When he opened his eyes what seemed like moments later, new, gray light stole around the edge of the blinds. He tried to straighten his cramped legs but the bed frame prevented them from unfolding.

A strange sound had awakened him. Had he really been asleep? And what was he hearing?

Singing? Yes. A woman's voice. Dassa's. Full-throated but muffled, as if she were outside. Pik buried his head, but sleep had left him. He had to stretch his limbs.

He yanked the cover off the bed and wrapped himself in it as he stood. Tried to open the blinds, but couldn't figure out how to work them. Of course. Nothing on Gannah was sensible. He gave up.

Bare feet slapping on the cold, gritty floor, he followed the sound of the singing.

The house was as circular inside as well as out. A narrow hall ran around a small center area that Dassa called the grayroom, though she didn't explain its purpose. The various other rooms branched off that hall, each with at least one window and a curved exterior wall. It was merely a matter of walking around the circle until he located the source of the sound.

He found his way into the dining room. Its window, without blind or drape, looked onto the patio where they'd eaten last night.

The Gannahan was out there, but that wasn't what first caught his eye.

A coating of ice glazed the woods, glimmering in the dawn like stars in a gray sky. He knew Gannah to be a place of stunning contrasts, but he'd never expected burning sun one day and frostbite the next.

Dassa was out there in the freezing weather without a coat. Not only singing, but dancing, breath billowing. With her head thrown back and arms raised, it reminded him of her position when she prayed before meals.

He spied a book lying open on the dining room table. A book with the binding on the left. On Gannah, that meant a Bible. She must have been reading it, worked herself up into a fit, and dashed outside to indulge in this preposterous dance.

He felt a little sick at the thought that he was alone with this mad creature.

She did look savage, having changed from her civilized clothes into the stereotypical wild-Gannahan attire. Both men and women were usually pictured in dark blue or black pants of some sturdy and unfashionable material, cut in a crude, loose-fitting style. Usually they wore a short tunic, decorated with embroidery for men or smocking for women. Her tunic now was heavy and long-sleeved. Her ankle-high, dull-finished shoes covered the entire foot, and the pant legs were stuffed into the tops. No sense of decency at all.

Ears frowning, he watched through the window. She sang in Gannahan gibberish, but her motions were easy to interpret. She was worshiping. Praising the God who had wiped out her entire race. She danced for joy when she should have been shaking her fist and cursing. The Yasha, or Bara, or whatever she called him, stole all she had, all she was, all she ever hoped for. He'd cruelly wrenched her whole life away, trampled her into the dirt and spat on her. And she worshiped him.

She was stark raving mad.

Behind her, the awakening sun's rays suddenly burst upon the world, illuminating the ice-laden trees. Rainbows glowed from every leaf and twig as the glittering forest echoed Dassa's joyous praises.

It was a glimpse of astonishing beauty, and Pik gaped. But rather than being speechless with appreciation, he quaked with a surge of unexplainable terror. He'd never felt so isolated, so separated. He was alone not only in this untamed, unknowable world, but estranged from the entire universe.

On rubbery legs, he turned away from the glowing vision, staggered back to the bedroom and fell onto the mattress, covering his head with his hands.

26

Pik's bloodshot eyes widened in shock at what they saw in the mirror.

His face, though less red than it had been last evening, was streaked with brown from the tea he'd smeared on the sunburn, and blisters swelled beneath the stain.

Worse yet, a stubble of beard emerged through the mess despite the hair-inhibiting lotion he slathered on religiously twice each day. And since batteries didn't work here, he probably couldn't even use his razor.

He found it in his bag and pressed the On switch. Nope. No good.

Pik's peeling ears tilted sadly. He'd never been in such a spot. How could he apply cosmetics over whiskers? But how he could *not* wear cosmetics, with that terrible stain on his skin? He smoothed lotion over his bristles. One way or another, he'd have to cover those streaks. How had he allowed her to convince him to smear tea on his face?

He had to admit, though, the crude treatment eased the pain. Unlike this lotion, which made his eyes water from the sting.

He slumped in defeat. There was no one here to see him but the Gannahan, and he certainly had no need to impress her. He washed off the lotion, taking care not to rub too hard, and smeared on more tea. Soothing. He just hoped she was right about the stain not being permanent.

While he performed his ablutions, Dassa came into the house after an apparently successful hunt for food. When Pik joined her in the kitchen, she was assembling an omelet made from two large yellow eggs she must have snatched from some bird's nest, a nasty-looking assortment of freshly harvested herbs, and a red fungus the shape of a Glenmarrian's ear.

She looked up and smiled. "Good morning. Sleep well?"

"Passably, thank you." Pik mixed his powdered breakfast shake with bottled water, glad he didn't have to eat things picked off the ground or excreted by a bird. He knew his forefathers subsisted on that sort of diet, but thank science for freeing his generation from such an awful fate. It's a wonder the species survived.

When he sat at the table across from Dassa—who deemed it necessary to sing another prayer first, as if she hadn't done enough of that earlier—he lost enthusiasm for his sterile, scientific meal. The mix was the same brand he'd been drinking the whole trip, but today it seemed gritty and tasted vile. Quite a contrast to the rich aroma of Dassa's breakfast.

She rolled the steaming omelet into a tube and ate it with her hands, then licked her fingers with evident pleasure. After that, she cleaned her teeth with another of those minty twigs. She chewed it up, flossed with the fibers, and left the masticated pulp on her plate.

Pik's stomach turned. He imagined a roomful of grunting Gannahan savages in their grotesque embroidered shirts, elbows on the table, eating with their hands, then gnawing their sticks like gikdogs. To think, if not for Karkar ingenuity, these slobs would have conquered the galaxy.

While he contemplated the matter in disgust, a belch rose from his stomach, tasting like artificially flavored strawberry bile. He tried to wash the taste away with distilled water, but it didn't help.

Dassa's stomach gurgled audibly, and she winced.

The doctor knew the signs of intestinal distress when he saw them. "Are you ill?"

"A little. Excuse me." She hopped up and hurried down the hall toward the bathroom.

Pik remembered her prediction that the food probably wouldn't agree with her. Why did she eat it, then?

For something to do while she was gone, he cleared the table and washed the dishes. He burped again, and the taste almost made him gag.

He was drying the omelet pan when she returned, looking a little pale. He surveyed her with a professional eye. "Are you all right?"

"You did the dishes? Why, thank you!" She put away the clean plates he'd laid on the counter. "Yes, I'll be fine. It's taking a little time for my system to adjust to real food, but I'm over the worst of it. Kind of you to ask."

"I am your doctor, after all. Or at least, I used to be. Are you feeling well enough to do what you came here to do?"

She picked up the bottle of juice she'd opened last night and emptied it into a glass. "Absolutely. Good thing, too. We haven't time to waste." She sipped the juice with an expression of bliss then extended it toward Pik. "This is wonderful. You should taste some."

He picked up the bottle and sniffed the opening, and his mouth watered. "How can I taste it? It's gone."

"I'd be happy to share this with you."

And get sick too? "No, thank you." He set the bottle back down. "So what are your plans for today?"

She drained the glass. "I want to collect clothes and other things from the house. Then I'll dig some roots, take cuttings, and gather soil to plant it all in. I don't know yet how well Gannahan plants will grow under artificial light, but I'd like to experiment."

Pik grabbed the empty glass and washed it along with the juice bottle. The Gannahans might not have used alcohol, but he'd seen a collection of bottles like these at the palace that would put a wine connoisseur's cellar to shame. He almost regretted not trying a sample when he had the chance. "And after that?"

"We'll go to the library in Ayar."

He replaced the clean, towel-dried glass in the cabinet. "Ah, yes. Your quest for history."

"I have a number of things I want to pick up there, but it's much more than just a library. You'll enjoy the visit."

The only thing he'd enjoy about this visit was ending it, but he didn't want to be rude. "I suppose a library would be as good a place to spend the afternoon as any."

"You probably won't want to leave. Meanwhile, feel free to poke around here. If you see something you like, it's yours."

His ears twitched. "I wouldn't take your things." As if he'd even want them.

"Why not? The *Swordfish* crew is getting souvenirs. Why shouldn't you have something to take home? You might even be able to sell it and make a bundle."

She had a point. Her living expenses, her education, and this extravagant trip were entirely financed by the sale of her late husband's belongings. From that perspective, he sat on a dragon's hoard. With the dragon dead. "How much can we carry on the shuttle? Do you know its weight capacity?"

"Dmitry assured me we can safely stuff it to the rafters. I hope he's right, because I intend to do it."

Pik reconsidered, but it still didn't seem right. "How can you give these things away? That lahab of Hoseh's, for instance. It's a national treasure. How can you part with it so casually?"

"I do not give it casually." She spoke slowly. "Leaving it to rot on an unpeopled planet achieves nothing. It can bring no one back. Parting with it enables me to one day return, bringing more people with me. It's an investment in the life of Gannah."

He snorted. "You can't actually believe that. Who would come? No one would leave a safe, decent, civilized life for… for this forsaken place."

"They will." She smiled. "I have it on good authority."

Pik's ears jerked. Positive thinking was all fine and good, but Dassa was delusional.

While Dassa dug and gathered, Pik explored the house, garage, and grounds, but he made sure the Gannahan was always in sight. He also kept an eye out for wild animals. Several smallish creatures did make wary appearances, but none stuck around for long. Dassa seemed able to communicate with them, both verbally and through motions, and the conversations didn't appear to be friendly. But at least the animals left them alone.

The more he looked around, the more interesting things he found. Knowing space was limited, he couldn't decide what to bring. But this was only their second day here. Maybe later he'd find the perfect souvenir.

The morning sun chased away the chill, and before long Pik was warmed through. Dassa gave him a hat of Rosh's to keep the sun from burning him further. It was the same sort Knapsack wore on the road, a crazy thing with a wide brim all around. It looked barbaric, but it kept the sun off.

He'd grown bored following Dassa around, and his stomach was rumbling when she closed the lid of a truck compartment over the last of the things she'd gathered, then wiped her hands on her pants and looked up at Pik. "I could use some more of those fish. Shall I catch some for you, too?"

Mentally inventorying the contents of his backpack, he hesitated. It would be hard to watch her eat another good meal while he choked down a lab-created food substitute, but he was afraid of what might happen if he ingested anything Gannahan.

On the other hand, Dassa's distress had only lasted a few hours. "How sick did that supper last night make you?"

She shrugged. "It wasn't life-threatening."

"The library we're going to after lunch has bathrooms?"

"Of course."

He stiffened his back with resolve. "Catch me some fish, then, and catch me a lot of them. If I'm going to be ill, I might as well make it worth my while."

On the patio an hour and a half later, Pik leaned back in his chair, the brim of Rosh's hat shading his eyes. He watched the blue-green leaves of a nearby tree dance in a breathy breeze as he chewed a fresh-cut mintwood twig and waved an insect from his face. "I was just thinking about my favorite Karkar meal."

Dassa put her chewed mintwood on her plate and picked up her napkin. "Oh?"

Ears smiling, he envisioned the scene. "My mother used to make the most delightful kcht balls, lightly browned and simmered in a tangy rallalta sauce, served on a bed of yellow nnahsnnahs. That, with a salad of fermented zikzak, and jellied yteeeek for dessert, has long been my idea of the perfect meal. But this—" Pik nodded at the table before him. "This makes it seem like swill. Never have I tasted the like of this meal."

She chuckled. "I hope you'll still have pleasant memories after it hits you in the gut."

"I can't imagine being sick enough to regret this. At last I understand why you find all other foods so disappointing. How long does it take before one's system adjusts to Gannahan fare?" He was already looking forward to whatever exotic delights she'd rustle up for them next.

"Usually fourteen to twenty-one hours, but who knows? I'm sure you're the first Karkar ever to set foot here."

Pik slid a mintstick fiber through a gap in his teeth and removed an errant morsel of something still delicious. "No self-respecting Karkar would consider it."

"You're here."

"I quit respecting myself when I realized my father was a Terrestrial." He sucked the last few drops from his empty goblet. "Any of that juice stuff left?"

Dassa picked up the bottle she'd opened for lunch and poured him the rest. If this was a common, every-day beverage like she said, he was afraid the good stuff, should he ever have occasion to indulge, might send him into paroxysms of delight.

"I never dreamed a non-alcoholic beverage could be so satisfying to body and soul."

"Actually, this one is mostly water. The first bottle I opened was less dilute. On Gannah, juice blending is as refined an art as winemaking or brewing is on oth—" She stopped in mid-sentence and stared at him.

Pik spun around to see what monster lurked behind him. Seeing nothing amiss, he turned back to her. "What's wrong?"

She blinked, still looking at him in something like shock.

"Are you quite all right?"

At last she seemed to come to herself. "You've breathed the air, drunk the water, and eaten the food grown in the soil."

"Yeah, so what?"

"According to the old saying, that means you're a Gannahan."

His ears sneered. "I've also swum in the ocean on Eutare. Does that make me a Eutarian seal?"

Her laugh sounded mirthless.

"I shall never be a Gannahan. That is a preposterous suggestion, like everything else involving superstition and religion, which are one and the same. Completely preposterous." His manner was languid, particularly for a Karkar. For some reason the flare of indignation he should have felt lay smothered by the contentment of that amazing lunch.

She shook her head. "Gannah is in you. From now on, nothing will ever be the same."

Pik laid his mintwood pulp on his plate. "I was never, am not now, and never will be a Gannahan."

She gathered the dishes without looking up. "*Never* is a big, big word."

27

After lunch, they returned to the palace, where Pik helped Dassa load the shuttle with the things she'd collected. Then he crammed himself into the tiny truck bubble again and they took the Ayar Highway toward the capital city.

While she drove, Dassa explained how Gannahan cities were laid out. The central chatsr, a circle of buildings around a plaza, served as the main downtown area. From this hub, two or four spokes of roadway emerged, each leading to another chatsr. The larger the city, the more of these circles subsequently branched out. A major city like Ayar had several dozen, whereas some small towns had only one or two.

Each chatsr had a particular function. Since Ayar was the capital city, the central section was for government offices, as were two of the four circles attached. Other chatsrs were residential, and some housed various businesses, but three kinds of buildings were found nowhere on the planet: banks, because there was no such thing as money; schools, because education was not institutionalized; and churches, because no Gannahan ever thought to build a structure with such a limited purpose. Congregations met in homes, parks, auditoriums, or other locations.

As they neared Ayar, Pik pointed toward what looked like concentric rings hovering above the city. "What are those? Elevated railways?"

"They're roads. Gannahan railways are all underground, and there are plenty of them. There's no need for people to use surface vehicles like this very often, and for those who do, city traffic is kept at a minimum by keeping the bulk of it overhead. You can drive to the city and park beneath whatever chatsr you choose, but to get around from one circle to another, you must either walk or take the rail."

The highway rose gradually until by the time they reached the most outlying chatsr, they were well above the buildings, yielding Pik a clear view of the city. And the destruction he saw struck him with new force.

When they were at Dassa's house, it had been easy to imagine people living nearby, unseen. But looking down at the vacant metropolis, he couldn't forget that millions had died on this strange planet. Hundreds of millions. Pik couldn't fathom the deaths. The solitude—the knowledge that there were only the two of them on this vast, empty globe—nearly crushed him.

It seemed impossible, but there it was. Unending desolation that stretched to the horizon and infinitely beyond.

Dassa was silent as well. A glance her way revealed a face taut with pain. The weight of her loss thinned her lips, bleached her complexion. Not knowing what to say, he said nothing for several minutes.

Staying on the outside ring of road, the little vehicle skirted one cluster after another of empty buildings in disrepair, overgrown lawns, abandoned vehicles, unkempt gardens and forlorn playgrounds, all devoured by rampant vegetation and taken hostage by wild animals. A pack of bushy-tailed canine-looking creatures roamed like a gang of thugs, scattering in alarm as the truck passed above them. A grazing herd of humpbacked beasts with enormous flat feet turned and looked up. On the road ahead, a family of brown furry somethings waddled along in the opposite lane, their mother scolding them to stay in line.

If not for the recent neglect, the whole city would have looked like a park. Pik saw no tacky business districts, no substandard housing, nothing to break the theme of natural beauty and quality workmanship.

Pik broke the silence. "Are you trying to impress me by avoiding the bad parts of town?"

She glanced over at him, brows raised in a question. "There are no bad parts."

"Of course there are. Every city has run-down neighborhoods."

"Only when people don't have money to maintain them. That isn't an issue on Gannah. When something needs to be fixed, you call a repairman."

A flock of birds swooped down on one of a different species, which they commenced to torment without mercy. Pik turned his eyes away, sickened by the bloody sight. What a place this was. "Who paid the repairman?"

"Nobody pays him, just as nobody pays the storekeeper for his goods nor the factory worker for his labor nor the doctor for his services."

"You mean you could walk into a store and take what you wanted without it being charged to your account?"

"That's correct."

"Sounds like chaos."

"On other planets it would be, but it's worked on Gannah for thousands of years."

Dassa maneuvered the truck around a cluster of abandoned vehicles. Pik didn't want to look what was inside them nor imagine why they were left there, and she continued the discussion without interruption.

"Housing and possessions are made available according to your educational level. People at Level Three or below are entitled to modest homes and basic provisions. Fours and Fives shop in nicer stores and have larger houses. Sixes and Sevens are entitled to better quality yet, and Nasi have the best of everything."

He pointed to a residential area to their right. "You were a Nasi, but your house was nowhere near as nice as those down there."

Dassa nodded. "That's because Rosh was only a Five, as was I when we married. I might have been the toqeph's daughter, but that entitled me to nothing beyond my own level." She sighed. "Other than to call the toqeph 'Abba' and eat at his table. But besides that, Rosh and I loved that house. We could have had a nicer place once I continued my education, but we liked it there and wanted to stay."

Pik's ears sagged, perplexed. "What if a person were lazy and didn't want to work?"

"That does happen occasionally. In such a case, the offender is visited by a local constable to ascertain if there's a legitimate reason why he's not contributing to the good of Gannah. He's warned to find something to do. If he fails to obey within a reasonable time, he is conscripted."

"Conscripted?"

"Sent to work wherever he's needed, whether he likes it or not."

Pik felt sick. "You still had slavery?"

"Only under certain circumstances. No one's born a slave, nor made such for no good reason. Nor are they kept in chains or mistreated. Their families can go with them wherever they're sent, and they're all properly fed and housed."

Pik struggled to find words in the standard tongue to express his contempt for such a concept. "That's barbaric. It's horrifying. It's…"

"Is it worse than confining the poor to ghettos? Or rewarding deceit and villainy with wealth and power? Or administering uneven justice based on money or position? Or—"

"I get the picture." Pik's stomach cramped, and he tried to reposition himself more comfortably in the small space. "Our system isn't perfect, but at least slavery is banned throughout the League."

"Officially, yes. But debt keeps people bound in a different kind of slavery. I'm not saying our ways are perfect, but they are more just." She waved at the scene before them. "And prettier. Look out there. No billboards, no garish advertising, no tacky buildings."

"I've been noticing. This was a beautiful, uncluttered city." He tensed as another cramp seized him. If he ignored them, maybe they'd pass. "But how could a system like that work? Competition is healthy. It encourages people to excel."

"Craftsmen take pride in their work for the prestige and satisfaction it gives them. There's no need for manufacturers to cut costs, so everything is well made. Beauty, efficiency, and durability are the goals, not profits. And, of course, the good of Gannah. That's the first aim of every endeavor."

"Sounds like the Karkar Oooptukar, or what the Terrestrials call Utopia."

"Another common legend, like the constellations?"

Pik paused before answering. "Perhaps." He hoped she wouldn't launch into some ridiculous religious interpretation.

His ears winced when she did. "Those legends spring from a universal yearning for Christ's Kingdom, you know."

Pik's low moan was partly from annoyance, but mostly from the pain in his gut.

Dassa looked over at him. "Feeling the effects of that lunch already?"

"I'm afraid so. How far are we from that library?"

She pointed toward a flat hilltop to the left of the elevated road, beyond the city's boundaries. "A few kilometers yet."

Pik squinted at what appeared to be a whole town in flames, but with no smoke. Just a bright, intense burning. "How do you define 'library'?"

She laughed. "It's not on fire, it's reflecting the sun."

"What's it made out of?"

"A lot of glass."

The building glowed so brightly against the blue sky that when Pik looked away he saw spots. His stomach gurgled. "You sure it has a bathroom?"

"Several of them. Barring problems with the road up ahead, it should only take a few minutes to get there."

She accelerated until the truck fairly flew. Pik closed his eyes and tried to relax against the cramps, reminding himself of how good the lunch had been. Yes, it was worth this small discomfort.

Some time later he opened his eyes when he felt the truck slow. They'd descended to ground level and were entering the library's parking area. It seemed small for such a large structure, but he guessed most people accessed the library by underground rail rather than on the surface.

The building rose beyond them, a glistening, multi-story, round-cornered jumble of seemingly disorganized juttings and ells.

"You can't tell from the ground," Dassa said, "but it's in the shape of a leaf from the Tree of Life at Armown."

Pik craned his neck. "Is the whole thing glass?"

"No, but it looks like it, since a solarium runs around the entire perimeter."

The building was reached from the parking area by a walkway through a wooded strip surrounding the library. But Dassa took the liberty of driving directly to the building on what appeared to be a service road. She pulled up in front of the main entrance at the end of a long, narrow glass tube, which she called the leaf's stem.

It felt good to throw open the truck door and unfurl his cramped limbs, but the movement made his stomach churn dangerously.

As they walked toward the entrance, Dassa kept looking around as if expecting something to jump out at them. "I hope the doors are set to manual."

"What do you mean?"

"Ordinarily they're motion sensitive and open when you come near. But if that's the case, any animal tall enough to set off the sensor could walk right in. I hate to think what sort of damage they could do."

"To us or to the library?"

"The library. Books can't defend themselves."

Pik wasn't sure he could, either, and he was relieved when the doors didn't open at their approach. But when Dassa pressed a button on a post nearby and the doors remained closed, her brow furrowed with concern. "If they don't work, we'll have to come up with another plan."

Great. Pik's need for a bathroom was growing urgent. "Break a window? Oh, I forgot. Gannahan glass. So what do we do?"

Dassa put her ear and fingertips to the door. "Press that button. I'll see if anything's happening."

Pik pressed, and she nodded. "It's humming, so there's power going to it. Maybe—whoops!" She jumped back as the door slid open. "I guess it was just a little sticky."

They entered and the door closed behind them. Pik hoped it would be willing to let them out when they were ready to leave.

They passed through the stem and emerged into the solarium, a swath of jungle curving away both left and right. The leaf-littered carpet felt like living ground beneath his feet. He couldn't resist the impulse to stoop and examine it more closely.

"It's not really natural soil, but it looks like it, doesn't it?" Dassa said. "Especially now, with everything so messy."

Pik supposed messy would describe it. Most of the trees on either side of the walkway were leafless, and the plantings beneath and around them were either wildly overgrown, or shriveled and dead. Brown husks of vegetation lay everywhere, entwined with vines, skewered with long, bladelike leaves, or overlaid with drifts of delicate flowers.

"What's that sound?" he asked

"Deborahim." Dassa went to a profusion of yellow flowers, over which crawled and hovered several bulky insects. "Hard at work. I'm surprised they're still alive."

Pik tagged along, curious. "Are they like bees?"

"They are. If not for them, the blossoms wouldn't be fertilized. I hope some of the fruit trees in the other lobes are still alive."

"Bees in the library? Didn't they sting people?"

He stepped back in alarm when Dassa snatched one out of the air.

"Gannahan insects neither sting nor bite." She opened her hand, and the bee walked around her palm, rubbing its wings as if to remove the contamination of her touch. "Some kinds wreak havoc on crops or food stores, but other than their voracious appetites, insects are harmless. It's the mammals and birds you have to watch out for."

Pik's stomach cramped. "And the fish."

The bee left Dassa's hand and flew back to its work. "There's so much to see here," she said, "it's hard to know what to show you first. Let's follow the vein. You can look at the directory and decide where you want to start."

None of that made sense to Pik until he followed Dassa through a glass tube to their left and entered the main body of the building.

The walls lit up as they entered, but these weren't ordinary glowlights. Along both sides of the tube, lighted pictures appeared in the glass, invisible until someone approached. Pictures and diagrams and writing.

"This must be the directory you were talking about." Pik scanned the foreign information, trying to spot the men's rooms with an urgency that mounted by the moment.

"Yes. It shows what each lobe of the leaf contains, arranged according to category. The solarium is along the edge, and the library proper is in the main part of each lobe of the leaf. There's history and geography, which will be my first destination. Here are the sciences—you'll want to check out the medical section, I'm sure. Natural history, religion, music, art—"

Pik stiffened in pain, sweat beading on his forehead. "All I want is the men's room."

"Oh, I'm sorry. Here, look." She pressed a pedal on the floor. The directory flickered out then reappeared in the Standard Tongue. "We're here." She indicated the area where the stem entered the leaf. "And here are the closest restrooms. Right up ahead." She gestured down the tube.

Pik hurried in the direction she pointed, trying to avoid doubling over. "Where will I meet you?" he asked without turning around.

"Don't worry about that, take your time. I won't abandon you."

He thought he heard compassion in her voice, but he didn't stop to think about it. Those fish he'd had for lunch were biting him on the inside, tearing out great mouthfuls, from the feel of it. He dashed through a doorway, hoping it was the right room.

It was. Good thing, too. He didn't have time to keep looking.

28

D assa watched Pik disappear around the corner.

She felt as if she'd been dragged from a dream into an unthinkable reality. In her imagination, the task of rebuilding had been challenging. Now, she saw it was hopeless.

Worse yet, the future husband in her dream was brave, strong, and confident, a man with a gentle smile and sparkling eyes. Not a wan, oversized, blank-faced Karkar with sub-Cephargian character, the timidity of a child, and the disposition of a wounded keleb.

If she'd been honest with herself, she'd have acknowledged all along what the Yasha intended. But now He made it too clear for her to deny, and every fiber of her being yearned to rebel. Marriage to the Karkar — the one thing she couldn't do — was the very thing she must do. How could the Yasha require such a thing?

Dassa wandered down the tube, dreading the thought of going further into the library or into her future. None of the people she used to look forward to seeing would be here. Faces paraded across her mind. Librarians. Friends she'd studied with, mentors who had guided her. Maintenance people, cooks, and servers. Gone. All of them. It was a big planet, a big galaxy. How could there be no Gannahan left in any of it?

Thou art Gannah, my daughter.

She trembled. *It is too heavy, Lord. I cannot bear it.*

Then give it to Me.

Dassa found a reading room, stumbled to a couch, fell to her knees, and melted into tearful prayer.

ooking up at last, she became aware of the time. She must have been here nearly an hour. She rose, rubbing her knees.

Where was Pik all this time? For once, the question evoked no revulsion. Rather, an amused fondness mixed with concern. Odd that she hadn't heard a squawk out of him the past hour, for squawking was what he did best.

She went to the corridor near the men's room, but he was nowhere in sight. Not liking the odor emanating from the room, she tapped on the door. "Pik?"

"I'm here," a weak voice answered.

"Are you all right? Do you need anything?"

He didn't respond, and she waited a few moments before repeating her question. "Are you all right?"

"Not…not really."

She opened the door a crack and nearly retched at the smell. Then, holding her breath, she went in.

He lay on the floor in a pool of sweat, shivering. A puddle of vomit sprawled nearby. The dirty tiles, not cleaned in four years, grimed his face, and his trousers were darkened by bloody feces.

"What sort of medicine," he croaked, clutching his middle, "can you get your hands on?" He jerked in a spasm of pain. "Or something to make me die quicker? This is hell."

She surveyed the situation. "I'll be right back." She turned left, her mind whirring, and took a gulp of fresh air once in the hall.

How many Gannahans had she watched die, or seen their bodies after the fact, lying in their own filth? It was an image, and an aroma, she would never shake. And now here it was again, fresher than fear.

But Pik wasn't dying. He only thought he was.

She took another deep breath. "I shall speak to him, Lord. In Your language."

Guessing she could find what she wanted at the nearest restaurant, she hurried down the corridor until she came to the dining area, then passed into the kitchen, where she tore open cabinets and drawers. Concentrated tamar juice. Spoon. Cup.

One cabinet hummed as if motorized, and a drawer was stuck shut. She guessed some stray deborahim had built a hive in it. Forcing it open, she saw she was right, and with a spoon from another drawer scooped out a dollop of sticky pink honey, wax and all. "Sorry, deborahim, I won't take much."

Dassa turned on both hot and cold faucets to drain the stale water from the pipes. Once it ran clear, she filled a kettle and popped it into the quickheater for tea.

She found cleaning supplies in a back closet and ticked off her needs in her mind as she rummaged. Floor mop, rags, sponges, deodorizer. Towels. She thought some more then took a couple of tablecloths from the dining area.

While the tea steeped, she carried her loot to the room where she'd recently prayed, set everything on a couch, and pushed it down the hall to the men's room, then went back to the kitchen. After pouring the tea into a thermal pot, she stirred in some honey.

She carried the tea and the juice to the couch and set them on the floor beside it. Then she gathered the rest of the things and took them into the bathroom.

Pik was no longer on the floor, but the door to a toilet stall was closed and his long feet, half naked in their silly open-backed shoes, showed beneath.

"I brought you some things," she said as she mopped up the mess on the floor.

A gasp came from behind the stall door, followed by, "What are you doing?"

She poured out deodorizer. "When you're able to come out, you can take off your clothes. There's a tablecloth here you can wrap up in until I can get your bag from the truck. You have a change of clothes in it, don't you?"

"Yes."

Terrible sounds came from the stall, and the deodorizer failed to sweeten the air. "I brought some towels. You can clean yourself up then go out into the hall. There's a couch out there for you to lie on."

More awful noises. "Why?"

"Because it's better than lying on the floor."

"No, I mean…never mind."

Dassa cleaned the floor and two of the sinks, then laid the tablecloth and towels on one of them. After that she cleaned the commode in the stall next to Pik.

"Next time you need to go, use this one. Meanwhile, I'll go out to the truck and get your clothes. Leave your soiled ones here for now, I can wash them later."

He moaned something that sounded like, "Thanks."

Leaving the cleaning supplies in the bathroom, she hurried out, eager for air.

Dassa stopped by the couch, picked up the bottle of tamar juice and took a sip. It was potent enough to make her gasp, but it sent a beautiful warmth spreading from her stomach through her whole body.

Though most often used as a flavoring, tamar juice also had medicinal properties. It wouldn't cure Pik's stomach troubles—only time could accomplish that—but it might help revive him.

She poured several spoonfuls into the teapot then took off jogging toward the main entrance.

At the end of the leaf's stem, she saw the truck through the glass. A scruffy pack of kelebim surrounded it, sniffing. About the last thing she wanted to see.

On Earth they had a saying about a dog being man's best friend, but Dassa couldn't relate to that. No Gannahan animal was ever a man's friend, and canines were among the least trustworthy of the whole vicious lot.

Ten of the slavering creatures milled around the truck, growling with hackles high, probably riled by the foreign odor of Karkar. The largest, struggling to climb into the truck's bed, succeeded as Dassa reached the door.

She didn't relish a fight, but she had to get Pik's clothes. He couldn't spend the rest of the week wrapped in a tablecloth.

The monster in the truck grabbed Pik's bag in his teeth and shook it, slobber flying. She'd have to act fast.

Dassa pressed the button to activate the door, which seemed to consider the matter for several agonizing moments before opening. By the time it finally did, twenty keleb eyes had turned to her and each animal had assumed a menacing crouch. Except the leader, which dropped Pik's bag, put his front paws on the edge of the truck bucket, and bared his teeth.

Hoping they'd respect her authority as toqeph, she waved her arms. "Begone!"

A half-grown pup put its tail down and skittered away then stopped at a distance and barked. The others held their ground.

Dassa moved forward. When two of the animals lunged, she sliced one's throat with her lahab and broke another's jaw with a boot to the teeth. She moved so fast the others fell back, snarling but uncertain. The younger ones had never seen a living human before, and it was unlikely even the oldest had ever met a Nasi.

While they hesitated, Dassa slipped into the truck, slicing the chief's face when he snapped at her. She slammed the door on another when it drew near in its leader's defense.

One keleb dead, another rendered harmless. Eight more to deal with. But she was safe for the moment.

The big black and gray animal in the bucket lunged against glass bubble, smearing it with blood from his dripping face. The others, emboldened, snarled and jumped against the truck until it rocked. She pulled the electrodart from under the seat then lowered the far window enough to maneuver the weapon's muzzle in the crack. It was an easy matter to pick off three kelebim from there. No wasted charge, one shot per kill. She went to the other window, where she finished off one more. The rest kept moving, making themselves more difficult targets. Going from one side of the truck to the other, she killed two more.

The electrodart exhausted, she felt under the passenger seat for the other weapon and came up empty-handed. That's right. Pik had slipped it into his bag when they were at the house yesterday.

The bag that was in the back with Top Dog, who frothed with frenzy.

Dassa watched the two animals for a moment, sizing them up. The tan one wasn't so large, but the leader was more accessible. She'd deal with him first.

With the smaller one on the side of the truck nearer the library, Dassa threw open the far door. When the big keleb leapt for her, she grabbed its throat, threw it to the ground, and severed its neck with her lahab. Blood spurted as the brute writhed and spasmed in death, and Dassa turned to face her last opponent.

Its leader fallen, the last animal took off. Dassa vaulted into the truck bucket and grappled with Pik's bag, searching for the other weapon. There it was.

She looked up. The keleb disappeared into the wood surrounding the library. Dassa leaped to the ground and ran after it, tasting blood. She reveled in the adrenaline rushing through her veins, the power of her legs to run, her hands to kill, and her mind to outwit the enemy. This was what it meant to be a Gannahan. She'd never felt more alive.

Dassa caught a flash of tan through the trees. The keleb had reversed his retreat and sneaked toward her, barely visible in the brush thirty meters away. She smelled his fear, even at this distance.

She slowed to a jog then stopped. Though she wasn't winded, she bent over as if catching her breath, lahab tucked in her left hand and the electrodart in her right, hidden behind her back. She sensed the animal grow bolder and step out of the trees, but she didn't look up. Its panting grew louder as it neared, but still she didn't move. When she could hear its nails clicking on the pavement a few meters away, she stood upright and flung the lahab. The animal leapt, then jerked back and fell as the blade buried itself in its throat.

Holding the electrodart at ready in case the beast should move, she approached and made sure it was dead. Then, smiling in satisfaction, she retrieved her lahab and cleaned it, then turned back to the truck.

Her smile faded at the carnage she'd left in her wake. Already buzzing with flies, animal carcasses littered the driveway. The truck looked like it had been driven through crimson mud. She glanced down at her hands and her clothing, sticky and splattered. The vigor flowing through her body drained out like blood.

She had killed and enjoyed it. Pursued it, lured it, wallowed in it, then looked for more. She was, every cell of her, the bloodthirsty cutthroat everyone thought she was.

She'd just spent an hour in prayer, rising holy and pure and ready to love the unlovable. Smug and self-righteous, she'd performed the sacrificial rites of servitude. Then in a flash, she filthied herself with slaughter, proving herself the worthy heir of Hoseh the Horrible.

The Gannahan sun glared hot upon her, raising the smell of blood from the pavement and the smell of death from the beastly bodies. She threw her head back and shouted at the sky. "I only wanted Pik's clothes!"

The sole answer was a cry of a da'ah circling above, calling its friends to the feast the toqeph had prepared for them.

She closed her eyes against the burning accusation and lowered her head. She was what she was. As was Pik. They were equally flawed, unable to redeem themselves, dependent on the Yasha's grace.

Ten kelebim she could vanquish. But she couldn't kill the truth.

One by one, she dragged the beasts' carcasses across the drive and laid them at the edge of the wood. When she was finished, streaks of red pointed toward the evidence of her fall from grace.

The fountain near the library's entrance wasn't working, but enough rain water lay pooled in the base that she could wash herself off. She went back to the truck and retrieved Pik's bag. Her bloody hands had dirtied everything in it. So much for clean clothes.

It was she who was unlovable. Not Pik.

"I'll be back," Dassa had said, and then left Pik on the bathroom floor. He hoped when she returned, it would be to finish him off. But being a Gannahan, she'd probably only prolong his agony.

Pik castigated himself for his foolishness. He should have known Gannahan food would kill him. Despite this planet's beauty, it was every bit the hell it was rumored to be. But he'd realized it too late. Scolding himself couldn't change what was happening.

Nor could being a specialist in exotic diseases.

This was the rarest condition of any he'd encountered. No doubt he was the only one in the universe to die of it: a Karkar with Gannahan food poisoning.

The pains grew too urgent to be ignored, and he crawled back to that wretched commode, where it seemed he'd spent the last year of his life. The crazy thing flushed as soon as anything entered the bowl. And it flushed with water, not chemicals, and sideways, like a rushing stream. It was pretty alarming when you weren't expecting it. But by now he knew it all too well.

How could there be anything left in him? There seemed to be no end to it. Nor to the pain. If he lifted his head, the room spun like a centrifuge. He didn't want to fall off again.

He was surprised when Dassa returned, though he couldn't say why. He remembered her words as he'd hurried away on his search for the men's room: "I won't abandon you." And she hadn't. She'd come back.

And she cleaned the floor.

This was not something decent people did. Robots kept Karkar floors clean, but it hadn't always been that way. At one time floor scrubbing was the lowest of menial professions, performed only by the grossly impaired, those unable to perform any other function. If something was spilled, it was covered by special floorcloths until the scrubber could come. Nowadays, though, even the most inferior people had bots to do the job. A Karkar would no more manually clean a floor than clean a waste can with his tongue.

But here was Dassa, heir of Atarah King, cleaning Pik's vomit from the floor. He'd have stopped her if he'd been able, but all he could do was weep in shame as he passed who-knew-what into the streaming commode.

Some time later, he sat on the clean floor to remove his ruined clothes and mused that for all her strange and disturbing attributes, this Gannahan did have some good qualities.

Clinging to the sink, he pulled himself up. As he washed, he recalled his previous fantasies about seducing her.

If he weren't so ill, he might have laughed at himself in retrospect. She would obey her Yasha no matter what. Even when it meant denying herself pleasure. Or humbling herself to clean a floor. Had the Yasha told her to do that? She must have thought so, for she would never have done such a thing otherwise.

Yes, whatever else she was, she was faithful to her god.

Faithful. True to her word. Incapable of lying. These were attributes of a civilized people, which everyone knew the Gannahans weren't.

Yet on Karkar, the highest of all civilizations, genuine honesty was rare. He remembered his mother saying, "It's best not to lie, but if you must, the least you can do is sound sincere."

His mother. She'd hate him forever for dying on Gannah. Why had he done it?

His mother. If Dassa had told anyone how much he missed her, he'd never hear the end of it. But no one mentioned it, so he knew she was true to her word.

True to her word. She would bring him clean clothes from the truck.

Too exhausted to wring out the washcloth, Pik left his clothes on the floor and the towels on the sink, wrapped himself in the tablecloth and shuffled out into the hall, where he sank onto the couch.

He had a vague but uncomfortable feeling he didn't deserve the kindness the Gannahan was showing him, though he wasn't sure why not. Almost as if he'd wronged her somehow. But that couldn't be. He'd saved her life. He'd sacrificed everything—including, it now appeared, his life—to come back here with her. By Kankakar, she *should* be nice to him.

But as he shivered under the tablecloth, his gut burning, his head spinning, a cold sweat sliming his body, he somehow felt he deserved this.

29

When Dassa returned, Pik lay huddled on the couch in the hall, his tea untouched.

She called his name softly as she poured him a cup.

He must have heard her approach, because he didn't act startled. "What time is it?"

"About sixteen fifteen, League Standard Time. Take some tea. It'll help prevent dehydration, and the tamar juice and honey I put in it will give you energy."

"Nothing to settle my stomach?"

"Tea sometimes helps, but as sick as you are, it probably won't." She didn't add the obvious fact that since eating Gannah-grown food was the cause of his troubles, no Gannah-grown potion could cure it. "All we can do is keep up your strength until this runs its course. Which it will."

Pik moaned as he sat up. "I wish I could believe that." He pulled the tablecloth tighter around himself and reached for the tea.

"Be careful, it's hot."

Those six-fingered hands looked strange wrapped around the cup. And how could he drink with that immobile face?

He managed somehow. "Tasty."

"Plain eseb tea is kind of bitter, but fancied up like this it's not bad."

He sipped again. "Not bad at all." He tensed up suddenly, no doubt from another stomach spasm, but took a third sip.

"I, ah, haven't had a chance yet to look for the things I wanted. If you don't mind, I'll leave you here for a while. There's more tea in this pot. You should probably drink as much as you can."

"Did you get my clothes?"

"Yes, but it might be better to wait a bit."

"You might be right." He set the cup on the floor and lay down again. "And I think I'd better wait before I drink any more."

"That's fine. I'll be back in a while."

Dassa washed Pik's dirty clothes in a deep sink in the kitchen and sponged the bloody fingerprints from those that had been in his bag. She removed a few pans from their hooks above the stove and hung the clothes there to dry. She had less luck spot cleaning her own garments, as Gannahan fabrics weren't as stain-resistant as Pik's synthetics.

After a quick check on the sleeping Pik, Dassa headed into the main part of the library at last, where she kept busy until well after dark. It felt horribly strange to be alone in this vast building, formerly so full of bustle and life. She hadn't finished with what she'd come to do before calling it a day.

She made Pik more tea then brought him the clothes she'd spot cleaned for him. The others were still damp. While he was in the men's room getting dressed, she found another couch in the lounge and slid it down the hall near his, where she fell asleep under a tablecloth almost as soon as she closed her eyes.

Pik slept and was sick, sipped tea and was sick, slept and was sick again, all night, all the next day, and into the second night. Dassa wasn't always beside him, but the teapot never ran dry. Once, a bowl of clear, rich-flavored broth appeared, and another time a small, tangy fruit she said she'd picked in the solarium. On the second evening, his dashes to the bathroom grew less frequent, and by morning his ordeal appeared to be over.

Dassa smiled down on him when he awoke. "Are you tired of tea yet?"

Pik pushed off the tablecloth and eased himself into a sitting position. The room hardly swam at all. "Not the way you fix it. I think it's the only thing that's kept me alive."

"You wouldn't have died. I don't think. Anyway, breakfast is ready, such as it is. There's quite a bit of food in the restaurant, but not much you'd want in your stomach first thing. How about some more of that baqar broth and a biscuit?"

"A four-year-old biscuit?"

Dassa chuckled. "No, just baked. The kitchen staff had everything sealed to keep out the bugs, and the flour was refrigerated so it didn't go rancid. There's none of that butter you like, but we've plenty of honey."

Pik's mouth watered, and not from nausea. "I think I'm up for the task."

He rose carefully then staggered after Dassa, afraid to move too fast.

"The problem with being tall is your head's at such a dizzying height," Dassa said.

Pik blinked in surprise. "You do read my mind, don't you?"

She answered without turning around. "Your face doesn't show much, but your body language is usually quite vivid."

Looking at her shapely form up ahead—to which her uncouth Gannahan garments gave tantalizing allusions without revealing too much—Pik remembered with embarrassment the fantasies he used to entertain about how they might spend their time on the *Swordfish*. How many of those thoughts had she discerned? And how could he have thought such things about her? She was so foreign, so unrefined. And so—he hated to think it, but yes—so pure.

In the abandoned dining area, a table was set and decorated with fresh flowers. Dassa had cleaned only one small area, but it was enough.

Of course she had to sing the blessing before they ate, but she kept it short, and for the first time, Pik could appreciate the melody's haunting beauty and the quaint charm of the tradition. His stomach rumbled with anticipation, not pain, and the breakfast fit into it as a kjohng in a kjuhkng.

"How are you doing?" Dassa licked honey from her fingers with that disturbing purple tongue.

"If a belly could smile, mine would."

She tipped her head, her expression almost coy. "Could your face smile, do you think? If you'd let it?"

"Of course not."

"I know a full Karkar's can't, but your face is less stiff than is typical of your people."

Why must she destroy the beautiful morning with reminders of his shameful heritage?

"It's Karkar enough."

"Oh, it's plenty Karkar. But I think if you'd allow yourself, you could smile. Maybe not a big silly grin, but a little upturn, don't you think?"

"I don't think. Why would I want to, anyway? Those grimaces you people make look ridiculous."

She wiped her hands on a damp napkin. "Don't you like to see your father smile?"

A dull pain stabbed Pik, not in his gut, but deeper. He took a sip of tea. "What's on the agenda today?"

"I'd like to see you smile." Dassa demonstrated with a smile of her own. "Not today, perhaps, but one day."

"The only way you'll see that is if you alter a photograph."

She laughed then handed him a sprig of mintwood. "Have a stick, Pik."

He took the twig, hoping it would banish the sick taste from his mouth. "I might pick my teeth like a barbarian, but don't expect me to sit cross-legged at the table and eat with my hands."

"You should try it. It's relaxing, good for the digestion." She took a gob of chewed wood pulp from her mouth and placed it in her empty teacup. "And speaking of digestion, I can give you a jar of sand to take home with you."

"Ah, splendid. There's nothing like sand to comfort the stomach."

"Don't laugh. Whenever a Gannahan travels Outside, he takes along some sand from the beaches of the Isles of Yam. It's almost as fine as dust, and a small pinch each day will keep his system attuned to Gannah, so when he returns he won't have to adjust to it again."

"I'll never come back here and neither will you. Gannah is dead. Too far gone for resuscitation."

She skewered him with one of those sharp green glares. "Gannah lives as long as I live. And I'm pretty healthy." She began clearing the table. "But you asked about my plans. I can show you around the library a little this morning. Then after lunch we can check out the airport. Tomorrow we'll fly to Yabbashah. I'll want to start as early as possible, so we can't waste time in the morning looking for a plane."

"What's at Yabbashah?"

The look on her face was hard to read, and she paused before answering. "You'll see when we get there. Tonight, we can stay at

Armown. There are plenty of beds there, and I think we could both use a shower."

He rose from the table. "A shower sounds good. What did you want to show me in the library?"

They left the dining area. "We won't have time for you to do much exploring. I hoped you'd enjoy the science department in particular, but I pulled out a few things to take back to the ship. Though the medical books are in Gannahan, I plan to translate them for you on the *Swordfish*. I've also got information on computer, but Gannahan computer language isn't compatible with what the League uses, and I couldn't get a Translator to work. I'm not sure what you'll be able to do with it. Maybe you can find someone who can adapt the Tappu to a League system and translate the files."

Pik was about to ask what a Tappu was when she said, "That's the type of computer system the libraries use."

She led him at a brisk pace past the entrances to various rooms and wings. Pik's legs ached like he'd walked several kilometers by the time they passed through the entrance to one of the lobes of this huge leaf-shaped building.

"Rather than carry everything all the way back through the building," she said, "I stacked what I'm taking home by the door at the end of this lobe, then parked the truck outside." She gestured toward somewhere ahead of them.

"Sounds like a good idea."

"But, um, I have to warn you" — she tossed a hesitant glance up his way — "the truck is a little messed up."

"How can you mess up a vehicle at a library?"

"When I went out to get your bag the day before yesterday, I had to fight a pack of kelebim for it."

On Gannah? Who'd have guessed. "I hate to ask. What's a kelebim?"

"They're kind of like wild dogs. They were sniffing around the truck when I came out, and one of them was in the back with your bag in its teeth."

"Splendid. So you killed them for it, is that what you're saying? And that's how you messed up the truck?"

She nodded, avoiding his eyes. "The rain yesterday washed off the worst of the blood."

Remembering the quick work she made of the Cephargians, Pik felt his breakfast turn to cold stone in his stomach. He sighed. "I suppose you only did what you had to do."

"That's the way it seemed at the time. Afterward, though, I wished I'd let them take your bag. It wasn't worth killing for."

Surprised at her somber tone, Pik glanced down at her stricken face. What did she have to regret? "That was my bag! And they were just dogs."

"Yes. They were just dogs. But... well, never mind. Let me show you what I got you."

They passed rows of shelves, display cases, computer desks, tables, and more passageways in quick succession, until they reached an exit at the far end of the lobe.

Dassa went to the stack of boxes. She pulled out a book, bound at the top.

"It's a book," Pik said. "I mean, an old-fashioned paper volume. When you said 'books' I was expecting something electronic." Not that he minded. A bound book was a rare pleasure, and a whole box full was a treasure.

"We have those too, but I was afraid we'd have trouble with the readers. I think print books will travel better." She translated the title, "*Anatomical Chemistry*," then flipped through it to show him.

It was full of indecipherable writing, along with pictures and diagrams. "I thought you might find it interesting, once I get it translated." She handed it to him and picked up another. "This one is on nutrition. It tells how particular compounds in various foods contribute to human health. Our lack of disease is in large part due to our diet, you know. The subject has been studied extensively over the centuries, until we now know exactly what to eat, in what amounts and in what phases of our lives, for optimal health and longevity."

She pulled out a third book. "*The Medical Practitioner: A History*. And this one, *The Healing Processes*. I've never read it, but it should explain what happens when we go into a semi-dormant state to effect self-healing. I know you've been wondering about that."

Pik felt light-headed. "Do you realize… I mean… If I could find out what made your people so exceptionally healthy… Why, this could bring the practice of medicine into a whole new era."

"I thought you might like them. There are other things in this box too. I didn't know what you might like. And a few of them, less specific to Gannah, are written in the Standard Tongue. All Gannahans are at least bilingual, you know. We learn the Standard Tongue from childhood."

"Why? I thought you were isolationist."

"Just because you didn't see us doesn't mean we didn't see you. Gannahans have lived and traveled Outside for generations. But we didn't make ourselves known until fairly recently, because our presence tended to make people uncomfortable."

While Pik examined the contents of the box with growing delight, Dassa disappeared into the depths of the library. About the time he began to wonder where she'd gotten to, she reappeared, carrying some small items.

"You asked me awhile back about games," she said. "Here are a few. This handheld might not work off Gannah, but you can try it." She set it down on the stack of boxes, along with three round, silvery discs resembling coins. "Math, logic, and memory games." She held up two more discs. "These, I can show you now. Come on."

Pik followed her around rows of bookshelves, down a short corridor and into a hall with several round doors along it. "Game rooms," she said, and entered one.

"Remember I told you about the Festival of Voices and how the last event is a big dance that everyone participates in, and it goes on for hours?"

"I recall you mentioning something about that."

"Well, it takes a very long time to learn the Festival dance. Children aren't permitted to participate, but they learn it as they're growing up so they'll be ready to dance with the adults when they're old enough. One of the greatest joys of my life was my first dance, when I was sixteen."

Pik glanced down at her pain-tightened face, trying to imagine her as an eager sixteen-year-old. He couldn't. "Okay, so what about it?"

She held up the discs. "These aren't really games, they're training sessions. This is one for children just learning the steps. And this one"—she twiddled the disc between her fingers—"is my favorite. It's a dance-along. I thought—that is, if you're interested—we could do the training so you could learn the steps, then we could play the second one and dance with the holographs."

"With the what?"

"Holographic images doing the dance. We can do it with them."

Dancing with Dassa had been on Pik's mind many times, but he wasn't sure he wanted to share her with a roomful of holographic Gannahans.

She must have read his hesitation. "You want to try the training one? If you don't want to go any further, we don't have to."

"Okay. Let's see how it works."

"It's easy, of course, because it's for children. It starts with the foot positions. All you have to do is put your right foot on the yellow spot and your left foot on the green one. I'll set it for two so I can play along with you. There'll be an instructor hologram, so you can see how it's supposed to look while you're doing it. And of course the song will be playing, so you can see how the steps fit the music. Ready?"

With an unexpected surge of anticipation, Pik nodded. "I guess so, sure."

Dassa slipped the disc into a slot in the wall by the door, punched a few keys on a pad, and the room darkened. Then the image of a smiling Gannahan female appeared in front of them, saying something unintelligible in a voice obviously geared toward children.

"Don't worry," Dassa said. "You'll be able to figure it out."

"Got it."

The room lightened, and Pik found himself in an amazing mountain grotto with sharp cliffs rising on all sides, full of steps and terraces and dwellings.

"The cliff city of Arawts," Dassa explained, "where the Festival is held. The natural acoustics in the plain are amazing."

Before she'd finished speaking, the music began, a simple tune played by a flute-like instrument. In front of Pik, two spots, one yellow and one green, appeared on the floor, which now looked to be made of a pale, sandy stone. A quick glance toward Dassa showed that she had a set of colored spots, too. They each stepped onto the appropriate colors, and the dance began.

It was tricky at first to follow the spots, but he soon picked up the pattern and came to anticipate where they would lead him next. Dassa already knew the steps and danced with confidence and grace, using arm movements the instructor at the front of the room hadn't taught yet.

After a few minutes of practice, the music and the visual backdrop faded away, and the instructor spoke again, making gestures with her arms.

"Same as with the feet," Dassa said. "Right hand on the yellow, left on the green. When there's a blue dot in the center of the spot, palms go up. When the dot's red, palms go down."

"Blue up, red down," Pik repeated. And the dance began again.

Since he already had the foot movements down pat, he could concentrate on the gestures, placing his hands in the spots of light suspended in front of him, now beside him, now up, now down. Instead of watching the instructor, he watched Dassa. He noticed her arms were positioned straighter than his, and her hands extended beyond the spots. Ah, of course, her arms were longer than a child's, which was what this game was designed for. Pik took his cue from her, stretching his arms through the spots instead of placing his hands on them. Yes, that felt better. Probably looked better too.

More body movements were added, then more steps and more gestures. Every time the instructor came on to give explanations, Dassa translated. Before long Pik found it absorbed his complete attention. He wondered how a child could learn it all. And this was just a part of a dance that continued without pause for two hours? Only on Gannah could something so grueling be conceived.

By the time the disc ended, Pik's energy was fading.

"What do you think?" Dassa asked when the cliffs faded from view and the room lights came on.

Pik wished he didn't sound so winded when he answered. "I think your Festival of Song—"

"Voices. Festival of Voices."

"Yes. It must have been fascinating. But I don't think I'm up to dancing with your holographs quite yet. That kids' tape wasn't exactly child's play. How old a child is that game for?"

"Eight or ten. The games that teach the slower sections of the dance are simpler, but the last movement is my favorite. You don't want to do this other disc?"

Pik wished she'd chosen a slower section to start with. It wouldn't have been so tiring, but more than that, he'd like to slow dance with her. "Go ahead and put it in. I'll watch you."

"You sure you don't mind?"

"No, really, I'll sit here and watch the show." He folded himself onto the floor, now revealed in its true form, that of a dense, short-napped carpet.

"All right then, but be forewarned, this one's no kids' game."

Pik wondered what that was supposed to mean, but he didn't ask.

She slipped the disc into its slot, punched a couple of keys, and the room was plunged into darkness.

Pik heard music, faint at first, then growing as the light returned, until he sat in the vast plain below that cliff city amidst a sea of dancing Gannahans.

He clambered to his feet, almost thinking he'd be trampled, though he knew the images had no substance. He stared at them, his pulse racing. The song surged through his ears, into his heart and through his veins.

The images were the most solid, lifelike holographs Pik had ever seen. He could scarcely tell the difference between them and Dassa, who took her place among them. They moved as one, their colorful garments darkened with perspiration. They glowed with exertion, their brows beaded with sweat, and their faces—Pik couldn't keep from staring at those faces. As with any peoples, no two were alike, but young or old, man or woman, fair or swarthy, each radiated a pulsating, passionate joy more deep and inexpressible than Pik had ever known.

He felt an unfamiliar power course through his body, standing his hair on end. The dancers supplied their own music, singing with rapture, in intricate harmonies he couldn't hope to follow. He pressed against the wall, trying to get out of their way, but he was trapped in their midst. They danced over him, about him. Wildly, yet with perfect discipline. As if channeling some power beyond themselves to which they yielded their bodies with willing abandon.

Pinned to the wall by the force of their emotion, Pik's eyes moved from one savage face to another. He thought he recognized two of them from photos in the toqeph's suite. He looked at Dassa, indistinguishable from the holographs in her appearance, movements, and expression. These were her people, her flesh and blood. This was Gannah, in all its beauty and color and vigor, united in common tradition, language, and blood, rejoicing as one in…in what? What made them dance? What put such rapture in their hearts, in their faces? What absolute certainty directed their steps?

Their voices soared to unbearable jubilance, their music rising above Pik's soul, incomprehensible. He imagined he could smell their sweat as they danced about him with no hint of weariness, fueled by a passion bubbling within like an eternal spring.

Many of their faces were wet with tears as well as sweat, and it came as no surprise when Pik realized that his eyes also streamed. The song built to a climax until Pik thought his chest would explode. Then the Gannahans, turning with hands and faces upraised, sank to their knees as one. Their voices grew muffled as their bare heads touched the ground, hands and forearms flat before them, their fading song echoing off the surrounding cliffs.

The images dimmed, the room darkened, and when the light returned, Dassa alone remained, face down, sides heaving, her body shaken by deep, silent sobs.

30

On the drive to the airport, Dassa finalized her plans. There should be several suitable planes in Hangars G and H. She'd find a functional Mahar 440, or maybe a Qol. Yes, that little Qol XT she last flew would be perfect. She'd check it out thoroughly, make sure it—

As she rounded a bend and the airport came into sight, she stopped, stunned.

This was the main transportation hub of the planet, where all underground, surface, and air systems converged. But in its entire, vast expanse, only one structure remained standing—a hangar at the far side of the airport, its half-detached roof flapping in the wind. Skeletons of ruined buildings staggered up from piles of rubble amid a carnage of broken-winged aircoaches, some lying on their backs like poisoned insects. Acres of debris lay strewn across the runways.

Dassa's mind whirred as she surveyed the scene. How would they get to Yabbashah? There wasn't time to drive, even if the roads were unobstructed. Which they probably weren't. The railroad below ground wasn't an option, since Dassa didn't know how to get a train functioning. Nor could she know the condition of the rails between here and her destination.

"What in the world happened?" Pik asked. "Looks like King Kong had a temper tantrum."

She silently mulled their options.

"I didn't know Gannah had giant gorillas."

Dassa looked over at him. "Huh?"

"King Kong. An old Earth tale about a giant ape that ran about terrorizing the world. They must have made fifty movie versions."

"Mmm. Gannah has no primates." She plotted an indirect course across the destruction to the one remaining hangar. It looked like they'd be able to drive all the way.

"Are they all extinct?" Pik asked as the truck moved forward again.

"No, there never were any."

"That's unusual."

She answered without much thought. "I suppose so. Back in the days before evolutionary theory was finally debunked, the Darwinists would have found it quite a conundrum."

"But I suppose you still believe the foolish old myths about Adam and Eve, Aktak and Eeeeio, Atarah and…and whatever the Gannahan equivalent, placed in the Garden by God. "

"Em." Dassa maneuvered the truck around mounds of rubble.

"What?"

"Atarah and Em. In the Garden. Which is what *Gannah* means, by the way."

"What?"

"Garden." She concentrated on negotiating the obstacle course. "Gannah is the garden Atarah and Em were placed in by God."

Pik was silent for a moment. "I see. Was there a snake?"

"No. There are no reptiles of any sort here." Why the pointless questions?

"Interesting. Karkar at least has lizards." He held on as the truck made a sudden swerve around a pile of jagged metal. "This place is a mess. Where do you think you're going?"

"To that hangar over there. That's where I left the aircoach."

"What aircoach?"

Sorrowful memory lay like a leaden blanket on Dassa's chest and she tried to exhale it with a heavy sigh. "Everyone at Armown was dead, and I couldn't raise anyone on the communications systems. Anywhere. So I took a small aircoach and flew all over, looking for signs of life. Couldn't find any. Just chaos. And lots and lots of bodies."

She thought she felt sympathy in Pik's pause. But when he spoke again, his words didn't reflect it. "And that's the hangar where you left the plane. Do you actually think it's okay?"

"Why not? The hangar's still there, isn't it?"

"More or less. But tell me again why it's so important we go to — wherever it is we're going."

"Yabbashah. I can't tell you again, because I never told you the first time."

"Why are you being so secretive?"

She threaded the truck between rows of crumpled toppellors. She'd have to tell him sooner or later, but she'd rather not do it now. "Must have been one monster of a tornado that went through here. More likely, several."

"What's at Yabbashah? If I'm going to fly across a corpse-filled planet, I think I'm entitled to know why."

"You're right, you are." She pulled up in front of the nearly-roofless hangar, shut off the truck and gazed at Pik, still uncertain of the best way to approach the subject. "And I'll tell you, when the time comes. For now, I've got to make sure we have a way to get there."

The sun hung low in the crimson sky when Dassa hovered the truck into the palace courtyard. Nearby, the shuttle sat undisturbed on the pavement.

She'd found the aircoach intact, its batteries registering full. The Yasha be thanked, every system she examined checked out fine. For the next two hours, she and Pik had labored together, opening a wide swath from the hangar to the back runway, which, miraculously, was clear. Pik's size came in handy, and she was grateful for his strength in wrestling with the larger pieces of debris. The effort took its toll, though, after his illness. He drooped with exhaustion as they pulled up to the shuttle.

With the sun setting behind Armown's walls, they unloaded the things they'd brought from the library and packed them wherever the shuttle had a vacancy.

"I hope that's all you're bringing, because we're pretty well full," Pik said.

"Almost. Just one more thing."

"How big is it?"

"I have no idea."

"Will it fit in here?"

Bent over in the back of the landing craft, she turned and scowled. "I told you, I don't know how big it is. But if it won't fit, we'll have to leave some of this behind. It's the most important thing I'm taking."

"I thought you came for all that history stuff? Anyway, we're not leaving my books, I'll tell you that. Let me grab a couple now, I'd like to look at them this evening. And you said this box is food, so you'll want to bring it in."

"Right. And I want the things for Sylvia and Dmitry in the front, so I can unload them first." She had a sudden thought. "Wait a minute, I want to see something." She searched for the leather pouch in the box of goblets. "There was a rumor about these ancient lahabs. I'd like to see if it's true."

Pik rolled his eyes. "What? That they make Karkars bleed?"

"That's not a rumor, it's a fact. But remember how I said a lahab is both a weapon and personal identification?"

"You said it's got your name and a short genealogy etched on it."

She pulled out her own lahab. "Right. But look, the modern ones also have a photo ID." She pressed an indentation beside the center button as she pointed the lahab toward the side of the shuttle, and her headshot appeared, projected on the ship's charred shell. "I was younger then, but there you go. That's me."

"That's a neat trick. You're thinking Hoseh's does that, too?"

Dassa slipped her lahab away and pulled Hoseh's from the pouch. "We'll find out." She studied it with reverence, turning it over, feeling for some sort of pressure point. "Ah. Maybe this will do it." She pressed, but nothing happened. Pressed again, with an added forward motion of her finger.

And nearly dropped the lahab as she jumped back in surprise.

Pik let out a cry of alarm. Atarah Hoseh Charash himself stood before them, a full-body, lifesized, three-dimensional holograph, dancing from the startled movement of Dassa's hand.

"Whoa, that was a bit more than I anticipated," she said, pulse racing. Yearning to study the image further but not wanting to give Pik a heart attack, she released the button and the towering king disappeared.

Pik's eyes bulged. "First you try to poison me, now you want to scare me to death. What do you have against me?"

With an indulgent sigh, Dassa put the lahab in the box and stowed it in the shuttle before closing the aircraft's cargo door. "Nothing. I'm sorry, I didn't expect a life-size projection. "

Pik gathered his books and his backpack, Dassa picked up a bag of personal things and the box of food, and they headed for the main entrance.

"I'll have a hard time getting that image out of my mind." Pik glanced over his shoulder.

Wishing she'd taken a longer look, Dassa tried to remember the hologram's details. "He was an imposing man, wasn't he?"

Pik opened the massive, carved door. "Yes. And I hope that's the last I ever see of him."

"I'll fix us something to eat. Maybe supper will make you feel better."

The glowlights welcomed them, and Dassa led the way.

"I'd offer you a guest suite," she said as they walked, "but I don't care to sort out which have skeletons in them and which don't. We can both sleep in the royal residence, but there's only one bedroom."

"I'd rather sleep on the bathroom floor than share a bed with a dead Gannahan."

"I think we can find something more comfortable than a floor."

In the residence, they laid their burdens on the dining room table, where she unloaded an assortment of foodstuffs from the box. "I'll show you how the shower works. I imagine it's a little different from what you're used to. All the power seems to be working, so you might even have hot water. While you're doing that, I'll fix us something to eat."

After supper, Dassa spread out a paper map on one end of the table. Her black hair, still damp from bathing, hung in tight, spiral curls as she studied the familiar geography. She nearly trembled with excitement and dread at what she was about to reveal.

Across from her, Pik leafed through a Standard-Language book entitled *League of Worlds Economic Systems Explained.* "Intriguing to look at the subject from the Gannahan perspective. But I can't say as I care for the way it's bound at the top."

"It's all in what you're used to. What do Karkar books look like?"

"We have no paper books. Computers are more efficient."

"So is hydroponics. But food grown that way isn't fit to eat, and electronic books are no fun to read."

"If not for hydrofarming, Karkar would starve."

"I understand that. I only mean that efficiency often has its costs. Usually the price is pleasure. Sensual satisfaction. Artistic appeal."

Pik glanced up from the book. "Space is at a premium, and the resources necessary to produce paper and ink are too valuable. Electronic books are all our environment can afford, more's the pity. Because I agree with you. I like the old print volumes better." He paused. "However, we do not lack for sensuality."

She avoided his eye, trying not to use too much imagination on that one. "I'm sure that's true. You merely find it in different places and express it in different ways."

He laid the book aside. "When are you going to tell me why we're going to Yammashah?"

"Yabbashah." On the map, she pointed to the large island off the southwest coast. "It was a fabulous resort spot at one time, with the mildest climate on the planet. But it was the first of Gannah to die."

He rose to get a better look. "How so?"

"The explosion occurred somewhere around here." She drew an invisible circle with her finger on the extreme left edge of the map, far out in the ocean. "And Yabbashah," she tapped the island, "was the first to feel the effects. Ishvah Hanoch Adin, one of the Nasi who helped me when I first returned from my quest, was Governor of Yabbashah. He told me the cloud was the most intense there, and people died quickly. Many in the first day. Their muscles deteriorated within hours."

"Why was he still alive then?"

"Because he wasn't on Yabbashah at the time. He and Natsach Gunni Jachin, who also met me here when I returned, had been at a meeting in Dedan with three other Nasi. Trying to figure out how to prevent my father from doing what he did."

She looked up at Pik then, who studied her with that same, unreadable expression he wore in every situation. Even his pale eyes, as blank as a bird's, revealed nothing.

"You're an unusual creature, Dr. Pik. And though it pains me to admit it, I'm developing a bit of respect for you." The thought had been forming for quite some time, but putting it into words jarred even her.

"What?" His ears twitched.

"Hidden behind your eternal Karkar whining, you have more character than you let on. More, I think, than you allow even yourself to believe."

"You're making less sense than usual."

"You didn't try to save Gannah from the plague just because it was your job. You were prepared to heal every one of us if you could. Not only prepared, but determined. Not out of duty, but out of compassion." She probed him with her meah, and what little she could read gave confidence to her words. "It grieved you when you saw the devastation here, didn't it? You were horrified to see you'd arrived too late."

Pik straightened. "I don't know what you're talking about."

Why would he not accept her compliment? Was it Karkar guilt for helping a Gannahan? "And the way you taught me all the little things about the manners and customs in League society. You didn't need to do that. You could have left me to fend for myself. But you wanted to see me succeed."

"You're a quick learner. There wasn't much teaching involved."

"I know how vain the Karkar are, how they value comfort and routine and dislike new situations. But you left your home planet and never looked back, separating yourself from all things familiar despite your mother's vehement objections. That shows unusual daring. And now this trip. When I think about it, I can scarcely believe it. You left all the comforts of civilization, a prestigious job, everything you ever knew and cared about, for the sake of this mad adventure. But you meet every challenge and keep looking for more. I used to consider you a coward, but you're not. I have no doubt you could face down an angry dowb if you had to."

"I most certainly—"

"Oh, you'd complain about it—loudly—but you'd stand up to it. Then, after shooting it in the throat, you'd berate it for ruining your day."

Pik's voice rose a half notch. "You know nothing about me. Nor about the Karkar. We are the most noble of peoples, the very image of culture and refinement—"

"Yes, and humility." She stifled a smile. "But I'm mortified, Pik. I thought myself insightful and you superficial. Now I see the reverse is true. At first I looked only at that fake face you put on and found it irksome. I didn't see the man behind it. I have misjudged you. Please accept my apology."

Pik blinked, his ears expressing some emotion Dassa couldn't read. Then he stood. "I cannot. Your apology is not accepted. Now, if you will excuse me, I shall go sleep on the divan in the sitting room. The bed is rightfully yours, Madam Toqeph."

That ear-twitch must have been guilt. But why compound shame upon shame? She'd thought even a Karkar would have more class than to scorn an honest apology. But his response didn't change what she had to do.

"Wait. I need to tell you what we're doing at Yabbashah."

He stopped but didn't turn around. "I do not care. I'm just along for the ride."

"You do care. Why do you pretend you don't?"

He finally deigned to turn to her. "If you have something to say, then say it. But if that last speech of yours is any indication, it's likely to be nonsense."

"I'll show you. Come." She led the way up the stairs and into the office, where she opened her father's diary.

Pik looked down at the computer. "How can you show me anything in that? It's written in Gannahan."

"You won't need to read it." She found the entry she was looking for, then put the computer in voicemode and selected the Standard Tongue. "You can hear for yourself in my father's own words."

She looked up at Pik with sudden concern. "But maybe you'd better sit down first."

31

"Third Adar, in the Year of the Stewards Eight Hundred Eight," intoned a compugenned male voice. The Gannahan accent and inflection made Dassa want to weep.

"Today we have opened a new era in history. The year 808 will be remembered as the year Atarah Degel Jachin changed the color of Gannah in the galaxy's eyes. The year we will make the first payment on our debt to those whom we have wronged.

"Our father Atarah Hoseh dreamed of making amends to the planets his armies despoiled. For some it was too late, for the peoples were annihilated. To others, especially the Karkar, he hoped to apologize and repair some of the damage. It was his most fervent hope to eventually share with them the glorious Gospel of Salvation, that they, too, might have eternal life in Jesus Christ, King of all Kings and Redeemer of all humanity. But the plague, just punishment though it was, prevented him from carrying out his purpose. Now I, heir to the Wise, have found the key to restoring to the Karkar a small measure of the dignity our fathers brutally tore from them in Hoseh's day.

"It will be with the greatest joy and the humblest hopes that I, Atarah Degel Jachin, shall return the Kankakar Jewels to the people of Karkar."

Sensing the doctor's violent feelings in reaction to what he was hearing, Dassa stopped the voice. "Shall I go on?"

The only visible sign of distress was his ears, which tilted backward. Sharply. "Please do." His voice cut like a lahab.

Dassa resumed the recital, but the cold anger she felt pouring from him gave her a chill.

"It is my prayer," the voice went on, "that the return of their treasure will enable the bitter Karkar to hear the message of hope. How sweet it will be to see the Word of God have free course among them, bringing new life and transformation. What glory it will bring to God when Karkar and Gannah are brothers together in Christ."

Pik sprang from his seat with a suddenness that caught Dassa off guard. He snatched up the computer and threw it to the floor, then turned to her, amber eyes blazing. "You lied to me! You filthy, lying little monster! You told me the Jewels weren't here!"

"I didn't lie to you—"

He balled up his fists and took a step closer. "How dare you say such a thing!"

"I never lied to you—"

"You lied when you said you didn't have the Jewels." He waved his arms. "You lied when you said a Gannahan can't lie. Every word that's ever come out of your mouth was a lie."

"Pik, listen—"

"You insult me! Your planet insults me! You and your planet insult my people! You think you can make amends by giving to us what's ours to begin with—"

"Wait, Pik—"

"You knew all along where the Jewels were, you knew all the time! I should never have trusted a blood-drinking Gannahan."

Dassa stepped back to give room to his rage. She managed to rescue her father's computer from being trampled, though it looked like it was already ruined. Before she had a chance to examine it, he snatched it from her hands and threw it down again, this time crushing it beneath his oversized foot as he pelted her with poisonous insults in his own violent language.

As if in slow motion, Dassa watched that ridiculous open-backed shoe, polished to a mirror shine, grinding the life out of her father's last words. The Karkar shrieking raked her like a dowb's claws until she tasted the blood of hatred.

She could take him down with the flick of a finger.

But when she looked up at his florid face, its placid expression a jarring contrast to his vehement words and actions, she saw his torment. Karkar or not, the age-old Earth battle raged within him, with his beleaguered soul the prize.

He is no dog, her Yasha reminded her. *Hand not his soul to the Enemy.*

Seeing what was at stake, her hatred ebbed, but the tide of Pik's anger rose. He kicked the computer across the room then grabbed Dassa by the throat. "You'll never lie again, you filthy Purpletongue."

She grasped his wrist with both hands and tensed her neck muscles against the pressure of his long fingers, but made no effort to fight him off.

"We'll see what lies that tongue tells when your larynx is crushed. Can a Nasi breathe without a trachea?"

He forced her head back until she thought her neck would snap. She scrunched her eyes closed when she saw two fingers from his other hand rushing toward them.

"And what will you do without those evil green eyes? How will you violate my thoughts then, you forning witch?"

Fighting against instinct and training, she kept her feet on the floor and dropped her hands to her sides. Even if Pik rendered her speechless and blind, she wouldn't kill him. His grip cut off her air. Her eyes felt ready to explode, but she refused to raise her hands. As her Yasha commanded, she would not deliver this soul to the Enemy.

A roaring filled her ears, a fog rolled across her consciousness and she felt herself falling. Pik's voice no longer tore the air. Was she now deaf as well as blind?

She gasped for breath and found her windpipe unobstructed. The pressure was gone from her eyes, and she opened them as she pulled herself up to sit. Her head hurt and her vision was blurred, but she could see. She leaned against the desk and closed her eyes again while she listened to her rasping breaths, each one coming easier than the last as her trachea returned to its proper shape.

Finally she swallowed, then opened her eyes and looked around the room. Pik was gone, but she heard his footsteps on the stairs.

Shakily, she picked up the ruined computer and set it on the desk, then went upstairs to the dining room. She lowered herself into a chair. Took a sip of water. After a successful swallow, she ran tentative fingertips along her neck. It felt tender, but nothing appeared to be permanently damaged.

When her legs felt strong enough to hold her, she went to where Pik sat on the divan, face in his hands. He didn't look up when she sat beside him.

"I have never lied to you." She wanted to sound firm, but her voice quavered. "When I told you I didn't know where the Kankakar Jewels were, it was the truth. I didn't know, not then. It wasn't until two years ago, when I was studying your planet's history, that it occurred to me. I wondered why my father was so bent on raising those warships. Why would he go against Atarah Hoseh's decree? Obedience is what's important on Gannah, not worldly treasure, and my father revered the Yasha."

Pik never moved. Just kept his bony elbows planted on his legs, his face hidden behind long, guilty hands. He gave no indication he knew she was there, even when she spoke the hated name of the Yasha.

She continued, her voice still sounding bruised. "Once I guessed what had happened, why he had raised the ships and what he planned to do with the recovered Jewels, I made arrangements to come here to find them and to finish what my father began. What Atarah Hoseh wanted to do, but never could."

She paused, casting her meah toward him, seeking entrance. The door was closed, but behind it she sensed bitter cold. Shame. Despair. Solitary Pik, shivering in the darkness alone.

She stood up and looked down at him, but he still didn't acknowledge her.

"Better get some sleep," she croaked. "We leave at first light."

The sitting room was dark, except for the dim glow of the moon outside the window. Pik lay on the divan, staring at his hands, barely visible in the ghostly light. Two hours ago those hands had behaved like things possessed. He'd watched them grab and squeeze and press, and couldn't stop them.

Holding the Gannahan by the throat had excited him. Seeing her flinch, feeling her muscles tense, sensing her fear, fueled whatever vestigial hunter instinct drove his hands to behave in such an uncivilized way. He wanted to disable his Gannahan enemy. To render her harmless forever. Though trained and sworn to save lives, his one desire had been to snuff hers out.

Good thing his training got the upper hand. With her dead, he'd never have gotten off the planet.

He remembered her sparking green eyes and the murderous set in her wild face after killing the Cephargians. That's what he'd felt, for an instant. He was no better than she.

Pik's Terrestrial and Karkar halves argued like bickering spouses: I'm better than the filthy Gannahan. She yielded to her baser impulse, but I stopped myself. I could have killed her, but I chose not to.

Do you actually believe that? You won't even smash a spider, let alone kill a person.

But I could have, didn't you see? She was helpless and squirming in my hands.

Helpless? She chose to let you kill her. It was never in your control.

Pik didn't argue with himself any longer. He knew it was he who had been helpless. Lost in his rage. Blind in his confusion, helpless to know what was happening, or why, or what any of it meant.

Unlike him, she was a trained killer. Why, then, had she made no move to defend herself?

He'd never understand her if he lived to be a hundred.

32

The aircoach rumbled like a big, satisfied cat as it taxied out of the hangar and down the cleared path to the runway. But Pik didn't comment. Neither did he mention the riotous hues of the sunrise, nor the morning song wafting on the breeze, nor the sweet freshness of the dawn. He noted them, but he held his peace.

He didn't ask if she knew what she was doing as she turned the coach onto the runway and adjusted various controls.

He made no complaint when they bumped down the overgrown tarmac at an alarming rate of speed. He had nothing to say when the aircoach lifted off without incident and made a quick ascent into the blue. And he kept his relief to himself when she pulled down a shade to block the merciless stare of the heartless Gannahan sun.

Other than a mumbled resemblance to "thank you" when Dassa handed him breakfast, Pik hadn't spoken since he'd called her a liar and shouted all those other cruel and inaccurate things. Last night he'd done everything wrong. Until he figured out the right thing to say, he'd say nothing at all.

He marveled at her apparent lack of resentment. But the faint bruises on her dusky neck screamed accusations, and his eyes avoided them. Instead, he kept his gaze on the scene passing beneath.

Pik loved to fly. It put everything in a different perspective. He liked the lofty sensation of seeing the big picture, of scanning the landscape as it truly lay rather than the bits-and-pieces view of the surface-bound observer.

But the images unfolding below were unlike any he'd ever seen. There was no tidy graph of a Karkar city encased in a comforting dome. He saw no bushy order of an Earth city with its trees interspersed throughout. No close-cropped verdant parks, no patchwork of farmland, no arteries flowing with traffic. What passed below was a wild planet rushing into the home of a fleeing foe. The humans had fought it off for millennia, only to succumb at the end.

And Gannah gloated. Its grinning teeth and savage claws and creeping tendrils would tear down and bury everything within the decade. Humanity's marks would be reduced to buried bones and crumbling ruins.

An unnatural gleam flashed through a rainbow of trees, and the leaf-shaped library glimmered into view. Pik stared in awe at its functional design. It was art at its highest and best. From the texture and color of its roof surface to the perfect detail of its shape and dimensions, it looked like a living leaf edged and sparkling with dew. Pik felt an inexplicable glimmer of pride to have been in such a magnificent edifice.

He gazed at the leaf until it was out of sight. But he still didn't say a word.

Dassa sang with the music playing from some device she'd brought along. Ordinarily Pik found that sort of thing annoying, but he welcomed it this time, for it absolved him of any obligation to converse.

What remained of the city fell behind, and Pik realized he liked the strange, Gannahan music. Her versatile voice complemented rather than interfered with it. Relieved that his fingers had done no lasting damage, he settled back in his seat and closed his eyes. He hadn't slept much last night. Every time he dropped off, he'd jerk awake, gripping the bunched-up blanket like a throat.

He awoke with a start when the singing ceased and Dassa let out an exclamation. Something pelted the aircoach.

Pik sat up and looked around in a panic. The plane was under attack by a cloud of small, angry-looking birds.

"Gazal." Dassa pointed the plane's nose downward. "They don't like us invading their airspace."

Pik forgot he wasn't speaking to her until the words were out of his mouth. "Does this happen often?" He was sure he saw hatred in those shiny, pin-head eyes as they flew beak-first to their deaths against the aircoach.

"It's one of the biggest hazards of air travel. Usually you can see them coming and get out of their way, but this group caught me napping."

She executed a stomach-churning series of lurching directional changes until the plinking of their small bodies against the plane faded away, and Pik's heart rate slowed in equal proportion.

"If those things get in your engines, they'll bring you down." Dassa turned on some sort of windshield-cleaning device to scrape off the feathery splatters, then pointed to a gauge on the panel. "Good thing the bird-blades are working."

Pik didn't ask what those were, but she explained anyway. "They whir around the engines during a gazal attack. If a bird tries to get past them, it gets cut to pieces. They slow the engines' efficiency, but they help keep you in the air. I guess it's safe to shut them off now." She pressed a switch, and a dull hum, unnoticed before, ceased its droning.

The skies had been clear when Pik closed his eyes, but Gannah's cheery mood must have passed. Pik regarded the heavy cloud cover and wondered how Dassa could have expected to see the birds coming.

"They showed up on my instruments," she said as if reading his thoughts, "but I didn't notice them until it was too late. I should have been paying attention instead of singing. If you were my flight instructor, I'd be in big trouble."

Pik didn't answer.

"I hope we're not in big trouble anyway."

Pik still didn't respond, but he fervently shared that hope.

Hours later, Dassa's voice awakened Pik from a drowsy reverie. "What's that over there?"

She consulted her instruments. "If that's land, my autonavigator is leading me astray."

Pik peered through the window but saw nothing until the plane banked and headed north. Then, if he strained his eyes, he could make out a dim outline shimmering in the distance.

According to the map she'd shown him last night, Yabbashah was at the extreme southwest corner of Gannah's land mass. If they'd passed south of it the next land they'd see would be the continent's far eastern coast on the other side of the globe. Assuming their power held out.

The thought that she'd almost taken them out to sea infuriated him so much he again forgot his vow of silence. "How could your autonavigator not work? You must have set it wrong."

"No, I triple-checked it. That's not the problem. Electronic devices are never reliable on Gannah, and it doesn't pay to rely on them too heavily."

The spot of land grew closer until Pik could see a wide, sandy beach, and farther inland, what was once a town, its outlines blurred by rampant greenery like the other cities they'd flown over.

"The coasts of Yabbashah were mostly used for vacations and retreats," Dassa said. "In the northeast there's the port city of Yattiyr, and also a center for oceanographic research. That's where we're headed. The middle of the island was mostly cattle ranges. I imagine we'll see big herds down there still. They're wild and don't depend on humans for their survival."

It wasn't long before Pik saw a cluster of brown spots like dense freckles on green skin.

"There's a herd," Dassa said. "A good sized one, too. If we had the time, I'd bring a few steaks back to the *Swordfish*. The crew would love it."

"Yes, and so would you. The butchery, I mean." The memory of her inexplicable refusal to fight back last night was still fresh in his mind, and he knew his comment was uncalled for. But it was out of his mouth now, he couldn't take it back.

Nor did he want to. Her lack of bitterness after what he had done stung worse than a slap to the face. How could she act as if nothing had happened? Why didn't she treat him with contempt?

But those questions were secondary to the larger one. Why was she so intent on returning the Kankakar Jewels? And why had her father sacrificed the entire planet to find them? He felt like a character in a play with no plot.

They passed over kilometers of smooth, grassy plains dotted with sparkling blue lakes and etched with spidery silver streams, before the aircoach lurched and the engine noise changed.

"Uh-oh." Dassa scanned the instrument panel. She punched a few buttons, pulled a lever repeatedly, and uttered something Pik guessed was a Gannahan curse.

"What's wrong?" He didn't want to know, but he had to ask.

"One engine's out, and the other's looking pretty shaky. I've got to land this thing."

Pik's felt the blood drain from his face. "You mean we're going to crash?"

"No, I mean we're going to land. A crash is what I'm trying to avoid."

"So what happened? What's wrong with the engine?"

She looked grim. "Could have gotten gummed up with pieces of those birds. The mess must not have worked its way far enough in to cause any problems until now. I suppose I should have landed earlier to check it out."

"And I suppose you should have avoided the birds to begin with instead of singing. And you should have flown directly to our destination instead of taking the scenic route and almost missing the island altogether. Seems to me you've done everything wrong this whole trip."

"Seems to me you should have stayed on the *Swordfish*."

The green plain drew closer with frightening speed and Pik braced himself for a hard landing. "No doubt about that. In fact, I should never have left Karkar."

"That would have saved us both a lot of grief."

At least she was getting her spunk back. Pik stared out the window. "You're putting us down right in the middle of a herd of wild cows."

"Instruct them to move, then. I have little choice where we land."

She kept the descent level. The cattle, all in the same chocolate brown uniform, looked up at them without alarm. Some trotted back a few paces before stopping and turning to watch, and others didn't bother to move until the plane drew close enough that Pik could see their jaws working.

As he wondered what kind of damage a collision with a cow would do to an aircoach, the largest one bellowed, and the whole herd took off running.

Though Pik liked flying, he hated landings. Especially emergency landings in a Gannahan cow pasture. The ground was nowhere near as smooth as it had looked from the air. They touched down, bounded up, touched down again, then bounced wildly along the grass until Pik thought his teeth would jar loose.

When Dassa finally brought the thing to a stop, he opened his eyes. He hadn't even realized he'd closed them. "Are we alive?"

"For now."

She tipped her head back with a heavy sigh. "This is not what I envisioned."

"No joke."

She threw open the cockpit door, shouting, "This is not what I envisioned!"

Pik fumbled with his door latch. "We've already established that."

"You don't understand." She jumped to the ground. "We have twenty-two hours to find the Jewels and return to the *Swordfish*. But I'm not certain of their location, and the shuttle is 1500 kilometers away. If we do not reach it…"

Pik finally got his hatch open. "What do you mean you don't know the Jewels' location?"

"Had you not damaged my father's diary beyond repair, I could have gotten the coordinates."

Pik clambered out. "You don't know where they are? You brought us all this way, and you don't know where they are?"

She didn't answer, and Pik wanted to shake her. He came around the plane to find her looking at the sky. "You don't know where they are?" he shouted.

"I have a pretty good idea." For some reason she seemed more calm now. Why? Their situation had certainly not improved.

"We shall get there one step at a time," she said. "The Yasha has granted us a safe landing. Now all that stands between us and the Jewels are some thirty kilometers and an angry bull."

"What angry bull?"

Dassa pulled an electrodart out of the plane and gestured with it. "Over there. The one whose conjugal pleasures we just interrupted."

Pik looked. Across the field stood an enormous beast, even bigger than a Karkar holejeojinkooeikika, huffing insults at them and pawing the ground. "Those horns have got to be a meter long."

"Impressive, aren't they? I hope we shall not have the chance to examine them more closely."

"You're going to kill him?" Pik asked, hopeful.

"If I do that, his harem will attack. No, I'll try to reason with him. You'd better stay here. If there's trouble, try raising the *Swordfish* on the radio. If you can get through, they might be able to transport you up."

"What do you mean, if there's trouble? You're a Nasi, aren't you? Didn't you kill ten wild dogs a couple days ago?"

"A big pack of kelebim is less lethal than a small herd of Yabbashah bison."

As they spoke, the bull put his head down and charged. Pik watched in dry-mouthed terror as she gripped the weapon and started running toward the beast. Who would run *toward* a charging bull?

The bull must have wondered too, because he slowed to a trot, then sauntered, then stopped.

When he stopped, so did she. They stared at each other across the field, about fifty meters between them, the cows watching with tail-flicking curiosity, and Pik by the aircoach, agape.

She raised her arms and shouted something in Gannahan. If the bull understood, he wasn't impressed. He put his head down again, scimitar horns waving a warning.

A cry stuck in Pik's throat when Dassa began running straight toward the beast as if trying to impale herself, but he released his breath when the bull unexpectedly lifted its head, turned and ambled away.

Pik expected Dassa would stop, but she kept running until the bull increased his pace to a trot. She pulled up and stood for a while, watching him lead his harem away. Then she walked back to the aircoach, pausing now and then to look back over her shoulder, but the bull didn't resume his belligerence.

"Okay," she said, as if the incident were nothing out of the ordinary, "now on to Yattiyr. I think we can make it by nightfall. Let's grab our bags and go."

"Walking? You're not going to try to get the plane running?"

"Not unless you're an aeromechanic. I can check to make sure things work, but if they don't, I can't usually fix them."

"I can't either."

"Then we walk."

She handed him an electrodart in a holster. He strapped it on, feeling silly. Then they slung on their packs and started across the field.

The grass lay in stiff curls, catching his feet. Pik was glad to have Rosh's hat between him and that tropical sun. But within minutes, his clothes clung to his sticky skin.

And then there were the shoes. Pik slipped and stumbled and the wiry grass cut into his heels and ankles, while in front of him

Dassa walked nimbly in her hideous brogans. He wouldn't have wanted anyone to see him wearing them, but he wished he had a pair.

As if feeling his eyes on her feet, Dassa turned around and looked at his. "Those are the most senseless shoes I've ever seen. Your feet will be in pieces before we get to the trees."

"I'll have you know I paid a great deal for these. They're handmade of the best kalakala."

Dassa pulled out her lahab and cut a slice in the shoulder of her tunic. "If you paid more than five Leaguepounds, you were robbed."

She grabbed the cut sleeve at the top and tore it off, then ripped a thin strip from the edge.

"What are you doing?"

She knelt in front of him. "Pick up your foot."

"What?"

"Pick up your foot. This won't be as good as decent shoes, but it should hold up long enough to get you through the rest of this whipgrass."

She slipped the sleeve over his shoe and up his lower leg, leaving the shining point of the toe poking out, then tied the sleeve around his shin with the strip she'd cut. She tore off the other sleeve and repeated the process with the other foot.

Pik felt even more foolish than he looked as they resumed their trek. But his feet had better traction now, and the sharp grass didn't penetrate the sturdy fabric.

Once it was evident the bull would leave them alone, Dassa started to jog. She kept up the pace until they reached the trees at the edge of the field, where she finally paused. Though they'd jogged for twenty minutes, her breathing was no heavier than if she'd been on a brisk walk. But Pik collapsed onto a rock, gasping.

He dripped with sweat, his chest heaved, his heart pounded, and his face flamed from his exertion.

His spats were nearly disintegrated, and he pulled them off. He examined his heels and ankles, stinging and reddened with countless tiny scratches.

Then realizing Dassa had almost disappeared into the trees, Pik jumped up and hurried after her, the fear of being left behind chasing away his weariness.

33

The Isle of Yabbashah might have once been a fabulous vacation resort, but for Pik, it was purgatory.

Clouds of tiny insects swirled like mist, crept into his eyes and ears and nostrils and crusted in the corners of his mouth. The rocky ground tortured his feet. They climbed one steep incline after another, skidding down the other side through sharp-edged scree. The one time they paused for a drink, a weaverrat the size of his hand dropped from a branch to the ground beside him. Three-legged birds of every size and color screamed and threatened, and vague but ominous mammal shapes skittered from tree to tree just out of sight.

Two relentless hours later, Dassa pointed to the desolate city far below them. "There it is. Yattiyr."

Pik looked down the sheer drop-off at his feet and tried to discern what she saw in the distance, but said nothing. Partly because he was angry with her, but mostly because he had no breath left for speaking. His clothes were sweat-soaked, grimy, and torn, and his eyes burned from the salt of his perspiration. It would have been a relief to fall off that cliff to his death.

She scanned the ridge then pointed toward the right. "Looks like the remains of a road over there. I'll bet it takes us where we want to go."

Pik couldn't see it but followed along, every step an agony.

Some sort of voracious, moss-like vegetation seemed to eat the pavement. It formed a spongy carpet, like a dense forest of tiny, soft fir trees. It wouldn't have been unpleasant to walk on, except it was slippery on slopes. Even Dassa had a difficult time keeping her feet under her on the steep descent to the city.

Once they emerged from the trees at the foot of the hill, the shade-loving moss pulled back from the sun and the pavement became pavement again. The town they passed through seemed even more desolate than Ayin, for other than birds overhead, there was no life to be seen, not even animals. The sea air smelled putrid, like death.

Pik felt near death himself, but kept lifting his feet and putting them down, following Dassa, whose pace had never slowed. His medical eye told him that being on Gannah had brought her to complete recovery at last.

Moving through a haze of exhaustion and pain, eyes on the ground and head bowed, Pik contemplated the irony. The poisonous air of this place had wiped out her race, and now it rejuvenated her. Some organic concept about life springing from death worked in his brain. A seed falling to the ground and dying, only to germinate and grow. A winter-brown prairie blooming with color at the kiss of a warm spring rain.

Where did these thoughts come from? He knew only indoor things. He'd never even kept a houseplant. He tried to pull back the curtain of stupor closing over his mind, but instead of opening, strange images played across it like moving pictures without sound. The audio was supplied by the slap, slap of his feet, Dassa's brisk steps, the near-human cry of circling birds, and the ever-nearing sound of the surf.

Dassa slowed then stopped. Pik lifted his gaze to where she looked.

It required every shred of his remaining strength to keep from collapsing at the sight.

Some distance offshore, moored to floating docks apparently designed for the purpose, towered an ancient, barnacle-encrusted Gannahan warship. It was the same malevolent shape and hideous design as portrayed in the horror movies of his childhood, but larger, more solid, and more terrifying, even in its impotence. Pik thought of the number of deaths its inmates had caused—and the number of skeletons that must, even now, lie molding within it—and trembled.

He tore his gaze away and looked at Dassa. She seemed as overcome as he. Though that specter represented the crippling of his people, it was the utter annihilation of hers.

Then his ears frowned as fresh anger revived him.

"You said it exploded!" Bitterness made his voice crack.

"I said one of the ships exploded. I didn't say which one."

"How many did they pull up?"

She walked to a bench overlooking the water and lowered herself onto it. Pik chose another nearby. Before them was a railing, curving around the edge of a drop-off. A stairway to the right appeared to descend to a lower level, just above the sea.

"Successfully? I believe only this one." She gestured at the ship. "Their first attempt. The second exploded as it surfaced."

She glanced at the sun. "We're running out of time. What did the diary say?" She pressed the bridge of her nose between her fingers. "He wrote how they raised the first ship and pulled it to Yabbashah. Then docked it here. I don't know what he told the people, how he explained what he was doing. Perhaps he didn't. No one would have questioned him. At any rate, when it was docked, he entered the ship alone, and after a great deal of searching, he found the Jewels..."

Her voice trailed off as if she were trying to remember. Pik thought with a jolt that she probably wasn't remembering, she was making it up as she went along. What a masterful storyteller — she actually had him convinced for a while.

What did she hope to gain from this cruel deception? It was the sort of bottomless wickedness only a Purpletongue could conceive. Killing him quickly afforded too fleeting a pleasure. No, she'd make him go slowly, feed off his suffering.

Dassa rose and stood by the railing, talking to herself in Gannahan and gesturing. As if reviewing the events, she pointed to the ship, moved her finger around, then motioned as if the character in her monologue were leaving the ship and coming toward land. She put her hands on the rail and repeated a phrase several times, contemplating, then leaned over and looked at the ground below. Repeated the phrase again then added another, with an upward inflection as if asking a question as she leaned farther to get a better look.

Then she stood upright and turned to Pik. "I might have found them. Let's go see."

He looked up at her then out at the warship in the harbor. Under no circumstances would he sit alone in view of that monster. Particularly with the sun lowering in the sky. She was down the stairs and out of sight by the time he struggled to his battered feet and shuffled after her, tensing with every torturous step until the numbness took over again.

At the bottom of the stairs a small plaza spread across a terrace, with the ocean lapping below.

Nearby, the hillside beneath where they'd just stood contained a door, and Dassa headed toward it. "The diary said he put the Jewels in the closet under the stairs. Do you suppose this is what he was talking about?"

"Why would there be a closet here?" It might be a cruel charade, but Pik felt too weary to resist playing along.

"For the maintenance people to keep tools, trashcan liners, that sort of thing. If this isn't where he put the Jewels, I don't know where else to look."

"Then by all means, open that door."

Though it was prominently marked as locked, she tried. But either it was stuck, or its lock was more than symbolic, because the knob wouldn't turn. After several tries, Dassa felt around the base of the knob, wiping away crusted filth.

"It really *is* locked," she said. "That must mean we're at the right place."

"But what do we do for a key?"

"If it was the toqeph who locked it, only the toqeph can open it."

"Great."

"It is great. I'm the toqeph." Whatever she'd been feeling for around on the door, she must have found it, because she pressed her ring against a smudge at the base of the knob. When she tried the door again, it opened without difficulty.

Janitor's closets, apparently, didn't rate glowlights. It was like entering a sepulcher. Dassa left the door open wide, but the balcony above blocked the evening sun. She felt along a ledge above the door, pulled her hand back in recoil as if it met with something unpleasant, then reached up again and produced a portable light source.

Its glow was dim and faded quickly, but it illuminated a rectangular shape occupying the right half of the closet. Amidst a dust-caked and web-draped assortment of canisters and tools stood a wheeled cart, upon which rested an ornate chest inscribed with Karkar markings.

Pik's head swam. Then the light died, and they stood in darkness again.

With the Kankakar Jewels in front of them.

Dassa's voice sounded choked. "Let's get this out of here."

Not daring to believe what he was doing, Pik helped Dassa maneuver the heavy cart through the door and onto the plaza into the light.

He stared at the chest. Ran his fingers over it. Traced the faint markings with trembling hands. Wrapped his arms around it and laid his cheek against its cold, gritty surface.

"Aren't you going to open it?"

Pik slowly stood upright. "Open it?"

"How do we know this chest isn't empty? It's of Karkar origin, to be sure, but what if it isn't the Jewels?"

Of course, that was it. She was still torturing him. Letting him think they'd found the Jewels, only to snatch them away again. "You open it," he said, and stepped away.

"It should be your privilege."

Pik envisioned her opening the chest and exposing his people's treasure to the Gannahan sun while he stood idly by. "Perhaps you're right."

He examined the chest again. Only excellent Karkar construction and superior Karkar materials could have survived burial at sea for eight hundred years. But what of its contents? Was the chest full of sea water? Were the Jewels corroded past recognizing?

Pik pried at the gnarly, encrusted latches, and they crumbled in his hands. When he lifted the lid, the hinges cracked in half.

But he hardly noticed once he saw what lay inside.

34

Pik's legs buckled, and he sank to his knees, clinging to the ancient coffer to prevent total collapse.

The trunk's interior was dry, its contents in perfect condition.

Still kneeling for fear of swooning again, he reached inside and opened an ivory case encrusted with green gems. And wept. The ektkaj-stone tiara of Queen Nakkik glittered in the fading Gannahan sun, its glory blurred by his tears.

Pik's arms rested in the chest, his body paralyzed by disbelief and awe while his mind shuffled thoughts at dizzying speed. The Kankakar Jewels, recovered. In his very hands. When he returned them to Karkar, he would be famous. Respected. Legitimized.

And fabulously rewarded.

He rose with difficulty and fingered the legendary treasures. The brooch of Hgl. A shimmering string of sacred sjnaaaxix stones. The fabled Osnodeen pendant. Countless other gems whose names and histories he didn't know. Time felt suspended, place didn't matter. All that existed were Pik and the Jewels.

Gradually he remembered Dassa. He glanced toward where he'd last seen her, but she wasn't there. Looking about, he found her on a nearby bench, her face buried in the crook of her arm resting on the bench back.

She sat only a few meters away, but the distance between them had never seemed so far.

Pik closed all the cases, repacked the chest, and laid the heavy lid on top, though it would no longer fasten. Time seemed to have stood still while he examined the treasure, but in fact the day had waned. The shuttle was half a planet away, and they must return to the *Swordfish* tomorrow. His troubles weren't over quite yet.

He turned to Dassa.

She lifted her head but didn't look at him. Face wet and eyes reddened from weeping, she spoke to the pavement in front of her. "I suppose we can eat now."

Whatever Pik might have expected her to say, that wasn't it. "Eat?"

"I was determined not to stop for dinner until we found the Jewels. And here they are. After dinner, we can figure out how we're going to get them out of here." She stood, nodding toward the ancient warship looming off shore. "But not here. I can't eat in sight of that."

"Where will we go?"

"Does it matter?" She grabbed the cart's handle and pulled it toward the stairway. "Let's just go."

Pik lifted while Dassa pulled, and step by step they walked the chest up the curving stone stairs to the city level. Then they wheeled it along the litter-strewn pavement until they rounded a corner and the warship was no longer in view. Around the next bend, they found the remains of an outdoor café. Dassa turned a table upright, took off her backpack and slung it onto the table. "I'll have dinner ready in a few minutes."

She produced a flimsy-looking handful of shiny metal sheets, which she unfolded and assembled in less than a minute to make a small oven. Next she unwrapped a thin square of something, folded it in half and laid it in a small, shallow pan, which she slid into the bottom of the oven. Within seconds, the material was glowing red. Then she took out a glass container of last night's soup, removed the lid and slid it onto the rack. On the oven's top she laid several leftover biscuits wrapped in foil. "Not much of a dinner," she said, "but it's getting too dark to forage for more."

While their supper warmed, they found water to wash in, and from the café cabinets they helped themselves to bowls and spoons, as well as a jar of some sort of pickled mixed vegetables. Ordinarily, Pik would never have dreamed of eating leftovers that had been jostling in a backpack beneath the hot sun all day. But since nothing was ordinary on this planet, he made no objection. Just ate in silence.

There wasn't enough food to satisfy him, but he made no objection to that, either. His mind still struggled with the fact that the Kankakar Jewels were real. And in his possession.

Dassa ate quietly, her gaze resting on the Karkar chest.

The silence made Pik uncomfortable. "I don't understand how the water never got into that trunk," he finally said, polishing off the last biscuit.

"The diary said it was in a sealed vault. A little water seeped into the vault over the years, but the chest was never submerged. Its latches and hinges just corroded from dampness."

"Ah. That explains it."

"What I don't understand is how those baubles could be worth three hundred million lives."

The dumplings from the soup turned to stone in Pik's stomach as his gaze went to the chest.

Dassa gathered their dishes and folded the collapsible oven, already cool. "Now to find transportation."

"How are we going to do that?"

"I don't know. But the Yasha wouldn't have brought us this far if He weren't going to take us all the way."

Pik's ears jerked back in annoyance. If he ever got off this planet alive, he never wanted to hear the name of Yasha again.

"You don't believe me?"

"About what?"

"You don't believe the Yasha will provide our transportation back to the shuttle."

"No, I don't. But you're resourceful in your own right. If we make it back to the *Swordfish* in time, it will be thanks to you, not to some mythical deity."

She slung her pack over her shoulder. "I am resourceful, yes — because the Yasha is my Source."

"You see things your way, I see them mine."

"Good. And you take your treasure" — she gestured toward the Karkar chest — "and I'll take mine."

Pik grasped the cart's handle. "And what might your treasure be?"

"I pray one day you will share it with me."

Pik's ears tilted. He would never understand this woman. Wise and practical one moment, wholly irrational the next. Unable to form a response to her inanity, he pulled the cart in silence down the deserted, crumbling street, too spent to move but too elated to stop.

It was fully dark when she pointed to a sign up ahead, which only a Gannahan could have read in that light. "Ah, there's an airport six kilometers from here. Now that I know where we're going, let's find a vehicle so we don't have to walk all the way."

"I like the sound of that."

Though unwilling to be left alone, Pik's feet would take him no farther. He waited by the cart while she went looking. Several anxious and lonely minutes later, she returned in something resembling a delivery van. With two flat tires. She got out and opened the back of the van. "The hover mechanism isn't working." She pulled down a ramp. "But it will get us there."

They wheeled the cart into the vehicle and secured it in place. They also found extra straps, which they used to refasten the trunk's lid.

Neither of the van's headlamps functioned, but Dassa maneuvered around obstacles in the road as if she could see them.

"You must have good night vision," Pik said.

"Of course. I am Gannah."

"Then why do your buildings have glowlights?"

"That's a good question. Personally, I never liked them, but most people do. I guess you could say they're a nicety, a frill."

After the last airport he'd seen, the airstrip at Yabbashah surprised Pik. A fraction of the size of the one at Ayin, and all the buildings were intact. But no aircraft was to be seen. With each empty hangar they passed, Pik's panic mounted. What good was it to recover the Jewels if he had to spend the rest of his life with them here?

Nothing to worry about, he reassured himself. Even if they didn't make it back to the *Swordfish*, Dmitry would tell someone they were here. Another ship would be sent for them, someone would find them eventually. Wouldn't they?

No, he shouldn't think that way. Think positive. Dassa was smart, she'd find a way.

"They must have flown people out to seek help on the mainland," Dassa mused aloud. "And never returned."

They found a strange little affair in the fourth hangar, with both top propeller and wings. But Dassa didn't trust it. "I've never seen anything like that before. Let's keep looking. I'd rather fly something I'm familiar with."

Fearing they wouldn't make it back to the shuttle in time, Pik glanced back reluctantly as they drove to the next hangar.

They found a toppeller there, which Dassa said couldn't take them far enough. A plane on the other side of the building had been renovated and turned into a home by an enterprising family of furry creatures, whom Dassa refused to evict.

And the rest of the airport was empty. Dassa gave a weary sigh. "I guess we'll have to try that weird peller-type thing."

They drove to the fourth hangar again and climbed out of the van for what Pik fervently hoped was the last time.

He stared at the hybrid contraption. "What is that thing, anyway?"

"I have no idea. Looks experimental. Probably homemade. Look, there's a sign on it."

A large sheet of heavy paper was affixed to the windshield. Dassa pulled it down and took it outside, where the light, though negligible, was better than in the hangar. Brow puckered, she read it to herself then grinned.

"What does it say?" Pik asked. He couldn't imagine what could put a smile on her face at a time like this.

"It's a note from the man who left this here for us. Loosely translated, it says, 'Honorable Toqeph. This coach is of my own design. I flew here from Yad. The Yasha hath told me the toqeph and a visitor shall have need of it. Thou shalt find the batteries at the powerports and operating instructions within the cockpit. I am honored to serve the toqeph. Glory to the Yasha, His name be praised, I go to Him soon. His devoted servant, and thine, Hatita Eliab Chen."

Pik grunted. All this Yasha-talk was getting under his skin. "Do you suppose it still runs?"

"Of course it does." They hurried back into the hangar. "Ah, Mr. Hatita is still here."

"What?" Pik glanced around then looked where she pointed. In the gloom, he could barely make out a shape against the far wall as Dassa headed for it.

As Pik drew closer, he realized it was a cot, upon which rested skeletal remains. The man must have flown the plane here, written the note then lain down to die.

She knelt beside the body and pulled the man's lahab from his clothing, apparently verifying his identity. Then she returned the lahab and rejoined Pik at the plane. "That man had a treasure no one could take."

Pik's ears twitched. "What treasure?"

"The Yasha's forgiveness."

He was glad she didn't elaborate, but Pik couldn't help ponder that inexplicable statement as they loaded the Jewels into the back of Hatita's contraption.

Though the lights didn't come on when they entered the cockpit, Dassa was able to read the instructions posted at various locations on the instrument panel. She smiled. "He was very thorough. Let me get the batteries."

Pik buckled himself in and waited while she exited the plane. He tried to think of some medical cause why his skin should be crawling, his heart pounding, and his mind begging him to bolt.

There was no reasoning with this planet. A warrior trained to kill submitted to an attack without a struggle. A dying man, obeying the imagined command of a nonexistent deity, delivered this plane for Pik's own use four years later.

But most boggling of all was that he, Pikpeeeeekpiktootakpik-kakazghaghanmattsson, the uncategorized product of the unfathomable union between incompatible races, was in possession of the Kankakar Jewels.

The reality fluttered just out of Pik's grasp. And he feared what it might look like once he captured it.

Dassa slammed the engine hatch shut and returned to the cockpit. The lights came on when she opened the door. "Looks like I hooked everything up right." After another perusal of the dead man's instructions, Dassa pressed a button, turned a switch, and the machine grunted, groaned, and shook into wakefulness.

"The Yasha provides," Dassa said with a smile as she studied the controls. Then she pushed a lever forward and the craft rolled toward the hangar's entrance. She said something in Gannahan—thanking the dead man, Pik guessed, because he picked up the name "Hatita"—and they taxied onto the runway.

Pik had never felt so solitary. The little plane's lights made an infinitesimal glow in the empty airport, the only artificial light on all this vast planet. And though he sat in close quarters with another living being, he felt as if he were alone with the light, racing along the runway, then jumping off and reaching for heaven. A heaven as inky and unfathomable as the blackest hell. A heaven that pressed down upon him with its terrible immensity, but from which he would forever be separated. The precious Jewels notwithstanding, Pik knew that wherever he traveled he would be always alone, cut off from all life, the sole resident of his own personal, lifeless planet.

As if delighted to be freed from the hangar, the plane hummed as it soared over the dark island. "I think she'll get us there, Doctor," Dassa said.

Pik tried to find a comfortable position for his aching bones in the cramped space. Why hadn't the Yasha told a giant to build a plane instead of an average-sized Gannahan? Despite his discomfort, the contented drone of the engine and the gentle rocking made his heavy lids close. "I think she will, Madam Toqeph."

When he next opened his eyes, the air was filled with a glittering haze as the sun flexed its morning muscles.

Dassa checked her course for the hundredth time. Still dead-on. Then, hearing him stir, she looked over at the sleeping Karkar grotesquely pretzeled in the Gannahan-sized seat. He'd be mighty stiff by the time he finally pried himself out of there.

His eyes narrowed to slits, he raised a long-fingered hand against the glare.

"Sun wake you up?" she asked.

With a wordless groan, he twisted to look behind the seats at the chest, its gilded Karkar characters winking in the sun's sleepy rays. Apparently satisfied, Pik faced forward, folded his arms across his broad chest, and nodded off again.

Why were drowsy creatures so appealing? Even this ungainly Karkar. If he could see himself, though, he'd be appalled, for Gannah had not been kind to him. Kilos had melted from his powerful frame. His droopy clothes, creased in all the wrong places, bore several rips, and their original colors were barely discernible beneath the dirt. His long feet were swollen masses of crusted cuts. His cheeks and chin sprouted a short yellow beard, and the whole of that grimy, expressionless face was peeling from sunburn and striped with sweat. A vivid hat line encircled the top third of his head, and his untrimmed blond hair, now darkened with dirt, lay flattened in several unnatural directions. What she wouldn't give for a camera.

She chuckled, envisioning his horror next time he looked in a mirror. Why couldn't he understand that it was the inner man that mattered, not the facade? With her meah, Dassa probed the half-

Karkar's dead spirit, dismayed by its refusal to awaken, and once again prayed for his soul.

He showed no change as a result, but the change in her own heart made her worship the Yasha in awe. Somehow, through no effort of her own, between their forced landing in the cow pasture and the flight through the night, she'd grown almost painfully fond of this impossible man.

What a strange, blank face, its muscles relaxed in sleep. She focused on the straight, thin lips, now chapped and split. Could they pucker and kiss?

Best not to venture there. Dassa shifted her gaze to the rainbow of foliage skimming below, and the familiar ache of loneliness swallowed her whole.

35

After a week of fearing they might never return, Pik let out a long sigh of relief as the bay doors closed behind the shuttle and Dassa maneuvered the craft onto its pad. Relief, yes. But no elation.

When he opened the hatch, a blast of cold air poured into the landing craft, and the *Swordfish*'s crew rushed into the shuttle bay.

"Holy excretions, tall guy!" Lawbby exclaimed as Pik unfolded himself from the cockpit. "What happened to you? Pardon my language, Lady Toqeph, but the doc looks like he's been mud wrestling with a grizzly."

"I shall be fine." Pik straightened his stiff limbs. "Is there no heat on this ship?"

"Still whining, I see." Dmitry was already poking around in the mountain of things they'd crammed into the back of the shuttle. "You should have left him down there. It would have made more room for cargo. I can't believe you broke gravity with all this weight. Why'd you bring this ugly old chest back?"

Pik's heart lurched when Dmitry plucked at one of the straps securing the lid on the Kankakar Jewels. "That's mine, Captain, and I'd thank you to keep your hands off."

Dmitry looked up at Pik through narrowed eyes. "Sure, Sunshine, it's all yours, but it's in the way. What say you get it out of there so we can get at the good stuff?"

The load had shifted during the flight, and Pik struggled to unwedge the cart. The others ignored him, asking Dassa questions, not lifting a finger to help. Finally he wiggled the chest free and pulled the cart from the shuttle.

"Your things are next," Dassa told Dmitry and Sylvia. "I brought everything you asked for, and more. Lawbby gets souvenirs too. I've got something for everyone."

"Really? What did you bring me?" Lawbby asked. They crowded around as Dassa entered the cargo hold to hand things out.

Pik interrupted their happy chatter. "Excuse me, Captain. Do you require this to be irradiated?"

Dmitry looked up in irritation. "Of course."

"These are the Kankakar Jewels."

The captain and crew froze. Then Dmitry laughed, followed by Lawbby a second later.

"You had me going for a minute there," Dmitry said.

Lawbby guffawed. "The Kankakar Jewels are about as real as unicorns."

"He's not kidding," Dassa said.

The laughter ceased as if squeezed by the throat.

"I shall pass this through the irradiation chamber, then secure it in the cargo bay," Pik said, gratified at their silent, open-mouthed response, "where I trust it will not be disturbed."

Dmitry leaped forward as if startled from slumber. "Let me help you with that."

"No need. I shall see to it myself." Pik turned away and pushed the cart through the shuttle bay doors, the discomfort of his battered body temporarily forgotten in the satisfaction of the moment.

His gratification didn't last long.

The Jewels sat cold and lifeless in the ship's belly, bringing Pik no warmth as he shivered in the sunless, artificial climate. They added no pleasant taste to the travelrations he once considered acceptable fare. The treasure provided no company as the solitary hours stretched on. Nor could it soothe the uncertainties that plagued his subconscious mind.

The others kept busy with the toys Dassa brought them. From the way Dmitry fawned over Hoseh's lahab, you'd have thought it was worth as much as the Jewels. Sylvia squealed at the stemware with inordinate rapture. For Lawbby, Dassa brought an electronic game system and a handful of games, which were unusable until they could be adapted to an Outside power source. But the sailor holed himself up in the maintenance lab until he'd succeeded in making the system work. Once he performed similar magic on the movie player Dassa brought back, the crew was never bored.

Though Pik would soon be the most famous man in the galaxy, Dassa was the favorite on the ship. They invited her to play the games she'd brought, or watch a movie, but she often declined. Instead, she spent most of her time translating Gannahan medical texts for Pik. True to her word, as always.

Pik often joined their activities, though they seldom made it a point to invite him except as an afterthought. The movies could be played in the viewers' choice of languages, but the Gannahans' idea of theater arts was different from what Pik was used to, and most didn't appeal—except for a couple of the comedies, which made him laugh until the others yelled at him to quit braying like a donkey.

The games were physical and usually instructional, much like the dancing disc Pik and Dassa had played in the library. Lawbby and Dmitry rigged a cubicle in a corner of the cargo bay for a game room. It was cold there, but the activity helped to warm them.

Lawbby's favorite was basic fencing, a sport he said he'd always wanted to learn. Because the game was intended for practice rather than instruction, Dassa brought along protective gear and foils for two so she could give him lessons.

At first, Lawbby played the new games—fencing and otherwise—with the glee of a child. But after he'd mastered basic fencing, he wanted to learn more and pestered Dassa to duel with him. Occasionally she obliged, but most times she begged off, suggesting he challenge Pik to a game of hmmmjckt instead. Offended at her condescension, Pik wanted to refuse but was too bored and lonely to turn him down on such a shaky principle.

"Too bad you didn't bring any advanced fencing games," Lawbby said one day at lunch.

Dassa folded her empty travelration wrapper. "If you must know, I did."

"Why didn't you say so sooner?"

"I meant to get beginner and intermediate, but I accidentally grabbed one from the most advanced class. I didn't mention it because it would be way over your head."

"You're pretty handy with a foil," Dmitry told Dassa. "Is the game too advanced for you?"

"I may have been able to play it years ago, but I wouldn't do very well these days. "

Pik stifled a burp. "I'd like to see you play."

The others clamored their agreement until she relented. "As long as you don't laugh at me. I was never an expert."

"I'm sure you'll do splendidly," Pik said, "since you're a cutthroat."

"Throats are off-limits with a foil."x

After lunch she fetched her equipment, and the others joined her in the makeshift game room to watch the show, each pressing into a corner of the tiny space to keep out of the way. After wiring her foil to the electronic sensor, Dassa stepped into her jacket and slipped on her glove. "This game follows Gannahan rules rather than Standard. Instead of calling a halt at each touch, the director calls out who scores but doesn't stop the play. The bout continues until one competitor scores fifteen touches. Because the play never stops, it gets pretty intense. Ready?"

Dmitry's eyes sparkled with interest. "Whenever you are."

She affixed her mask, picked up her foil then inserted the game disc into the player.

The room went black.

When the lights came on a second later, Pik found himself standing beside a tree-shaped pillar in the throne room at Armown. In the background, people sat around the long central table, which was laden with the remains of a feast. But Pik focused on the full-sized hologram standing before him.

The burly Gannahan, muscles bulging beneath his fencing attire, seemed more lifelike than the flesh-and-blood ship's crew who stood in the corners of the game room, their faces distorted by the images projected upon them. Pik thought they looked as scared as he felt when Dassa's challenger raised his foil.

The holographic fencer was tall for a Gannahan, thick-limbed and powerful but graceful as a cat. And his bearing suggested he meant to take no captives. Weapon flashing, he stepped to his line, and Pik's stomach knotted with unreasoning fear.

Dassa stepped to hers, standing as determined and tall as her petite form allowed. Pik's skin prickled with anticipation—he'd seen her fight the Cephargians and had little doubt she could beat this monster.

The scene was scary, though. Even the director, as Dassa called the referee, was an unnerving sight, with his strange Gannahan clothing and fierce Gannahan face. He raised his arm then called out something in a harsh, commanding voice.

The holographic opponent jumped to the offensive. Pik knew little about this sport, but there was no doubt who had the upper hand. In a matter of seconds, the director called out something that sounded like, "Naga!" and gestured toward Dassa's opponent, awarding him a point.

The bout continued without interruption, and Pik forgot the fight wasn't real. The combatants' weapons flashed and clanked, their bodies danced forward, backward, lunging. Both fencers, actual and virtual, panted and gasped. The intensity of the battle built and Pik's tension with it, as again and again the director called, "Naga!" usually pointing to the untiring hologram.

With only three points to his nine, Dassa fought as if for her life, and Pik held his breath until he felt faint. In the opposite corner Sylvia covered her eyes, while the virtual spectators pounded the table and cheered, chanting something like, "Ah-ree-li, Ah-ree-li!"

Pik imagined desperation in Dassa's movements as the bout wore on, but her challenger remained confident, repelling her attacks, countering them, slicing through her defenses like a scalpel through flesh.

The score was fourteen to six when, in backing away from a forceful thrust, Dassa stepped off the boundary strip, and the director awarded the fifteenth point to her competitor.

She lowered her foil with a sigh of heavy dejection then pulled off her mask. Her opponent removed his as well and shot her a gut-chilling look of triumph with eyes as green as her own.

Such an expression of pain crossed her face, Pik wondered if it were possible for a virtual sword to wound. Without thinking, he hurried toward her as the scene faded. Stretching her hands toward the dimming warrior, she moaned, "Areli!"

The room went dark as Pik reached her side, and he heard her choke on a sob.

"Are you injured?" Pik asked.

"Of course not." Her voice quavered as they were transported back to the makeshift game room with the returning of the lights. "None of that was real."

"It sure seemed real," Lawbby said. "Excretions, that was quite a bout."

Sylvia emerged from her corner clinging to Dmitry. "It was awful! I'm shaking all over."

"Most amazing game I've ever seen," Dmitry said. "So real it was spooky! Do you have any more like that one?"

Dassa dropped her foil and mask to the floor and fled the room, leaving the others staring after her in surprise. After a moment's consideration, Pik followed.

He soon caught up. "Dassa," he called, but she didn't turn around. "What was that all about?"

She reached her quarters, and the door slid shut behind her.

He stood outside. "Dassa, what's wrong?"

Silence. No, not silence. A muffled sound. A sound of… could she be weeping?

Pik paused, wondering what to do. Finally his curiosity got the better of him. "What happened back there?" When no invitation was forthcoming, Pik entered anyway.

Sitting on the edge of her bunk, she wept in the dark.

He turned on the light. "I don't understand. So you lost. It was just a game."

She wiped her eyes. "It was Areli."

Pik sat beside her. "What does that mean? What's an areli?"

"Not what. Who."

"All right then, who?"

In halting, tearful sentences, she told him. "He was my eldest brother. My father's favorite. He was so proud of him. I remember when they filmed him for that game. I was about fifteen. It took days. He fenced dozens of opponents, incorporating every conceivable move. It was all then programmed into the game so that whatever the person playing the game did, his hologram could respond. He was the best fencer on Gannah. He was best at everything. Two weeks after he made that game, he began his Nasi quest. He never returned."

"He what?"

"He left on his quest and didn't come back. His body was never found, but my parents both knew it the moment he died. So did his fiancé. They felt it in their meahs. My father was never the same after that." She wiped her nose. "And that's just it. If Areli hadn't died, those ships wouldn't have been raised, and all Gannah would be alive today.

"Why did he have to die? Why did he fail, and why did I succeed? He'd never failed at anything before. I'm his baby sister, I could never beat him at anything. My father said it best. He said when Areli fell, the future of Gannah fell with him."

She struggled for control, but her tears prevailed. "I didn't know he was the fencer in that game or I would have left it on the planet. Someone put it in the wrong slipcover. Areli! How could you have left us? Why did you die?"

"I doubt it was his choice."

"Of course it wasn't. But it shouldn't have happened."

"And who should have prevented it? Blame your Yasha, not Areli. Like all the rest of your people, he was an innocent victim of your precious 'Savior's' whims."

She leapt up and pointed to the door with a quavering finger. "Get out!"

Pik rose. "Your blame is misplaced. Impressive as your brother was, he was just a man, and your father was the same—a flawed human. The real fault lies in the one you claim is perfect."

"Out!"

"I do not understand you." Ears twitching in irritation, he retreated to his own quarters. There he huddled, shivering beneath his blankets, seeing the sword fight before his open eyes, and the fierce, green gleam of the victor's.

How could a man like that have failed his final quest but little Dassa succeeded? How could such a mighty people all have died? If the Gannahan God could provide Pik with an aircraft four years in advance, why could he not have saved the race that worshiped him?

And why did Pik now think of him as real? God was no more material than the fencer in the game.

He couldn't be.

Pik considered the universal story in the stars and shivered all the more.

36

The *Swordfish* flung ever farther from Gannah, and Dassa's sorrow increased with the distance. Cutting herself off from her home planet was like severing limbs from her body, and in her meah, she bled tears.

Pik, on the other hand, swaggered with self-importance as he checked on the Jewels several times daily. He hovered over the ship's every activity as if willing the vessel to reach Karkar more quickly. If he spoke to Dassa at all, it was to insult her. She avoided him by keeping to her room, translating Gannahan medical texts into the Standard Tongue.

Since the swordfight with Areli—she cursed whoever put that game disc in the wrong cover—despondency overwhelmed her. Pik's remarks about blaming the Yasha made sense. Sometimes she sat in the command center beside whichever crew member was at the helm and stared in silence at the stars, contemplating their Creator. Her Creator. His plan—if He had one. Her place in it—if her survival wasn't a random fluke. And when she felt a stirring in her meah, she slammed the door on it. She didn't want to hear anything the Yasha had to say.

In her mind she roamed her desolate, cobwebby house, visited her boys' empty bedroom, looked at their dust-obscured photos on the piano—and realized that the clearest memories she had of them were those pictures. Their warmth and smells and voices were nearly forgotten. As for Rosh, all that was left of him was an ache in her heart and a few objects yet to be sold.

And his handwriting in the margins of his Bible.

She still opened it every day and struggled to read. Once, the words had seemed alive, written personally to her. Now they were mere ink on a page, characters in a foreign language. She longed for things Gannahan. Gannahan voices, dancing, laughter, flashing eyes and grinning faces.

All gone forever. Her whole life. Gone forever.

The voice in her meah invaded her brooding. *Remember My promises.*

Promises. All she could look forward to was a life of exquisite loneliness, dragging a whining Karkar along like an injured limb. He was right. Her Yasha was exceedingly cruel.

It is time to put on thy shoes.

Those were not the Gannahan words she'd wished for. *Begone. I will not hear it.*

It is time. Put on thy shoes.

She knew what He meant. As the apostle Paul wrote in his letter to the church at Ephesus, a believer's feet were to be shod with the preparation of the gospel of peace. But how could she share the gospel when she wasn't sure she believed?

If I am not real, how then do I speak with thee? Do I exist only in thy imagination?

Nay, I could not imagine anything like Thee.

True. As the next galaxy is beyond the reach of thy arm, so far am I from thy comprehending. But you believe, or you would not answer Me.

Then I shall answer no more.

Lawbby looked up as Dassa hopped from her seat and fled the command center. "Was it something I said?"

Neither could Jonah escape me. Whither shalt thou go from My presence?

Dassa scowled. "What would Thou have me do?" she asked aloud. And nearly ran into Pik rounding the corner.

"What?" he asked.

"I wasn't speaking to you."

"There's no one else here."

"Oh, never mind. It's not important."

It is of utmost importance. Speak to this man. His eternity dependeth upon it.

She scowled at Pik. "I mean, I was speaking to the Yasha."

"Where is he?" His ears twitched. "I don't see anyone."

Her initial irritation at his sarcasm fled before a flood of certainty. Pik might be blind, but she wasn't. "He is here. Were you looking for me?"

Pik's face was serious, even for a Karkar. "Yes. Do you have a moment?"

She sensed an urgency in his demeanor. "I have many moments. And they're yours."

In her meah she knew her kind words, rare as they'd been lately, rattled him.

"How about a hot chocolate?" he asked.

Dassa smiled. "Sure."

In the galley, Pik handed her a steaming chocolate and poured something warm and alcoholic for himself. They sat at the table together.

Pik wrapped his twelve fingers in their worn and mended gloves around his cup and stared into its depths as if to divine the future. "We enter Karkar space in two days."

"Yes, so Dmitry said. And I've been thinking about that. Before we embarked, when I said we'd have no need for formal attire, I was mistaken. I should have suggested you bring something appropriate to wear when you return home with your prize."

"I brought a good suit. Though I didn't expect to need it, I couldn't imagine traveling without one."

"Good. I brought formal wear as well."

Pik hesitated. "I go to Karkar alone."

"But I wish to present the Jewels to your Kaaqakaanikakak Council. With apologies to all your people, on behalf of my ancestors. I have my speech already prepared."

"I know. But I cannot permit that."

"You what?"

"Recall my fury when you told me you knew the location of the Jewels. Now envision that madness multiplied by a hundred and twenty-three billion. That is the rage that would greet you when you set foot on my planet with my people's sacred relics."

She imagined, and quailed at the thought.

Pik's thin voice was quiet. "I cannot allow that to happen."

Dassa searched his face, her meah probing for a spark of something within him. Something she might connect to. But his spirit was dead, as always. "You care for my welfare?"

"I wish to avoid a riot. The Jewels might be damaged in the fracas."

She smiled but sobered quickly. "But my apology. I must offer it. My speech…"

"They would kill you before you uttered the first word."

"At least let me give you a written copy to take with you. Do you think the Kaaqakaanikakak will read it?"

"They'll probably tear it to bits, then burn its remains and spit on the ashes." He shrugged. "But I'll give it to them."

"Your people sound quite hospitable."

"Under ordinary circumstances we are the most gracious of hosts."

She leaned forward. "I should like some day to find out."

"That would be foolish." He shook his head. "Put it out of your mind."

Despite their arguing, once this grumbling Karkar debarked to his planet, the ship would be lonelier — her life would be emptier — than ever before. Her throat swelled, nearly choking her words. "I will respect your wishes. The last thing I would do is cause more trouble for your planet than my people have already given them."

They sat in silence, sipping, for several moments before Pik spoke again. "But when I return the Jewels, they'll ask many questions. And I will not know all the answers."

"Such as?"

"Primarily, why are you so bent on returning them? They caused the death of your entire race. Why not throw them back in the sea to rot forever?"

Dassa put down her cup and looked Pik in the eye. Usually when she did that he looked away quickly, but this time he studied her face.

"My father was wrong to raise the ships, and he died for his error. The Nasi, and all the rest of us who knew his plan, should not have allowed him to pursue it. To form a united front to oppose the toqeph would have been unprecedented, but it was what we should have done, and I believe we all knew it. The guilty died because of that failure — all but me, anyway. And the innocent dependents who entrusted their lives to their toqeph and his Nasi died as well.

"But despite the error upon multiplied error, my father was right in one thing. The gospel of Jesus Christ should not be kept to ourselves, but must be shared with all who have never heard it. Once I understood my father's motives, I had no choice but to finish what he'd started. For me to deny your people the opportunity to hear the gospel after all my people suffered for that end, would be the greatest desecration of all. I realize it will be a long time before a Karkar will listen to anything a Gannahan has to say, but returning the Jewels is a significant step toward getting their attention."

Pik's ears flattened with emotion. "And I am supposed to tell them that? That your planet died to get our attention?"

Dassa almost smiled. "It worked, didn't it?"

He leaned back in his chair and fixed her with a penetrating stare. "I do not understand you."

"I do not believe it was merely for the sake of your people that my ancestor Hoseh or my father Degel desired to return the Jewels. If the embittered people of Karkar were to receive eternal life in Christ through the immeasurable grace of God, think what an impression that would make on the rest of the galaxy."

She paused to watch his reaction. There was none, visually. Prodded by the voice of the Yasha, she continued. "But you are not just another Karkar. You matter very much to me. And even more, having a human soul, you matter to God. Whatever your people may choose to do, you have a decision to make for yourself. Despite your feelings toward Gannah. The decision does not involve you and me, it's between you and God."

Pik opened his mouth, but she answered his retort before he spoke. "Yes, there is a God. And yes, you do believe that. Yours is a practical, logical mind. All the evidence in the universe testifies to His existence. The fact that we cannot grasp His ways merely proves our inferiority. If we could relate to Him as an equal and understand Him with our finite minds, He would be no God."

Dassa sensed that, despite Pik's calm expression, a spiritual battle roared within, and her heart raced with alarm at its ferocity. "Yield to the Lord," she urged. "You think you fight to preserve your freedom, but don't you see? Surrendering will grant you liberty. For all eternity."

Pik slowly rose, towering above her. "I cannot."

They spoke no more of the matter until the *Swordfish* orbited Karkar, and Dassa went with Pik to the shuttle bay to see him and his precious burden off.

She watched as he loaded the chest into the landing craft's hold, allowing no one to help him. Lawbby waited in the shuttle at the controls.

"Are you sure I cannot go with you?" she asked.

"It would not be wise."

She nodded. "I suppose you're right."

"That happens from time to time, you know."

"Yes. Many times."

He emerged from the shuttle and stretched the kinks out of his back, looking down at her from his great, sorrowful height. "I shall give your message to the Kaaqakaanikakak. That is all I can do."

"There is one more thing." Her eyes searched his, and found his thoughts impenetrable.

"And what is that, Madam Toqeph?"

"Consider the story in the stars. And how it applies to Dr. Pik."

He gave her a long look. "I shall never understand you." Then he climbed into the shuttle and closed the hatch.

Dassa left the bay, his words ringing in her ears like a slammed door.

37

On Karkar, the name Pikpeeeekpiktootakpikkakazghaghan-mattsson was soon revered by every citizen. In the rest of the galaxy, the simpler "Dr. Pik" became a household word. The Karkar government paid his considerable financial debt to the League Bank, and the High Command forgave him for abandoning his post at the Paris Center for Disease Control.

Pik remained on Karkar, accepting the adulation that was his due. He kept busy, establishing a new research facility dedicated to unraveling the secrets contained in the recovered Gannahan medical texts.

He lived with his mother – who was proud of him at last.

After her death from a massive heart attack a year after his return, he remained in her flat. It didn't quite feel like home, but neither did anywhere else. The thought of living alone frightened the Solitary Pik, and he pretended his mother was still there.

He dreamed of Gannah, or the Gannahan, frequently. Those were the only things he saw in color. All else in his mind, in his world, was drab.

Though he granted no interviews, one enterprising reporter managed to reach him by phone.

"I'm conducting research for a book," the man said in a rapid Karkar squawk, "and recent data about the dead Gannah is impossible to come by. I was hoping you could help me. You will, of course, receive due acknowledgment."

Pik's ears frowned. How did this bozo get a call through? Heads would roll in Communications Security. "I can't help you. I suggest you contact the Gannahan herself."

"Don't hang up, Dr. Pik, please! I'm not interested in that barbarian's slanted view, I want a more accurate perspective. You're the only Karkar who's ever seen Gannah. Can't you tell me about it? What did it look like? How did you survive your ordeal in that desolate hell?"

Pik's finger hovered over the disconnect button, memories of Gannah scrolling through his mind. The energizing scent of the air as he stepped off the shuttle. The icy prisms clinging to the glistening trees that first morning. The empty courtyard at Armown, flag snapping in the breeze above the tower. The virtual plain of wild-eyed savages dancing with joyful abandon at the Festival of Voices—and the lone survivor's heaving sobs when the fantasy ended and the lights came on.

"Gannah is not dead," he said and terminated the call.

An hour later, his personal assistant, Kohz, found him reading one of the books Dassa had given him. Not a medical text this time, but an anthology in the Standard Tongue entitled, *Story in the Stars: Selected Writings of Atarah Hoseh Charash.*

"Sorry to bother you, Doctor," said Kohz, "but there's someone here to see you. I told him you were taking no visitors, but he was quite insistent."

Pik lifted his head and blinked, orienting himself to the present world. "Hmm? Who is it?"

"An Earther, sir. I believe a doctor of some sort. He says his name is..." Kohz paused, struggling to pronounce the unwieldy sounds. "Nat tszun. Or something like it."

Pik sat up in surprise. "Mattsson? Dr. Lars Mattsson?"

"I believe that was the name. You know him, then?"

"Of course." Pik put down the book. "I'll see him."

Kohz's ears stiffened with interest. "Shall I offer our guest a glass of akkg? As a foreigner, he might not—"

"By all means. He'll know what to do with it."

Kohz's face was placid, but curiosity twitched all over his ears. "As you say, sir."

"Lars Mattsson is my father. Come to pay his respects upon the death of his wife, no doubt."

"I didn't realize—"

"That the rumors are true? That my father is not Karkar?" Pik unfurled from the roomy lounge chair.

"No, sir… Well, yes. But I thought your father was deceased."

"Not unless my visitor is a cadaver." He headed for the bathroom. "If that's the case, I'll see him in the morgue. Otherwise, please tell Dr. Mattsson I'll be with him shortly."

Kohz gave a dutiful nod and left the room.

Three minutes later, Pik emerged from his office.

The aging Earther who perched on the edge of an oversized chair in the waiting area looked strongly familiar, but he didn't match the father of Pik's memory. This man was smaller, grayer, more stooped.

"Oaaha, a ada," Pik said, the Karkar rendering of, "Hello, my father."

The elder man rose, displaying the first smile Pik had seen since leaving the *Swordfish*. "Dr. Pik, I presume. Quite a place you've got here. Your very own research facility! I hope you'll be able to find the time later to show me around."

"I'd be delighted to give you a tour. It's not quite completed, but some departments are operational."

"I'd like that."

They clasped one another's arms in the traditional Karkar greeting then embraced in a tentative Earthish hug. "You look well, a ada."

"Thank you. And you look splendid. Splendid indeed." He looked up at his son with a face full of pride, then sobered. "But I...I'm sorry about your mother. I left as soon as I heard, but, well, you know the time involved in space travel."

"Say no more. I'm just glad you came."

It was true. Pik hadn't realized until hearing his father's name how he longed for someone to talk to. Someone not Karkar. Very strange.

But stranger yet was the conversation they had two days later, after visiting his mother's memorial. Due to the limited space in Karkar's domed cities, the dead were not buried, but were dehydrated and compressed, their brick-like remains used to construct a decorative wall in each city's memorial garden.

After visiting the garden, the men sat in Pik's dining room, partaking of the traditional funeral meal of zhaghatszokeetkoa soup and khhkzg bread. According to custom, they shared a bottle of wine vinted the year of the deceased's birth, drinking directly from the bottle.

"Your mother lived long enough to provide us a good wine." Dr. Mattsson licked his lips with satisfaction as he offered the bottle to his son.

Pik put it to his mouth. "Long and well," he said then drank.

"I'm sorry our marriage didn't work out," his father said, "although I guess it's not surprising, coming from different worlds as we did. Love can overcome a lot, but not those odds."

Pik nodded. Something about this man drew him, as to a familiar comfort. But the familiarity wasn't a mere breath of childhood memory. Something about his father reminded him of… of Dassa. How that could be, he couldn't fathom, but the more time he spent with him, the more he sensed it.

And the more the similarity comforted him. "I'm sorry too. I should have liked to have known my father better."

"And he you. I suppose your mother didn't have much good to say about me."

"Nothing whatsoever." Pik took another sip of wine, then put down the bottle. "But in the past two days, I've found most of her information unreliable. No doubt her memory was impaired."

"And no doubt I've mellowed with age. There's something to be said for experience. Speaking of which, visiting Gannah must have been an amazing one. When I heard you'd gone there, I thought it was a hoax. Leaving your post in Paris and taking off in an illegal vessel with that Gannahan woman? What got into you?"

Pik shrugged. "I'm still not sure. She made the offer, I weighed my options, and knew I'd be crazy to go. But I went anyway. Even today, I can't explain it."

His father laid down his soup spoon. "What was it like? I've looked for articles about it or interviews with you on the subject, but I haven't been able to find any, even on Karkar channels."

"Is that what this is? An interview?"

"Not at all. I'm your father. You needn't talk about it if you don't want to. I can understand if you'd rather forget the whole, awful experience."

"I shall never forget it." Pik stared into his empty bowl, brown zhaghatsz grease clinging to its edges. "Nor was it horrible. Not entirely, anyway."

"How did you manage to recapture the Jewels, can you tell me that?"

"I didn't recapture them. She took me there for the express purpose of giving them to me."

His father leaned back in surprise. "That's not the way I heard it."

"But that's the way it was. I had nothing to do with obtaining them, I was merely the delivery boy."

"Why would she do such a thing?"

"I didn't understand her explanation. Some sort of twisted Gannahan logic no sane person could follow."

"Hmm." The elder man nodded. "I hear the Gannahans were a peculiarly religious sort, following some primitive brand of Earthish Christianity. Did you see any evidence of that there? Did they have big churches, Terrestrial-style religious icons, that sort of thing?"

His father's familiarity with the subject surprised Pik. "Yes and no. The Gannahan woman is very religious, as you say, and I believe a great many of the others were too. But they considered a 'church' to be a group of people, not a building. She said she was amazed at the elaborate structures on Earth called churches that cost so much to build and maintain but which are used only once or twice a week. She said the money spent on them could have been put to better use."

"Interesting. Leave it to an outsider to see something so obvious."

"She also stressed that the Gannahans didn't consider their faith a 'religion,' but a personal relationship an individual had with the one they called the Bara, or Creator. They imagined they communicated with this mythical being on some pseudo-profound level. Moreover, they shunned religious icons of any sort, considering them heathenish and idolatrous."

"Very unusual."

Pik's sudden loquaciousness on the subject surprised even him. "Gannah is a place of great contradiction. They valued education so much that even the lowest classes were literate in two languages, but there was no such thing as a school building. Violent crime was extremely rare, though every citizen was a trained killer. Their technology was highly advanced, but the simplest or our electronics are useless there. Nothing about that planet makes sense."

"Did the woman…did she speak at all of the Bara? Did she tell you about her faith?"

"Constantly. It grew quite tedious."

"But she actually believes it, after all that's happened?"

Pik looked across the table at his father, noting a peculiar feeling in his middle that had nothing to do with the meal they'd just shared. "Apparently so. Why?"

The elder man cast a quick look around. "Can we speak plainly? There are no servants to overhear?"

"Privacy is one of the privileges of my position as savior of the Kankakar Jewels."

"Which reminds me. I should like to see them while I'm here. Would that be possible?"

"I will arrange it. Ordinarily you wouldn't be allowed into the Viewinghall. No foreigner has ever laid eyes on the Jewels except the filthy thieves who stole them, and the Kaaqakaanikakak would like to keep it that way forever. But for the father of the Jewels' redeemer, I'm sure they'll make an exception."

Dr. Mattsson rubbed his hands together. "Wonderful. I can scarcely believe they're back after all these centuries. And intact, too, you say? I'm floored. Speechless. I always knew you were destined for greatness. But I think…I think greater things even than this await you, if…"

Pik watched his father, curious.

"You say it's safe to speak plainly, so I will. About your mother's death. As I said, I'm sorry our marriage failed. And that as a result, I failed you as a father. But she's now just a memory. A brick in a wall. Serving Karkar as part of a beautiful edifice."

"Yes. I understand all that."

"I know you do. But do you also understand that you yourself are not a Karkar? That when you were conceived in your mother's womb, you received an eternal soul?"

Pik went weak and his father's face shifted out of focus. "You sound like you've been talking to the Gannahan."

"Ah, so she did tell you this?"

Pik's anger pulled his senses back into focus. "What do you know of it?"

"The Gannahan's faith originated on my planet, you know."

"Yes. We discussed this already. But it's unlicensed and intolerant of other religions. That's why it has long been illegal to propagate or practice it on this planet. And why the rest of the League has recently outlawed it as well."

"I know that. Are you going to have me arrested, or may I continue?"

Pik sighed. "No, no. Please go on."

"All right, then. I am a scientist. And an incurable skeptic. I question every convention, every assumption, every accepted belief. Because science, as you know, is always evolving, always changing. If not for questioning, no progress would be made. I consider it my duty as a scientist to never be content with our present knowledge."

"I share your passion. That's why I founded my research center. The Gannahan's view of health is a whole new perspective, one that bears further investigation."

"Your work is exciting, and I congratulate you on your fresh thinking. That's one of the ways your mother and I were incompatible. She adhered to the traditional Karkar ways in every respect, never had an original thought in her life. Except, of course" — he smiled — "when she married me. But even that was my idea, not hers. The only reason she agreed was to hurt her mother, who disowned her for leaving the planet to study. That, and the way I plied her with Eutarian brandy. Its reputation for causing errors in judgment is well deserved."

"Yes. It's been recently classified as a poison."

"And poisonous it is. But once she came out from under its influence, she returned to her old, convention-bound ways. She could put up with my nonsense to a point, but when I began considering the possibility that a Divine Creator might actually exist, she reached the limit of her endurance."

"Can't say as I blame her for that."

"She told me either come to my senses and drop the subject, or leave her, you, and Karkar behind me."

Pik's rage bubbled near the surface. "You chose some aberrant religious philosophy over your son?"

"No. I tried to forget about it. To please her. To hold the family together. But the more I tried to put it out of my mind, the more obvious God's existence became. All the evidence points to it. I couldn't get away from it. Everywhere I turned, God was there."

"I fail to see — "

"But you will. You will see. Either in this life or the next. But in the next life, it will be too late. That was the final straw for your mother, when I realized that as my son, you needed to hear about God. And I tried to talk to you about it. I didn't know then what I do now — I hadn't had the opportunity to study the Bible at that point. But I felt compelled to teach you what I did know.

"She charged me with child abuse. I was quickly convicted and banished from the planet, forbidden to see you again until the death of the complainant. That's why she moved to another dome when you were six. Too many people in Agkztikkokikanon knew what had happened. She wanted to give you a fresh start without your father's shameful shadow hanging over you. Your father, who has since prayed for your soul every day of his life."

Something in the elder man's face—Pik supposed it was love—made his rage fade to an irksome resentment. "This all fits with what I recall. With what Mother told me, and what she didn't say. But three times I met with you as an adult, off Karkar, and you never made mention of any of this. I'm glad you didn't, because I don't care for the subject. But if this was such a pressing matter to you, why didn't you bring it up before?"

Pik's father shook his head. "I was afraid, sorry to say. I never felt free to discuss it. Now, though, I almost feel I'll burst if I don't lay it out on the table."

Pik took another drink of wine—more than just a sip this time—then spoke without looking at the man across the table. "The Gannahan woman insists that when a person believes in this Yasha of hers, this Savior, who I assume is the same as the Christ of the Christians—she says when a person believes, the Spirit of God enters in somehow and lives within that person. She also says one believer can see the Spirit within another."

His father nodded. "I understand the Gannahans possessed a sensory apparatus that Earthers lack. It was only through that means that they could see spirits within other people. An Earther who belongs to Christ is, in fact, indwelt with His Spirit, but we cannot see Him. The Gannahan saw Him in me immediately, however."

Pik looked up. "What do you mean? You've met her?"

"Several years ago. I was at a conference in Calgary. I'd heard about her, of course, about how you'd saved her life, and I wanted to meet her. I was curious. So I found her at the university. I never told her who I was. That is, I gave her my name, but there was no way she could know I was your father."

"You actually met her?"

"I did indeed. We had a wonderful talk."

"Did she mention me?"

"I don't recall that she did. But I was careful not to bring you into the conversation, because I preferred that she not know our connection. I thought it might inhibit her openness."

Pik's ears frowned. "I see," he said, though he didn't. "What did you talk about then?"

"About Christianity, mostly. It wasn't a long talk, but it was certainly delightful. Like a cool drink for a dehydrated body."

Reminded of that satisfying Gannahan spring water, Pik understood the concept of pure refreshment. "But can only Gannahans see this alleged Spirit?"

"Sometimes an Earther can sense it too. The Spirit within one person will sometimes make a connection with the same Spirit in another, but the awareness isn't as strong in an Earther as in a Gannahan. Why?"

"Because since you came to visit, something about you has reminded me of Dassa. I couldn't put my finger on it. Perhaps this perverted misconception you share has something to do with it."

Dr. Mattsson looked startled then slapped the table and laughed. "Did you hear yourself? With one breath, you say you can sense the Spirit of God in both of us—not by the power of suggestion, but with your own observation—then you call the whole thing a perverted misconception. Get your head out of the so-called science of Karkar, man, and into the reality of life. Give me one concrete, scientific reason why there cannot be a Creator who made Karkar, and Earth, and Gannah, and everything else in this whole inexplicable universe. Give me demonstrable facts, give me formulas and equations. Prove to me those stars beyond the dome above us, and the chhmgkfly crawling on the window beside you, just developed on their own. Out of nothing, by accident, with no design or guiding force. Calculate the odds of that happening."

"That's not the sort of thing that can be proved..." The things Pik had been reading in Hoseh's book shuffled through his mind. All of a sudden they made sense in a way that disturbed him profoundly.

"But the evidence *does* support the existence of a Divine Creator, doesn't it?"

"I, ah, I have my doubts about that..."

"Doubts? Wonderful! That's where it all begins. Tell me about your doubts."

Pik slowly rose. "I've enjoyed our chat, but I have some things to attend to at the office. I'll see you this evening."

He took two steps then stopped and turned before moving on. "Thank you, a ada."

Two days later, Pik and his father stood in the Viewinghall, staring in awe through the glass at the Kankakar Jewels. Breathtaking as the baubles were, Pik's eyes kept darting to the photo of himself in the case beside them, commemorating his presentation of the treasures to the Kaaqakaanikakak upon his return from Gannah.

He'd cut a striking figure that day, dressed in the most fashionable xuxsuit the Karkar clothiers had to offer. How good it had felt to be back in civilization. To be among his own people. To be honored as he deserved for the great hardship he'd endured in bringing the Jewels back to their rightful home.

Out of the corner of his eye, he saw his father studying the display before them, his face beaming with pride in his son.

Pik's great bubble of glory slowly deflated. What was there to be proud of? The people of Karkar were no better off with the Jewels than they'd been without them. They suffered the same diseases, the same sorrows, the same trials. And when they died, they merely became bricks in a wall. An edifice to emptiness.

Is that what we're here for?

The great Pikpeeeekpiktootakpikkakazghaghanmattsson had secured his place in history, all right. He'd henceforth be known as the most grandiose narcissist ever spawned on a planet of pompous windbags.

Pik suddenly longed for genuine immortality.

He looked at his wizened Earthish father, and in a wave of dizzying revelation, he realized he already possessed it.

The only question was, what he'd choose to do with it.

Five standard-years, eight months and sixteen days after Dassa watched through the porthole as the shuttle carried Pik and the Jewels to Karkar, she bustled about her apartment, cleaning up.

Perhaps in her next class she'd introduce some of the simple courtesies Gannahan guests extended their hosts. Terrestrial guests expected to enjoy a hostess's hospitality and then depart, leaving her to clean up after them. On Gannah, the hostess sat and rested while her visitors rendered the place spotless. It didn't seem reasonable to Dassa's Gannahan mind that she should have to clean house both before their arrival and after they left.

Reasonable or not, her heart was full of praise for her Yasha. She sang as she scraped the dirty dishes, saving the scraps to compost for the plants in the tiny greenhouse on her balcony.

Though the League had outlawed the practice of any unlicensed religion and punished proselytizing with stiff fines and prison sentences, Dassa enjoyed a rare freedom. In her capacity as professor of Gannahan Studies at the League University in Calgary in North America, she could teach the Gannahan religion as an elective academic subject. After two semesters, fifteen students had made professions of faith in Christ. Twelve were her students, and three were friends they'd brought to audit the class. The meeting in her home today had been a "study session" during which the students participated in a Gannahan-style worship service followed by a traditional Gannahan luncheon.

As close to traditional as she could muster, that is, without real Gannahan food. At least her mintwood tree was thriving, and she gave each guest a twig to chew before they left.

Halfway through loading the dishwasher, she got a buzz from the lobby.

She spoke through the messenger. "Who is it?"

"A shadow from your past," a reedy voice answered.

Her smiled broadened. She prayed for Pik daily, and he'd been so much on her mind the last few hours she almost felt he was in the room with her.

"Come on up." She punched in the code so he could enter the building.

Her hands trembled as she continued loading the washer. "Silly thing," she scolded herself. "He probably just wants to gripe about something."

But in her meah, she felt… No, she must be imagining it.

The buzzer sounded as she dried her hands. She hung up the towel and opened the door.

Pik stood even taller than she'd remembered, though his new hairstyle lay flatter than his old brush cut.

"The famous Dr. Pik! What brings you here?" She tipped back her head to look him full in the face.

"I finally understand you," he said. And his whole face smiled.

Author's Note

I don't anticipate mankind will ever travel through space as described in this story. I don't believe there is life, let alone human life, on other planets. And I don't believe that Psalm 19 and the Scriptures mentioned in this book's Chapter 21 apply to extra-terrestrials. All that is pure fiction.

But the stars are real, and so is the Creator whose handiwork they show and the knowledge they speak of. That's what this whole thing is about.

Several years ago, I ran across a fascinating little book called *The Gospel in the Stars* by Joseph A. Seiss. Originally published in 1882, it was reprinted in 1972 by Kregel Publications. Because of the antiquated language, a trek through its pages is a painstaking endeavor. But the content is intriguing, and it became the inspiration for this story.

I never set out to create a fantasy world called Gannah, nor new races of humanity, nor anything else so grand. I just wanted to illustrate some basic truths that apply to everyone, everywhere, no matter what stars they live under.

Karkar—its language and its people—merely represents me having fun.

However, in creating the language of Gannah, I employed *Strong's Exhaustive Concordance of the Bible*, borrowing the Hebrew words used in the Scriptures for the concepts I wanted to convey and adapting—probably more like corrupting—them to create some Gannahan words and proper names. *Gannah*, for instance, comes from the Hebrew word for garden. Here are some others:

Ayin – color

Armown – palace

Atarah – crown

Bara – Creator

lahab – blade

meah – sometimes translated bowels or intestines, the word was used in the Scriptures to indicate the place where sympathy and soft feelings originate; the seat of emotion; the heart

metheq – offering

nasi – prince

Natsach – musician

toqeph – authority, power, strength

Yasha – Savior

As Pik discovered when he took an honest look, the universe presents convincing evidence of the existence and transcendence of God. Wherever you come from, I hope you've enjoyed this tale and will give due consideration to the story in the stars.

Yvonne Anderson
www.YsWords.com

Fly Through the Gateway to Gannah
For Some Serious Sci-Fi Adventure!

Book 1 – *The Story in the Stars*

Though heirs to an ancient cosmic feud, he must save her life, and she must… well, she doesn't want to think about it.

Book 2 – *Words in the Wind*

Marooned in a place where reality and fairytale are flipped, Dassa wonders if "home" ever really existed.

Book 3 – *Ransom in the Rock*

How much is a life worth? And who will pay the price?

Book 4 – *The Last Toqeph*

Will Adam right an ancient wrong and lose his inheritance? Or ignore the truth and lose his integrity?

Return to Gannah

Book 1 – *Grace in the Gale*

On the planet Gannah, two lonely teens comfort each other — and the resulting storm blows their plans off course and rips their families apart. There's only one thing that can hold their lives together.

Book 2 – *Truth in the Tempest*

Feeding on open lies and subtle deceptions, the storm that began in *Grace in the Gale* grows into a tempest that buffets the whole province of Ayin. Where can Caleb and Dorona find refuge? And will this turmoil ever end?

Book 3 – *Cry in the Cliffs*

Coming in 2027.

Also by this author:

The Four Lives of J. S. Freeman, a story that spans three volumes:

One of the most prominent names in the lore of the planet Umban, J. S. Freeman is as mysterious and controversial as the island of Freemansland from which she came.

How does one rise from the shrouds of obscurity to become one of the world's most influential figures? In this series, Freeman breaks her long silence and tells the whole tale. Come and see. The truth she tells is better than her fiction.

Book 1: *Stillwaters*
Book 2: *Citizen*
Book 3: *Free*